IN THE GARDEN OF THE DEMIGOD

BITTERGATE TRILOGY
BOOK THREE

EMILIA LEE

For Gardeners and Older Siblings
May you reap the best of what you sow.

1

Leo Quince wasn't sure that he enjoyed being bit by a vampire. He didn't mind the pain of it; it didn't hurt exactly, but burned a little like a cat scratch. He'd been warned about the venom, that it would heighten some senses and dull others, supposedly a highly erotic experience. At the moment, though, it was just making him feel dizzy, and a little hot. That could have been the other bodies in bed with them. Or the sex. A hand, neither the vampire's or his own, was sliding beneath the waistband of Leo's shorts, and he groaned, the vampire's fangs withdrawing from his neck while the hand wrapped around the base of his cock.

Limbs heavy, face flushed, Leo leaned back and let himself be stroked and touched. As a rule, Leo sought out sex that was going to overwhelm his senses and allow his brain to turn off, but this had gone a step too far. He was losing cognizance, which he didn't really care for, and it was making him anxious, his stomach queasy. Being totally senseless was how people got caught. Not that Leo was ashamed of what he did in the bedroom, but there were reputations at stake. Not his own. Still, he needed to be careful.

In a haze, he rolled out of bed, away from grasping hands, and stumbled to the dresser where there was a pitcher of water on a tray with several glasses, and two unopened bottles of champagne. In the mirror, he could see that behind him his friends Evie and Paul were being assisted in an amorous embrace by a woman with jet black skin and crystalline green wings that emitted small puffs of sparkles as she rubbed herself against Evie's hip. The vampire, Indigo, was feeding off a young woman that Leo hadn't seen come in. She was touching herself and moaning, and another man was touching himself as he watched her.

Leo poured water into a champagne coupe and downed the whole of it in two gulps. His trousers were on the floor near his feet, so he stepped into them, pulling them up unevenly, his shoulder crashing into the dresser. No one noticed. Or if they did notice, Leo didn't. He wanted to go outside, take a breath of cold air. It had been a long weekend. His knuckles were sore from fighting. He was worried about his brother Sidney, who Leo had been fighting for, and about their father finding out. They'd won, of course, but that wouldn't really matter to Congressman Quince who was more concerned with appearances than he was about the well-being of either of his sons. Leo wanted to talk to someone, but, as usual, there wasn't anyone to listen.

Before, he had been enjoying talking to Asterion, the prince (apparently) of the fae realm of Andurnei. But Asterion had left a half hour ago and hadn't come back. He had said he was going to join them, and Leo had been interested. In him. Just that he was pretty. And he seemed nice. They'd talked a little bit since they'd met the night before. And rumor had it he was quite an attentive lover. Maybe tonight just wasn't an orgy sort of night. Maybe one partner would suffice, or no partners at all, but either way, looking for Asterion gave Leo an excuse to go. He scooped a shirt and jacket off the floor that he hoped were his, tugging them on as he left.

Elmmond House had taken on a hazy glow, like the gas lamps had all been turned up too bright. Leo was bumping off corners, tripping upstairs, the sound of the string quartet below eking and echoing up the walls, strangely thin. Downstairs was too crowded. He'd never find anyone down there.

That didn't make sense. Nothing was really making much sense. It had the shape of sense about it, but that was all. It was hard to concentrate. Leo was hot still, his skin just on the precipice of sweating. He wanted touch. He wanted no touch. He wanted to take his clothes off. He wanted the heavy weight of a massive parka to curl up in. Overstimulation had never been so unpleasant, which was disappointing, as he often enjoyed it. But not tonight. Bodies were funny that way, he supposed. So were desires. At the moment, Leo wanted someone to hold his hand, wrap an arm around him and tell him it was all going to be alright. The people he cared about were safe. He was safe, but he didn't feel like it. He was jittery and getting paranoid. He kept thinking he heard someone behind him on the staircase, but there was nothing. No one.

Finally, Leo made it to the landing at the top of the staircase and gasped. Twelve glowing doors lined the hall. They were open wide, and people and creatures seemed to walk through them as though they were taking an evening stroll in the park. Leo wavered down the hall, peeking into each open door. Looking for Asterion. Looking for Andurnei. Looking at everything else.

"Andurnei?" A woman asked. Had he said the name of Asterion's realm aloud? It didn't matter. The woman was a goddess with maroon skin and softly pink hair. She leaned against a doorway, and smiled at him, and Leo felt a strange fluttering of affection in his chest. "It's through here." Her golden dress shimmered across her ample curves, and, bewitched, Leo stumbled through the glowing archway into the gentle dusk beyond.

2

Ares Silva had forgotten what day it was. It was a bizarre mistake to make, but one that had been a long time coming. Generally, Ares followed the seasons, the cycles of the moon, and the growth of the plants in Leyland Hall's expansive gardens. He didn't have to keep track of days when he had no friends and no one else to account for except himself. Calendars held things he'd rather forget: the sting of seeing his brother's birthday come and go, his uncle's and aunt's, knowing they were all living their lives without him a literal world away. Even still, in the hottest weeks of summer, he thought of his brother Dom, a mid-July baby, and wondered who he was celebrating with, and what he looked like now, and what kind of a man he was.

It wasn't mid-July now, though. Of that he was totally certain. The north winds had brought a chill over the last few weeks, a bit early by his reckoning. Ares had begun to prepare for the first frost, laying down extra mulch and getting the cold frames out of the short shed that he'd built to store them. He'd been distracted by the change in weather and what it meant for the groundskeeping he undertook by Leyland Hall. He hadn't realized it was Ascension night, or he would never have come into town.

Fitzwilliam's was Ares' watering hole of choice, primarily because of how quiet it normally was. It was off the main square in Laurel Grove, down a narrow close that kept most people with horses and carriages away. But that night the spillover from whatever festival was going on in the square was making the small room boisterous and cramped.

Somehow Ares made his way to the end of the bar, his normal stool available next to a pair of cackling elves, not barely four hundred years between the two of them based on how silly they'd gotten on Marty's finest ale. Ares ordered a drink, and when Marty finally delivered it, they arched a cut black brow in Ares' direction.

"Surprised you came out tonight. Thought you didn't like crowds."

"Somebody get married?" Ares asked. He usually knew about weddings. Seven years ago, he'd convinced the lord of Leyland Hall that it would generate goodwill to donate bouquets to his tenants' ceremonies. Ares' roses were the biggest and most beautiful in any country garden from here to the Eastern Sea and were highly sought after. The dahlias and lilacs did particularly well too.

"And whose wedding would generate such a crowd?" Marty asked, rolling their eyes. "It's Ascension night, Ares," they said with a shake of their head, the additional 'dumbass' at the end of the sentence unsaid but fully audible. Ares scowled down at his drink. He'd attended exactly one Ascension party in his life, and he certainly wasn't about to do himself the damage of even incidentally attending another.

Usually, Marty lingered to talk. Ares brought the kitchen gossip from the Hall, and Marty shared the relevant news from town; an equivalent trade, generally, with neither of them required to impart any detail of their own lives, which was how they both preferred it, Ares assumed. But tonight, the bar was too busy even for the briefest of chitchat. For every patron that left the building, two more entered. Ares finished his drink quickly and got to his feet, dropping his coin on the table before weaving through the crowd of patrons toward the door, allowing his size and scowl to do the large part of the heavy lifting for him.

The night was cool, and the relief of the wind on the back of his neck made Ares sigh as he stepped out into the narrow street. The main thoroughfare that led back to the square was crowded. People strode by singing along to music that was spilling out from somewhere else, some more popular bar. Truly, a waste of a trip into town. He couldn't even risk a stop by the fountain in Minister's Circle, where he liked to go, especially on summer nights, to look up at the stars. Not that he was starving for places to look up at the clear autumn sky. Leyland Hall had a perfectly lovely view, especially out past the orchard in the rolling hills of the hunting fields. But no matter how far he made it from the big house, no matter how well he tended the gardens and livestock and took ownership over their harvests, the fact remained that Leyland Hall was still a prison.

He didn't get to feel bad about that, he reminded himself as he turned left down the alley, forming a simple map in his mind of which streets he'd be avoiding on his way home. If Leyland Hall was a prison, it was one he'd sentenced himself to. He'd made a choice ten years ago, and there was no use regretting it or resenting it or having any kind of emotion about it whatsoever. What was done was very much done. Fifty more years of toiling, forty if he was lucky, and then he'd die and be buried in the orchard beside his mother. That, at least, would be quiet.

The streets, on the other hand, were anything but. He'd drifted too close to the main square where voices were raised in celebration, greeting travelers who'd waited a year or more to be able to return, and the last hurrahs of those who were soon to leave. Ares doubled back, going west before he could turn east, knowing he'd chosen correctly when voices began to fade away on the autumn wind.

Except the quiet allowed Ares to hear a different sound: the noise of a scuffle. A voice cried out and was silenced quickly by the sound of flesh hitting hard against flesh, and a grunt of pain. Ares paused mid-step, half to determine if anyone else had heard the commotion, half to see if he could tell where it was coming from.

"Get off me! Get the fuck—" Another hit. Hard. The sound came from an alley to Ares' left where a trashcan clattered to the cobble street.

Ares was a big man. Two hundred and eighty pounds and six foot three, he cut an imposing figure, even if there were times when it was particularly inconvenient to do so. This was not one of them. He shoved his hands in the pockets of his canvas jacket and squared his shoulders before striding purposefully into the alley.

Two men had a third man pinned to the brick wall. A fourth fellow was staggering, barely keeping himself upright, an arm wrapped around his stomach as he wheezed. The man being held against the wall had his cheek pressed against the brick, an assailant's hand pressed against his jaw, slick with the blood that was dripping out of his nose. Still, his eyes widened as Ares' shadow fell over the scuffle, his attackers taking an extra beat to notice.

"Fuck off," Ares growled. It was enough to turn everyone's attention toward him, and Ares didn't smirk, though he very much wanted to.

"You've got no business here," said one of the men, ripping his hands out of the victim's trousers. Hopefully pockets. It was dark and Ares couldn't quite tell, and the fact that he couldn't tell made him angrier. "You fuck off!"

"Are you going to make me?" Ares asked, praying the answer was yes. The Ascension had put him in a bad mood and, no matter how foolish it was, delivering a beating to a bunch of assholes who deserved it would go a long way to putting him in a better one.

The three men looked at each other and seemed to come to some conclusion. The man, doubled over and still wheezing, charged at Ares headfirst, and it was an extremely simple thing to wrap an arm around the man's torso and flip him up, over Ares shoulder, letting him land with a painful sounding crack on the sidewalk. The other two men stilled, their expressions wide-eyed, as though they'd thought he was just big and not strong. The man who held the other to the wall loosened his grip, his mouth hanging open in shock, and it was enough that his victim could twist and sucker punch him in the stomach. His assailant doubled over with a grunt; the punch had been solid and well thrown. Ares approved. The man staggered back, reaching for his friend, whose eyes were now darting between Ares and their would-be victim.

Ares jerked forward with his shoulders, like he was going to reach out and grab for them, and they both turned tail and fled down the other end of the alley. Their victim staggered forward off the wall, hand coming up to stem the flow of blood from his nose, or perhaps to hide his huff of relieved laughter.

There was no question to Ares why this man had been targeted. He was handsome and well-dressed, though really, he was half undressed. Deep brown curls framed dark eyes that were glossy with drink and tilted down toward the knot of a previously broken nose. His shoulders were broad and might have been hidden by the narrow tailoring of his jacket, if it hadn't been hanging open across his chest.

"Are you alright?" Ares asked.

"Did you kill that man?" he asked, nodding toward the man who was still laying behind Ares, face down on the ground. Ares shrugged, and then sighed, turning and bending down to check for the assailant's pulse.

"Did they take anything from you?" Ares asked.

"Are you turning out his pockets?"

"I'm trying to see if he's dead," Ares scowled. There was blood, but also a heartbeat. The man groaned, and Ares stood and kicked him gently in the ribs. "He'll be fine. Serves him right, anyway."

"True," the man said, with a considered nod. He sniffed, scrunching his nose slightly, before bringing his fingers away and looking at the blood.

"Can I walk you somewhere? Are you staying in town?"

"No," the man said, looking around the edge of the alley curiously. "Or... I don't know exactly. I hadn't planned on it."

"It's not a good idea to go wandering around out here half-drunk and with no destination."

"Those men. Before they attacked me, they'd told me they could take me to...well..." the man's cheeks began to darken as he trailed off, his hand lowering slowly to press against his neck. "Is there a prince who lives near here?"

"You're looking for the Lord of Andurnei?" Ares asked, a little surprised. They were a good half hour's walk from Leyland Hall.

"I don't know." The man shrugged. "I suppose so." Then, two things happened at once. The man clapped his hand to the side of his neck, making a pained sound, and then his knees buckled.

Ares only just caught him around the waist, hoisting him up. The man's eyes had glossed over, head lolling to the side as he dipped in and out of consciousness. The side of his neck was swollen, and in the center of a blue-ish looking lump, were bite marks. A vampire.

"Oh, Godsdamn," Ares sighed, hoisting the man up into his arms.

"Sorry, I don't—" the man slurred.

"When did you get bit?" Ares demanded, sweeping the stranger into his arms and stomping out of the alley, back toward Fitzwilliam's.

"I dunno."

"Was it one of those men in the alley?" The man didn't answer, his head coming to rest on Ares' shoulder. Ares cursed, loudly, and the man startled. "What's your name?" Ares demanded.

"Leo," the man mumbled.

"Leo, stay awake. Can you do that?"

"I'm not sure."

"Well try."

"Am I dying?"

"Hopefully not," Ares grumbled, as he picked up his pace.

3

Marty stuck their head out of the back door, looked at Leo, whose veins were purpling beneath the light peach skin of his neck, and told Ares to take their biggest horse, an Andurneian draft, which Ares needed a small stack of wine crates and the help of a barback to mount. With a grunt, Ares hoisted Leo out of the barback's arms and into his own. It would have been more convenient to take a cart, but speed was of the essence, and once they were out of town, Ares kicked the horse up into a gallop, giving it a long lead on its reins, as he held Leo to his chest.

They followed the river north, into the woods, moonlight glinting off the surface on the water. Leo jostled in Ares' arms, his nose still bleeding, sweat beginning to bead on the center of his chest. Ares ungracefully transferred the reins to the hand that was clutching Leo's taut waist and pressed his palm flat against the center of Leo's chest.

Ares' magic felt slippery, fish-like, twisting away from him as the pounding of hooves and trying to keep his own balance, as well as Leo's, and everything else, swam in and out of his perception. Healing magic had been the first kind he'd learned.

It had just been a while since he'd used it on anything that wasn't rooted in the ground. It drew up heavy and slowly, sinking golden into the warm skin of Leo's chest, and then vanishing as Ares had to duck beneath a branch. Leo coughed, his body jerking forward, then collapsing back. Ares exhaled, frustrated. At least he could see, in the glow of the moon, that Leo wasn't flushed, sweating, anymore.

After a few more minutes, the moon grew brighter, and Ares looked up surprised to find the trees were already beginning to thin. He tugged on the reins, turning them right, over the cliffs, as opposed to left, down to the water and the beach that lay below the bluffs.

"What's happening?" Leo murmured.

"A vampire has properly fucked you up," Ares said, curling forward over Leo as the horse charged downhill.

"I don't think it was on purpose," Leo said. Ares snorted. He didn't trust a single magical creature as far as he could throw them. It wasn't precisely true, but it felt true in that moment, as it had in many moments before. "Where are we going?"

"To see Mae. She's an alchemist. If anyone can fix you, it'll be her. I just hope she's still up."

Mae's house was in a valley between two large hills, on a cliff overlooking the beach. The river was a couple of miles wide as it stretched out before them, flowing steadily southward. Ares juggled Leo and the reins, slowing the horse, coming right up to Mae's wide front porch. Lights inside the wide wooden structure glowed green and blue and purple, floating and flicking on and off, off and on. Crickets chirped, even though it was too cold for them, and there seemed to be a constant scuttling in the tall browning grasses that blew in the steady breeze off the water.

"Sal!" Ares called. "SAL!"

Sal shimmered into existence, their ghostly form hovering

behind the railing of the porch. Their hair was longer, shaggier, than Ares had seen it in quite some time. They tucked it back behind their long, pointed ears.

"Do you have any idea what time it is?" Sal demanded.

"I need to see Mae. It's an emergency!" Before Ares could blink, Sal had swooped over to hover beside him. They looked down at Leo with a furrowed brow.

"Vampire."

"That's what he says. Though I've never seen a bite swell up like that before."

"I'll get her," Sal said, and then they were gone.

"What was that?" Leo asked. "Was that real? Was that a person?"

"Sal?" Ares asked. "They're real."

"Why're they blue?"

"Moonlight?" Ares guessed. Then he thought about it for a moment. "Spiritual energy. Maybe." That sounded more likely. Leo wrinkled his nose. Then he winced and groaned.

"God, I feel like shit."

"I bet you do," Ares said. "You look like shit." It wasn't precisely true. Even bloodied and glassy-eyed, the man was pretty, with a square jaw and heaving chest, like something out of one of Ares' brother's smutty pulp novels.

The door to the house swung open, and Mae strode out, tying a silk robe around her waist. Her long auburn hair was up in curlers, her cheeks ruddy and speckled with freckles, and she had wide leather gloves on that flapped around her wrists as she charged through the garden and over to Ares and the horse.

"Hand him down here," she said, her voice even more gruffly Scottish than usual. He really had woken her up. As gently as he could, Ares passed Leo's body down. "Well," Mae said to Leo, as she started carrying him toward the house. "Look at you. Halfway through a marking. Fascinating stuff."

"Mae," Ares jumped down from the horse. "He's not a science experiment."

"I'm just saying it's fascinating is all. Come on, then. I'll need you to set him right. Sal can take the horse to the barn."

"Oh, but I wanted to watch!" Sal said, reappearing on the porch as Ares took the steps two at a time.

"Then you'd best hurry up with the horse," Mae replied, tersely. Sal vanished in with a huff, and Ares followed Mae into the house.

Mae's décor was something between an old beach cottage and a scientific death trap. Fishing net hung down from the ceiling, draped with glowing crystals tied to strings, and a giant portrait of a lewdly painted mermaid hung above the fireplace. Mae led Ares through the living room and down a narrow set of stairs, into the basement, where things were more clinical look-ing, all pale stone and metal, but no less messy.

"Move those papers off the table, Ares. There's a lamb." Ares shuffled her papers to the side, and with a grunt of effort, Mae hoisted Leo up onto the table. Then, without a word, she went over to the long counter against the far wall and began pulling open cabinets.

Ares took a breath. It was a relief to have done his part. He might have even left if Mae hadn't already asked for his help. Mae was the smartest and scariest person he knew in this realm or any other, and he was happy to hand off this man and his half-swollen neck to Mae for whatever treatment she managed to conjure up.

Ares leaned forward, wondering if Leo had finally dropped into unconsciousness; he'd stopped talking several minutes ago. Instead, Leo's brown eyes were darting around, wide and frightened, his chest heaving, blood drying on his chin. He looked terrified, and Ares felt a bit like a prick for having just been considering getting back on his horse and going home.

He swallowed, and reached up, putting a hand on Leo's shoulder.

"It's alright. Mae's brilliant. She'll figure out what's wrong with you."

"What's wrong with him is he's got a neck full of vampire venom," Mae said, her back still turned, "and he's not been turned or properly marked, so it's poisoning him. He'll start hallucinating soon, I'd wager."

"I'm not already?" Leo's voice was weak. Mae laughed as she walked over, holding two bowls. She set one on the table beside Leo's head. The bottom was filled with a milky white substance. The other held some sort of seeping poultice.

"Ares," Mae said, her bright blue eyes fixing on him across the table. "I need you to suck the venom out of his neck."

"You need me to do what?" Ares demanded. Mae rolled her eyes.

"Are you hard of hearing now? The most effective form of venom extraction is to suck it out. The enzymes in saliva react with the venom to keep it fluid for longer and—"

"No, no. No," Leo shook his head, barely. "Too dangerous."

"Not for him it's not," Mae scoffed. "Divinity is a natural neutralizer to undead component fluids. Worst thing that'll happen to him is a tummy ache. I'm still going to have him spit it in here." Mae was looking at Ares again, gesturing to the white liquid in the bowl. "It's a stabilizer. Not every day I get the chance to collect relatively fresh vamp venom, you know."

Ares glanced down at Leo, who was looking up at him with wide eyes, still fearful, but now curious. Curious about Ares. That was literally the last thing Ares needed.

"Fine," Ares sighed. "Let's get on with it then."

"What's his name?" Mae asked.

"Leo," Leo and Ares said in unison.

"Leo, be a dear and turn your head toward me. That's a

good boy." Mae patted him on the cheek as he complied. Ares' stomach roiled. Mae glanced up at him. "Go on," she said with a nod.

"You don't have any other instructions for me?"

"Don't swallow?" she shrugged. "Once you get your mouth on, you may need to push on the swelling a bit. Just to get it going." Good Gods. Ares took a deep breath and leaned forward.

He could taste the salt on Leo's skin, the subtle iron tang of blood. Ares ran his tongue over the bite marks, and then he sucked. Leo twitched, a full body shudder, and some small, errant part of Ares' mind was pleased that neither of them were enjoying this. He didn't want it to hurt Leo, but pain was less intimate, somehow.

Ares pressed against the swollen edge of Leo's neck, and a sweet, bitter tasting liquid spilled slowly onto Ares' tongue. It reminded him of biting into an orange peel, the scent of citrus, and a rancid taste. He lifted his head up and grabbed the bowl Mae had left on the table, spitting into it. The venom was a deep purple, but in the milky liquid already in the basin, it turned a strange, almost unnatural shade of indigo.

A cabinet crashed shut and Mae strode past them with a curse.

"I've got no clean vials down here. Keep going. I'll be right back."

Ares huffed and lowered his mouth to Leo's neck again. He sucked and Leo let out a small, choked whimper. Ares put his hand on Leo's shoulder, trying to brace him. The bridge of Ares' nose brushed the firm line of Leo's jaw, and Leo shuddered again. Ares raised up and spit into the bowl. The swelling had already gone down significantly, and Ares could see the slight flush of a bruise left by his own mouth on Leo's throat. Leo had twisted onto his hip, curled in on himself. Ares frowned.

"Does it hurt?" he asked.

"Is it almost done?" Leo grunted, through what sounded like gritted teeth. So, it did hurt. He could probably get the rest in one more mouthful, if he pushed.

"Almost," Ares replied.

⁊

ARES' mouth pressed against Leo's neck. His soft lips, the stubble on his chin, the earthy scent of his skin. Leo trembled, clenching his fist and swallowing down a moan. Vampire venom heightened sensation and created a sense of euphoria, he'd known that going in, but now Leo was doing his damnedest not to writhe against the table. It did hurt, but it also felt so fucking good. Ares' fingers were thick and pressed hard against his shoulder, and his neck and the suction of his mouth was just on the sharp side of pleasure. The hair on Leo's arms was standing on end and he was aching. Ares did that thing with his tongue, soothing it slowly over the sensitive bite marks and Leo groaned.

He couldn't help it, which was unfortunate. Sweat beaded on the back of his neck, arousal coursing through him, leaving him dizzy. Ares drew back, and Leo curled in on himself further, hoping to hide what had to be his very obvious erection. The sound of Ares spitting into a bowl wasn't helping. Nor was the way Ares was now running his fingertips over the sensitive skin of Leo's throat. Leo wracked his brain for anything that would kill his arousal, reaching desperately for the exhaustion that was beginning to cloud his thoughts, now that the pain was starting to subside. Passed out was better than orgasming on the table over some big man who was only trying to stop Leo from turning into a vampire. Time and place and all that.

"Are you okay?" Ares asked again. There was an archness in

his tone this time that wasn't there before. Leo desperately willed himself to drop into unconsciousness.

"Here we are!" The woman, Mae, rustled back into the room with a clanking of glassware. She didn't seem to notice or care that Leo had basically curled himself into a ball. She nearly rested her bosom on his face as she leaned over to look at his neck. "Ares press here. I'll catch the rest in this." The glass that she held against his neck was like ice, and it did wonders for dulling his arousal, leaving him with a low, uncomfortable burning in his skin. Sweat prickled against his hairline, and suddenly unconsciousness didn't seem like it was so far off.

"A little fever," Mae said. "Not surprising. He had such a strong reaction. He might be allergic—" and then Leo passed out.

4

Gods.

Damn.

Ares stared down at Leo's unconscious form. Leo's flushed cheeks were paling, the bruise Ares' had given him purpling on his throat, the fang marks like two small bug bites in the center. Ares' neck was hot, his own cheeks flushed, as Mae pushed a cold compress against Leo's forehead.

Ares didn't know why he was so unsettled. He'd just saved a man's life, so why did he feel like his own skin didn't fit properly? Why was Leo's groan still echoing in his ears? Hairs stood up on the back of Ares' neck. His cock twitched.

Ares yanked the mental door shut on his arousal. No. No way. Not happening. Not worth even entertaining the notion. It was the closest he'd been to another person in ten years. His body had gotten carried away with itself. And that was over now. He took a step back from the table.

"What are you going to do with the venom?" he asked Mae. She shrugged, rolling Leo gently onto his back.

"Dunno. I've read that it can be quite a potent catalyst in love potions. The sensation heightening properties, I suspect, can be chemically altered to—" She kept talking as a gentle wave of relief washed over Ares. Of course, vampire venom aroused. Ares knew that, and he'd forgotten, but that explained it. Mae grunted as she tried to move Leo's limp body, and Ares stepped forward again to help her. As though he'd been afraid of a little arousal. Foolishness. He almost laughed.

"Where do you want him?"

"I was going to put him on the couch upstairs. We'll need to keep an eye on him until he wakes up. And for at least a day or so after that."

"I can come back for him on Monday, if you like," Ares said, scooping Leo up into his arms. He was heavier than Ares had realized before. Mae snorted and started toward the stairs.

"Oh, not me, love. I can't watch him. I'm off to Harnwell for a conclave. Leaving early tomorrow morning. He'll have to stay with you." Ares frowned as he followed her up.

"I can't."

"Oh? Big plans?" Mae's voice dripped with sarcasm. Ares scowled at the back of her head.

"I have work. I can't be playing nursemaid to some wayward—"

"Oh, he won't need much minding. Just make sure he's not over-exerting himself."

They reached the main floor, and Mae led them into the living room, gesturing to an old couch. Ares laid Leo down, and Mae threw a thickly knitted blanket over him. Then she went to the mantle and scooped a handful of silver powder out of an urn that sat beneath the painting of the orgasmic mermaid. Mae tossed the powder into the grate without a second glance, and a fire burst to life in the fireplace.

"Whisky?" she asked, gesturing Ares toward one of two armchairs. He sighed.

"Please." Mae nodded and disappeared into the kitchen.

Ares took a deep breath as he sat and tried to think about what he was going to do now. Arguing with Mae was like arguing with the wind, and he wasn't going to be able to leave Leo with her. He *could* just leave Leo in the cottage while he went about his normal work. Ares didn't love the idea of having someone in his home unsupervised. Not that he had anything particularly precious, but it was just his space, that was all. No interlopers. No strangers.

Mae came back in, handing him a tumbler at least four fingers full. He smirked, shaking his head as he took a sip.

"I might take him up to the hall," Ares said to Mae as the thought occurred to him. "Warren can keep an eye on him. And he was asking about Kephisto anyway. They probably know each other." Ares certainly didn't want anyone who associated with Kephisto in his house for too long. Mae pursed her lips.

"I suppose you could."

"What?" Ares demanded.

"No, nothing. If he knows Kephisto, it's very likely he'd rather be at the hall than at your house anyway."

"Exactly," Ares nodded, pleased that they were on the same page. Mae sat silently, staring at Leo, tugging Ares' attention to him. Leo's chest was rising and falling more steadily now. He almost looked relaxed, the squareness of his jaw and shoulders softened by unconsciousness.

"He just doesn't seem like the type, is all." Mae said after a long moment.

"What?"

"To associate with Kephisto. He seems... well, he seems nice."

"You spoke to him for two minutes, and he was delirious," Ares arched an eyebrow. "You don't know anything about him, except that recently, he got bit by a vampire." Mae rolled her eyes.

"I have a sense about these things, Ares. And it's a good thing I do, because otherwise I would've written you off a long time ago."

Ares huffed, but didn't have any sort of rebuttal, because she was right. Instead, he leaned back in the chair and sipped his whisky, dragging his eyes away from Leo to stare into the fire.

5

Leo woke up with a crick in his neck and horrible cottonmouth. Blinking open gluey eyes, not really taking in the room yet, just willing shapes to congeal into meaning, Leo did his best to retrace his steps and found that there were no outstanding gaps in his memory. Leo knew where he was (mostly) and how he'd gotten there (generally), which was surprising because he felt like he'd been drunk, hungover and drunk again. He pushed himself up on the stiff couch with shaky arms and looked around.

It was as though a hunting lodge and a beach cottage had had an unfortunate child. Dark planks of wood made up the high walls, and heavy looking fish netting hung, perhaps artfully, if he was being generous, from the ceiling. The mantle was banded in by two ornate golden candlesticks, and hanging high above it all was a mermaid being brought to climax by what appeared to be two starfish and some apparently sentient kelp. Or was it a tentacle? Leo squinted at the art, cocking his head to the side, as though that would make it make more sense. It just stretched the ache in his neck, and he winced.

"Oh, good. You're up." Leo jumped as Ares stepped into the

room from a narrow hall. He was holding a large earthenware mug in one hand, and if it was full of coffee, Leo would gladly dunk his head in it. "We need to be getting back to Leyland Hall. Mae's lent us her dogcart."

Only about a third of that made sense, and none of it sounded like Leo was getting breakfast.

"Coffee?" he asked, voice rough and tongue moving like sludge. Ares looked down at Leo with an eyebrow lifted, whether in question or in judgement, Leo wasn't sure.

Ares was big. Leo tried to focus on Ares, get a read on him, something he prided himself on being rather good at, but it was hard not to get distracted. Ares was broad shouldered and tall, with a round stomach, olive skin and a head of short, soft-looking black hair that looked like it would have curled if he'd let it get long enough. Ares' sleeves were rolled up and his thick forearms were covered in twisting vines, tattoos, they must have been, though they shone like scars and weren't so far off from his skin tone. But then, if they'd been scars, there couldn't have been so many of them. Ares was interesting, and it took Leo a moment, several moments, to remember that he was supposed to be trying to get a sense of Ares as a person, not get distracted by the sight of Ares' stubble and the memory of how it had felt pressed against Leo's throat.

"There's some in the kitchen," Ares said finally. "Can you walk?" Leo hadn't tried, though he supposed now was as good a time as any to do so. He threw off a heavy knitted blanket and slid his feet down onto the floor. His knees tried to knock together like a newborn foal's, but he took a deep breath and steadied himself against the arm of the sofa. When he looked up, he was surprised by how close Ares had come, almost within arm's reach. Ares' brow furrowed, but he didn't say anything.

"Where's the kitchen?" Leo asked.

"Through there," Ares nodded toward the way he'd come in. Leo went, slowly, and he could hear Ares following along behind him.

The kitchen was through a small butler's pantry, and was wide and bright, with a large circular table beneath a red and purple glass chandelier that dripped crystal flowers. It reminded Leo of his mother. He smiled and cast his gaze around on the cluttered countertop for anything that looked like a percolator.

"Have a seat," Ares said, sliding past Leo and going to the cabinets. Leo did as he'd been told, watching as Ares got another mug down and poured a coffee as big as his own. He put it down on the table in front of Leo without a word. Leo looked up at him and smiled.

"Thank you," he said, deeply meaning it. Just lifting the warm mug felt like relief.

Ares made a sound like a small cough had stuck in the back of his throat. Before Leo could ask if he was alright, Ares had turned on his heel and was walking out of the kitchen.

"Hurry up. We're leaving in ten minutes."

THE RIDE to Leyland Hall in the borrowed cart did nothing for Leo's stomach. By the time Leo could make out the hulking stone edifice in the distance, he was breathing very purposefully through his nose, trying hard not to throw up. Ares hadn't spoken a single word to him since they'd departed from Mae's house, and Leo had gotten nauseous before he could properly formulate any questions. He'd taken to using Ares' shoulder as a fixed point on the horizon, his eyes trained dutifully on the soft curve of the muscle there and where it met Ares' neck. When Ares began to speak, it took Leo several seconds before he realized that Ares was speaking to him.

"...to the front of the house and get a footman. They'll make sure Kephisto knows you're here."

"Kephisto?" Leo managed to ask. He didn't recognize the name.

"You said you were looking for the Lord of Andurnei." Ares looked back over his shoulder, his heavy brow furrowed in a frown.

"Ah. Right. Prince Asterion?"

"Prince Asterion?" Ares repeated. Then he shook his head. "Paravel is a full day's ride from here at least." A full day in this fucking cart? The very idea made Leo's stomach clench, bile creeping up the back of his throat. "I can't take you all that way. You'll have to talk to Kephisto about borrowing a horse."

"Fine," Leo said. He sounded terser than he meant to, but Ares didn't say anything, and Leo wasn't really managing to think anything aside from an unending stream of curses. This is what he got for messing around with creatures and magic and things far outside his realm of understanding. After what had happened to Sidney, he should have kept his distance. But also, what happened to Sidney hadn't seemed like it was all bad. Jonas and Asterion and the others, they had been fun. Funny, handsome. Interesting. It was just that Edmund Morrow fellow who'd been so evil.

Leo sighed. None of that mattered now, and it was no good making excuses. He'd get out at Leyland Hall, and instead of trying to find his way to wherever Asterion was supposed to be, he'd just go home. When he looked back on all of this, years from now, the entire weekend would just be a random misadventure. A funny story to tell at parties, *'I got bit by a vampire once, you know,'* and no one would believe him.

The white stones that made up the driveway in front of the hall clacked loudly against the wheels of the dogcart. Leyland Hall was tall and dark grey, with high windows and four circular towers, one at each corner. It looked like it couldn't decide if it wanted to be a manor house or a castle, and either would have been dour and unwelcoming. Still, the garden beds along the front of the house were pristine, flowering in oranges and reds, long stalk-like plants that looked like pikes. Leo swallowed. When he glanced up at Ares, Ares was already looking down at him.

"Feeling alright?"

"A little nauseous," Leo admitted. Ares nodded.

"They'll set you right," he said, gesturing toward the building. Leo knew when he was being dismissed, and got to his feet slowly, willing them to hold him up. He got a firm grip on the side of the cart, and then it rocked beneath him as Ares hopped down out of the driver's seat and held out a hand for Leo to take. Ares' palm was warm and dry, his grip steady, and so, with more confidence than he felt, Leo hopped down onto the drive. The small stones shifted under his feet, and Ares steadied him with a gentle hand against his ribs. Leo gave himself an extra moment to get his balance. It was, oddly, the most at ease he'd felt since he woke up that morning. Leo took a deep breath, and slowly, Ares drew his hands away.

"Thank you for your help," Leo said, looking up at him. Ares inclined his neck stiffly, his expression going rigid, obviously uncomfortable. "I probably would have died without your assistance. I wish I had some way to repay you." This was true, but also, Leo wanted to see what Ares would say, since he'd barely said anything to Leo all morning. He'd been kind the night before; Ares had braced his hand against Leo's shoulder and helped, when he could have left. He'd come into the alley when he could have just walked away. It didn't quite square with the brusqueness that he seemed to be putting on like an ill-fitting coat.

"Good luck," was all Ares said before he pulled himself back up into the dogcart and tapped the horses into motion, driving them away around the corner of the house.

6

butler in emerald green livery showed Leo through a tall, grimly appointed foyer, all grey marble, crowned by a massive, unlit silver chandelier, and into a small receiving parlor on the right side of the room. There were a couple of uncomfortable looking couches, bookshelves full of books that were in precise, untouched rows, and several of the ugliest, gaudiest floral sconces Leo had ever seen.

Leo tried to explain to the butler that he was truthfully just looking for a way back to Hindry, that he didn't need to disturb Kephisto if there was some other way home, but the butler seemed haggard and didn't acknowledge anything that Leo had said.

"Someone will be with you in a moment, sir," the man muttered, affecting a small, insincere bow, before backing out of the room.

Leo took a deep breath and could taste the air, staid and unmoving as it was. Clearly this room was little more than a holding pen, and Leo had half a mind to walk out and see if he could find someone who would actually listen to him. He did a couple of laps around the sitting area, trying to get his knees back in working order. On his fifth or sixth turn about the room, a brief glance in the long silver mirror that hung across from the windows brought Leo up short. He winced at his reflection, no longer wondering what was taking the butler so long. The poor man was probably trying to muster up some sort of security forces. Leo managed to pat down his curls, forcing them into some semblance of order, and he hid the worst of the wrinkles on his shirt, and the tears in the fabric by keeping his suit jacket buttoned.

He was still fighting with his rumpled collar when, over his shoulder, he saw a carriage arrive on the front drive. This was no dogcart. An ornate, intricately carved black conveyance, pulled by two stately looking grey horses, brought Leo over to the window proper. Voices echoed in the foyer, and Leo stepped back. He tried to settle himself on the sofa and look as though he belonged there, in case someone else was about to be brought into the parlor.

Deep breath. Sit up straight. Smile. Good first impressions were everything, and whoever this person was, Leo was ready to greet and gladhand until they agreed to get him home.

After several moments, the parlor door opened, and a short man with dark hair swept inside and then came up short, blinking in surprise at Leo. Edmund Morrow was dressed all in black, except for the garish shine of seafoam satin that flashed from beneath his cape. The last time Leo had seen Edmund Morrow, Morrow was standing over Leo's brother, holding a knife dripping in Sidney's blood. Even if that particularly horrible image hadn't been seared into Leo's brain for the rest of his life, he'd recognize that stupid moustache and his swoopy coif of hair anywhere.

Leo stood quickly. Morrow, with a gleeful smirk twisting his thin lips, wasn't likely to help Leo get home any time soon.

"Mr. Quince, isn't it?" Morrow asked, striding right to the

edge of what Leo might have considered his personal space. "What are *you* doing *here*?"

"I came to speak to the prince," Leo said. It wasn't exactly true, but Leo doubted this man's meddling would go so far as to interrupt a royal appointment. Morrow's eyebrow arched.

"On what business?"

"None of yours," Leo replied sharply. Morrow's smirk flattened.

"You broke my nose," Morrow accused.

"It looks fine to me." Leo said. "But I'd be happy to try again, if you'd like. Maybe this time it'll stick."

Morrow studied Leo closely, with a scrutiny that prickled against his skin. Then, his smirk returned, gaze snapping toward the window. He took a step, coming up even with Leo's right arm, and placed his hand on Leo's right shoulder. Leo didn't flinch, but before he could brush Morrow's hand off, a searing heat pulsed against Leo's chest. It was sharp and hard, like a solid right hook. Leo's shoulder jerked back, and he grunted in pain. Yesterday's bruises sung.

Morrow's grip on him loosened, and a whipcrack of energy burst from the bottom of Morrow's palm. This was harder and stronger than any punch, and Leo lurched backward, gasping in pain as his shoulder was wrenched out of socket. He stumbled, his legs colliding with an end table, sending him flat on his back.

Leo scrambled with his one good arm, desperate to keep himself upright and moving as Morrow advanced on him with a sick, rictus grin. Leo's back hit the bottom of a bookshelf, and he winced, as Morrow crouched down in front of him.

"Well, isn't this a curious turn of events? And no Jonas or Asterion here to help you."

"Back off," Leo snarled through gritted teeth. Morrow chuckled. Opened his mouth to speak. Leo put all of his weight on his good arm, leaning as far back as he could and then kicked Morrow. He'd been aiming for the groin, but his angle was bad, and only managed to connect with Morrow's upper thigh. Still, Morrow staggered, almost falling, teeth bared in an unhappy growl. He regained his balance and managed a firm kick to Leo's ribs. Leo wheezed, and Morrow spat at him.

"Stay there. I'll deal with you in a moment." His voice was harsh and hollow, and Leo felt a surge of furious anger that this man had harmed Sidney. It was more fortifying than the fear that crept around the edges of his senses, sharpening his hearing to the sounds of Morrow storming from the room. "Keep this door locked!" he bellowed, probably in the direction of a nearby footman. "No one in or out! Where's Kephisto?" Leo heard the door close hard and a latch click.

He scrambled to his feet, bracing himself against the book-shelf. His dislocated arm was throbbing, and he clutched it to his chest, doing his best to hold it steady, ignoring the ache that was pressing in at his temples. What kind of power did Morrow have? More than Leo had guessed. Worse than that, Leo had no leverage. He'd been operating on goodwill alone since he'd arrived in this world, and it didn't seem like it was going to get him much further. Leo cast his eyes around the room, looking for options, ways out, and his gaze settled on a heavy looking statuette in the shape of a woman holding a torch high above her head.

Good enough.

Ribs burning, shoulder aching, Leo reeled forward. He grabbed the statue with his good arm, and then rebalanced himself under the weight of the thing. It was properly heavy and in other circumstances he would have hefted it with two hands. Leo cradled the thing between his chest and his arm and went for the window. He twisted his torso as best he could to get momentum, biting back the sounds of pain that inched up the back of his throat. There was no way he'd be getting a second chance. With a grunt that he couldn't stifle, Leo flung the statuette through the window. Glass shattered, and Leo heard movement outside the door as he half climbed, half tumbled out, landing in the glass shards and the flower bed below the sill. Voices behind him called out, yelling, as Leo got to his feet and ran.

7

After stopping by the house to get Matilda, Ares unhitched the horses from the dogcart and let them wander out into the pasture with the cows. The weather was beautiful, perfect for letting the animals stretch their legs, and for him to occupy himself with mucking out the barn. A morning of hard work would scrub the memory of Leo's handsome smile from Ares' mind entirely. He hoped.

Tacked to his front door had been a note from Fen, the cook up at the big house, thanking him for the herbs he'd delivered the day before and reminding him that Kephisto was hosting a hunting party that weekend. Sometime in the next day or so, he'd need to oil the guns and check the far fences and gates near the woods, to make sure everything was in good shape. It was more work than usual, but if the weather stayed decent, it should be manageable. A couple of the ewes were pregnant. He'd need to look in on them as well.

A to-do list kept Ares' head on straight. It always had. There were things to get done, and not a lot of time to get distracted by pretty interlopers who were stupid enough to get bit by a vampire and then attacked in an alley. Not that he was thinking of anyone in particular. Just that it was good not to get side-tracked. Too much to do to worry about anything as inconsequential as what Leo might be doing right now.

So, the stalls. They weren't in bad shape, and Ares was just turning to the hay pile to put down fresh straw, when he heard the first gunshots. Self-preservation made him go still, trying to sense direction and intention. Hunting was a favorite pastime of Kephisto's, but it was unusual to hear shots so close to the house. Pounding footsteps and loud, heaving breaths, made Ares lift his pitchfork as Leo came sprawling through the open door of the barn. One arm was cradled to his chest, and a cut dripped blood down his cheek.

"Hide me!" he panted. "Please!" The crack of another gun had them both flinch. Leo looked like a rabbit about to bolt.

"Hay," Ares said, pointing with his fork. Leo staggered gracelessly, spilling himself behind the pile of yellow straw that Ares had been stockpiling for the coming winter. So much for not getting distracted.

No sooner had Leo tumbled to safety, two guards, one armed with a flintlock, stuck their head in the open barn door.

"Don't go firing that thing off near the pasture!" Ares shouted at them. "Spook the sheep and there'll be hell to pay from me, you hear?" The men, both young enough to have been taught by the rest of the staff to avoid the wrath of the surly groundskeeper, backed away quickly, their attention turning south where the rolling fields stretched a good distance. A man on foot would have been easy to spot, unless he was hiding behind a cow, but Ares kept that thought to himself and speared another forkful of hay.

He'd just finished laying down the straw in the second stall, when he could hear another set of footsteps coming along the dirt path. Ares didn't bother looking up this time until a throat was cleared. Edmund Morrow stood in the doorway, his arms clasped behind his back, as though Ares was one of his pupils, and he was conducting an examination.

"Can I help you?" Ares said, foregoing the 'sir' that he knew Morrow wanted to hear. The man's face was pinched in a sour expression, and his eyes were scanning the rafters and the stalls, narrowing as they made their way back down to Ares.

"A man *you* brought to the house attacked me and broke a window," Morrow's voice was low and furious. *Impressive, Leo.* Ares suppressed a smile.

"He said he was here to speak with his majesty. I'm in no position to discourage any of his Lord's many admirers," Ares said, his eyes wide with what he hoped was a look of totally innocent compliance. Morrow seethed, his glare hot with anger.

"Where did you find him, Silva? Now."

"He was in town last night. He asked if I knew where the Prince of Andurnei lived and I said I did—"

"You have put the prince in danger," Morrow spat.

"Again, Viceroy," Ares raised a hand halfway between supplication and a shrug. "I am but a lowly groundskeeper. By your own orders, I'm to do nothing but tend to the—" Morrow strode into the barn, stepping almost up to Ares, nearer than he'd been in years. His chest was puffed out in what they both knew was an empty threat.

"You are to protect these grounds."

"Not the men who reside within them. Your care and keeping, and Lord Kephisto's, is above my paygrade. And far outside my interest."

"Did you see Quince come by here? Yes or no?"

"Two footmen went south into the pasture about five minutes before you arrived. If you look now, you'll probably still be able to make them out among the sheep."

"If you're lying to me—"

"I could swear on my mother's grave, if you like," Ares replied, his tone arid. He'd be happy to do so, partially because he hadn't lied and partially because his mother had no grave. Morrow scowled at him.

"You're a stupid, insolent brute."

"Always a pleasure to see you too, Viceroy," Ares said with a thin smile. "Now if you'll excuse me, I have work to be getting back to." For a beat, Ares thought Morrow was going to say something else. To actually push him. But Ares continued to scoop hay, and after a moment more of glaring, Morrow turned on his heel and left the barn, stalking out in the direction of the pasture.

Ares swallowed, spit thick in his throat, and let out a long, low exhale through his nose. Hate made him act funny; in ways he wasn't usually proud of. He always ended up wishing it would come to blows. How satisfying would it be to actually lay fists into the man. But Morrow could do anything to him but touch him, and they both knew it. Needling his jailer wasn't smart, but it was as good as Ares was going to get.

"I'd stay put for another few minutes," Ares said to the emptiness of the barn, assuming Leo could still hear him. There was no response. Ares didn't look up when Morrow and the footmen walked past the barn, though Ares could feel Morrow's gaze hit him as he went by. Ares waited until the sound of their footsteps had faded, and then another three minutes beyond that, before he walked over and closed the barn door, then went to the far side of the haystack.

Leo was half buried, curled on the floor, with his right arm still tucked tightly against his chest. Hay stuck out of his dark brown curls, and Ares could see tear tracks in the dirt on his face, though thankfully he wasn't crying now. His teeth were gritted, and his eyes were tight with pain.

"Sorry," Leo said.

"Does that hurt?" Ares asked, nodding toward Leo's shoulder.

"It's not a kiss," Leo said, pressing himself up slowly with his good arm. The sleeve of his jacket was torn. Blood stained his white shirt across his chest.

"I guess they didn't want you to borrow a horse," Ares stepped back, giving Leo space. He'd have offered to help, but he wasn't sure what would be most helpful. Leo grit his teeth and braced his feet against the dirt floor of the barn.

"I didn't get far enough to ask. Morrow saw me first." The bitterness in his voice was so strong Ares could almost taste it in the air.

"He doesn't like you much," Ares said, bending forward, taking Leo's good hand and helping him upright. "What'd you do?"

"To myself?" Leo winced. "Or to him?"

"Either."

"I broke his nose. But before you think too poorly of me, I promise he deserved it."

"If we're being honest, it makes me like you more."

"Ah," Leo gave a small chuckle, running a tongue over his chapped lips, and for a moment Ares' concentration slipped, his full attention changing with a rapidity that made his stomach turn over. Leo's mouth was a hard line of pain where it should have been soft. "He tried to kill my brother."

It was such a sufficiently surprising statement, that the weird arousal Ares had been struggling to comprehend was fully shuttered. He blinked at Leo.

"What?"

"It's a long, stupid story and my arm hurts. Can you pop it back in, or did he do some dumb fucking magic on me that means my shoulder will be dislocated for the rest of my life? In which case, do you have a strong enough stomach to amputate?"

Ares snorted at the outburst, found it endearing despite himself, and then stepped to Leo's side. He wasn't a doctor, but he could feel the place where the joint needed to go, and he had popped a couple of his own fingers back into place before. How different could it be? Ares ran his hand up the inside of Leo's chest, beneath his jacket, ignoring the spot where his palm hit tacky blood.

"What did you do here?"

"Cut myself going through a window," Leo said. Ares shook his head, stifling a snort of laughter. He had to concentrate if he was going to ignore the heat of Leo's skin, the firmness of his chest, the planes of warm muscle along his ribs as he slid his other hand up Leo's back. He'd like to be touching Leo sometime when Leo wasn't injured. He'd like to be—

No. Good Gods. What was wrong with him?

"Is it bad?" Leo asked. Ares cleared his throat. Focus.

"I don't think so. But it is going to hurt."

"No shi—" Ares shoved Leo's shoulder back into place, and Leo let out a low, deep, moan of pain, his knees buckling. Ares caught him, wrapping an arm around his waist, holding him up as Leo struggled to keep his legs beneath him, his face buried in Ares' shoulder. "Fuck!" Leo hissed. Ares could feel Leo's breathing, hot and heavy, through the fabric of his shirt, damp against his neck. Leo's fingers dug into the meat of Ares' arms, and Ares let Leo steady himself, while he ran through a mental list of other chores he had to get done today and reminded himself that Leo was certainly, obviously, more trouble than he was worth.

"Let's go back to the house," Ares said, stepping back as soon as he thought Leo would be able to keep himself on his feet. "My house, I mean. You need ice and I've got more work to do."

"I can help," Leo said. "I think at this point, it's safe to say I owe you one."

"You can't help. And you don't owe me anything. You need to go back to wherever you came from." Ares laughed and went to the barn doors, pushing them open again. He whistled for Matilda. Leo groaned, turning his arm slowly at the shoulder.

"I'm from Bainbridge," he said. Bainbridge? Ares swung around, surprised.

"You're not from Andurnei?"

"No. Not at all."

"How'd you get here? Where did you get bit by a vampire in Bainbridge?"

"I wasn't in Bainbridge at the time. I was at a house party. The Elmmond House party," Leo said. Ares nearly lost his own footing. Mistaking Ares' shock for confusion, Leo shook his head. "It's this big manor house on—well that doesn't matter. It's in a town called Hindry—"

"I know where it is," Ares said. "I'm from—" Pieces of their conversation began clacking against each other in Ares' head, a complete picture trying to form from disparate parts. "Wait. You met Edmund Morrow in Hindry?"

"At Elmmond House," Leo said. "He tried to kill my brother."

"Why?" Ares demanded. It was like his own worst fears were coming out of someone else's mouth. Matilda trotted into the barn and pressed her shoulder against Ares' knee. They were supposed to be walking back to the house. Ares bent down and scratched her behind the ears, and then straightened up and gestured for Leo to follow him; they went out the paddock gate as Leo explained.

"To be honest, I never quite got the full lay of the situation. Sidney, that's my brother, said something about a soul sealing? Or stealing?" Ares grunted. They were essentially one in the same, and it shouldn't have come as any shock to him that Morrow had been trying to take someone else's soul. "Anyway, there was a lot of blood and it seemed to me like Mr. Morrow wasn't too worried about Sidney surviving the whole thing." Ares nodded, keeping an eye on the path back to the cottage and the horizon toward the house as Leo continued, telling Ares all about how he'd received the invitation to the house party, and hadn't intended to see his brother there at all. They made it into Ares' cottage. Ares dug through the icebox for a couple of the reusable flax seed cold packs Fen had given him and tried to ignore the panic ringing in his ears, drowning out Leo's inane chatter. His head still in the freezer, Ares heard Leo say: "we went to this diner—" and Ares' heart caught in his throat.

"Which diner?" he interrupted abruptly, grabbing the pack and straightening up all at once.

"Oh, Silver something, I think. The food was great. Do you know it?"

"The Silver Platter?" Ares came over and handed Leo the ice pack, sitting heavily on the couch opposite him.

"That's it," Leo nodded. Of course that was it. The Silver Platter. His family's restaurant.

A thousand questions leapt into Ares' throat. Who had been working that day? Was his brother there? They'd probably sold the place. Gods, he would hate it if they'd sold the place. Ares ran a hand over his face, trying to get ahold of himself. Did he really want to know? Any of it? When he'd left Hindry and come to Andurnei, he'd told himself he wasn't ever going to look back. That was the cost of the choices he'd made. Knowing would only hurt, one way or another.

It was then that Ares realized Leo had finally stopped talking. Ares looked up to see that Leo's gaze had narrowed and was fixed on Ares. Ares could feel his cheeks flush. Was there a way he could backtrack on the minor panic he'd just had? Maybe Leo had the good grace to pretend Ares hadn't just collapsed onto the sofa at the mention of a random diner. Maybe—

"You do know it. Oh!" Leo's good hand came to cover his mouth, and he stared at Ares, his eyes going wide. "Oh my God. Are you... Are you the owner's brother? Silva. The brother who's been missing for ten years?" Ares felt like he was going to be sick. He braced his arm against the back of the couch and heaved himself upright, ignoring the tremor in his knees. "Ares," Leo said. "Your brother is... I mean, he's looking for you."

It stuck like a knife in his chest. Dom was looking for him?

It couldn't be true. Ares turned toward the door.

"Stay here. I have work to do."

8

Ares stalked outside, desperately gulping in deep gasps of air. Panic. It was almost unfamiliar to him now. The last time he'd felt like this was—

Ten years ago. When the gravity of what he'd done finally hit him. He was really and truly alone in Andurnei and would be for the rest of his life. He'd expected to be sad. He hadn't expected that it would feel like his whole body was rejecting the decision, allergic to it. His chest tightened, stomach curdled, teeth clenched, shoulders trembled. Viscerally, he didn't want to do what he'd already done. But he had no choice. He'd thrown up in the hedgerow and kept going.

Logically, it was sort of funny to feel it all again now. At the mere mention of his brother. As though Dom hadn't crossed his mind before now; Ares thought about Dom all the time. But it was different to hear Leo talk about him. About the diner. About Ares' former life like it was all still real and there. Like he could reach out and grab it, if he tried.

They should have forgotten about him. Ten years was a long time to look. A long time to keep hoping. Ares had thought he'd be a distant memory by now. A fond one, to bring out at the holidays, admire and put away again. He didn't want to be searched for. Even if they found him, he couldn't go back.

All the problems he'd identified and codified and solved by his disappearance would come roaring back the moment he stepped foot earthside. It was better this way. It was better. And maybe if he kept repeating that the entire walk to the edge of the forest, he'd calm down.

Slowly, sensation came back. The solidness of the ground beneath his feet; the rush of a cold breeze against his face. It was barely still warm out, the coolness of impending dusk right behind the last of the sun's warmth. Winter was approaching fast. He could hear it in the chilled creak of the branches above his head, the rustling of the leaves in the orchard. If he let himself, he could feel the changing energy in the air. The cold meant hibernation, the animals and plants would rest, and Ares would hunker down in his cottage apart from the other servants of Leyland Hall, alone once again. Leo would be gone by then. Ares needed him gone. He was far too…

It was a shame that the first word that came to mind was 'pretty.' 'Dangerous' was better, and more accurate. Getting tangled up with Morrow, no matter the reason, meant that the man was more stupid than brave. Ares himself was proof of that.

Not to mention the vampire thing. And what was Dom doing, talking to the sorts of men who consorted with vampires? He didn't really know what sort of men that meant, but in his mind, it was certainly a negative trait. Dangerous, again, probably. And that might have been more concerning than all the rest of it put together. Ares would send Leo back to Hindry with strict instructions to stay far, far away from Dom.

When he got back to the cottage, Ares would open a portal to Elmmond House and be done with Leo, the entire encounter little more than a snag in the weave on the tapestry of Ares' life.

Somehow that decision brought Ares back to himself. He'd made it all the way to the far boundary of the pasture in a daze, and he only now realized that a section of the stone wall that bounded the sweeping forest was crumbling in a few places, and several large stones had rolled off the top. Ares paused, putting his hand in the gap, feeling the rough edge of stone, and took another breath, looking out at the expanse of trees. The hunting party would ride this way, which meant Ares needed to patch this wall before the weekend. Ares could already hear Kephisto proclaiming that a broken wall had embarrassed him in front of his guests. How many similar holes had Ares missed because he'd been distracted by Leo? Ares scowled, squinting back the way he'd come. There were other gaps. Several of them. It was time to send Leo back home and get to work.

ARES YANKED the door closed hard behind him when he left, and Leo jumped. The big black dog that had followed them into the house from the barn looked up at Leo with an expression that Leo interpreted as, 'see what you did?' before she hopped up onto the sofa and lay down with an audible huff.

Leo took a deep breath and looked around, trying to get his bearings, feeling guilty, and not liking it. The cottage was lovely, though. Whitewashed walls were covered on nearly all sides by wooden bookshelves, stacked with tomes and potted plants and lanterns and a variety of other bric-a-brac that Leo couldn't help but be intensely curious about. Carefully he made his way around the room, peering at everything. He found two shelves of ledgers, each filled with charts and numbers, crop yields, perhaps or some other gridded something. Leo hadn't seen any evidence of a proper farm on the property, but they had walked through a verdant back garden as Leo had rambled on about Sidney and Hindry until he'd put his foot in it.

Mentioning Dom Silva and the diner had been... well, it hadn't been a mistake. He would have done it eventually, but he could have done it more tactfully, he supposed. Still, how was he supposed to know the man would be anything other than relieved? Trying to swallow his unearned feeling of guilt, Leo put the ledger away and then moved to the next shelf. There, a set of about twenty books, a little more than an inch thick each, bound in brown leather, were squished together, like Ares was determined not to give them a second shelf.

Leo selected one at random and tugged it out with effort. They really were jammed in. He flipped it open to a detailed pencil illustration of a bird. A warbler, maybe? He turned the page. Chickens. About three pages of them. Then a woman, with round cheeks, smiling, and short hair. For a moment, Leo wondered if she was someone of particular importance, but then, the next page was filled with other faces, a line of hunched shoulders along a bar at a tavern, a fountain in the center of a cobblestone square.

Every book on the shelf was a sketchbook, each filled with careful, delicate illustrations. They were unfairly beautiful. The weight of the lines, the soft angle of shading, added up to images that lifted off the page. Leo was no artist. The doodles in the corners of his legal briefs looked much the same as they had in law school and college and even elementary school. But the thought that big, burly, gruff Ares was an artist surprised him. The sketches were mostly of nature, occasionally of architecture (the planning of what looked like a greenhouse enchanted Leo for nearly a quarter of an hour,) and every so often there was a burst of portraits, as though Ares only encountered people in barrages and then not at all. Who was this man Ares Silva? And what was he doing here?

Leo had intended to explore the rest of the house, but by the time Ares returned, Leo had made himself comfortable on the floor, his back up against the back of the couch, flipping slowly through the fifth or sixth of Ares' sketchbooks. The big, black dog had curled up next to him, but even so, she was about as long as his leg. They both looked up as Ares closed the side door.

Before Leo could move, Ares strode around the side of the sofa and nearly tripped over them. He came up short, scowling, fingers tightening where he'd caught himself on the back of the couch. Leo flipped the sketchbook closed.

"What are you doing?" Ares demanded.

"Reading." Leo tried for breezy. Tried to ignore the heat in his cheeks. Were sketchbooks supposed to be private?

"Get up," Ares grumbled, stepping over Leo and the dog in one broad stride. "It's time to go."

"Go where?" Leo asked, scrambling to his feet, bracing himself against the back of the couch as the dog nearly took him out at the knees in her rush to follow Ares out of the room.

"Back to Hindry," Ares said. Leo followed the dog through an archway that led to a lovely foyer, red tile on the floors, and dark wood beams across the ceiling that matched the banister, barring in the stairs to the upper floor. For a moment, Leo thought they were going to go out the wide front door, with its glazed glass panel giving the light of the room a sort of wave that reminded Leo of opening his eyes under water, but then Ares turned toward a door on the right, opposite the bottom of the stairs. He took a half step back, as though he was sizing up the doorframe, and then he tugged a short wooden handle out of his pocket.

When Ares flipped open the knife, Leo stiffened. Whatever he had expected (and he wasn't sure if he had been expecting anything at all) it hadn't been that.

"What are you doing?" Leo asked. Ares slashed open his own palm without wincing. "Christ! What are you doing!?" Leo demanded, charging forward, wondering if he would be strong enough to wrest the knife from Ares' hand. Instead, Ares handed it to him, handle first.

"Hold this. And be quiet. I'm trying to think."

"Uhh—" Leo was going to protest, but then Ares was already moving, dipping his finger into the blood in his palm, and then tracing symbols around the edge of the doorway. Three on each side. One on the center of the floor on the threshold of the two rooms. Leo barely registered that the doorway led to a small study, a couch and a desk filling the bulk of the space in the room, when Ares blocked his view, reaching up to trace a deep red sigil above the door. He took a step back, frowning at his work. For a long moment, nothing happened. Was something supposed to happen? Or was Ares having some sort of nervous breakdown. Leo cleared his throat. "Ares, are you—"

Ares put his hands on the doorframe, on top of the center sigils and pushed hard.

The doorway turned opaque, pearlescent, like someone had dropped a curtain over it. The frame glinted a sort of metallic sheen, and for a moment, Leo thought he heard a hum, like a distant electric motor had turned on. Ares wiped his palm against his trousers, smearing blood against his thigh as he turned toward Leo.

"There you go," he said. "Have a nice... life, I suppose." He gave Leo a painfully insincere, thin-lipped smile, and stepped back, gesturing toward the door, like he was a waiter seeing Leo to his table.

"What the hell is that?" Leo asked. Ares scowled.

"It's a portal. Back to Hindry. You're welcome."

"It looks like a sheet."

"It looks like a—" Ares' eyes twitched toward the doorway. "That's a hallway."

"That's not a hallway," Leo said. Ares huffed and stepped up next to Leo, turning toward the door again.

"That's the hall of the upper floor at Elmmond House. Look at the sconces!"

Ares had clearly broken with reality. It was Leo's fault, surely. He really shouldn't have brought up Ares' brother.

"Do you want to go sit in the living room for a minute? I can get you some water."

"What I would like, more than anything in this world or any other, is for you to leave," Ares said firmly. He took Leo by the elbow and pulled him forward. Leo let himself be pulled, feeling the warmth of Ares' blood soaking through the thin fabric of his dress shirt, ignoring the tight ache in his shoulder. This was madness. But Leo still felt responsible for it. Ares tossed Leo's arm toward the doorway, and Leo stumbled forward, the pearlescent sheet rippling with the changing light. He straightened himself up and tugged on his shirt sleeve. This might have been magic, but it wasn't Elmmond House. It wasn't a hallway. If he pushed through the white barrier, Leo would find himself in that narrow study beyond. He spun around and looked at Ares, who grimaced.

"What should I tell your brother, if I see him?"

Ares' deep brown eyes narrowed. His shoulders squared, and Leo put his weight on his back foot, ready to dodge the blow he was certain was coming. Ares was on him in a step and a half, a heavy fist closing around Leo's lapel, hauling him close to Ares' chest.

"You won't speak to my brother again. Or to anyone in my family. Understand?" The fury was coming off him in waves, his grip tightening as Leo searched his face for reason. Why was Ares doing all this? What was he hiding?

"I'm not sure you can stop me. If you stay here, and I go through," Leo nodded toward the doorway. "Unless you were planning on coming too." Ares growled, and Leo gave the best shrug he could, considering he was being lifted up onto his tiptoes by the front of his jacket. He could smell Ares' sweat and something verdant beneath it, that reminded him of the scent in the air before an early summer storm. It was, overall, a stupid time to get distracted, but then Ares shoved him backward, and instead of falling through the white sheet onto the floor of the study, or even into the hallway at Elmmond House, Leo's back smacked against something hard.

Ares stumbled forward, his elbow folding, bringing him chest to chest with Leo against the very solid doorway. His eyes widened in shock, and Leo could see that they were flecked with bright silver. Leo's feet dangled, inches off the floor, pinned to the unyielding nothingness behind him by Ares' chest and stomach. Leo ignored the zip of arousal that shot down his spine. It was the position, that was all. And Ares' furious, heaving breaths against the side of Leo's neck.

"How are you doing that?" Ares demanded between gritted teeth.

"I promise you, I'm not doing anything at all."

"You came through a portal!" Ares dropped Leo and took a step back, pushing a hand through his hair. "Didn't you?"

"Yes," Leo said. He had. "I told you, I was looking for—"

"Prince Asterion of Andurnei. I remember. Did you sleep with him?"

"What?" Leo was so confused. And now he was blushing. "No. No, I didn't—"

"Then how did you," Ares stopped short and pushed both of his hands against his eyes. "The vampire. Of course." He let out a loud, frustrated groan that made Leo feel uniquely like a burden. Which he hated.

"Would you please explain what the hell you're talking about? In full sentences, maybe, so I have a fighting chance of understanding?" Ares groaned again, dragging his hands down his face.

"You're not marked anymore," Ares said. His cheeks were flushed, and his tone said that this was all Leo's fault, even though Leo still wasn't sure what he'd done.

"Marked?"

"Humans have to be marked to pass into other realms. The vampire bit you. Put its venom in you. So you were able to come through. But now—"

"Now, you and your Alchemist friend took the venom out, so I can't go back? Is that it?" Leo demanded. Ares nodded, leaning against the round end of the banister, sliding down onto the bottom step of the staircase. Leo's mind was racing. He hadn't intended on getting stuck in Andurnei. He needed to get home. There was work, his office, campaign events for his father. Christ, if he missed the donor's dinner at the end of the week, he'd never hear the end of it. "So, how do I get marked again? Another vampire?"

"Gods," Ares huffed, rolling his eyes. "No, it doesn't have to be. Most creatures with access to magic have some ability to—"

"Like you, then?" Leo asked. "Mae said you had divinity or something. Are you a God?"

"It's more complicated than that," Ares said quickly. Evasively. If Leo had Ares on the stand in a courtroom, it was exactly the moment where he would have pressed. Unfortunately, he was starting to panic. Nuance was less interesting to him than it had been minutes before.

"Can you mark me?"

Ares looked at Leo with another wide-eyed expression, jaw hanging slightly slack, and for a moment Leo thought that Ares might not have been breathing. Ares' gaze dropped as he pulled himself to his feet, braced on the edge of the railing. He strode past Leo and swiped his still bleeding palm against the doorframe of the portal, smudging a sigil. The white sheet blinked out of existence, and the study was returned to its rightful place.

"Stay here," Ares said, grabbing his boots and not looking at Leo. "I need to go up to the house for a moment."

"No, wait," Leo began, but before he could protest properly, Ares was already out the door.

9

res tore through the narrow servant's halls, turning sideways to avoid the maids wielding baskets of laundry twice as wide as they were. After the last two days, it seemed impossible that things at the house were unchanged. Still, when he found the head butler, Mr. Oswald polishing silver in the pantry, Ares almost collapsed in relief at the mundanity of it all.

"Mr. Silva," Oswald nodded in Ares' direction, the half circle of grey hair like a thick laurel wreath around his pale, balding head. One very thick eyebrow arched in Ares' direction. "How can I help you, sir?"

Formality was Oswald's singular mode of operation, and Ares had come to rely on his consummate professionalism over the years. It wasn't unkindness; never that. But in the way that Ares used tasks to keep himself occupied, Oswald used his work to keep himself entirely at an even keel. This was not the first time Ares had burst in on him unannounced.

"I have a problem," Ares said. Oswald nodded toward the pantry door, and Ares leaned back and pulled it closed, barely hearing the latch click before everything that had happened with Leo spilled out of Ares' mouth like a bursting dam.

Oswald's attention stayed fixed on the silver, his movements steady and practiced, even when Ares ended with the conversation about marking, which was really not a topic Ares had ever imagined he'd broached with Mr. Oswald, who was at least eighty-five in human years, if he was a human at all. It had never seemed polite to ask.

"So, the boy can't get home, and he can't come up to the house, and Master Morrow will kill him if he finds him. Is that the lay of it?"

"Yes," Ares exhaled.

"Very bold of you to be telling me, then. Who's to say I won't go to Master Morrow directly with this intensely incriminating information."

Ares sagged, exasperated, as Oswald shot him a mischievous smirk.

"I know what you think about Morrow."

"I'll deny it to the grave, Mr. Silva. And with my word against yours, I know who they'd believe."

"Oswald, what do I do?"

"Alondra comes through a week from today. Send him back with her. Travelers can bestow marks easier than most," he arched an eyebrow at Ares, the *'obviously'* unspoken, but there all the same. Ares leaned his head back against the nearest cabinet. Of course. Alondra. He'd forgotten she'd be at Leyland Hall so soon. He was losing track of days. "Until then, we'll tell the staff that Lord Kephisto has finally approved my request for an assistant groundskeeper. Mr. Julian Flint will be staying with you in the cottage until he learns the ropes. Should do nicely."

Ares forced himself to exhale. It was a decent plan. And it only had to work for the next six days. Ares had enough work to do to keep himself out of the house and away from Leo for a week. In the fields and pastures. He had to prepare for the hunting party, and winter was fast approaching.

"You do need an assistant," Mr. Oswald said. "Might as well use the boy while he's here."

Something deep below Ares' stomach twisted. Just like it had when Leo looked Ares in the eye and asked to be marked. When Ares had pressed his mouth against the hot skin of Leo's throat. Gods. He needed to put as much distance between them as he could.

"I'm fine," Ares said.

"I'll send one of the fabricators down for his measurements for a few sets of work clothes. I'll be glad to know you have someone helping you. I was trying to sort out who I could spare."

"I don't need any help," Ares insisted. Oswald finished the forks he'd been polishing and started on the spoons.

"Don't be foolish, Silva. It'll go faster with two. Now, is there anything else?"

Ares knew he was being dismissed and shook his head, bowing out of the pantry with his thanks. He took the way out through the kitchen, looking for Fen, the cook, but she wasn't in. By the time Ares made it to the cottage, it was on the heels of a fae fabricator with teal tinted skin and long shining golden hair. Ares couldn't remember their name but he let them in all the same, ushering them into the foyer with a grunt and a broad gesture, hoping that Leo hadn't wandered off again. Ares wasn't sure if he was relieved or worried when Leo came into the foyer with a tea towel tossed over his shoulder. He stopped short at the sight of the fabricator, and Ares swept in.

"This is Mr. Julian Flint, my new assistant. Mr. Flint, this is..." he dragged his gaze up to the fabricator, whose eyebrow lifted slightly in offense.

"Cerise."

"Cerise," Ares continued as though that wasn't a stupid name for a creature who'd tinted their own skin blue. "They're one of Lord Kephisto's fabricators, and they're here to size you up for some work clothes. His room is just there," Ares gestured toward the study, ignoring the fact the doorframe was still streaked with bloody sigils. Cerise was fixated on Leo, and Leo was watching Ares with a skeptically arched eyebrow, like the next thing out of his mouth was going to be an argument. Damn him. Ares took Leo by his uninjured shoulder and steered him into the study with gritted teeth. "Just one moment, if you don't mind," he said to Cerise, closing the door behind them.

"Julian Flint?" Leo hissed the moment Ares turned around. "What the hell are you talking about?"

"I have a way to get you home, but it'll take a few days. Until then, and so Morrow doesn't *kill you*, we're pretending you work here. Understand, *Mr. Flint*?" Leo's brown eyes were narrowed, his lips pursed, jaw set. He looked furious, and what did Ares care? Soon he'd be gone. And Ares would have done more than his share of helping the idiot bastard.

"How long?"

"Six days."

"Stop storming off," Leo demanded. Ares froze. How dare— "Because I don't like this any more than you do, but if you don't fill me in on what the hell is happening, how can I help?"

"I don't need your help. I need you to stay out of trouble, and then I need you to leave."

"And not tell your brother where you are. Or what a massive prick you've turned into."

"Don't talk about my brother," Ares said, his voice exactly as low and dangerous as he'd wanted it to be. Then he turned on his heel and stormed out of the room.

10

Leo stood, silently fuming, with his arms outstretched, while Cerise measured him like any other tailor. Everything was so ridiculously fucked, and Leo was mostly angry with himself. He should have been more careful, that was all there was to it. And now he was stuck in this cottage, with nothing to do but wait until whatever was coming in six days actually happened. He would miss the campaign dinner, and he could already hear his father's snarling contempt that would be waiting for him when he returned.

"I should have something ready for you in about twenty minutes," Cerise said, startling Leo out of his preemptive dread. "In the meantime, I might recommend a shower."

Leo snorted and Cerise left with a judgmental lift of their eyebrow, exiting out the front door of the cottage, touching the doorknob with two fingers, as though they were worried about something infectious. Leo let out a long breath and let his shoulders slump. A shower would be lovely. He only had to find it in him to politely ask Ares where the extra towels were kept.

When he walked into the kitchen, Ares' head was in the icebox, his hulking form bent in half, shuffling things around.

"Where would I find a spare towel?" Leo asked. Ares jerked up and slammed his head against the bottom of the freezer door. He grunted and looked back at Leo with a scowl.

"Linen closet is at the top of the stairs on the left. Bathroom's on the right. Don't go into my bedroom."

"I wouldn't want to," Leo grumbled, turning around and heading up the stairs.

The shower, fortunately, was heavenly. The water was hot and strong, and sluiced the grime and sweat and blood from his skin with ruthless efficiency. The pipes and shower head were hung over a massive claw foot tub, and all of Ares' soaps were lined up along the windowsill, where frosted panes let in light and the shapes of distant trees, shifting slowly with the wind. Leo breathed in the steam and forced himself to let go of some of his frustration. He prided himself on being good at finding solutions to problems, and if there were no solutions, his next best bet was the silver lining. His mother had taught him a long time ago that every bad situation had one, and so he would just endeavor to find it.

He could try to think of these next six days as a vacation. Work had been bustling since June, and his father's nascent Senate campaign had already been brutalized by the press as a premature power-grab by a middling Congressman. Things were stressful back home, and Hindry was supposed to have been a place for him to let off some steam. Between Sidney and the vampire, Leo had failed at relaxing, but now maybe he could. There was, he giggled to himself, nothing more relaxing than hiding in an asshole groundskeeper's house, trying to avoid a murderous, insane magician who wanted to kill him.

Leo turned off the shower and dried himself. He looked at the pile of dirty clothes on the floor and decided he'd wait to dress until Cerise returned with his new clothes. They'd said twenty minutes, and he'd been in the bathroom a while. Surely, they'd be back soon. Leo tucked his towel around his waist and examined his reflection, the bruise on his neck and the way he needed a shave soon. Hopefully Ares wouldn't mind lending him a razor.

Leo stepped onto the landing, which was really all there was to the second floor of the cottage, and was surprised by a delicious, savory smell drifting up the stairs. Meat and garlic, and God, he hadn't eaten all day. Leo held onto his towel, hurrying down the stairs, with only food on his mind and collided with Ares at the bottom of the steps.

"Sorry!" Leo backed up, as Ares managed to rebalance the parcel of clothes that was held in the crook of his arm. Ares looked Leo over vaguely, his scowl unchanged, but for a moment, Leo swore that there was heat in his gaze. He remembered the feeling of Ares' tongue against his skin, his rough stubble, his firm grip. Leo swallowed. Ares held out the parcel to him.

"Here," Ares said. Leo took the bundle, surprised by how much there seemed to be in it. It was heavier than he'd expected. "Hurry up. Dinner's almost ready." And without another word, he turned and stalked back toward the kitchen.

Leo dressed in an undershirt and trousers, ignoring the almost constant rumbling of his stomach. There was no dresser in the study, only the couch and the desk, a small set of shelves between them. Leo made room for his clothes on the top of the shelf, and then ran the towel through his hair again, curls springing, unruly, in all directions. Which was fine. There wasn't anyone here to impress.

As he walked through the living room, the dog appeared, walking alongside him as he stepped into the kitchen. The space was warm and cozy with yellow tile and black stone countertops. In the corner was an alcove, just large enough for the circle table and four chairs wedged around it. Dried herbs hung in each corner, and all around the room, open shelves held plates and pots and jars of dried goods and all manner of cooking utensils. Ares stood at the stove, scooping something out of a large pan and onto a thick bread roll. Leo was nearly drooling.

"Do you like cheese?"

"Sure," Leo said, embarrassingly eager. Ares huffed, almost certainly laughing at Leo's expense, and Leo could not have cared in the slightest. "Can I help at all?"

"Sit," Ares said, nodding toward the table. Leo did as he was told; he'd be as docile as a lamb if it meant he was getting fed.

The sandwich that Ares set in front of him very literally brought a tear to Leo's eye. Roast beef, onions, peppers, with melted cheese on top, served on the thickest roll Leo had ever seen. Ares could be as rude and snappish to Leo as he wanted. Leo could take it.

"Are you crying?"

"No," Leo sniffed, picking up the massive sandwich with both hands and taking a bite. He groaned in delight. Tender, garlicky, cheesy goodness. He actually was going to cry. Ares rolled his eyes and walked away.

"Beer?"

"Please," Leo gasped between bites.

"Slow down, or you'll choke," Ares said sharply, but Leo ignored him and knew he'd die a happy man. Ares set the beer down on the table and then sat across from Leo. It took Leo three more bites and a long drink of beer before he realized that Ares was watching him.

It wasn't like before, when he thought he'd felt a touch of heat to Ares' gaze. This was a sizing up, a measuring, more incisive than most. Leo set his glass down and tried to meet Ares' eye, like he hadn't just been moaning orgasmically over a sandwich. Think of this like a courtroom. Prosecutor. Defense.

"See something you like?" Leo arched an eyebrow, trying to imbue the phrase with sarcasm a bit too late. What was wrong with him? Ares made a derisive sound in the back of his throat.

"What do you do when you're not causing havoc and breaking people's noses?"

"I'm a lawyer," Leo said. Ares leaned back in his chair, looking smug, as though he had guessed it, which he absolutely hadn't. "And you're a groundskeeper?"

"Well spotted."

"And for the duration, I'm a groundkeeper's assistant. What does that entail?"

"Staying out of my way, and not getting into more trouble with Morrow."

"You don't seem to like him very much," Leo said. If he'd wanted to keep pressing, he shouldn't have leaned forward and taken a bite of his sandwich, but he couldn't help himself. Ares didn't respond though, only took a bite of his own sandwich, chewing slowly. Leo watched him swallow. "And, while I'm happy to stay out of your way, I don't think it'll lend much credence to the lie we're telling if I don't seem to be helping you with anything. You'll have to give me a couple of tasks to do at least."

"Unfortunately, I don't have any contracts that need looking over at the moment. No motions to file." Ugh. He was such a prick. Leo tried to breathe his frustration out through his nose, and it didn't help much. He had half a mind to ask Ares about his brother again. About why he was here and not back in Hindry. But that would almost certainly be the end of the conversation.

"Look, make fun of me all you want, but if you want me to stay out of trouble, the easiest way to ensure that is to give me something small to do. Doing nothing will stand out. You want

Morrow to ignore us, then we should be as innocuous as possible."

"Are you an expert in being ignored?" Ares asked, taking a swig from his beer, and hopefully missing the flush of embarrassment that flooded across the back of Leo's neck, and crept toward his cheeks. He grabbed up his own drink for something to do.

For Leo's whole life, unless he was doing something actively being remarked on, he was ignored. No one cared about what he'd done until he had succeeded or failed. It was almost magic, in a way. Leo's father wouldn't notice that Leo was gone until he didn't show up for that stupid dinner. At work, it would be when clients called someone else, angry that Leo hadn't called them back. Sidney, well... He would notice, but Leo had been absent from his life for so long intentionally that he couldn't blame Sidney for not minding; that wasn't so much being ignored, as turning invisible. Which Leo did intentionally by doing exactly what was expected of him at all times. Which was how he knew it would work.

"How's your shoulder?" Ares asked. Leo took a deep drink of beer, trying to get his head on straight.

"Stiff. Achey. It'll be fine in a couple of days." Ares scooted back from the table and got up without a word. Leo sighed and slumped back in his seat. Before he could decide whether he wanted to weep or sleep, Ares returned, sliding a glass bottle the size and shape of a double shot onto the table beside Leo's beer. The liquid inside was blue and shimmering, very obviously magic in a way that was almost laughable. Like a cheap stage trick. "What's that?"

"Medicine. It'll help."

"How much should I take?"

"All of it. Just toss it back. It doesn't taste like much. Mae makes it." Leo scooped up the bottle and held it up to the light.

"What's in it?" he asked. Ares shrugged.

"You'd have to ask Mae."

"You trust her," Leo observed, popping the thick cork out of the top of the bottle with his thumb.

"If I hadn't, I'd have died a long time ago." Ares replied with a smirk that changed his face so drastically, that Leo almost didn't recognize him. "And frankly, last night, she probably saved your life too."

"To Mae, then," Leo said, holding the blue stuff aloft. "Hopefully she'll never tire of helping wayward idiots." Ares chuckled, his round cheeks crinkling his eyes, smile broad and handsome. Leo smiled too and then tipped his head back and drank.

Whatever it was tasted vaguely of blueberries and not much else. Leo still chased it with his beer before realizing he maybe shouldn't have.

"Is that—?"

"It's fine," Ares said, with a gentle shake of his head. "At worst it'll make you tired. I imagine you already are. You can have the study, if you like. Though Matilda might fight you for the sofa."

"Matilda?"

"That great beast," Ares said, his smile warm again as he nodded toward the large black dog who was laying unsubtly in the doorway, watching them with wide yellow eyes. "She's about three inches away from being shunned for begging, and she knows it. When I snore too much, she sleeps on the sofa in the study."

"Do you think Cerise thought to make me pajamas?" Leo wondered aloud, grabbing for his sandwich again. Ares rolled his eyes, though his smirk remained as he got up to take his empty plate to the sink.

11

Leo woke to a short, sharp knock on the doorframe. He lifted his head, groggy, looking toward the door, as Matilda did the same, resting her chin on the arm of the sofa.

"He's looking for you," Leo mumbled to the dog.

"I'm looking for both of you," Ares huffed. Leo could see the shadow of him through the crack in the door, and some animal part of the back of his brain made his muscles tighten. Unfortunately, this alerted him to a crick in his neck. Leo had barely finished tasting his food the night before when he sank into a deep and dreamless sleep on the couch in the study, no concern at all about position. He was far too old to do that again. "Get up now if you want breakfast. Once I'm done loading up the cart we're leaving whether you've eaten or not."

"Where are we going?" Leo asked, even as he began to untangle his limbs from the blankets, while Matilda got to her feet.

"You said you wanted to help, so you're helping. Dress warm," Ares said. "It got cooler overnight." For a moment, Leo thought he caught Ares' eye through the crack in the door, but then he was gone, his footsteps fading down the hallway. Leo pulled on the same clothes he'd shucked after dinner the night before, and then pulled a thickly knit navy sweater on over the top of that. He glanced around for shoes, remembering Cerise holding their measuring tape up alongside Leo's feet, but didn't see any, until he opened the door and saw a pair of simple black work boots, too small to be Ares', sitting beside the front door.

In the kitchen, a thermos of coffee was on the table beside a single plate that held a breakfast sandwich that looked so good, for a moment Leo thought it might be a trap, like the ones stupid cartoon animals fell for in comic strips. The biscuit was light and golden brown, the sausage was three quarters of an inch thick, cheese melty, egg perfectly crisp around the edges. If this was meant for Ares and Leo ate it, Ares would kill him and Leo would have no regrets. He was relieved when a cursory glance around the kitchen revealed a dirty plate in the sink, crumbs on the ceramic. Ares had already eaten, so Leo would happily take the bait.

The first bite was so good that Leo moaned and sank back against the counter. Unfortunately, that coincided with the exact moment that Ares came in from the patio. Leo felt a small prickle of embarrassment, but the egg and cheese was melting against his tongue, hot and sticky, and so Ares could roll his eyes judgmentally all he wanted. Leo was in heaven. And it was Ares' own fault for being such a damn good cook. Ares shook his head and whistled for Matilda, who came bounding out from somewhere. Ares gave Leo a pointed look as he stepped outside.

"Grab the coffee and hurry up," he said, just before the door clicked shut.

Leo savored his breakfast for slightly longer than he imagined Ares would tolerate and received a glare for his trouble when he finally made it outside.

"Thank you for the sandwich," Leo smiled. Ares ignored him, grabbing the handle to the cart and starting down the paved path that led behind the house. So, they were back to sourness. That was fine. Leo could wait for Ares to warm up again.

They walked for a bit in silence, as Leo tried to take in the arrangement of the property behind Leyland Hall. The barn and pasture were beyond Ares' cottage to the south. The other side of the flower garden was lined by an orchard contained within a high stone wall. He could see the fruit on a few of the trees, something he didn't recognize, small and deeply purplish red like a grape, but they were bright against the green leaves and the soft grey clouds that littered the sky.

Leo didn't know enough about orchards to comment that it seemed odd to have it walled in so thoroughly. None of the other gardens were so protected; the flower garden had a decorative iron fence, and all of Ares' vegetables were behind split rails or pickets. The stones were large, and the wall was nearly six feet tall. Did orchards have some natural predator that Leo didn't know about?

As they turned off the paved path, onto a dirt road toward a distant line of trees, the sun came out from behind the clouds. The rays caressing the back of Leo's neck relaxed him, and he sighed in contentment before he could stop himself. Ares gave him a sideways glance, eyebrow lifted.

"I don't get to spend a lot of time outdoors," Leo explained. "I'm a lawyer, like I said. In Bainbridge. Not a lot of sun." Ares didn't comment, turning his gaze back to the dirt path as it began to wind south. "Where are we going anyway?" Leo asked.

"That stone wall over there," Ares nodded. Leo could see it clearly. About three and a half feet high, and noticeably shorter in places. "Needs patching. There's to be a shooting party here this weekend, and they'll come through this way, into the forest."

"And they care about how the wall looks?" Leo asked. Ares sighed.

"Perhaps lawyers don't understand that the work of a groundskeeper is to keep the grounds of a property. The wall is my job."

"No kidding," Leo muttered.

"How's your shoulder?" Ares asked, gruffly.

"Fine," Leo said. Then he rolled his arm and was surprised to find that his shoulder really was fine. Not even a twinge. "Really fine. That stuff is amazing." Ares nodded, a small smile drifting across his chin as he turned back toward the cart.

The work was hard, but the good kind of hard, where Leo knew the aches he would feel in his muscles at the end of the day meant that he'd accomplished something. He didn't get to experience that much anymore, occasionally at the boxing club. But he enjoyed it, truly. He hefted stones or held them in place while Ares spread mortar around them, stabilizing them, recreating what had once been a straight line across the top of the wall.

They stayed quiet, but the work seemed to loosen up Ares as well, his movements easy and practiced, his scowl fading as they worked their way along. He didn't even comment when Leo stopped to shuck his sweater and grab the thermos from the cart. Leo sipped and then offered the coffee to Ares who took it with a nod of thanks. Leo tried not to stare as Ares' throat moved, turning his gaze toward the trees, trying to find the source of the steadily growing birdsong.

"Starlings," Ares said. "Or something very much like them."

"It's getting cold. They don't migrate?" Leo asked. Ares shook his head.

"All of the animals here... in this world, I mean... they're just a little bit different than ours. Slightly off. Not in a bad way, they just—" he paused and then pointed toward Matilda, who was about ten yards off, sniffing something in the grass. "What sort of a dog do you think she is?"

"A herder of some kind," Leo shrugged. "Great Pyrenees, maybe? I don't really know breeds."

"I think she is a Great Pyrenees," Ares said. "Except, one of my aunts used to have Great Pyrenees, and Great Pyrenees aren't black. It's not in the breed."

"A mutt, then?" Leo suggested. Ares shook his head again, and handed the coffee back to Leo, who placed it down in the cart.

"It's just something to get used to about this place. Everything is just on the far side of what you expect."

"The lords of the house, and the carriages and—" Ares nodded.

"Fen told me once that the fae got obsessed with Earth between 1820 and 1900 and never looked back. They took the aesthetic pieces they liked and got rid of the rest."

"Well, all the opium and absinthe probably made humans a much more agreeable bunch. Is the green fairy real?"

"I take it you've seen her," Ares replied, judgement back in his tone, though he was smirking as he bent down to heft a large stone onto the top of the wall.

"Once or twice, but I was absolutely out of my head at the time. She certainly didn't try to dislocate my shoulder like that one up at the house."

"Oh, Morrow's not fae," Ares said. "He's a human." Leo frowned, stepping forward and holding the stone in place as Ares began to spread mortar.

"Not possible. I saw him doing magic."

"Humans can do magic," Ares said. "You just have to," he hesitated, rolling his bottom lip between his teeth as though he was searching for words. "You have to get access to it first."

"How?" Leo asked.

"I wouldn't know," Ares' attention was trained on the stone as though this wasn't the twentieth one they'd replaced, all the ease gone. He looked like a witness on the stand, trying to avoid a prosecutor's questions by not meeting his eye. Leo let him have it. It was the first conversation they'd had that wasn't primarily Ares snipping at him, and Leo was more interested in a truce than he was in information.

"I don't think I ever thanked you for giving Morrow such a hard time yesterday," Leo said as they moved to the next section of wall that needed patching.

"He's a bastard. I would have done it whether you were there or not."

"What did he do to you?" Leo asked casually. "What's your history?" There was a long pause, Ares grunting as he slid the stone into place. His eyes met Leo's as he rested a hand on top of the wall.

"He threatened my brother," Ares' tone was flat, but Leo could practically hear the rage behind it, could see it in the set of Ares' jaw. Another conversational blockade; Leo definitely wasn't going to bring up Dom Silva or the diner again. He took a breath, sighed and shook his head.

"No one truly appreciates how hard it is to be an older brother. A good one, I mean. It's easy to be a bad one, probably. Though, it's easy to be bad at most things." Ares didn't respond exactly, but he did make a huff of sound that might have been agreement, and Leo was determined not to let the conversation slip away. He rambled on as they continued to work, about how he'd followed in his father's footsteps after their parents' divorce primarily so Sidney wouldn't have to.

"Sidney's smart," Leo enthused. "Brilliant even. But he's not cut out for politics. His head's always been in the clouds. In the stars, more accurately. Somewhere far out beyond the realms of common sense. He's the sort of fellow that just plows forward toward whatever he wants until he reaches it, whether he ought to or not."

"A family trait, I gather," Ares said beneath his breath. Leo laughed.

"On the contrary, compared to Sidney I'm practically the picture of moderation and discretion." Ares laughed at that, a throaty, deep sound, that had Leo beaming.

"Your brother sounds incredibly intimidating."

"He's more menacing than he looks," Leo agreed.

"Another family trait," Ares said. Leo's eyes widened as his brain processed the words and scrambled to decide whether they were meant as a jibe or a flirtation. Ares cleared his throat, stepping ahead, bending down for another rock, and it took Leo a full fifteen seconds to catch up with him. When he stood, Ares' expression was neutral again, his attention on his work. Leo swallowed and let it go by, thinking that he was going to be a master of conversational diplomacy by the time his stay with Ares was over.

They worked in silence for another half an hour as the sun inched higher in the sky. By lunchtime they were nearly done. Leo had shucked his flannel, tossing it in the cart with his sweater, and Ares had rolled up the sleeves of his thermal, sweat glistening temptingly on his neck. There were some apple trees at the edge of the woods, and Ares reached up and plucked them a couple. Leo hoisted himself up onto a completed patch of wall and enjoyed the sweetness of the fresh fruit and the warmth of the sun on his arms and his face. Ares ate as he walked the length of the rest of the wall, dusting old mortar off the rocks with his hands, and Leo closed his eyes and let himself listen to the starlings and the sound of his own breathing. When Ares came back, he was humming a tune that Leo had never heard before. Leo listened instead of asking what it was, and Ares continued humming as they finished their work and walked back to the cottage.

12

The sun was setting as Ares dragged the hose across the yard to fill the poultry drinker. Matilda was rounding up the chickens and the crickets were still singing, confused by another day of pleasant weather.

Ares and Leo had made it home a few hours ago. He set Leo to gathering the squash and had gone back out to coppice some of the hazel at the edge of the forest for firewood. Experience had taught him that these few mild days wouldn't last much longer, and they'd want the extra kindling soon up at the house.

It had also been a good excuse to get away from Leo for a couple of hours. Not that the man had been anything but agreeable, almost irritatingly so. Ares didn't trust it. Leo was too smart, probably trying to lull Ares into a false sense of camaraderie for some unsavory purpose. He was a lawyer, after all. And a flirt. And he had looked unfairly good sitting on the stone wall, sweat sticking his undershirt to the knots of his spine, the bulge of his shoulders. Ares overfilled the poultry drinker and water splashed onto his boots.

When he made it back inside, kicking his wet shoes off on the patio, there was a strong smell of bacon emanating from the kitchen. Ares took a deep breath. Matilda paused at his side and looked up at him, her head cocked to the side as if to say 'aren't you going to go see what he's doing?'

"Why don't you go see what he's doing?" he muttered to her. Matilda blinked, then opened her mouth, yawning widely before she hopped up onto the sofa. Ares sighed and walked across the living room, pausing in the doorway to the kitchen. Leo's back was to him, his curls damp on the back of his neck. Multiple pans were sitting on the stove, and a pile of potatoes were on the cutting board. Ares cleared his throat, and Leo whipped around, wooden spoon raised guiltily in his hand.

"What are you doing?"

"Making dinner," Leo said. Ares cocked his head. "I found these potatoes in the cellar. Thought I'd make chowder."

"You know how to make chowder?"

"I found a cookbook."

"I thought I told you to stay away from my things." He hadn't. But he had meant to.

"When you're busy what should I do? Sit silently with my hands in my lap and wait for you to come back and boss me around?"

"Ideally," Ares replied, forcing the smirk from his face. "That's what assistants are for."

"Well, it's a good thing I'm not really your assistant then, isn't it? Dinner will be done by the time you're out of the shower," Leo said, turning back to the stove.

"Are you sure a fancy boy like you knows how to cut a potato?" Ares needled, just because. It had been a long time since anyone had cooked in his kitchen, apart from Ares himself.

"I've managed this far," Leo said, not looking up, the rhythm of his knife slow and steady against the cutting board. Ares stepped closer, watching his technique.

"You could go faster if you held the potato from the end.

With your fingertips." Ares suggested. Leo paused, full lips pursing slightly as he moved his hand into the perfect position to cut one of his fingers off. "Not quite," Ares stepped up behind him, cupping the back of Leo's hand with his palm, tucking Leo's fingers back out of the way of the knife. "Like this. Now cut." Leo chopped, while Ares slowly moved their fingers back, and it wasn't until they reached the end of the potato that Ares realized how close they were. He could smell his own shampoo in Leo's dark, thick curls. The firm heat of Leo's shoulder pressed against the center of Ares' chest. Ares dropped his hand and tried to take a casual, unbothered step back, so that Leo couldn't feel the way Ares' heart was suddenly pounding. His cheeks were on fire, and he felt like an idiot. Hadn't he just said not to fall for any of Leo's tricks? Stupid. Ridiculous.

"Like this?" Leo asked, placing another potato on the cutting board and glancing back at Ares as though they hadn't just been too close for comfort. Ares barely looked at Leo's hand.

"Yes. Exactly. Just be careful." And he hurried out of the kitchen and headed up the stairs.

Gods, what on earth was wrong with him? One day of companionship, and Ares was trying to make friends again? He had enough friends, and he certainly didn't need a friend like Leo. Reckless and mouthy. Someone who picked fights with Morrow and got bitten by vampires. No, thanks. Ares' life was dangerous enough all on its own.

In the bathroom, Leo had left a small puddle beside the tub, and Ares scowled at it. And at the wet washcloth on Ares' hook in the shower. He turned on the water and got undressed, trying not to think about Leo. About Leo in his kitchen, cooking dinner. About Leo, naked, in Ares' shower.

It was all wrong. Leo wasn't cut out for the life Ares led: spending days in the garden and patching walls and chasing chickens. No matter how good it had looked on him. He was all law offices and fancy dinners. Definitely, he'd be as good-looking in a suit as he had been sitting on the wall, smiling in the warm sunlight. And the day before, when he'd come down the stairs with only a towel around his waist—

Wait. No. Ares wasn't going to think about that.

Ares closed his eyes and turned up the heat on the shower, letting the water scald his skin, hopefully burning some sense back into his brain. If he ignored that he was half-hard, his erection would go away. Leo was nothing to him. He wasn't handsome. He was dangerous. Ares didn't want him. Ares was just lonely. A ten-year dry spell would have that effect on anyone.

He opened his eyes, and Leo's washcloth on Ares' shower hook was the first thing Ares saw. Ares had the sudden, bizarre urge to take the washcloth and rub it against himself. And that was too deviant by half. There was nothing wrong with jerking off in the shower, but there were limits.

There were, weren't there?

Ares took himself in hand, trying to be efficient about things. He stroked himself the same way he always did and stared at the tiles, trying not to picture Leo's palms splayed against them. The way Leo would sound if Ares bent him over in the shower and took him hard and fast, his pretty mouth wide in a gasp of pleasure that would echo against the walls.

Or, Gods, Leo on his knees, his lips stretched around Ares' girth. Ares' fingers threading through damp curls. Leo swallowing deep, whining, moaning, bright brown eyes fixed on Ares. Leo's rough stubble against Ares' palm. The pad of Ares' thumb against Leo's bottom lip.

Ares came with a groan that was absolutely too loud for a house with more than one person in it. He braced himself against the wall for several seconds, heat staining his cheeks, as he tried to tell himself that he was done. He'd let himself indulge in the fantasy that was so far removed from anything that he could ever have, that it was going to leave a sour taste in his mouth for the next few days. And served him right. He knew better than to let himself get carried away. A man like Leo and a fool like Ares? It was downright laughable.

Ignoring the persistent tingling in his skin, Ares finished his shower and dried off without so much as glancing at the damp towel on the hook behind the door. He got dressed, his stomach rumbling every time a whiff of the delicious chowder Leo was cooking made its way up the stairs.

By the time he made it back to the kitchen, the table was set, and Leo had managed to get a splash of sour cream on the collar of his shirt. Which Ares ignored. It became slightly easier to ignore when the soup turned out to be delicious.

"No need to be so impressed. I can read, you know," Leo said, sopping out the bottom of his bowl with a biscuit left over from the ones Ares had made that morning. Ares didn't respond, but he did get up and serve himself seconds.

"I'm going to be doing some work in the big house tomorrow," Ares said as he sat back down with his bowl. "Do you think you can manage to keep your hands to yourself until I get back?"

"Because it was so terrible that I looked at your incredibly secret cookbook?" Leo huffed, rolling his eyes. "Honestly, Ares, it's like you're keeping a horde of pirate gold beneath the floorboards. How much damage do you possibly think I can do?"

"Oh, I wouldn't want to speculate," Ares said. Leo rolled his eyes, his cheeks turning a pretty shade of pink as he pretended not to smile.

"Why don't I come up with you, then?"

"Yes. That seems wise. You made such a good impression on the lord of the manor last time."

"I didn't technically meet the lord of the manor, did I?" Leo replied, his tone as arched as his eyebrows. Ares huffed.

"You really can't sit quietly for a single afternoon?"

"I like to keep busy." Leo met Ares' gaze, challenge in his eyes. The intensity of him was enticing. It lit something in Ares, made him want to push back. Made him want to give in and see what Leo would do when he came across Morrow again. Leo was dangerous; Ares recognized it, because it was the same danger he'd spent the last ten years avoiding. Maybe longer than that. But he'd only needed to dance with it once to have it ruin his whole life.

"It's a stupid risk. One you're not taking."

"I'm not afraid of him." Leo squared like he was going to throw a punch, his bottom lip jutting out in a pout. Idiot. Ares shook his head.

"You should be afraid of him."

"You're not. Even if he is threatening your family."

Ares inhaled, his chest suddenly tight. He wasn't afraid of Edmund Morrow, that was true. Not anymore. Fear had changed over the years, thickening into something much more potent: first rage and then hate.

"I'm not afraid of him," Ares admitted. "But caution and fear are different things. He can still do damage. And he enjoys breaking things. If you're smart, you'll be careful."

"The way you backtalked him in the barn yesterday was far from cautious." Ares grabbed his napkin and wiped his mouth.

"I don't have to be cautious," Ares said, getting to his feet. "He's already taken everything from me that there is to take."

Ares had wanted to shut down Leo's line of questioning, which was why he'd been honest. The truth was ugly and uncomfortable, and he hadn't wanted Leo to answer. But Ares hadn't expected Leo's beautiful mouth to crumple into a frown, his eyes wide with curious concern. He hated the way Leo was looking at him now, so Ares walked away, dumping his empty bowl into the sink.

"Thank you for dinner," Ares said, as though that would take the edge of tension out of the air. The tension that he'd purposefully placed there. For a long moment, neither of them moved, and then, before Leo could speak, Ares left, heading for the stairs and the sanctuary of his bedroom.

13

Leo dressed for bed in the narrow space between the couch and the desk in the study, trying to sort through all the disparate pieces of Ares like a puzzle. He was reserved and stand-offish, but only when he wasn't being brave and kind. Every time Ares revealed even the slightest bit of a personal detail, he immediately ran away. Morrow had threatened his brother, and taken everything from him? What could those two things mean in conjunction? Dom had seemed well enough. Did Ares have another brother? Leo took a deep breath and listened for a moment to the sounds of the house. Ares' footsteps on the landing, and then the bathroom door closing. The quiet chirp of crickets outside Leo's window. Leo sighed.

Leo's ability to get a good read on people had always been a point of pride. It was a useful tool in the courtroom and the campaign trail, and he knew he was good at it. Which was why Ares constant obfuscation was frustrating. What was Ares' history with Edmund Morrow? Why didn't Ares want his brother to know where he was? Why had he come here in the first place? What was he hiding?

The door creaked open as Matilda nosed her way in. Leo

patted her on the shoulder as she made room for herself beside him, looking up at him expectantly.

"It's bedtime," he said. She sniffed as derisively as any old biddy ever had, and Leo chuckled. "Look, I would have loved to stay up and chat, but your owner made it quite clear he was interested in no further conversation." He wasn't sure if dogs could properly roll their eyes, but Matilda almost certainly did before hopping up on the end of the couch and resting her large chin on the arm of the sofa. Leo shook his head, though, really, he didn't mind sharing.

And he didn't mind going to bed early. With a full stomach and sore shoulders, a day of real labor was finally catching up to him. He finished getting dressed and curled up on his half of the sofa, tugging the blanket down over himself and Matilda's lower half. He wondered about Ares again, about his motives and his reasons, for approximately thirty seconds before falling asleep.

In Leo's dream, his office at the law firm felt slightly more claustrophobic than it did in real life. The shelves felt higher, the door was closer to his desk, and Ares was standing in front of him, dressed in something like a suit.

Pages of inheritance and contract law were spread out across Leo's desk, and he caught himself mid-lecture about a topic he didn't quite understand. Ares watched him, arms folded across his broad chest, his mouth curled into the small, shit-eating smirk that he got when he was going to tell Leo something he thought Leo didn't know.

"What?" Leo demanded, irritability from reality carrying over into his dreams.

"I didn't ask you to explain it to me."

"You asked for my help," Leo countered.

"No, I didn't."

"Well, you should have," Leo snapped, getting to his feet.

"And if you don't want my help, why are you here?" Ares dropped his arms, grin widening, crooked.

"That's a good question, Mr. Lawyer."

Really and truly, Leo had had enough. Leo rounded the corner of his desk and grabbed Ares by the elbow, with every intent of tugging him toward the door. But the moment his grip tightened, Ares swung toward him, grabbing Leo by the waist, pushing him back against the bookshelves.

Ares' chest was just as firm as it had been in reality. And so was his grip. Leo whimpered, realizing, finally, what sort of dream he was having. Ares crowded Leo against the shelves, hoisting Leo up so just the tips of his dress-shoes touched the ground, and when Ares kissed him, Leo sank into it before he could stop himself.

Grabbing Leo by his lapels, Ares manhandled Leo around the office, pressing him up against the wall and the desk, stripping Leo with ruthless efficiency. Before Leo quite knew what was happening, he was bent over his own desk, wrists pinned to the small of his back in one of Ares' large hands. Ares teased him, rough and then soft and Leo writhed and squirmed and begged. Ares smacked his ass hard, and Leo woke up as he came, spilling in his shorts. He lay in the dark for a long moment, chest heaving, before he had his first coherent thought.

Shit.

Leo leaned up, relieved to see that Matilda was no longer at the other end of the sofa. Her baleful yellow gaze would have made him want to die of embarrassment. *How dare you think those things about my father?*

How dare he, indeed. And how long had he been asleep? Between his own exhaustion, the orgasm, the dark, Leo was feeling as disoriented as if he'd been bitten by a vampire again.

He got up carefully, stripped and redressed, before creeping up the stairs to wash out his shorts in the bathroom sink.

What was wrong with him? Ares was handsome, yes. Ares was big and gruff and maybe those things appealed to Leo on an objective level, sure. And maybe Leo had been a little too willing to let Ares hoist him off the ground again. But this? He hadn't orgasmed from a dream since he was fifteen, and it was absolutely an embarrassment. Ares didn't even like him! At least, Leo didn't think so, and Leo was not in the market for fantasies about people who would just as soon throw him out on his ass as invite him into their bed.

Leo finished cleaning up and went back downstairs, flopped down on the couch, closed his eyes, and immediately thought about the dream again. About Ares taking control, taking what he wanted, taking—

Leo opened his eyes and rolled over. Enough was enough.

But it wasn't.

Visions of Ares appeared every time Leo closed his eyes, tossing and turning on the narrow couch cushions, until Leo finally gave in, letting the scene replay in his brain until he passed out from exhaustion. It didn't mean anything. It was never going to mean anything. It was just a dream.

14

Ares got up early the next morning and was surprised when Leo wandered into the kitchen in his pajamas while Ares was still brewing coffee. Leo didn't speak, just stood bleary-eyed and bed-headed in the doorway, until Ares turned to him.

"You're up early."

"I didn't sleep well."

"Oh." It was the first complaint he'd heard out of Leo, and it wasn't even angled at Ares, when it certainly could have been. Ares didn't know how to respond, and after they'd left things so awkwardly at dinner the night before, he almost felt like he should apologize. But then, would that only be stranger? "Well, if you want to make yourself useful, you could go let the chickens out and gather the eggs for breakfast. Basket's by the door." Not quite as kind-sounding as he'd hoped. Ares turned back to the coffee to hide his wince and listened to Leo's footsteps fade back into the living room.

Ares couldn't blame Leo for declining; Ares wasn't sure when he'd lost all ability to be even remotely cordial. He didn't have to fall in love with the man, but he could at least be kind.

'I'm sorry you didn't sleep well. Do you need another blanket?' How hard was that to say? Ares took a deep breath, working himself up to it, but before he could step away from the counter, Leo, now dressed, walked across the living room, pulling a sweater on over his head. He stepped into his boots before scooping up the basket and leaving through the patio door without a word.

Guilt sat strangely with Ares as he finished making coffee and started on toast and rashers. It wasn't his fault Leo hadn't slept well. Or at least... it might not have been. Ares, still sated from his shower fantasies, tired from a day of hauling stones, and his stomach full of a hearty meal, had dropped off to sleep immediately. It wasn't as though Leo had done that much less than Ares, all things considered.

While the sausages sizzled in the pan, Ares went upstairs to his bedroom and opened the hope chest that stood against the far wall beneath the window. He'd given Leo a pillow and a blanket, but he did have more, and better ones besides. He lay them on his bed to air out a little, and then went back downstairs to finish up breakfast, feeling like he'd at least be able to make an offer of more comfort when Leo returned.

Twenty minutes later, Leo stormed back into the house.

"How?" Leo demanded, furious. He slammed the basket hard on the table, and Ares looked over, eyebrows raised at the outburst. Leo held up his hands, and Ares had to purse his lips to stop himself from laughing. Leo's fingers, the backs of his hands, were scratched and nipped. Hen-pecked, as it were.

"What did you do?" Ares managed.

"I was getting the eggs!" Leo snapped, anger pinking his cheeks. "Every time I would reach under—"

"Reach under?"

"They're all sitting there—"

"Pick them up, Leo!" Ares laughed, shaking his head. Before Leo could explode, Ares walked over and handed Leo the cup of coffee Ares had been holding. Then Ares scooped up the basket. "There's toast on the counter and rashers in the pan. I'll be back in a bit."

"You didn't tell me I could pick them up!" Leo fumed, presumably to himself, as Ares was already halfway out the door.

To Leo's credit, a few of the hens were particularly feisty that morning, and Ares guessed that it was primarily the fault of the large grey thunderheads on the horizon. It was colder too, wind picking up from the west, blowing leaves from the forest across the pasture. By the time he'd gathered eggs and picked the ready greens and a couple of squash from the garden, it was beginning to drizzle. He ran the majority of his harvest up to the house, and while he was there, he had the forethought to ask one of the footmen if Morrow was still in residence. The answer was thankfully no. He'd gone the day before yesterday and wasn't expected to join the hunting party that weekend, much to Lord Kephisto's displeasure.

Ares' shoulders were damp from the rain, by the time he made it back to the cottage. Leo was still sitting at the kitchen table, coffee and a crumb covered plate by his side. He was reading a book, and Ares didn't say a word about where he'd gotten it from, as he went over to the stove and ran a dishtowel over his face.

"Eggs?" he asked, as he tossed the towel aside.

"I didn't know you could move the chickens," Leo said, flatly.

"And I should have known better than to send a lawyer to deal with a bunch of ornery hens," Ares replied, keeping his tone as light as he could. "They hate when it rains." Leo snorted, and Ares set to work on a quick fry-up. As he threw some cheese into the pan, he glanced back over his shoulder. Leo was still looking at the book, but he hadn't turned the page.

"Morrow's gone. I checked with Warren up at the house. So, with the rain and everything, I guess I could use your help after all."

"What do you have to do?"

"Cleaning and oiling the hunting rifles for the weekend. We won't want to test fire in the rain, but we can get the messy part out of the way today," he said, his attention on turning the eggs. Leo was quiet, and Ares glanced over his shoulder to gauge whatever reaction Leo might be having. He didn't seem to be having much of any reaction at all, just staring out the kitchen window past Ares shoulder. "Don't care much for hunting?"

"No, I..." Leo shook his head, ran his tongue over his teeth. "I was just thinking about the last time I went. I'm... it's not one of my favorite ways to spend a day. Never seemed particularly sporting, I guess."

"What sort of sport do you go in for?" Ares asked.

"Boxing," Leo replied.

"Watching or participating?"

"Participating," Leo said simply. It made sense. Or, at least, it explained the cut of Leo's physique. When Ares looked over at him, Leo only pointed to the bump in his nose with a smirk. "That's where this came from."

"So it's not the violence you object to," Ares posited. Leo chuckled.

"Rather me than some poor defenseless bunny."

"That's fair."

"Which would you rather do for an afternoon?"

"Neither," Ares said. "I'd rather be left in peace. Give the animals their space—"

"And the people," Leo added. Ares nodded.

"And the people."

"It really doesn't bother you to be alone, then? Out here by yourself... all this time?" Ares bit down on the inside of his bottom lip. The answer to that was complicated. Loneliness, he'd learned, was a faceted thing. Years changed its shape. So did visitors. Ares shook his head.

"Having a guest stay for longer than a night," Ares paused, tossing the tomato slices into the pan and then reaching for the salt. "I'm not even sure I remember what lonely feels like anymore," he lied, shooting Leo a small smirk over his shoulder. As though Leo's presence had done anything but shone a light on exactly how alone Ares was, and how it had changed him. Made him forget certain parts of himself. Like how to be nice.

Leo didn't smile back, his brow furrowed. Ares turned to the stove and tried to focus on what he was doing. The last of the sausage in next. Leftover beans last, letting them crack in the grease.

He dumped all the food onto one large platter and placed it in the center of the table. Leo closed the book, his eyes softening as he looked over the spread. Ares returned with two plates and cutlery, and then went back for the carafe and a coffee mug for himself. It wasn't fancy, but it was as good a way to start the morning as any he'd found. Leo seemed to perk up after downing a couple of eggs and shoving a mouthful of beans onto toast.

"Did you teach your brother how to cook? Or did he teach you?" Leo asked. Ares chuckled. Cooking, the only safe topic of conversation.

"My parents taught us both. I'm better at the griddle, but I never took to baking. That's all Dom."

"Sidney's an excellent baker," Leo said, with the same proud enthusiasm that Ares had gotten used to hearing the day before any time the topic came around to Leo's brother. "Our mother and her wife run a dry goods store in the town we grew up in, but they did baked goods too. Cookies, pies, cakes, that sort of thing. Sidney's well-versed. He makes these honey rolls..." Leo trailed off, nodding in contentment as he took another bite of toast. "I'll have to get your biscuit recipe for him."

"Biscuits are the only thing I ever got good at," Ares said. "It's an easy bake. Hard to mess it up."

"Well," Leo shrugged, a small smile finally tugging up the corner of his lips, "I'll give it a try and see what I can do." Ares smiled at Leo before he realized he was doing it. Not that there was anything wrong with smiling at him. Not that commiserating about their brothers and Leo's cooking skills was anything more than polite conversation. Ares used to be a master of polite conversation. Every day at the diner was spent making small talk with customers, not snarling at them or trading jibes. So why did this feel so different? Was he really that out of practice?

As they finished breakfast, Leo kept talking. Nothing of consequence, mostly about food and his brother and the places those two topics intersected. When Ares stood to take his plate and platter to the sink, Leo got up quickly and took the dishes from his hands.

"I'll do it," he said. "You cooked." It was then that Ares realized Leo had done the dishes the night before. And from breakfast yesterday... and for every meal they'd shared since Leo had arrived at Ares' house. "What time are we going up?" Leo asked, his back to Ares, his sleeves rolled up, hands already in the sink.

"I need to milk the cows," he said. "Check on a couple of sheep. After that."

"Alright," Leo said.

"Thanks for doing the dishes," Ares said, feeling dumb.

"Thanks for cooking." Leo didn't turn around, just grabbed for the soap, but when Ares left the kitchen, went to grab his canvas coat off the hook by the front door, he felt strangely as though he was running away again.

15

The armory room in Leyland Hall would have made Congressman Quince salivate. Leo had been honest when he told Ares how he felt about guns. There were better ways to spend an afternoon than chasing poor defenseless creatures around a paddock, even though he'd been on several hunts himself, mostly to appease campaign donors and that sort of thing. Still, even he could admire the aesthetic of the room, all dark wood cabinets, and wall-mounted rifle racks, holding the sort of decorative hunting guns that even his father could only aspire to own.

From one of the lower drawers, Ares had produced all the cleaning equipment they'd need, and he'd taken down one of the long-barreled rifles and shown Leo the process. Fitting it in the stand, adding powder solvent to the cloth that was pushed through the barrel on a small pike. There was more after that, oil and an external machine part lubricant, as well as wood polish, but Leo handed the guns off to Ares for those steps.

There were twelve rifles that Leo could see, and they worked quietly for the better part of half an hour, the pattering of the rain on the eaves filling the silence. Leo was feeling better. Food had helped, and it was nice to stay busy. The house was lovely, and he couldn't complain about the company. Until he looked up from the gun he was working on to see Ares, rifle butt braced against his hip, sliding an oily rag up and down the thick metal barrel of the gun. Leo blushed, shifting his stance to try and accommodate his sudden hard-on. He knocked the rifle he'd been working on out of its stand, barely catching it before it clattered to the floor.

"Alright?" Ares asked. Leo hazarded a glance at Ares and shouldn't have, his eyebrow arched in mild concern.

"Fine. Sorry. Just, slipped." Ares grunted as he hoisted the gun off his hip, and Leo was thrust directly back to his dreams the night before with unfortunate clarity.

"Do you want a break?"

"No. Nope. I'm fine." Leo managed to get the rifle back into the stand and began to clean with a renewed focus. The next time Leo looked up, Ares had a new rifle pressed into his hip, wiping drops of oil from the tip of the barrel with his thumb. Leo's blush was creeping up behind his ears.

"Actually, I might go get a cup of coffee—"

"I can bring you one." A sweet, chipper voice followed by a round cheeked woman with pale olive skin popped into the room. Black hair was wound in an elaborate braid around the crown of her head, and an apron covered the bulk of her outfit.

"Ah, yes," Ares said, his tone more formal, but not more gruff, as he made introductions. "Julian Flint, this is our cook, Fennel Rourke. Fen, this is Julian. I'm sure Mr. Oswald mentioned him to you."

"Barely," Fen grinned. "But Cerise filled me in. Welcome to Leyland Hall, Mr. Flint."

"Please, call me Julian." Leo wanted to shake hands, but was terrified that stepping around the counter would reveal an embarrassing tent in his trousers.

"Julian," Fen beamed, her cheeks rosy, "are you and Ares staying for lunch?"

"We don't want to put you out," Ares said before Leo could ask what they were having. Fen shook her head.

"Nonsense. We have more than enough. The first guests are getting in for the weekend, so we've made extra. Curry puffs and pan-fried salmon with a coconut and chili glaze. Roasted veggies. Spiced apple pudding for dessert." Great. Now Leo's mouth was watering.

"It sounds delicious—" Ares began, but Leo could already hear the exception that was coming at the end of Ares' sentence, and so he interrupted, unable and uninterested in keeping the desperation from his voice.

"We'd love to. Thank you so much."

"Flint," Ares said so reproachfully, that Leo's arousal couldn't decide if it was dying or flaring to life. He needed to get a hold of himself.

"It's raining," Leo arched an eyebrow at Ares. "How much else can we do?"

"I just hope it stops before tomorrow," Fen said. "We're going down into Laurel Grove in the evening to go dancing. Normally we've got Sunday night off, but since the party's this weekend, Mr. Oswald arranged for us to have tomorrow instead. It'll just be Warren and I and a couple of the others. Maybe Marnie and some of the valets who are in with the guests. You should come with us!" Leo didn't know who any of those people were, but a night out meant a night not spent sitting across the table from a man who Leo was having unstoppable sex fantasies about and who couldn't be bothered to give Leo the time of day? Yes.

"That sounds incredible," Leo said, with likely more enthusiasm than was necessary. Still, Fen met it with a wide, genuine smile.

"Great. Ares, what about you?" Leo almost laughed. He couldn't imagine Ares socializing. And, he told himself, he didn't care if Ares came along anyway. But Ares, for some reason, hadn't said no. Instead, Ares' mouth was hanging open in hesitation, his attention off above Leo's head somewhere.

"Uhh..."

What was he waiting for? Leo imagined Ares must turn these people down all the time. Unless he actually wanted to go. But didn't know how to say so?

"He'll be there," Leo said, abruptly, ignoring the heat that flooded into his cheeks as he turned back to Fen. "He'd love to come."

"I don't believe you!" She replied with such cheer that Leo couldn't help but laugh. "But I'd love it if he did. Come round to the kitchens whenever you're at a good stopping point. I'll keep the salmon in the warmer for you." And then she left.

The silence that fell in the room was heavy as the door clicked shut behind her. There was nowhere for Leo to look except at Ares, and he tried to do so as guilelessly as possible, as though he'd done absolutely nothing wrong. Ares sniffed and went back to wiping down the barrel of the blunderbuss, as though he was very used to having something of that size in his hand. If Leo was waiting for Ares to say something, he might be waiting all night.

"Did you not want to come?"

"Do you not want me to come?" Ares returned, as he went to hang that beast of a gun back on the rack.

"No. I just... I know it isn't necessarily your idea of a good time."

"And what," Ares asked, turning back toward Leo, "would *you* know about my idea of a good time?" It was the same tone he'd taken in the dream, and Leo's brain screeched to a sudden halt.

"No. I— Not that I know. It just seems like. I mean… Have you gone out with them before?"

"Staff doesn't generally last very long at Leyland Hall," Ares said, plucking the rifle Leo had been working on from the stand. "There's quite a bit of turn-over among the younger ones. People who take the job without knowing how capricious the lord of the house can be." Ares grabbed a rag from the table, finally looking back at Leo. "All that to say, I haven't been out with this crowd all that often. But I do go out, from time to time."

"Oh," Leo said, wishing he had anything else to add.

"I mean, I was in Laurel Grove when I first ran into you," Ares added, his expression shifting into a small, smug smirk.

"Well, good. I'm glad you're coming," Leo said. Ares snorted. "I am. It'll be nice to see if you're any less surly in the company of people you actually like."

"You make a lot of assumptions about who and what I do and don't like."

"It's all I have to go on," Leo shrugged. "The only thing I know about you for sure is that you're determined not to be friends with me."

"That is true," Ares agreed, though he was still smirking, clearly teasing in a way that Leo was desperate not to be charmed by.

16

The rain only got worse, bringing with it a bone-chilling cold that Ares had fully known was coming. Once they'd had lunch with Fen and gone back to the cottage, Ares had taken out his heavier waxed canvas coat that would keep the rain from soaking him through and went to the barn, leaving Leo alone in the cottage to fend for himself.

Which was fine. He was pretty sure he'd defeated his burgeoning crush on the lawyer, and he was proud to say that he was now totally unaffected by Leo's charm. Ares was almost definitely going to find a way out of going into town tomorrow night, and then it was only two more days and Leo would be back in Hindry and Ares would be in exactly the same place as he was a week ago. No harm done.

Ares hoisted a bag of feed over his shoulder and wondered why that didn't feel more satisfying. Everything was going the way that he'd wanted. He'd gotten his errant feelings under control. Leo seemed to have dropped his questions about Dom and Morrow and the rest of it, which probably meant he'd forgotten, and for the most part, Ares was back in his usual routine. His list of chores was the same, harvesting and sheltering and preparing for winter. He'd need to go out on horseback in the morning and check the trails for anything that would impede the hunting party: fallen trees or low hanging branches. Traps set by the local poachers he was at regular war with. Ares wondered if Leo had ever ridden a horse before. Not that Leo was invited along. Fancy boy like that, probably had friends who played polo or something on the weekends. Ares sniffed as the cows crowded him, trying to reach the trough.

Ares finished up in the barn just as the last of the daylight sank down below the horizon, turning the sky from grey to dark grey. Pulling his hood over his head, he went to tend the chickens and the goats. They were all fine, a little sour at being kept in the run all day, but none the worse for wear. He hadn't needed to check on them, really. The grounds of Leyland Hall were, for the most part, a well-oiled machine, because he'd built it that way over the last ten years. Ares' job was maintenance now. And that was good. Definitely not unfulfilling. Or route. Or boring. And even if it was those things, so what? There was no alternative. Discontent slithered beneath his skin and he ignored it as he crossed the patio, wiped his boots on the mat and stepped inside the back door.

A fire was rumbling pleasantly in the stone fireplace, and the smell of something delicious, rosemary and onions, cooked meat, wafted through the air. Leo, in an undershirt that strained across the planes of his chest, was sitting on the couch, one foot tucked under his thigh, leaning toward a book balanced on the arm of the sofa. Matilda, the traitor, was curled up against his hip. Leo's head rested on his hand, his fingers carding through his curls, tugging on them as he read. Ares was struck by the sudden bizarre urge to draw him. Leo was so comfortable, so engaged, so lost in his book that he hadn't even looked up when Ares came in.

And then, Leo did look up. His chestnut brown gaze was infinitely curious and thoughtful, and Ares wondered what Leo must think of him. He almost asked: *what are you thinking right now?* But then Leo smiled, small and genuine, like he was happy that Ares was there, and the attraction that Ares had been sure he'd dealt with pricked threateningly at the back of his consciousness. Ares' mouth was dry. He wanted to walk away, but his heels were rooted to the floor.

"I tried to make shepherd's pie," Leo said. "It should be done in about," he paused, glancing down at a pocket watch that was sitting beside his thigh. "Half an hour. Sorry. I wasn't sure when you'd be back."

"Smells good," Ares said dumbly. Leo's smile widened, and Ares' skin tingled uncomfortably, trying to warn him about the threat of another home-cooked meal. Which was silly. They were just roommates. Temporary roommates. Nothing more.

"Same cookbook as yesterday," Leo said. "I make no promises about the gravy."

"You don't have to cook for me."

"Well, it's not exactly an easy dish to make for one."

"No, I just mean," Ares fumbled. What did he mean?

"And I'm not going to use your kitchen to just make food for myself. That seems pretty rude, given everything you've done for me." Leo stretched, clasping his hands over his head, raising his arms, straightening his chest. His shirt rode up over a patch of dark hair beneath his belly button and Ares caught himself staring.

"You don't owe me anything," Ares grumbled, ignoring the heat that was creeping down the back of his neck. He needed to get out of the living room. Get away from Leo. Which was crazy, because he didn't like Leo. He didn't want Leo.

But he didn't want to leave either. He wanted to sit down and ask about what Leo was reading. He wanted to tease Leo about his cooking and make him smile again. He wanted. And that wanting couldn't, shouldn't, exist.

"I'm happy to cook," Leo said, his voice kinder than Ares wanted to hear. "Or clean." Ares scoffed.

"You're a regular Snow White."

"I promise, I won't let the songbirds in your house."

"Will you be singing instead?" Ares asked. Leo laughed, and Ares tried not to be too pleased about it.

"Consider my silence the ultimate repayment of my debts."

"Oh, no. Did I finally find a flaw in Leo Quince?" Ares smirked.

"If that's the only one you've noticed, you haven't been looking that hard," Leo said, still smiling, but only just, as his gaze fell to the book, still open on the arm of the chair.

Ares paused. It seemed like he'd touched on an actual sore spot, which he might have forgotten that Leo probably had. Just like Ares. Just like anyone. Ares cleared his throat, and Leo glanced up at him before Ares had quite figured out what he was going to say.

"I could use your help tomorrow morning, if you don't mind a little riding." Damn. That wasn't supposed to be it.

"Riding?" Leo asked slowly. Ares frowned.

"Horses?"

"Oh." Leo shook his head, his cheeks unusually and suddenly pink. "I can ride."

"Good," Ares said. "We'll need to check the hunting trails and make sure everything is clear."

"Maybe I can find some bluebirds while we're out, to help me do the washing up."

"I really don't want any bird shit in my house," Ares said. Leo laughed, his smile returning in a way that Ares should not have found quite so satisfying. And yet, it was the only thing he could think of as he went upstairs to take a shower.

The night passed in companionable and relative ease. They ate the unfairly delicious shepherd's pie, and then retired to the living room, where Leo went back to being curled over a book, and Ares gave in to his earlier urge to sketch. It was nice to have a still model for once, was what Ares told himself, getting lost in the small details, the curve of Leo's biceps, the ridge of his ribs, the stretch of the muscle in his neck. A muscle that Ares could still feel against his tongue, if he let himself remember. Which he didn't. And he wouldn't. A still model was what he was appreciating, that was all. When Leo's head started to droop, Ares declared it time for bed, and Leo gamely trooped off to get into his pajamas, as though he was actually going to do what Ares said.

Ares knew that shouldn't surprise him. When they worked together, Leo was happy to defer to Ares' expertise. Ares hadn't realized until just then, how much Leo had been following orders. Working on the wall, cleaning the guns, the whole wild plan that Ares had put forth to get Leo home. Ares had assumed that someone as handsome, as smart as Leo was, would have been too arrogant to take orders. And he certainly hadn't bent his knee to Morrow or been a pushover when he'd been attacked in the alley back in Laurel Grove. Did Leo trust Ares? Why would he? It didn't make sense.

Ares struggled to turn it over in his mind as he drifted off to sleep and woke up the next morning feeling a little hungover and a little lost. The fresh pot of coffee he came downstairs to helped his brain fog but didn't make him feel any less confused. And then they were out in the cold where the weather matched Ares' mental space, grey and misty, with lower visibility than Ares would have liked.

"Are you a good rider? Confident, I mean," Ares asked, as he and Leo walked up to the stables.

"Good enough," Leo said with a yawn. His hair was still damp from a shower and curled against his forehead. "I won't fall off, at least," he smirked up at Ares. "I've got strong thighs."

No. Ares was not going to think about that. And thankfully, to aid him, one of the stable boys ran out to greet them. Ares fell back to the rote, giving instructions and helping to pack saddle bags in the warm light of the barn.

Ares pushed his favorite wide-brimmed black riding hat down onto his head, and turned to offer one to Leo, who was already up in his saddle. Leo's strong thighs were well displayed in tight trousers, leather boots wrapping high up his calves. The cut of the peacoat Cerise had left Leo with, along with his straight back, the strong line of his jaw and his glistening curls had Ares struggling to get words from his brain to his mouth. Leo wasn't Snow White at all. He was the handsome prince, riding off to find some beautiful maiden in a cottage deep in the woods and sweep her off her feet. Ares could feel his hands gripping the brim of the felt hat too tightly. He needed to get ahold of himself.

"Cover your wet hair, Prince Charming," Ares grumbled, tossing the hat up to Leo. "You'll catch cold."

Oh god. Why had he said that?

And why was he trying to care for the man? He wasn't Leo's mother. Or his boyfriend. Ares mounted up, ignoring Leo's muttered response. Thankfully he seemed to take the "charming" comment as a jibe. With a short, sharp exhale, Ares settled himself in his saddle, catching his extra pack out of the air when the oldest stable boy tossed it up to him. He nudged his horse, an Andurneian draft mare named Agnes, into motion.

The misty morning air cooled his flaming cheeks, and he kicked Agnes into a trot, just to get out ahead of Leo. But before they'd gotten much past the orchard, Leo was at Ares' side on an older, beautiful grey Andalusian that didn't get much real use because Kephisto had bought it for ceremonial riding. The boys had probably put Leo on it to let the poor creature stretch its legs, but between the horses' regal baring, and Leo's, Ares was still feeling flustered.

Which was patently ridiculous. Leo caught Ares' eye, and Ares couldn't stomach it.

"Race?" Ares asked. Leo arched an eyebrow, a sliver of danger in the way his eyes narrowed. "The path is fairly straight toward the river." It was a transparent attempt to get away from him, one that Leo could have poked a dozen holes in, but after a moment, he grinned.

"Last one there makes dinner," Leo said, and then he leaned forward, kicking the Andalusian into a gallop.

Agnes was built for power, not speed, but Ares knew enough shortcuts to make the race interesting. He lost Leo in the trees at one point, as he turned Agnes through a small holly grove, where he had carved out the path himself. Ares ducked his head, the sharp sting of the leaves against his cheeks bringing him back to himself. Making him gasp. He heard Leo whoop in delight, far out ahead of him, and he urged Agnes on, back toward the path, coming up close behind Leo, as Leo pulled his horse to a stop at the edge of the river.

"I win!" Leo's face was flushed, bright and beautiful, as he swung down off his horse, boots crunching in the leaves. Ares grinned, following suit, dropping his reins once he was on the ground, nudging Agnes toward the river with a pat on her rump. When he turned, Leo was right in front of him, so close that Ares took a step back. "You're bleeding."

"What?"

"Here." Leo pulled a handkerchief out of his pocket and pressed it against Ares' cheek and Ares couldn't hear over the thudding of his own heart. Leo was close enough that Ares could smell his own shampoo in Leo's hair again, and the bright, soft scent of unfurling spring leaves. Leo's fingertips against Ares' skin were like coming inside to a roaring fireplace from the dead of winter.

And then Leo pulled the handkerchief away and stepped back, and the spell was broken. The leaves were rustling, the damp fog settling heavily in around them. Ares reached up and rubbed his thumb against his cheekbone, just to feel the burn of the cut.

"We went through the holly grove," Ares said. Then he cleared his throat. "You'll need to take your horse down to the bank. She won't know that she can drink from it. She doesn't come into the woods, usually."

"Right." Leo shoved the handkerchief back into his pocket. He turned away, scooping up the horse's reins in one hand, guiding her steadily down the embankment. Two days. Two days until Leo was gone, and Ares wouldn't have to feel this way anymore. So muddled and confused. Leo was nothing to him. Leo was a stranger, and Ares was getting flustered like a teenager, and why? There was nothing there. There wasn't ever going to be.

"Watch for snares." Ares called after him. Kephisto's land went right up to the edge of the river, so it was the favored location for hunters and other poachers to try their luck with the most plausible deniability. A quick scan of the leaf scattered ground, and Ares didn't see any of the tell-tale signs of encroachment: footprints, rope marks. It was probably fine.

Ares reached Agnes, patting her on the neck and checking her harnesses, for something to do. He wasn't going to glance over his shoulder and check on Leo. Leo was a perfectly capable adult, who didn't need constant minding.

Ares stepped back, glancing across to the opposite shore. The trees were thinner, younger, and for a moment, Ares thought he saw movement. Was it a person? Or had it just been a deer? He took a step forward and felt the sharp tug of magic in his stomach before he vanished.

17

There was a strange, whooshing sound followed by a muted snap, like someone had placed a silencer on a whip crack. When Leo swung around to see what had made the noise, he realized Ares was gone. Both horses had their ears pricked up, and Leo stiffened, trying not to panic. If he spooked the horses and they ran, he'd really be in trouble.

"Ares?" Leo said, loudly enough to be heard, but careful not to shout. He turned around. No sign of him. Slightly louder, then. "Ares?"

A sharp whistle broke the eerie silence, and Ares' horse turned her massive head, looking toward the opposite bank. Before Leo could do anything, the horse began to walk into the river.

"Shit," Leo muttered, abandoning his horse's reins, to try and corral Ares' massive mount. By the time he got within grabbing distance, he was knee deep in the river.

The water was frigid and sucked into his boots, slowing him down. Lunging forward, Leo managed to grab one side of the reins, but the horse was entirely unfazed by Leo's tugging, and continued forward, dragging him into the water up to his hips. The river wasn't moving terribly fast, but the current still buffeted Leo, pushing him against the side of the mare. Another whistle, long and sharp, and Leo, helped along by the fact that he was partially floating, managed to get a hand up onto the pommel. A foot in the stirrup. And then with a great deal of effort, he was up on the horse.

"Oh my god. Okay." He got a tighter grip on the reins and tried to turn her around. They were halfway across the river now, ankle deep even astride the horse, but she kept walking forward, unbothered by his yanking. "Horse," Leo leaned forward, patting her neck. "Please, please, go back." She snorted, and Leo finally felt the panic rise in his throat, as it dawned on him that he could not talk his way out of trouble with a horse. Leo swallowed, trying to shove his anxiety back down into his chest where it belonged. Panicking never helped. He twisted the leather reins in his hand, letting them bite his frigid fingers. The horse was not listening to him in any capacity, striding up on its own onto the opposite bank. "Ares?!" Leo called, louder this time, a last-ditch effort before he would begin cataloging other options.

The whistle responded. Louder now. In the trees. Leo tightened his grip on the reins, and then dropped them, as the mare turned, heading into the forest.

"Is that him?" Leo asked the horse. She continued not responding, but it had to be Ares, didn't it? Who else could it have been? Who else would the horse be listening to? "Ares!" His voice echoed back at him through the trees. And then, there was another voice.

"Leo, shut up!"

Oh thank God! Ares! Leo leaned forward as the horse slowed and then Leo saw him. Ares was sitting at an odd angle on the roots at the base of the tree. A gold, glowing rope bound him hand and foot, and there were leaves in his hair, like he'd rolled around on the ground.

Leo was so relieved, he swung down off the horse before she'd fully stopped, wet fabric chafing against his skin. He raced over to Ares, dropping to his knees in the dirt. His fingers were shaking, whether from cold or adrenaline, he couldn't say. It didn't matter. He scrabbled against Ares' wrists, tugging at the binding.

"What the hell happened?" Leo demanded.

"Stepped in a snare," Ares growled. Leo paused, fingertips thawing from the heat of Ares' wrists, and looked up at him. Ares' cheeks were flushed with anger, his eyes, such a rich dark brown, edged with silver around the pupil, so distinct it had to be magical. And Ares was staring at Leo with an intensity that made Leo feel exposed in a way that he didn't have words for. It was intimate, like all of Leo's panic and his relief was telling a story Leo had no control over. It was out of his grasp, all over his face, and in his heaving breaths and scrambling fingers in a way he should have hated. But he didn't. It felt like infinity, but it couldn't have been longer than a second.

The pads of Leo's fingers skirted around the rope. No knot.

"I need a knife." Leo stood, turning back to the horse, trying to remember which pack he'd seen Ares put knives in.

"Back left," Ares said. Leo went for it, the direction letting his brain come up with a relevant question.

"The snare transported you over here?"

"It's a portal snare. Magically imbued rope. It traps animals and then transports them off the property, so the kill can't be considered a poach." The disgust in Ares' voice warmed something in Leo's chest, and since when did hearing Ares' surly tones make him happy? Leo freed the knife from its sheath and decided it was just relief that was making him giddy. "I've chased them off more times than I can count."

"Talk about unsporting."

"It's fucking infuriating," Ares growled.

"What does Kephisto say?" Leo knelt at Ares' side again, and Ares held out his hands. Leo slid the blade between Ares' palms, cutting upward, and the rope fell, the magical glow vanishing immediately. Ares rubbed his wrists as Leo cut his ankles free.

"Kephisto wants any poachers caught and beheaded, but that's not very likely to happen anytime soon."

"Why?" Leo sat back on his haunches. Ares arched an eyebrow in Leo's direction, like Leo should have known better than to ask. But he couldn't let it drop. "You just said you've chased them off. You can't catch them?" There was a long moment, where Ares stared at him, like he was trying to decide if Leo was very stupid. Finally, Ares shook his head, getting slowly to his feet, bracing himself against the tree.

"I guess not," Ares' tone was mild, a verbal shrug. Leo doubted him very much.

"That's not treason?"

"What? Me not turning them in? Or the poaching?"

"Well, I meant the poaching—"

"It's thievery," Ares snorted. "At best. It's irritating. It shouldn't be a death sentence."

"Would Kephisto actually do it? Kill them."

"Yes," Ares nodded, his gaze firm on Leo again. "He would."

Damn.

This place was so bizarre. Not so much the magical fairytale Leo had imagined. Instead, everything was conniving and secretive and violent. And Ares in the middle of it all, protecting poachers in the same breath as he said he was chasing them off. Leo stood slowly, still trying to wrap his mind around the whole thing. More disparate parts. Ares frowned at him, and Leo knew he must have looked confused, but before he could open his mouth, Ares asked, "Why are you all wet?"

"Oh. I followed your horse into the river."

"Why?" Ares snorted. Leo rolled his eyes.

"I thought she was running away. But she knows your whistle."

"She's a good girl, Agnes," Ares grinned appreciatively, walking over to pat Agnes' snout. What Leo wouldn't have given for that grin to be directed at him. Wait, what? "She's smarter than most humans, I think." Maybe so. She was certainly smarter than Leo. He shivered, cold and wet, coupled with the jitters of adrenaline deferred. He turned and could just make out the Andalusian on the other side of the river through the trees and the lingering fog. He was going to have to wade back through the river.

"Come on," Ares said, waving Leo over. Leo went, trying to shake the shudder of chill that ran through him. Ares looked him over again and shook his head. "Let me give you a hand up."

"Don't be ridiculous," Leo said. "There's no reason for both of us to get soaked."

"I certainly wasn't planning on it," Ares snorted. "Get on the horse."

"What are you going to do?"

"I'm also going to get on the horse."

"Can she carry us both?"

"She's an Andurneian draft horse. She could carry both of us and a full wagon besides. And anyway, what are you, a hundred and fifty pounds soaking wet? We're not going far." Ares gestured to the saddle, one hand on his hip, as though Leo was dragging his feet for no good reason.

Leo had a good reason, and it wasn't because he didn't think Agnes could carry them both across the river. She was the biggest horse he'd ever seen. Unfortunately, the problem was that being pressed up against Ares in a saddle was far more appealing than it had any right to be, and Leo wasn't trying to add any additional confusion to his already dissonant mind.

"Is there an issue?" Ares held out his hand toward Leo, and Leo stepped forward, trying one last time to come up with a believable excuse and failing. The next thing he knew, Ares was bracing Leo's arm as Leo hoisted himself up into the saddle. The moment he moved his foot from the stirrup, Ares lifted himself up behind Leo with a grunt that made Leo's toes curl in his soaking wet socks.

Ares reached around Leo for the reins, his chest and stomach pressing against Leo's back as Leo exhaled slowly and bit his bottom lip. Focus on something else. How many campaign events had he missed so far? Could he recite his calendar from the last week? Could he, please, God, think of anything other than the warm solidness of Ares' bulk behind him. Ares clicked his teeth and Leo jolted in the saddle, rocking back against Ares as Agnes started toward the river.

"You'll have to go home and change. If you leave the Andalusian in the pasture, I'll have the boys come get her."

"I'll be alright," Leo said. He wasn't sure if that was true, exactly, but he didn't like the idea of being dismissed. And Ares' body warming his back was making Leo's head feel fuzzy.

"You like being soaking wet from the waist down?"

"I thought we had work to do."

"I've been clearing the paths in these woods by myself for ten years—"

"It'll go faster with two."

"I don't need it to go faster."

"You don't have all day. We're going down to Laurel Grove tonight, remember?" Ares sniffed, but didn't respond. Leo turned in his saddle to see Ares looking over his head at the river. "Remember?"

"I'm sure you'll manage without me," Ares said quickly. Leo chuckled.

"Oh, no. You're not getting out of it that easily."

"Who said I'm trying to get out of it? If I'm late, I'm sure you'll manage until I arrive." Leo lurched forward as Agnes stepped down the bank, and he grabbed the pommel to steady himself. Ares' arm, thick and stable, wrapped around Leo's ribcage and held him. Leo forced himself to breathe through his nose. Ares' thighs tightened around Leo's hips, and Leo swallowed down a sound he would have regretted making.

Not good. Every thought that flitted through Leo's head was not good. He wanted to reach down and grab Ares' thigh; he wanted to lean his spine back against the solid warmth of Ares' stomach; he wanted to scoot his hips back to see if Ares was even half as aroused as Leo was. He wouldn't be. Ares didn't like him. Ares was actively trying to get out of spending an evening with him. And Leo was losing his mind.

"Whoa, easy!" Ares' pulled Leo him back against him, as Agnes found a deep spot, and water crashed against their calves. Leo braced his hand on Ares' knee, leaning as Agnes found her footing and made her way up the opposite bank. His mind buzzed, desire making him lose the thread of their conversation. Ares' grip on Leo didn't lose any of its tightness until they were back on solid ground.

And then Ares' body was gone. He let go and hopped off the horse, helping Leo down before Leo understood what was happening.

"Go change. I'll be back before our excursion tonight."

"But—"

"Watch out for snares," Ares said. "If you go back the way we came, you should be fine." Ares was still standing in front of him, looking down at Leo without heat. Without desire. And why should there have been? It was Leo craving Ares' attention, and not the other way around. "Will you be able to make it on your own alright?"

Disappointment thrust Leo back into his own body. He was cold and wet. And he felt like an idiot.

"Yes," Leo said, ignoring the way shame made his stomach clench. "Yes, of course."

"Good," Ares skirted around him, climbing back onto Agnes. "I'll see you later." And then he was off, trotting Agnes back toward the path, leaving Leo to climb up on the Andalusian alone.

The thing was, and it was a very stupid thing but it was there all the same, people generally liked Leo. He was ignorable and innocuous, but in a positive, unobtrusive way. And when people were friendly with Leo, when they decided they liked him because he was a handsome man of little real consequence, they became more or less predictable. Predictable was nice because it meant that Leo knew where he stood with them, and what they were likely to do and say. No risk of anyone getting hurt, or of Leo doing any damage to himself or others. Predictability was logical and safe.

Ares was everything but predictable. He was cavalier in one breath and protective the next. Gruff and then flirtatious. Rude then polite. Worst of all, Ares wasn't ignoring Leo, nor did he seem to find Leo pleasant. Which was crazy, because Leo hadn't done anything to him except exist near him and cook his meals and be helpful. It didn't make any sense.

By the time Leo had finally managed to at least parse his own frustration, not that he had the faintest idea what he was going to do about it, he was coming out of the trees and up onto the grounds of the estate. Ultimately, he supposed, it didn't matter. He was leaving in a few days, and neither the way Ares felt about him, nor the way Leo felt about Ares, was going to matter in the slightest.

18

Ares arrived in Laurel Grove a very respectable half hour late. Clearing the trails had gone quickly, but he'd caught himself meandering toward the end of the path, thinking about—Well, it was embarrassing, really. The thought of Leo leaping down from his horse, falling to his knees beside Ares. It was a fantasy tempered horribly by how embarrassed Ares was that he'd stepped into a trap. That he'd needed help. Being a fool who couldn't take care of himself should have drowned out all of Ares' prurient desires. But Leo had looked so good doing it, every inch the questing knight, riding to Ares' rescue.

Doubly unfortunate was the fact that when Ares arrived at the pub, Leo was exactly as outgoing and amenable as Ares had feared. He talked with everyone. He flirted with everyone. He danced with Fen, and then with Warren and then with Marnie, and one of the new valets was looking at him the way Matilda looked at a bowl of leftover beef tips. Ares had taken up a post at the end of the bar, where he could see the group, and decided that if Leo hadn't been there, Ares might have considered himself 'having fun.' But then, if Leo hadn't been there, Ares wouldn't have been there either, which was not really a hypothetical quandary he was interested in exploring without drinking. And he certainly wasn't going to be doing any drinking if he was going to have to corral seven youngsters, and Leo, back to the estate before it got too late.

The bar they were at was temptingly close to Fitzwilliam's. It was possible that if he were subtle about it, he might be able to shuffle them all in that direction. Fitzwilliam's wouldn't have live music, though, and currently Warren and Marnie were teaching Leo the steps to a jig that the band was on their second round of. Fen hopped up onto the barstool beside Ares, holding a tankard as large as her head.

"Ares," she said, propping her elbow on the bar and leaning her cheek against her hand, as though they were in the middle of a long conversation. He couldn't help but smile at her.

"Fen."

"You came."

"I said I would," Ares said. Fen sniffed, which was a generous response, considering how many times he had blown her off in the past.

"What's going on with Julian?" Julian? Oh, right. Leo's alter ego.

"Uh, I believe Warren's teaching him the steps to 'Women are Like the Seas,'" Ares said, nodding in Leo's direction.

"No, I know," she said. "There aren't really steps to it. I tried to tell them. Anyway, that wasn't what I meant. I meant what's going on with you and Julian."

"Absolutely nothing," Ares replied immediately and with as much certainty as he could muster. Fen arched her eyebrow.

"Are you sure about that?"

"Fairly, yes." Ares took a breath, then a sip of his ale, which gave him strength enough to ask, "why?"

"He's done nothing but talk about you for the better part of an hour. I think he's totally shot his chances with Preston, Lord Kernsey's valet."

"Oh," Ares said, ignoring the warmth that was spreading low in his stomach. He glanced with renewed interest at the table where a few of the others were sitting and received a glare from a freckle-faced young man for his trouble. "I wouldn't take anything he says seriously. He's probably drunk."

"He's not that drunk," Fen said. "If he's drunk at all. I think he's only had two. There's really nothing going on with you two?"

"No. There's nothing."

"Alright," she said, her eyes narrowed. "Marnie quite fancies you."

"I'm a decade too old for Marnie, and you can tell her I said so."

"Oh, boo!" Fen smacked him playfully on the arm. "You're not being very much fun."

"I'm trying to make sure you all make it back to the hall in one piece. Oswald will have my head if I don't."

"Warren's gran lives a block and a half away and has already welcomed anyone who doesn't want to walk all the way back up the hill to stay there for the night. That's the old lady who was in here earlier."

"I didn't see her."

"That's because she's shorter than I am, and about ninety-three. I'm going to go give Marnie the bad news and Preston the good news," she said, hopping off her stool. She pushed her tankard at him. "Finish that for me. I don't want to puke on Warren's nan's sofa." Ares watched as Fen strode over to Marnie and Warren and Leo, wrapping her arm around Marnie's waist. Warren and Leo clinked beer bottles, and then heels, and Warren laughed, and the music changed and Leo started over to Ares. Ares finished off Fen's tankard before he arrived.

"There's room for you at the table, you know," Leo elbowed Ares' arm, his eyes bright and shining. Happiness had never looked so good on a person.

"I'm closer to the beer if I stay here," Ares replied. Leo snorted.

"Yes, but that means I have to work harder to swoop in like a charming gentleman and buy you one." Maybe he was drunk after all.

"Are you sure that's my fault? Or do you just struggle with pretending to be a charming gentleman?"

"Ouch!" Leo clutched his chest, mock stumbling back. "That hurts, Ares. Truly. You wound me."

"I'm not so worried," Ares replied, turning back to his empty tankard and wishing it had something in it. "You're resilient."

"There's only so much one man can take," Leo replied, his smile softening as he leaned his elbows on the bar. Sincerity was more dangerous than happiness, it seemed. Ares should have gotten up and walked away. He should have given in and gone to sit with the others, where at least proximity to more people would have stopped Leo from looking at Ares with his dark eyes all softly crinkled at the corners, his mouth curled into a small smile, even as he pressed his teeth down into the center of the beautiful, full bottom lip. Ares' heart thudded in his chest. His palms were sweaty. For no reason at all.

A round of applause went up from the crowd and the song changed. People were singing along, and Ares wasn't listening until Leo nudged Ares with his elbow again.

"This is it, isn't it? That song you were humming the other day. When we were working on the wall."

Ares listened. The lyrics to 'Jolly Mortals Fill Your Glasses' slurred together with the realization that Leo had been paying attention. Had remembered.

"Do you want to dance?" Leo asked. Ares nearly choked on the panic that rose in his throat. He did not want to dance. He did not want to hold Leo against his body in any capacity, and he desperately needed Leo, the idiot, the asshole, to stop looking at him with those wide brown eyes like he wanted something.

Ares pushed back from the bar, dropping off his stool, and headed out. He used his size to push through the crowd, a tangle of rowdy dancers, and shouldered open the door, a trail of cacophonous 'fa-la-la's' chasing him out into the darkness.

It had gotten colder. Ares stumbled into it, the wind making him draw up short. He'd run away. Again. That was stupid. And embarrassing. But he hadn't known that Leo was listening to him. Really listening. And would talk about him in a way that would ruin his chances with other men. And when was the last time anyone had asked Ares to dance?

Ares turned, ducking his head against the wind, and dipped down the alley between the bar and the shop next door, heading to Fitzwilliam's. It would be quiet there, and he could think. He desperately needed to think.

"Ares!" Ares stopped, bracing himself on the brickwork, cold beneath his palm, and turned to look over his shoulder, as Leo, tugging on a coat, jogged into the alley behind him. "Are you alright? What happened?" The moonlight was blue and caught in the dark swirls of Leo's hair as he frowned up at Ares. "I'm sorry if I—"

"No," Ares shook his head. "Don't apologize. I—"

"Are you not feeling well?"

"I'm fine."

"Are you leaving?"

"I..." Ares' gaze dropped to the fullness of Leo's mouth, grazing his neck, his chest, all the places Ares wanted to kiss him, before settling on the cobbles between their feet. "I was

—" The warmth of Leo's palm on Ares' cheek made him look up. And before he could protest or back away or sink into it, Leo kissed him.

Leo's lips were soft and warm, and he bent to fit below Ares' bowed head, bringing their bodies close. Why was this happening? How was this happening? Leo's palms fisted in Ares' shirt and Ares clutched the brickwork with one hand, unable to stop the moan of longing that spilled from his lungs into Leo's mouth. Leo drew back slowly, his tongue drifting over his bottom lip, as he stared at Ares with wide eyes.

Ares turned, putting his back to Leo before he could see Leo's expression change to one of disappointment, or worse.

"I'll see you back at the house," Ares said, hurrying out of the alley and up the hill toward home.

19

Over the past ten years, Ares had gone through various stages of self-loathing. Where he'd finally settled, found some sort of twisted inner peace, was in the idea that whatever he was didn't matter. Ares the man was inconsequential to the larger turning of the world. It was what he could do, what he'd committed himself to, that gave him a purpose. And purpose overrode childish things like desire. Purpose kept him in Andurnei. Purpose kept him from seeing his brother. Purpose was what should have stopped him from standing at the foot of his bed, thinking about the way Leo's mouth fit against his. The way Leo's fingers had twisted in Ares' shirt, pulling them together. Ares tugged the shirt off over his head and tossed it into the corner. He'd been home for twenty minutes and he still hadn't managed to catch his breath.

Downstairs, the front door opened. He hadn't locked it; Leo didn't have a key. Matilda got up from her spot on the rug beside his bed and padded down the steps. Leo's voice was soft when he greeted her. Ares couldn't make out what he said, but it made him ache for Leo all the same. Why did he have to be so goddamn kind? Handsome on its own would have been easier to avoid. Or turn into something animal; Ares was well practiced in shoving desire aside. Or he'd thought he was.

The bottom step creaked, and Ares' heart skipped a beat. His bedroom door was open, and leaping across the room to push it shut was stupid. Hiding from Leo, like Ares was a maiden trying to protect her virtue from a lascivious villain. Leo didn't look villainous. He stepped onto the landing, his cheeks flush with cold, his eyebrows knit together. He was still in his boots. Still looking like a handsome prince. He stopped in the doorway and looked in at Ares.

"You forgot your coat," he said.

"Thanks," Ares' voice was too gruff. Obviously a put-on. He turned to grab a shirt from his dresser, trying to hide his face again because he wasn't sure what was on it.

"I'm sorry, if I—"

"No," Ares said too quickly, not turning around. "Don't be."

"I feel like I can't—" Leo stammered, hesitated. "Do I scare you or something?" Ares swallowed, and didn't respond, pulling his shirt over his head. That was probably answer enough, really, but he didn't hear Leo leave. Ares glanced over his shoulder to see Leo leaning against the door frame, toeing off his boots.

"I don't think I invited you in," Ares said. Leo froze, his spine straightening slightly.

"Should I go?"

"You *should*." Ares reached for a sweater, as Leo bit his bottom lip.

"Do you want me to?" And that was an entirely different question altogether. One that Ares knew the answer to but couldn't bring himself to say. How could he tell Leo to stay when he was the one who kept running? He couldn't. He shouldn't. Ares braced one hand against his open dresser drawer and turned toward Leo.

"If I told you to leave, would you?" Ares asked. For a long moment, there was silence, Leo's eyes skirting over Ares' face like he was reading the next lines in a script. Deciding what to say.

"I'm exceptionally good at following directions," Leo replied. His voice was low, serious, like he was telling Ares a secret.

"You'll have to forgive my skepticism," Ares said, though there was no accounting for the roughness in his voice, the way he was desperate to hear what Leo was going to say next. Leo stepped forward, over the threshold of Ares' room. Ares took a half a step back, and Leo paused, his hand on the edge of the footboard of Ares' bed. His other hand he rubbed across the back of his neck.

"Ten years is a long time to sleep alone," Leo said mildly, glancing toward the bed. Ares knew his cheeks were pink. He tried to swallow, to retort, but the words got lost in his throat, as Leo began to unbutton his shirt. "Before I became a partner at the firm, one of the other junior lawyers, Paul, and I had a sort of arrangement."

Ares didn't know why he didn't stop Leo from talking right then. Maybe it was because Leo was keeping his distance, the width of Ares' bed between them. Maybe it was because Leo started to undress as he continued to speak.

"Paul met this woman, a widow. I'm not sure where. Some sort of charity event, probably. Paul is handsome. Dark skin, nice eyes, strong arms. I wasn't surprised when he'd told me that he'd taken up with this woman, but he said there was something different about the encounters he'd had with her, and he wanted me to come along."

Leo tugged off his shirt by his cuffs, leaving it draped over his shoulders for a brief moment before shrugging it off. In his white undershirt and dark work pants, he looked rougher. The broken nose, the way the cotton pulled across his chest, he looked more like a boxer. More like someone who might try and seduce a widow.

"She wasn't old. Mid-forties, maybe. And she was lovely. Kind, I mean. She had a big house in the city, and she rattled around in it all by herself. Her husband had died years before." Leo's hand strayed to his belt, tugging at the leather, and Ares shuddered slightly at the motion of it, the strength of his desire totally at odds with the story Leo was telling him.

"She wanted Paul. Who didn't?" Leo chuckled, unthreading his belt buckle. "I certainly had. But she... was struggling to touch him. She said it felt disloyal to the memory of her husband, even though he'd been gone for years. So, it was Paul's idea that perhaps," Leo finally looked back at Ares as he dragged a tongue over his lower lip. "Perhaps she might like to watch us. Tell us what to do. Use me as a sort of proxy."

Ares knew he was breathing heavily, but he couldn't seem to stop. Leo looped his belt over the edge of Ares bedpost and left it there, his gaze still on Ares. Ares wanted him and couldn't make himself step forward. Years he'd spent telling himself that desire was the enemy, still he trembled with it, hands shaking. Leo seemed to be waiting for something, and Ares was captivated. He needed Leo to keep talking. To explain.

"What did you do?" Ares asked. Leo shrugged.

"She undressed. Paul undressed me. She sat against the headboard and asked me to get onto the foot of the bed. Hands and knees," Leo pulled his shirt off over his head, running a hand through his hair as he let his shirt drop to the floor. He glanced at Ares with a small smirk. "She liked to be spanked, so she asked Paul to spank me." A surge of heat rumbled through Ares, jealousy tinging the edge of a want so strong, Ares nearly grunted with the way it hit him. "So, Paul did. Still fully clothed. While she leaned back against the headboard and touched herself." Leo stepped out of his trousers and his socks. His cock was rigid against the tight fabric of his shorts.

"All that to say," Leo said, finally taking a small step forward. "That I'm very good at following directions."

"Did you like it?" Ares asked. Leo nodded, his palm resting flat on the foot of Ares' bed. It was not a subtly delivered invitation, but...

But if it was for Leo's pleasure.

If Ares was still fully clothed.

It wasn't *that* intimate.

"Can I spank you?" Ares asked. Leo bit his bottom lip and nodded again, before stepping out of his shorts. His cock was long and hard, and Ares' mouth watered, and he thought, briefly, about how stupid it was not to just toss Leo down on the floor and have his way with him right there like he truly, deeply, desperately wanted. But then, Leo was climbing onto the end of Ares' bed, facing away from Ares, his head toward the door, and somehow not having to look at his face made it possible for Ares to finally stumble forward.

He reached out, his hand shaking, his heart pounding in his ears, and slid his palm slowly over the smooth, warm skin of Leo's lower back. The ridges of Leo's spine rolled as he twitched at the contact, and Ares smoothed his thumb over Leo's vertebrae. They'd already touched. He had his hands on Leo the first night they met. His mouth on Leo's throat. Ares' cock twitched, already heavy and hard. Ares flattened his hand, sliding up to Leo's ribs, letting his fingers feel the muscles beneath flex as Leo shifted. Ares exhaled slowly and then lifted his other hand, sliding it up Leo's thigh, over the curve of his ass.

Leo made a small, needy sound, pushing back against Ares' palm, and Ares smacked him lightly. Leo's gasp was audible, followed by a smooth hiss of pleasure that Ares could feel in his chest. He did it again, and Leo moaned. The sound went straight to Ares' cock. Ares leaned forward, pressing himself against the footboard. The next time Ares slapped Leo's ass, Leo panted, his head dropping forward between his arms, a whispered 'yes' heavy in the air between them. Ares slid his hand lower, his palm caressing Leo's balls and then forward, stroking the firm length of Leo's cock.

"Ares. Please." Leo's voice was ragged, his head down still. At that angle, Leo could see Ares stroking him. So, Ares did it again, sliding his thumb over Leo's slit, and then over the ridge of his cockhead. Leo moaned, his back arching, and Ares switched his hands, stroking Leo with his left, spanking Leo's ass with his right.

"Ares!" Leo's hands tightened against the sheets, his hips jerking forward. Ares ached to be against Leo. To touch his skin, breathe in his air, rut against him.

"Turn over," Ares said. Leo rolled onto his hip, and then flat on his back, his knees bent, feet on the mattress. "Move," Ares nodded toward the headboard, and Leo crawled backward, eyes bright and wide and eager. Every inch of him was gorgeous, and Ares wanted to taste him, to touch him, and so Ares climbed up after him. Lying beside Leo on the mattress felt presumptuous, but Ares did it anyway, only so that he could reach down and stroke Leo's cock. Leo groaned, arching his back, thighs spread wide as he pressed his head against Ares' bicep. His hair was as soft and thick as Ares had imagined it would be. Because he had imagined it, and it was stupid to deny that now.

Leo's gaze kept switching between Ares' face and the hand Ares' was dragging up and down his cock.

"Ares," he moaned, toes curling in the blanket. "God. Yes. Please!"

"What happened?" Ares asked, breathless, shifting his hip to take some of the pressure of his trousers off his own straining member. "With you and Paul and the widow?"

"Which time?" Leo's chest heaved as he squirmed, panting.

"Your favorite time," Ares growled, wanting to hear it almost as much as he wanted to see Leo remember it. Leo groaned.

"She fucked me with a strap while I sucked Paul." Leo's hand clutched at Ares' still-clothed thigh, as Ares stroked him faster. "Ares! I—I'm so—" Ares shifted his hand up, his palm tight around Leo's cockhead, and Leo bucked, his head pressing back into Ares' bicep. Ares let Leo fuck into his fist, tightening and loosening his grip until Leo thrust hard and came with a shout, spilling across his own stomach. He scrambled with his left hand, reaching desperately for the top of Ares' trousers.

The fear that had gripped Ares before was totally overwhelmed by lust. Consequences be damned; Ares could sort out all his feelings later. He pushed up, leaving Leo's head falling against the mattress. Ares' knees bracketed Leo's thigh, and Ares unbuttoned and unzipped his pants. His cock was leaking, throbbing, and Leo reached for him before Ares could lie back down, his fingers stilling moments before they wrapped around his cock.

"Can I—?"

"Yes," Ares said, before he could think better of it. As though it mattered now. He was already gone. Ares' back tightened, hips shifting forward, as Leo stroked Ares over his cum-slicked stomach.

"Ares," Leo was begging, rubbing against him, and Gods, it was everything Ares hadn't let himself want. Leo reached with his free hand and dug his nails into Ares' thigh in the same moment he jerked his hand all the way up the length of Ares' cock, and Ares spilled over Leo's chest. Leo moaned, biting his lip, eyes fluttering closed in pleasure, leaving Ares to look down at him, debauched and beautiful. Ares felt dizzy, and he leaned back, catching himself with an arm on the mattress behind him.

"Gods, Leo," Ares breathed. Leo barely nodded, his eyes closed, chest heaving. Ares rolled onto his hip, and then onto his back, tucking himself inside his trousers. He was still wearing all his clothes. He'd just come on a man that he'd been terrified of touching twenty minutes ago. A man he'd been running away from. And now the only thing that he was afraid of was how much he wanted to touch Leo again.

Ares forced himself to get out of bed. He went to the bathroom, grabbing Leo's washcloth off the hook and wetting it in warm water from the sink. Leo watched him come back in, one hand in his hair, his breathing still heavy. Ares began to wipe off Leo's stomach, studiously avoiding looking at his lips. Maybe jerking each other off was one thing, but kissing... kissing was still something else altogether. Even if Ares suddenly wanted more of that too.

"Was any of that true?" he asked. He was aware, now that he'd been sated, that the widow story perhaps mirrored his own too closely to have been a coincidence.

"Yes," Leo said, taking the washcloth from Ares' hand. He opened his eyes, watching Ares with an arched eyebrow. "Did you think I made it up?" Ares clenched his fist, resenting the blush that was flooding his cheeks. "I don't need to make up stories to get people into bed with me."

"That's not what I meant." Leo rolled his eyes and propped himself up on one elbow, drying his stomach with the corner of Ares' bedspread. Ares should have hated that. His teeth clenched when he realized he didn't. "What happened to her?" Ares asked. Leo sat up, his legs hanging off the bed.

"If she's real, you mean?"

"I was just—" Leo got up, and Ares stepped back, out of his way.

"I doubt you'll believe me, but this is true too, hand to God." Leo bent over, scooping up his clothes off the floor before he straightened up and looked at Ares. His eyebrow was still arched, but his smug smirk had gone soft at the edges, and it was the alley all over again. If they'd been standing any closer together, Ares would have felt compelled to back away. "She married Paul. Three years ago. I was a groomsman."

Ares knew he looked shocked but he couldn't help it. Leo shook his head, as though Ares' reaction was disappointing somehow, his mouth curling into a small sad smile. There was a beat of silence then, where Ares struggled for something to say, and Leo waited, like he was expecting something. And when nothing came, he sighed and left, striding, naked, out of Ares' room and down the stairs, clothes in his hands, gorgeous ass still flushed in the shape of Ares' hand.

20

Leo slept better that night, which was nice, even if he refused to think about why. He didn't regret what they'd done, he'd just thought...

He'd wanted Ares to soften toward him. Not much, Leo wasn't looking to change the tides or anything, but he'd hoped that being vulnerable, being honest, might have made Ares do the same. Or warm up to him a little bit. Or at all.

There had been moments of softness. When they'd kissed in the alley, or when Ares' hands were trembling against Leo's skin, where Leo felt like he could see through all the cracks in Ares' behavior. In those moments, Leo understood that Ares was scared and lonely and craving affection. Affection Leo was primed to give; he liked the man, despite himself. But Ares was wall after wall, and for every blockade Leo thought he'd jumped over, there were three more standing in his way. Ares didn't trust him, even though Leo had bared himself (quite literally) and maybe there just wasn't a way around that.

Cold seeped in through the cracks of the house, the weather unrecovered from the fog and drizzle of the day before, and the sky was a shade of grey that only ever occurred in fall. There wouldn't be rain, but there wasn't going to be any sun either. Beside a plate of biscuits that only had a slight residual heat to them, Ares had left a note for Leo, asking him to collect the squash from the garden that were ready to harvest and take them up to Fen. 'Hard skin,' the note said in parenthesis beside the phrase 'ready to harvest,' which was information which Leo both resented being given and also required. It didn't say anything about where Ares had gone.

Matilda must have gone with him though, because she didn't seem to be around anywhere, so Leo ate three biscuits, got dressed, and went to the garden alone. He started without a cart, and then had to go back to the shed for one, as there were plenty of squash and pumpkins that were large and seemed ready to be eaten. He wondered at the size of some of the pumpkins, which were so big that it seemed like a shame to take them off the vine. He put a couple in the kitchen, thinking about butternut squash and pumpkin soup. Not that he knew how to make either of those things, just that he thought he probably could. The rest he rolled in his cart up to the house, knocking on the kitchen door.

Fen answered with bags under her eyes, covering a yawn with her hand as she looked over the cart full of vegetables.

"Yeah, alright," she mumbled through her hand. "Bring them into the root cellar. Do you have time to carry them down?"

"Sure," Leo said.

"Top shelf," Fen said, gesturing with her thumb over her shoulder where a door was open to a set of stairs that led below the house.

The kitchen was nice. There was a heat to it, and the constant warm burble of chatter from the other cooks and the footmen and maids who seemed to come and go. When Leo finished, Warren was sitting at the counter in front of a bowl of stew, looking far better off than Fen.

"Where'd you go last night?" Warren asked, his eyes bright and cheerful as he arched an eyebrow at Leo, who only shook his head.

"Just went home early."

"Preston was looking for you," Warren winked. Leo rolled his eyes.

"He's what, fourteen years old?"

"Twenty," Fen closed the exterior door behind him and nudged Leo toward the table.

"Cradle robbing at its finest," Leo replied. Warren snorted as Fen set another ceramic bowl of stew down at an empty seat.

"Eat. It's cold out there."

"How old are you anyway?" Warren asked.

"Thirty-one," Leo said, grabbing a spoon, inhaling the delicious, garlicky warmth of the bowl in front of him.

"Really?" Warren demanded, incredulous. Leo smiled at him.

"Really. But it's kind of you to sound so shocked."

"You don't look it," Warren insisted. Leo nodded and took a bite of stew, swallowing a groan as the meat melted against his tongue.

"I stay hydrated, and my job keeps me inside," he said. "Good god, Fen. This stew."

"It's good, isn't it?" she said, without turning around from the stove. "Favorite thing to cook when I have a hangover. Start it early and it basically makes itself."

"How'd the rest of the evening go?" Leo asked. "You didn't throw up on Warren's nan's couch, did you?"

"It was a near thing," she replied as Warren laughed. They talked about the evening for a little bit, the butcher's son who Marnie had gone home with, and that one of the valets still hadn't made it back to the house the last any of them had heard.

"Got snatched by pirates," Warren said, in a tone that indicated it would serve the man right if that was the case. Leo stopped sopping the bottom of his bowl and glanced up.

"Pirates?"

"He's not serious," Fen shook her head dismissively. Warren pursed his lips.

"Uh, yes. I am."

"Smugglers aren't pirates. And even if they were, what would smugglers want with a valet?" Fen asked. Warren arched both eyebrows into his hairline and looked at Fen from the corners of his eyes, horrible deviancy clearly implied. Leo looked between the two of them as he attempted to decide which of them was over or underreacting.

"Do the pirates..." he hesitated, barely able to come up with something that didn't sound fully outlandish. "What? Kidnap people from the town? Rape and pillage?"

"No," Fen said. "Because they're smugglers and not pirates."

"But people have gone missing," Warren said. "People disappear sometimes."

"Warren's afraid of his own shadow. When he started working here, he wouldn't speak to Ares for a full six months."

"Well, that's understandable," Leo muttered, even as Warren protested.

"He's intimidating! Scary like! I mean, I know better now. He wouldn't hurt a fly, but—"

"Wouldn't he?" Leo huffed. Warren shook his head, but before he could speak a bell rang on the wall and he got up with a groan.

"That's me. Sorry! Thanks again for lunch, Fen. Bye Julian!" And like that he was gone. Leo looked at Fen, who was watching him with her head cocked to the side.

"What?" he asked.

"It did not escape my notice that you weren't the only one who left early last night."

"I don't know what you're talking about," Leo said, wishing for a bell to ring that could summon him away from this conversation.

"Ares can be a little gruff," Fen said. "Rude even."

"You don't say."

"But he's got a bad lot. Far worse than the rest of us. He's easily doing the job of three people. And Kephisto won't hire him any extra help. You're the first new person they've brought on in years to do anything on the grounds."

"Why not?" Leo asked. "I mean, is there—" Fen shook her head, leaning over the counter toward Leo. When she spoke again, her voice was low, her eyes darting toward the open door to the hall.

"What Warren said isn't entirely untrue. There are… smugglers. Shipments going out in the dead of night. People leave suddenly, almost before you even know they're here. We had bets on how long you would last."

"You think Ares is wrapped up in it somehow?"

"If he is, it's not by choice. Warren's right about Ares. He takes care of everything around here, and he might not be polite, but he's never mean. Not cruel like…" she trailed off, glancing toward the hall again. Leo had several good guesses as to who she might have meant. "Point is… I think they keep him alone on purpose. No help with his chores means he's got too much to do to have any time to make friends. Friends who might try to help him out of whatever they've stuck him in."

"Ares can handle himself," Leo said, though he wasn't sure he believed it. He'd never met someone so isolated that they couldn't bring themselves to touch another person, even when they'd clearly wanted to. And if Ares was caught up in something sinister, well, Leo didn't have to work hard to imagine how firmly Ares might push other people away to keep them safe. He remembered Ares storming into the alley the first night they'd met, putting himself in harm's way for a total stranger.

"Here," Fen said. "Let me make up a couple of bowls of stew for you to take back with you. Ares will need something hearty before the hunt this afternoon. And I have some scraps for Matilda." She turned away, reaching for crockery, leaving Leo to mull over what he'd learned, and tried to match it up with the Ares he'd been in bed with the night before. They weren't totally incongruous creatures, and some of the things Fen had said put the cracks Leo had seen into a slightly different light. Not so much that he could understand what caused them, or how to fix them, but he had a better idea of how deep they might go.

"Ah, Mr. Flint. How lucky you're here." A balding man, wearing a butler's livery with the bearing of a naval admiral, strode into the room. They hadn't been introduced, but Leo assumed this was the Mr. Oswald that Ares had mentioned. "We need an extra hand for the hunt today. The Earl of Cenfaire's valet was going to ride out with the party, but the young man's gone missing. Can I ask you to step in?"

"I'm not a strong hunter, sir." It was an understatement at best, and Leo thought he might've gotten out of it with Oswald's deep frown.

"You won't be hunting. You'll be attending the Earl," he said as though Leo was very stupid. Leo cleared his throat.

"Oh, of course, sir."

"Be ready and at the stables in half an hour," Oswald instructed, before scooping a biscuit off the platter and then striding from the room.

21

Horses were saddled and ready for the hunters to arrive at the stables. Ares had spent the better part of the morning and early afternoon bringing out the weapons from the armory, preparing the hampers and the first aid, helping the stable boys saddle the mounts, and trying not to let anything slip through the cracks, for his own sanity, and so he wouldn't have to hear Kephisto complain.

It was almost enough busy work to keep him from thinking about Leo, the night before, the kiss and everything after. He'd left before Leo had gotten up and Ares planned on being out of the house all day. The hunting party was twelve in all, seven hunters and five attendants, a bigger group than they normally rode with, so there was lots to do.

Ares, of course, was exclusively there to assist Kephisto, who arrived at the stables with the other aristocrats, looking less like he was departing for a hunt and more like he was departing for a woodland festival, with quite a bit of shine on a silver coat that was so tight across his shoulders it looked like it was nearing non-functional. His seafoam green hair was tressed up in a series of elaborate braids and long curls that would almost certainly smack him in the face if he turned his head too fast. Tending to Kephisto on a hunt was an easy job, since the Lord was an abysmal shot. Usually, he'd have Ares kill a few of pheasants for him and take the credit; as long as he was riding back with a brace of birds to his name, he didn't much care where they came from, and neither did anyone else.

Ares was just seeing rounding up the last of the attendants, though they seemed to be one short, when Leo walked into the stables.

His hair was combed back, and he was wearing a tweed waistcoat, brown work trousers, boots and a quilted jacket. His handsome prince outfit again. This time, though, Ares knew what Leo's narrow waist looked like beneath the waistcoat that cinched him in. The curve of his ass had fit perfectly against Ares' palm and the memories that Ares had been attempting to suppress all morning flooded back.

"Everything alright?" Warren asked. Ares jumped.

"What? Yes. Fine."

"You just cursed."

"No I didn't," Ares scoffed, his ears heating.

"You just said, 'Damn!' Five seconds ago." Had he? Damn.

"No, I just. I forgot something. Check on the other attendants, will you?" Ares said, starting toward Leo before Warren could respond. Ares drew up short, as Leo approached a different attendant, asking a question that Ares couldn't hear over the chatter. The attendant pointed Leo toward the Earl of Somewhere. The one whose valet hadn't shown up yet.

Certainly, the Earl's looks hadn't suffered for having no one to tend to him. His hair was a purple so deep that in shadow it looked black, and his skin had a warm, peachy glow to it, entirely wrinkle and blemish free in a way that marked him out as fae. His dark hair curled around a broadly smiling mouth, his moustache thick and well-kept, curled slightly at the edges, and then covering the sharp angles of his jaw and chin. He greeted Leo with a friendly, if exacting, military sort of wave, and began to speak with him with an animated expression. Ares hurried toward them.

"Mr. Flint," Ares said, after bowing to the Earl. Leo watched him, brown eyes bright and irritatingly playful.

"Good afternoon, Mr. Silva," Leo smiled. "Mr. Oswald requested I attend his Lordship on the hunt, since his valet has rendered himself absent."

"I very much appreciate it," the Earl's voice was deep and smooth, and Ares hated him suddenly and without cause.

"You hate hunting," Ares said to Leo, before he could stop himself. Leo blinked, then his gaze flitted toward the Earl, as Ares realized what he'd just done.

"I certainly hope that isn't true," the Earl said, graciously. "I would hate to make anyone feel—"

"Oh, no." Leo chuckled, an easy laugh that probably only sounded unnatural to Ares. "Mr. Silva only means—"

"He's bad at it," Ares said quickly.

"Abysmal," Leo agreed. "Couldn't hit the broadside of the barn. Mr. Silva was the unfortunate soul tasked to teach me. But I'm quite good at following orders," Leo said with a placid smile. Damn him. "I'm sure we'll get along fine."

"Time to mount up!" Kephisto called. Thank Gods. Ares left Leo and the earl with a nod, trying to swallow down the mortification that was making his head swim.

Luckily, these hunts always started in the same way, so Ares had a chance to get his bearings. There were certain spots where Kephisto liked to stop with the party, primarily to show off the beauty of his property, and they made it to each in turn. It was colder out than it had been, but the weather seemed to be holding, grey never quite turning to rain. After a bit they rode on, stopping near the river to water the horses. Some of the hunters moved in a group off to the north, where one claimed he'd seen a stag. The earl and Leo were among them, and Ares itched to go after them, trying to block out the sound of Kephisto boasting about the new yacht he'd recently acquired, by walking a little way off toward the mouth of the stream.

He needed to focus.

Most of the other hunters who'd gone after the stag returned in due course, but two hunters and Leo remained in the woods.

"Let's ride on," Kephisto told the others. "We'll catch them up ahead. The path winds around—" The path did wind around, but Leo hadn't gotten this far with Ares when they were out. And Ares wasn't sure the other two men had ever been at a Leyland Hall hunt before. Ares mounted his horse nervously, as one of the hunters made some pun about bagging a stag that didn't make sense, but had Kephisto and several of the others laughing, as they kicked their horses into motion.

Minutes dragged as they rode on. Ares scanned the horizon for any sign of Leo, the earl or their horses. No shots echoed off the trees, and as they moved up the leaf-covered hill toward the edge of the forest, worry began to crystallize in Ares' chest. The forest was dense further away from the path, and while Ares knew it well-enough, even he occasionally got turned around when he was distracted. And Leo was stuck babysitting some earl, who was probably more useless than not.

After half an hour had gone by without any sight of them, Ares' imagination was spiraling out of control. What if Leo had been shot? Gored by a wild boar? Fallen off his horse with no one but an errant earl to assist him? Ares always tried to stay well off Kephisto's radar, but anxiety had him swallowing propriety and good sense, nudging his horse forward to come up alongside the prince's.

"My Lord," Ares began tentatively, "maybe I should ride out

ahead to see if I can locate the earl. It's been nearly half an hour."

"Who?" Kephisto asked, frowning as he glanced over at Ares. "Oh, Jonquil, you mean? Nonsense. He's a military man. He'll be fine."

"I—"

"A fusilier I believe, for the Andurnien regiment in the ninth realm. Quite decorated, as I understand it, though apparently, he doesn't like to talk about it." Kephisto sniffed at this, as though not wanting to brag was bad judgement on the earl's part. "The way I see it, he's either killed the stag and is dragging it back toward the house, which would be dreadful, because you know how I hate venison. Or he lost the stag and he's forcing Bertrand to ride out with him until they find something impressive to kill—"

"Or," chimed in another hunter, his ruddy cheeks and slurred speech indicating his water skein might have, in fact, been filled with something stronger, "he's off with that pretty footman. Giving him something to attend to, I'd wager!" The leather of Ares' reins bit into his palms as he clenched his fists, fury buzzing in his ears, while the nearby hunters laughed. "Rumor has it, Jonquil's quite a way with servants! A gentle hand, they say." Kephisto chuckled, turning back toward Ares with a magnanimous smile.

"See there? Nothing to worry about. Perhaps Jonquil will offer the man a position as his new valet," Kephisto said. And perhaps Ares would find the earl and wring his neck. Kephisto cocked his head to the side, and Ares remembered to school his expression a moment too late. He nodded, keeping his head bowed deferentially, as he let his horse drop back, where he could ride with the other attendants.

In twenty minutes, they'd come to a clearing where they were stopping for lunch. Ares was going to ride out from there.

He twisted the reins around his palms until the leather bit into his skin again and tried not to think about why he wanted to find Leo so badly. Why the thought of Leo fucking around with some earl was almost as horrifying as the thought of him getting hurt. Ares had already taken on too much responsibility where Leo was concerned; it wasn't any of Ares' business. But he knew as they came into the clearing, that he was going to go looking anyway.

Fen had overpacked, of course, and for longer than he wanted to, Ares was busy with the other servants, portioning out the rations, while the hunters dismounted and strolled around, looking up at the clouds that were growing heavier, dense with rain. Just as Ares managed to get back to his horse, half a sandwich hanging out of his mouth, three riders came trotting out of the woods into the meadow.

Leo rode behind the earl and Bertrand, who had a rather large boar strung up between their two horses. The hunters cheered their arrival, everyone crowding around to admire the great, dead creature. Ares' throat knotted, as Leo steered his horse toward Ares and the far side of the clearing.

Leo dismounted gracefully, swiping blood off his hands, onto the sides of his trousers, his gaze distant and heavenward. When he closed his eyes, Ares watched Leo's chest rise and fall, relief and worry ripping away what was left of his appetite. Leo was pale. There was blood on the white collar of his shirt. When Ares came up alongside him, Leo pasted on a weak smile.

"Any more sandwiches left for us?" Leo asked, his neck craning toward the hamper. A smear of blood on the side of his throat. Ares' heart pounded in his chest.

"Leo. I mean, Julian—" Leo shook his head, his gaze darting over his shoulder, and Ares fell silent. The earl was looking their way. "Come with me." Ares grabbed Leo by the cuff of his jacket, and pulled him to the side, ostensibly to check on the horses that were grazing nearby. Leo followed wordlessly, which worried Ares even more. Once they were behind the horses, there was barely ten yards between them and a dense copse of trees encroaching from the edge of the forest.

Ares tugged Leo behind the largest tree and began to give him a once over for injuries. There was more blood on the inside of his arm.

"What's this? What happened?"

"It's from the boar," Leo sighed, slumping back against the bark and closing his eyes tight. Ares grabbed him gently by the jaw, turning his head to examine his face, his neck.

"Are you okay? Are you hurt?"

"I'm alright."

"You look pale."

"I'm alright, Ares." Leo put his hands on Ares' forearms and squeezed, steadying himself. After a moment he opened his eyes. His irises were the light russet brown of a wren, and his gaze softened as he looked at Ares. He opened his mouth, and Ares was certain he didn't want to hear what he was going to say. What he was sure was written all over his face. Ares let out an exasperated growl, half throwing up his hands, though Leo was still holding his arms. Leo's smile was small, not nearly so smug as it could have been, and maybe that was why Ares kissed him.

22

res pushed Leo back against the rough bark of the tree, pinning him there with his body and his arms and his mouth. God, his mouth. Ares kissed him deeply, head tilting slowly as pressed against Leo's lips, his tongue tentative against the seam of Leo's mouth. Leo put up no resistance. He never would with Ares, he thought. Ares wrapped his arms around Leo's waist, and tugged him close, heat spilling through Leo's tensed muscles like breath through his lungs, and he sank into Ares' embrace.

When Ares pulled back slowly, his brow was still furrowed in concern. Leo smoothed a thumb across Ares' temple, noting how much brighter and warmer the weather seemed in Ares' arms. Leo could hear the birds calling above his head and the air had the strong fragrance of fresh leaves and blooming flowers, damp moss and the verdant lushness of spring. Leo kissed Ares again. A brush of lips, Ares' fingers sliding barely into the hair at the back of Leo's neck. Leo shivered against him, shifting closer, wanting to feel the heat of Ares' skin beneath his palms.

"Are you okay?" Ares' voice was low and soft, almost drowned out by the wind in the bright green leaves above them.

"Better now," Leo breathed. Ares scowled at him.

"They didn't hurt you?"

"No one hurt me."

"He didn't... the others said Jonquil was—"

"I had to hold the horses for a bit while he and Bertrand hid in some shrubs about twenty yards away and did God knows what. I'm sorry to report for both their sakes it didn't seem to last very long."

"Oh," Ares wrinkled his nose in disgust, and Leo laughed. "What happened to you, then? Why are you so—"

"I told you," Leo pushed a small lock of hair back into place above Ares' forehead. "I don't enjoy hunting, and watching the earl kill and gut a wild boar was, uh..." he trailed off, curling in toward Ares' chest as he shuddered slightly at the memory of the field dressing. And the vomiting that had come after. Luckily, he'd been able to wash out his mouth with brandy from Jonquil's flask. And Bertrand had given him a couple of squares of hardtack for his stomach. They'd teased him, of course, but after, he'd been well enough to help them tie the boar up between their horses, leaving him with all the guns and additional supplies. They'd all been ill-balanced, but they'd made it back with their kill, so no harm done. At least, Leo had thought. Realizing that the worry on Ares' face had been for Leo made him a little woozy again. Ares' grip on his waist tightened and Leo leaned close, tilting his head up toward Ares' mouth.

Ares' gaze shifted, his head leaning back as he scowled at the mass of grey clouds congealing in the sky above the clearing, just visible beyond the spray of green leaves that stretched out above their heads. Green leaves? That was odd. The tree Leo was pressed against, and perhaps the next closest three in the little grove Ares had tucked them into, were as bright as if it were the first days of spring, twisting green ivy fluttering out of the cracks between the bark as if it had just sprouted.

"It's going to rain," Ares grumbled, before he glanced at Leo. If he noticed the eager way Leo's face was angled toward his own, he didn't say anything. Leo thought he saw the smallest hint of a smirk and then Ares was kissing him again. His mouth was gentle, pliant and brief against Leo's before he pulled away and started toward the horses.

"Did you see those trees?" Leo pointed over his shoulder as he followed Ares back into the meadow. Whatever had happened between them, they could talk about it later. And Leo was going to make Ares talk about it, that was for damn sure. But for now the foliage seemed a safer topic of conversation.

"What do you mean?" Ares asked, pausing to adjust the bridle on one of the horses, and then the saddle on another.

"I mean there were about four trees back there that were still green. Springtime green."

"We've been in a warm snap." Ares' tone was suspiciously dismissive. Leo frowned.

"A warm snap doesn't put leaves back on trees." He wished he'd been paying more attention when Ares had walked them over in the first place, but he'd been afraid he'd done something wrong, and half irritated that he didn't think Ares had saved him a sandwich. As it was, he followed Ares back over to the hamper, and when Ares leaned down and produced a wrapped sandwich for Leo, Leo thought maybe it was the best day he'd ever spent in the outdoors. Of course, that was when the thunder started.

The attendants all hurried over at Ares' whistle, and he immediately began to give instructions on how to most efficiently pack up and prepare for a quick return to the house. Then Ares was over among the hunters, as thunder rumbled louder, drawing even some of their attention. It was impressive, the way Ares took charge, and more than a little bit appealing. Leo watched Ares' fingers twist and tighten the bindings on the boar, then orchestrated a changing of horses, so he and Warren could take the kill, and the hunters could have their unburdened mounts to get out of the rain faster. All the while, Leo uselessly wolfed down a sandwich and drank from a water skein someone handed him. Just as he finished, everyone was mounted and turning back, ready to attempt to outrun the storm through the forest. Leo tugged himself up onto his mount, and he was off with the rest of them.

The storm that followed seemed to expand in size and strength as they rode on. Heavy raindrops began a steady rhythm and then a pounding one. If there hadn't been so many riders to follow, Leo almost certainly would have gotten lost in the thickest parts of the trees. By the time they made it back to the stables, they were all soaked, and in the chaos of the attendants and the hunters and the game and fowl that had to be taken up to the kitchen and the removal of weapons back to the armory, Ares caught Leo by the elbow and pulled him to the side.

Ares was drenched, but it didn't diminish his commanding presence in the slightest. Leo found he was envious of the droplets that slid beneath the collar of Ares' shirt.

"Go home," Ares said, his head close to Leo's, his breath warm on Leo's neck. "I'll be back in a bit."

"I can help," Leo offered, without a single idea of how he might do so. He just wanted to keep watching Ares work.

"It'll help me to know where you are," Ares said. Leo nodded, suddenly warmer than he'd been at any point in the last half hour, riding through the driving rain. He liked it when Ares took charge. Not that that was a surprise to him, necessarily, but even here, when it was a bunch of men and horses and an unexpected rainstorm. Ares pressed the key to the cottage into Leo's palm, and Ares' gaze dropped to Leo's lips. Before Leo could do something supremely stupid, like kiss Ares in front of a dozen people, Ares turned, cheeks flushing, and called gruffly for one of the stable boys to bring around a nearby wagon.

Shivering with arousal, Leo hurried down the narrow path toward the cottage. Rain came in sheets. Leo's hands were so wet that he fumbled with the key in the door, dropping it twice on the stoop before he managed to let himself in. He stripped in the foyer, as Matilda bounced and barked around him. Leo balled up his sodden clothes into a puddle-forming pile, before carrying the whole of it up to the bathroom in just his shorts. He left it all in the tub so that he could wash his hands in hot water, both to clean them and to bring some feeling back to his fingertips. He was just drying his hands, when he heard the front door open again, and Matilda charged back down the stairs.

From the foyer, came the sound of wet cloth hitting the floor, boots knocking against the wall. Ares moved loudly through the bottom floor, and Leo could hear him open the patio door, close it, then open it again. Leo grabbed a towel off the rack and swiped it over his hair, his pulse quickening, as Ares came up the stairs.

Standing on the landing, looking in the bathroom door at Leo, Ares was glorious. His chest shone with the damp and was slightly flushed with the cold. His shorts were stuck to his skin, the firm bulge of his cock visible beneath the soft curve of his stomach. Ares arched an eyebrow, as if Leo was the only one standing mostly naked, his gaze hot on Leo's skin. Ares tossed his ball of clothes into the tub where it landed with a flat, wet sound, and stepped over the threshold. The bathroom was small, but Leo could have made room. He didn't.

Leo stepped closer to Ares. He rested his fingertips at the top of Ares' belly where the hair on Ares' torso was dark and soft and warm. Ares didn't flinch, didn't move. He watched the slow slide of Leo's fingers, and his eyes flicked to Leo's face when Leo spoke.

"You were worried about me," Leo said. He'd realized it before, in the woods, but Ares had interrupted him. And anyway, it felt more intriguing now. "In the trees. You'd thought—"

"Based on what you've told me about yourself, it's not unreasonable for me to have a healthy amount of concern for your wellbeing."

"I thought you didn't like me," Leo said. Ares smirked.

"Who says I do?" Leo's hand slid low, fingers drifting over Ares' hip. Leo could see the rise and fall of Ares' chest, could hear the heaviness of their breathing in the quiet. Ares took Leo's hand off his hip and pulled him closer, kissing him hard. Leo shivered, his body feeling loose and tight all at once, the warmth of Ares' hands and body against him soothing his frayed nerves. Ares wanted this. He wasn't running. Instead, he lifted Leo off his feet, and pressed him against the bathroom wall, before dragging his mouth, his teeth against the curve of Leo's neck.

Ares' fingers dug into the sensitive flesh of Leo's spread thighs, sore from being on a horse all afternoon, though now the ache felt good, stretching his muscles, pushing him between discomfort and pleasure. Leo moaned as Ares licked the base of his throat, the calloused pads of his thumbs rubbing small circles against Leo's inner thighs.

"Ares," Leo begged, shifting his hips, just enough to feel his cock rub against Ares' stomach. Glorious friction. Ares nipped Leo's earlobe.

"What do you want?" Ares' voice was rough, barely above a whisper, his mouth pressed to Leo's neck.

"You," Leo panted, eager, aching. Ares grunted, hoisting Leo up slowly, their bodies rubbing together. Leo moaned, grabbing for purchase against Ares' shoulder. "Take me to bed. Please." Ares lifted Leo off the wall, carrying him into the bedroom with almost no effort which was exceedingly sexy. Rain lashed against the windows, but Leo barely noticed, his focus narrowing as Ares set him down on the mattress. Leo stretched out like a cat, his body sinking into the softness of blankets, as Ares stepped back to close the door.

Leo shucked his shorts, stroking himself, watching as Ares did the same. Ares' cock was big, in proportion to the rest of him and then some, with a thickness that made Leo's mouth water. It had been one thing to have his hands on it, but this felt like something more. The dam between them had burst, and Ares, who had been so timid, was now kneeling on the end of the bed, waiting. He watched Leo run his hand over his cock-head, like he was hypnotized by the motion. Somewhere, in the kinder, less sex-addled part of Leo's brain, there was a small voice that told him to take it easy. Ares' first time in ten years. Leo should be gentle with him.

Oh, but then Ares wasn't waiting anymore. Ares' mouth was on Leo's cock, and Leo's back arched against the mattress, as he tried not to thrust, skin tingling with want. Leo's hand twisted in the blanket, heels slipping against the coverlet, and then Ares grabbed Leo by the wrists and pushed Leo's arms above his head, into the pillows. Ares slid his tongue up the cut muscle of Leo's hip and Leo forgot how to breathe. God, he hadn't thought it would be like this. The hesitancy of the day before had been washed away by the rain.

"'I should go missing more often," Leo said. Ares bit him just below the ribs, just enough to make Leo yelp in surprise. "Brute," Leo huffed, smacking Ares on the shoulder. Ares lifted his head, brows furrowed in adorable concern. Leo was entirely charmed. "I was teasing." Ares rolled his eyes, cheeks pinking. "I promise, if I don't like something, I'll tell you."

"And you like a brute, is that it?" Ares asked. Leo lifted his brows.

"I mean, I haven't told you to stop yet." Ares snorted, shaking his head as he lowered it back to Leo's ribs, kissing Leo's stomach softly. Leo moaned at his touch, gentle though it was. Anything from Ares, anything at all, was good enough for Leo. Maybe it was because he'd been so standoffish for so long. Maybe it was because Ares had been so worried before, and Leo knew it now.

Ares sucked on the tender flesh just on the inside of Leo's hip and Leo whimpered, twisting against the sensation. Ares' wide brown eyes were watching Leo carefully, and Leo moaned and sighed, wanting more. Wanting Ares to want more.

Slowly, after a minute, Ares raised his head, lips pink and flushed. Leo could hear himself panting.

"If I'm a brute," Ares said, lifting his head, sliding up Leo's body, bringing their hips flush. "Then what are you?" Of course, quiet, reserved Ares wanted dirty talk. Leo smirked as he freed his wrist, reaching down between them. He curled his fingers slowly around Ares' shaft.

"Oh, I've been called all kinds of things," Leo purred, stroking Ares, watching him twitch, his eyelids fluttering closed at Leo's touch. "Deviant, of course."

"Of course."

"Devil, once." Ares' hips shuddered forward to meet Leo's fist. Leo lifted his other hand, dragging his nails down over Ares' nipple, making him twitch.

"Christ!"

"Never that," Leo smirked, mock thoughtful, thrusting himself between his palm and Ares' cock.

"You don't say?" Ares growled and then groaned, needy, as Leo rolled his hips. "Leo—"

"Get on your back for me." There was a pause, a beat that

went on for just long enough that Leo thought Ares was going to argue with him. Or leave again. Ares was watching Leo with such intensity, and Leo stilled, not certain what it meant. And then Ares dipped his head, his lips brushing against Leo's for just a moment, and Leo's breath hitched. It was so soft, delicate, that Leo wondered if he'd ever been handled so carefully before. Like he was something precious. To be careful with. It made him want to pull Ares closer, turn the touch rough, just to show him that Leo could take it. It made him want to stay still, be treated with care, like he was fragile. Precious.

And then Ares rolled off Leo, just like Leo had told him to.

23

I t was so hard not to stare at Leo's body. His movements all lithe and fluid, strong and steady. Everything about Leo screamed confidence and ease. How often had he done this before? And did Ares really want to know the answer to that? Not because he cared how many people Leo had slept with, but just because Ares wasn't sure he could manage to be blisteringly jealous of too many people at once. Leo leaned forward, bicep stretching as he reached for the bedside table.

"This side," Ares said, pointing the other way. He slid up on the mattress so that he could tug open the drawer, pulling out the small canister of oil he kept there and handing it to Leo. Leo turned it over in his palm, deft fingers unscrewing the lid as he read over the label. Ares wondered if Leo recognized Mae's messy script. The container was old, but Ares was fairly sure the oil inside was still good. He hadn't had any problems, but before he could fumble through telling Leo how possibly expired his lube might be, Leo got to his knees. And then climbed astride Ares' hips.

Leo's cock was flushed, long and resting against Ares' stomach, begging for Ares attention, but before he could grant it, Leo was leaning forward, biting his lip as he braced one hand against the center of Ares chest. When he made a soft little moan and slid backward onto his own fingers, Ares felt every muscle in his body tighten with want.

"Where were we?" Leo panted, his eyes meeting Ares', his small smile dangerous and gorgeous.

"Uh, I don't—"

"You're a brute."

"I'm a brute," Ares repeated, catching the thread, ignoring the ache in his cock as Leo worked himself open slowly. Ares slid his hand up Leo's thigh and felt the muscle twitch beneath his fingers, as Leo spread his legs wider, pressing into Ares's palm. "We were deciding what you were."

"Well," Leo said. "I don't mind 'slut,' but I honestly only really like it when I'm being spanked." Fuck. Muscles in Ares' hips jerked, as he forced himself to hold still.

Leo shifted back, stroking Ares' length, coating it with slick. Ares groaned before he could stop himself, pressing his head back against the pillows. He could feel the heat of Leo's body, the tightness of him, as Leo sank onto him. Leo whimpered, moaning, soft, gorgeous sounds that Ares wanted to kiss from his throat. He arched his back, one hand braced against Ares' stomach, the other sliding from Leo's own neck, down his chest. His muscles were taut as he dragged his hand over his stomach to the base of his cock. Ares groaned, watching as Leo stroked himself, rolling his hips, smiled at the sound of Ares' gasp.

"Oh Gods! Leo!" Leo whined when Ares said his name. Still rocking back and forth, Leo dragged Ares' hand up his thigh to settle on the side of his ass. Ares knew what he wanted. He thought he knew. Gods. Ares was not a virgin, but he was a little more than ten years out of practice. He was desperate to get this right.

Ares spanked Leo. Not hard, but enough that Leo clenched and Ares groaned, hips leaping.

"Again," Leo panted. "Ares. Please."

"Gods, Leo," Ares thrust up, more in control and Leo's eyes closed. "So gorgeous. A perfect little slut." He smacked Leo's ass, and Leo moaned Ares' name and began to ride him in earnest, one hand reaching back to brace against Ares' thigh. Ares was aware of every single place their bodies were touching, and he wanted more. "Fuck! You're so good!"

"I want you to feel good." Leo's body was slick with sweat, his eyes dark and hungry. "Tell me this is good for you."

"Perfect," Ares gasped, as Leo sank down on him again. "Leo, God. You're so perfect." Leo tilted his head back, neck stretched long and Ares wanted to be over him. To bite him. To mark him. "I want you. Leo, I want you."

"I'm yours," Leo gasped, his cheeks flushed. Suddenly, they were making eye contact, and Leo's breath was coming in short sharp pants, his movements shifting into something erratic. Ares grabbed onto his hips and Leo moaned. "Ares! I'm yours."

"You're mine," Ares said. Something strange tightened in his chest, as he looked at Leo, the ways Ares wanted him suddenly overwhelming. Leo jerked forward. Ares got his hand around Leo's cock and stroked him quickly, repeating himself, even though he knew he shouldn't. "You're mine."

"Ares!" Leo's orgasm tore through them both somehow. Leo cried out, clutching at Ares' skin, barely holding himself up as Ares fucked into him, Ares following moments behind.

Desire intertwined with something raw and potent in Ares' chest. A pit, like the sharpness of a hunger pang, had suddenly been sated, and Ares ignored the dampness that was prickling at the corners of his eyes.

Leo collapsed against Ares' chest, breathing hard, and Ares could barely believe he wasn't dreaming. Ares ran trembling fingers down Leo's spine, and Leo moved into the touch, shifting slowly up Ares' body, detangling them from each other. He landed on the mattress at Ares' side and curled against him, using Ares' bicep as a pillow.

Ares rolled onto his hip, watching as Leo's breathing began to slow. Ares was still insensible, he had to be, because the next thing he knew, he was dragging his fingertips down Leo's chest, feeling the heat of his skin, the steady beating of his heart. Leo smiled, eyes closed.

"I like when you touch me."

"You like being spoiled," Ares murmured, though he didn't stop.

"So do you, I think," Leo yawned. "I just have to trick you into letting me do it."

"Oh. Was that what that was?" Ares needled.

"Was it *not*?" Leo looked smug, arching an eyebrow. Ares chuckled, waiting for Leo to open his eyes and demand an answer. When he didn't do either of those things, Ares wondered if it was on purpose. Leo wasn't watching him, so Ares could react in whatever way he liked. And he didn't know how that made him feel. But he did lean forward and kiss Leo again. Leo moved against him, pressing into the kiss like he wanted to be closer to Ares. Like he wanted more of him, even though Ares had just been inside him.

'He *is* yours now,' said a treacherous little voice in Ares' head. 'Marked. Even if it's only for a little while.'

Ares slid his hand over Leo's hip and pulled their bodies together, letting Leo slide his leg between Ares' thighs, sighing into a deeper kiss. Soft. Intimate. Incredibly dangerous. Ares forced himself to let go, to roll onto his back. Cool air brushed his chest. Thunder rolled outside the window.

"I'm sorry I worried you this afternoon," Leo said again. Ares huffed.

"As long as you're alright, it hardly matters," he said. He could feel Leo's mouth against his shoulder, a smile. Then a kiss. Ares blushed, pleased. "Hungry?" Leo hummed.

"Will you be cross if I ask to eat in your bed?"

"Will I be cross? No," Ares sat up. "But you absolutely may not eat in my bed." Leo groaned, and Ares laughed as he stood and went for clothes. "Don't bother pouting. I'm getting dressed and I'm not looking at you."

"Then how did you know I was pouting?"

"Lucky guess."

Ares dressed in his most comfortable joggers and a soft, worn in flannel, leaving it open until he could duck into the bathroom and wipe Leo's spend from his chest. Then he made his way downstairs, rooting around in the icebox for a couple of minutes before deciding he probably had the right sort of leftovers for a decent frittata. Above him the shower went on, and for the briefest of moments, an egg in his hand waiting to be cracked, Ares thought maybe he should put everything away and see if Leo wanted company.

No. That was insane. He went back to work on the frittata and had just slid it into the oven when there was a knock at the front door.

Rain was still pouring down outside, and as the temperature dropped the patter of water had occasionally begun to sound like the whisper of sleet. Not exactly visiting weather, which meant it had to be someone from the big house. Ares frowned at the thought of having to go tend to something now. What sort of emergency couldn't wait until morning?

But when Ares opened the door he took a step back, in surprise. Alondra's dark eyes shone in the front porch light, ice crystals glistening on the edge of her black hood. She smiled at him, her silvery lips curving like the thinnest sliver of the crescent moon.

"Alondra," Ares stepped aside, and she came in, ducking her head, and tugging the hood back and off the curve of her milky grey horns. "You're a day early," he said, trying not to sound accusatory. Her smile widened, her head tilting to the side as though she hadn't heard him properly.

"I don't think so, love," she said, her voice soft, melodic. "I think you're a day behind."

24

Leo tossed his pillow against Ares' headboard, and then glanced over at Ares who was kneeling in front of a chest beneath the window. The lid was open, propped against the wall, and Ares was pulling out blankets.

"So, she stays with you then?"

"Sometimes." His voice was muffled as he bent over the side of the chest again. Leo had feelings about this vague admission. Unearned ones, primarily jealousy. Not that he thought Alondra was Ares' type, exactly. She wasn't beautiful or ugly. Or maybe she was just so different from any other being he'd ever met, that he didn't have a real frame of reference to categorize her, which he found very troubling.

She had broad shoulders, but her limbs, her frame, were all thin, and too long by a nearly imperceptible amount. Her skin was as white as paper. Perhaps even whiter than that, and had no warm undertones at all, as though she was cool, grey stone beneath her flesh. Her hair was a light periwinkle blue, and she wore it coiffed around her four slate-colored horns—two that bent back like ram's horns, and two that curled down around her ear and followed the line of her jaw, almost tusk-like.

All of that Leo might have been able to swallow. She wore small, wire-framed sunglasses all through dinner, and held her fork between her thumb and forefinger, like she would have preferred not to use one. But even that was nothing compared to the way she stared at Leo. Her gaze, though hidden behind those smoky lenses, wasn't fully obscured. And even if it had been, Leo would have been able to feel it boring into him from across the table. It unsettled him and distracted him from the dinner conversation, which he only noticed in that it flowed extremely easily between Ares and Alondra, with none of the stiltedness that he'd experienced in his first few days staying at the cottage.

"I'll be right back," Ares said, getting to his feet with a small pile of blankets in his hands. Leo had moved, temporarily, into Ares' room. It was unclear where Ares intended to sleep.

Leo felt strange. Pulled opened and examined like a dissected frog. He stared down at Ares' bedside table, letting his fingertips drift over the grain of the wood, trying to decide if his strange feelings were a result of the sex, or if they were because Alondra was here, and her presence alone implied a whole life of Ares' outside of Leo's knowledge. Which, that was a stupid thing to be having feelings about, because Ares had purposefully kept Leo on the outside in every conceivable way. Until today. Maybe yesterday.

Was that why he was feeling so put out? Because now that Leo was finally beginning to understand some of Ares' inner workings, to see what he liked and wanted, some stranger appeared and already knew it all.

The sex hadn't helped. Leo was always very careful to keeping his sexual encounters and his emotions separate from each other. Sex was a leisure activity. It was how he blew off steam, distracted himself from the drudgery of work and the horror of another hour spent campaigning for his father. It was supposed to feel good; it wasn't supposed to mean anything.

Ares had looked him straight in the eye and said, 'you're mine.' Even now, standing alone in the bedroom, it sent a shiver up Leo's spine, made him want to curl up beside Ares, be held against him. To be Ares'. Whatever that might mean.

And what would happen if Leo broke through all of Ares' walls? What if he kept doing this, and there was a man who wanted him on the other side? A man who worried when he was gone for too long. Someone who wanted to make sure he was okay, not because his work was lacking, or he was late to meetings or missing conference calls with donors. But just because they cared about him. Ares did care about him. Leo was sure of it.

Leo heard Ares coming up the stairs and tried to arrange his features in a way that didn't telegraph extreme emotional distress. Jealousy was easier. He could sort that out more quickly.

Ares stepped into the bedroom and nudged the door shut behind him.

"So," Leo said, one hand on his hip, the other still on the side table, "you and she?"

"What?" Ares asked. Leo widened his eyes and nodded toward the bed. Ares blinked at him, eyebrows lifting slowly. "Are you asking what I think you're asking? Didn't you tell me yesterday that I'd been alone for ten years?"

"Well, your manners indicated—"

"You can't have it both ways, Leo," Ares smirked. "Which is it? Am I a lonely, bitter old hermit, or am I a wicked seducer?"

"In my experience, you're very effectively both."

"Gods help me," Ares threw up his hands, turning away to pull open a dresser drawer.

"I wouldn't have to make so much up, if you'd tell me what I want to know." Ares turned to face him, his pajamas in his hands.

"What do you want to know?"

"Do you like me?"

"Gods." Ares rolled his eyes and then blinked at Leo. Then he frowned. "You're serious?" Leo didn't respond, irritated that he could feel his cheeks heating. "I don't make a habit of getting in bed with people I don't like."

"I don't either," Leo said. Ares' frown softened a little then, and he turned his back to Leo and began to undress.

"Well, that's good to know. What else is on your mind?"

"Alondra spends the night here."

"Is that a question?"

"Do— what's the nature of your relationship?" Leo asked. Ares snorted.

"I did tell you before, she's a traveler. A trader, I suppose. We don't really have anything like it where we're from. But she travels the realms, takes goods across. And people," he added, glancing pointedly over his shoulder at Leo. Leo swallowed. "The two of you can discuss terms tomorrow. I'll be out most of the day. I lost track of..." he trailed off, shaking his head as he turned back around. "Anyway, she'll take care of you."

"Where will you be?" Leo asked.

"Orchard," Ares said, going over to the far side of the bed and pulling back the blankets.

"What do you need to do in the orchard that will take all day?" Leo asked. Ares glanced up at him, momentarily surprised. Like he'd forgotten Leo was there.

"I tend to it," he said briefly, as though that meant anything. Leo considered pushing further, and then decided to ask an adjacent question that might net him an answer to both.

"This afternoon, when you pulled me aside and kissed me up against that tree... did you make it grow like that? The green leaves?" Ares held Leo's gaze for a moment too long, and Leo knew that he had. A thousand more questions sprung to mind, but before he could ask them, Ares cleared his throat.

"I can sleep downstairs."

"No. No." Fuck. He hadn't meant to scare Ares away. "No, this is fine. I don't mind."

"I snore," Ares warned. Leo shrugged.

"So do I." A smile ghosted across Ares' face as he glanced down at the blanket in his hand. Then, after a moment, crawled into bed. Leo stripped off his shirt and slid between the sheets, telling himself firmly that an offer to share a bed was not an offer to drift close to Ares, even just to leech his body heat. Sex was still sex. And feelings were still feelings. And they didn't have to impact each other in the slightest. Mysteries could and should wait until morning.

Ares turned off the light and, for a moment, Leo couldn't tell the difference between his breathing and Ares' in the dark.

"Alondra and I have been friends for a long time," Ares said quietly, and Leo was a little surprised that this was the topic Ares had chosen to address. "She was one of the first people I met here who wasn't Morrow."

"It's not really my business," Leo said, though the information felt as precious as gold, and Leo was desperate to hear more. "I'm sorry I pried."

"We've never slept together. Alondra and I. And before today, I hadn't... it was longer than ten years. For me. And I'd forgotten—I—" he stammered, faltering, and guilt threatened to choke Leo.

"It was fantastic." *I want you. Still. More now.* Ares huffed, and Leo knew he should have said it sooner. He reached across the space between them on the mattress and slid his hand into Ares' palm. Ares curled his fingers around Leo's, and after a little while, they both fell asleep.

25

"What are you doing?"

Leo woke with a start. He was curled in the center of Ares' bed, his torso wrapped around a pillow, and Alondra was standing at the bedside, leaning over him. Leo yelped and rolled onto Ares' side of the mattress and nearly off.

"Jesus Christ!"

"I've heard of him. Interesting man." Alondra straightened up. She was wearing a long jacket, with sleeves that draped down from her wrists. Her skirt pooled around her feet on the floor, and the top she was wearing had a strange cowl-like collar that seemed primed to swallow her whole. Everything was black and it looked like something a first-year design student would have called an avant-garde statement about death. Her sunglasses had small, black gemstones hanging from the center of the bottom rim of each lens.

"Can I help you with something?" Leo panted, pushing himself up to seated.

"Ares said we should talk," she said.

"Where is he?"

"The orchard." Alondra said with a frankly unreasonable amount of venom. Leo swung his legs out of bed, heart still racing.

"Alright. Uh, well. I'll get up, and we can—"

"We need to go see Mae," Alondra said, drifting over to Ares' dresser. Leo's clothes were all neatly stacked on top, and she began to shuffle through them.

"Mae?"

"You really ought to know Mae by now, if you're going to take care of Ares." Leo flushed at the suggestion.

"I know Mae. I mean, we met." Sort of. He had been a bit loopy at the time, but he remembered her, and her strange house. Alondra stacked a pair of black pants and a dark grey and navy flannel into a pile and tossed them on the end of the bed.

"Get ready," she said, floating out the door. "Your breakfast is cold, and we have a long walk ahead of us."

Leo dressed and brushed his teeth, coming downstairs to find Alondra wrapped in a long black traveling cloak. Matilda was sitting at her side and they both turned toward Leo as though he'd kept them waiting an incredibly rude amount of time. Leo went into the kitchen, grabbing a sandwich off a plate and looking around for any sign of coffee.

"I already have the thermos," Alondra called, irritation ringing out clearly through the house.

Two minutes later, they were walking across the paved back path toward the forest and the field that stretched beyond it. The sky was full of thick, grey clouds, and the wind was cold when it blew, leaves rushing across the path, the damp air carrying a tangible chill.

Leo ate as he walked, and when he finished his sandwich, Alondra produced Ares' thermos from somewhere within the folds of her cloak. Leo sipped, appreciating the warmth more than the caffeine. The autumn air combined with Alondra looming over him, had left him feeling uncomfortably awake.

"I have met Mae," he said. Alondra sniffed. "She helped me out when I first arrived. Ares took me to her. Is she some sort of doctor?" Ares had used a word to describe her, but it hadn't stuck in Leo's mind.

"An Alchemist," Alondra said. "Technically, I believe she works for the master of the hall, but really who can control an alchemist?" It sounded like a strange philosophical question, a logic puzzle one of Leo's law professors might have posed, and since he didn't have an answer for it, he kept silent.

A great gust of wind swept up from the west and shook the trees so violently that the sound of the leaves reminded Leo of the rush of waves at the beach. Matilda began to growl, her gait slowing, and Leo nearly stopped, as he looked around trying to find the source of her distress.

"It's alright," Alondra bent at the hips, one long hand reaching down to stroke Matilda between the ears. "It's alright, darling. I know you don't like it."

"What?" Leo asked. Alondra began walking again, coaxing Matilda along with lilting, cooing speech that Leo didn't understand, or perhaps couldn't hear over the wind. "What doesn't she like?" Alondra answered him with a sweeping wave of her arm, her hand outstretched pointing to the high stone wall above the path. The wall that surrounded the orchard.

"What does Ares have to do in the orchard?" Leo asked, once he'd jogged a few steps to catch up with her. Alondra looked over the top rim of her glasses at him.

"What does anyone do in an orchard?"

"Pretend I don't know," Leo grumbled. She looked sideways at him, like he'd asked her to take flight. "What's he doing in there?"

"Tending to the trees," she said. Then she looked away, her

gaze turned across the rising field that stretched south and west where it found the edge of the forest. "Ares should be the one to tell you about the orchard. It's his."

"His in that he cares for it?"

"His in that he bleeds for it," she said, abandoning the path and going straight across the fading, leaf strewn grass.

"Just in like, the sense of he works hard, or—"

"In the sense that he bleeds. You're not very bright, are you?" Leo scrambled to get in front of her, he reached out and grabbed her by the arms, stopping her in her tracks. The orchard wall was just behind them, not more than fifteen yards away. If he yelled loudly enough, Ares would have been able to hear him.

"What do you mean? Is he hurting himself in there?" Alondra's smile was small, amused and absolutely infuriating. Leo's fingers clenched in the extra fabric of her cloak. "Answer me!"

"I'm sorry, Leo," she said, shaking her head. "It's not my story to tell. He is hurting himself, but we can't stop it. Not right now. He knows what he's doing."

"I can stop him," Leo dropped his grip on Alondra, pulling away, storming toward the orchard. The very thought was unacceptable. Ares was already hurting so much, the loneliness, the anger. The idea that Ares was actually, physically injuring himself was abhorrent. Alondra's sudden grip on Leo's arm startled him out of his thoughts. He turned, aiming to yank out of her grasp, and she threw him to the ground.

Leo lay on his back, staring up at the horrible, colorless sky, and wondering how Ares would feel about Leo going for three rounds with one of Ares' few friends in this stupid world, when Alondra leaned over him, her lips pursed.

"Let's not do that, alright?" she said in the same tone he'd heard his mother use to tell a puppy to stop chewing on the corner of the rug. Before Leo could speak, Alondra raised a hand to stop him. "I appreciate how much you care for Ares. And I'll tell you what I can on our way to Mae's."

THE FIRST TREE Ares always tended was his mother. Her trunk was large, took up four plots worth of space, her roots curving like waves above and below the surface of the soft earth and moss. She always had leaves. Crimson and marigold in the fall, a rich jade in the spring. In his first few years here, he would spend hours sitting between her roots, sliding his fingers through the gaps between dirt and tree, holding her like he was still a child holding her hand as they crossed a street.

Ares had woken that morning with Leo's body curled next to his, his own arm, traitorous, draped over Leo's rib cage. Ares let himself be limp, let his body rise and fall with the rhythm of Leo's breathing. For all Leo's compactness, he was warm. He let off heat like it was excess energy to burn, generated by his endless questions or his willful good humor.

Ares carried that warmth with him into the orchard, draped over his chest like a suit of armor. If he could have, he would have wrapped it around his mother's trunk like a blanket to keep the chill off her roots. After what Morrow had done to them, Ares had forgotten what it was like to wake up warm.

26

Leo rubbed his arm; the places where Alondra had gripped him were still throbbing. She'd helped him up and they'd walked in silence, whatever story she was going to tell him about Ares apparently still percolating. Leo tried to swallow down his anger and glanced back again toward the orchard which had already disappeared over the horizon as they crossed into the forest. The thought of Ares back there bleeding, doing dangerous things that Leo didn't understand and no one seemed to want to explain was making him antsy and irritable. He shook out his fingers, dropping his hand from his arm, and looked over at Alondra.

"So, you said you were going to—"

"You seemed like you might prefer silence," she said, looking at him plainly, as though this was obvious. Leo scowled.

"I want to know what's happening."

"I wasn't here when Ares struck his deal with Morrow, but Mae was. She knows more about it than I do. What I do know is that it's an extension of the deal Ares' mother had with Edmund Morrow."

"His mother?"

"Yes," Alondra said. Leo pursed his lips, his mind flicking unbidden toward the dream he'd had about Ares. Not the sexual part, but the beginning, with inheritance law and contract disputes.

"So, what was the deal then?" Alondra sighed and looked off into the trees, turning her gait toward the north. Leo opened his mouth to insist but before he could, Alondra spoke.

"I think you should talk to Ares about that. It's—"

"Please don't say complicated," Leo bit. She arched an eyebrow at him. "I promise, I'm smarter than I look. And Ares isn't likely to explain himself to me anytime soon, and I think you know that."

"You're leaving though," she posited. "Today. With me." Leo's teeth dug into the flesh on the inside of his bottom lip. "Ares said you were. So do you really care? Or are you just nosy?"

"I don't know if I am leaving," Leo said. He wished he sounded more confident, but it was a sort of alarming thing to give voice to. He'd not really considered it before then. Or, he had, but not in such plain terms. Andurnei was strange, and he was growing ever more curious about how it all worked. And he liked Ares, even though he wasn't sure, or he hadn't been sure until last night, that Ares really liked him back. There were responsibilities he should have been tending to. Things back home. Things that made him money. Things that choked him and made him feel stifled and pressed in on all sides. In Andurnei, there were wide open spaces and breathable air and a ridiculous bear of a man who might need Leo's help and wasn't going to ask for it.

"Ares said you were leaving," Alondra repeated. Leo grimaced.

"Contrary to what he thinks, Ares isn't in charge of what I do. I'm perfectly capable of making my own decisions."

"He might kick you out."

"He's welcome to try," Leo snapped. Alondra chuckled, a strange almost throaty sound, and when Leo glanced over to see if she was alright, he was surprised to see her smirking.

"The arrangement Morrow and Mrs. Silva had is older than Ares, though not by much. Sons and daughters of Demeter are rare. Some of the old gods are more cautious about bestowing their gifts than others, and those that take on the burden of birth—"

"Ares is a son of Demeter? The goddess? From mythology?"

"Ah, so you do know some things." Alondra sounded bemused. Leo ignored her.

"They're real? Gods and—"

"There are facets of reality to many old stories," she replied placidly. It was too cryptic for Leo by half. He grit his teeth and tried to focus on what might be most relevant.

"So, Ares is what? A god?"

"A grandson, and part human. So, a demigod. The inheritance of magical abilities—"

"Ares can do magic?" Leo demanded. Then he remembered the doorway, the runes and the blood. But that magic hadn't worked? Alondra sighed.

"I thought you said you were smarter than you looked?"

"Demeter controls the harvest, right?" Leo said, ignoring Alondra and trying to remember the names of Gods that he'd learned in his Classics class in college. Where was Sidney when Leo needed him?

"Yes. Along with—"

"So, he what? Makes the plants grow?"

"He's a gardener."

"Alondra—"

"The gifts of Demeter are manifold. A variety of things impact the harvest. Weather, earth. And then there's the more metaphorical aspects as well. The idea of nurturing. Of giving and plenty."

"What can he do?" Leo pressed. Alondra shrugged.

"Whatever he can do, it's why Edmund Morrow has trapped him here."

"But you know?"

"It's multifaceted, as I said."

"And you're not going to tell me?"

"You do catch on quick."

"Why—"

"It's personal. Not my place. He has abilities. His mother had them too. Morrow wanted someone with those abilities, and he acquired them."

"Trapped them," Leo corrected, not realizing that his anger had returned until he felt the press of his fingernails against his palms, fists clenched again.

"Morrow made a deal with them," Alondra said. Leo bit his tongue. Deals and marks. He remembered viscerally, the contract Morrow had held over Sidney's bleeding body in the chapel.

"How can we help him?" Leo asked. Alondra smiled at that, her thin silver lips curling up on both sides.

"Does he want to be helped?"

"Oh, come on! You can't be serious!" She stopped walking and turned to look at him, stepping into his path so that he had to come up short. The creaking of the trees in the wind, the sound of waves, and the rush of blood roaring in his ears were becoming overwhelming. The world felt tighter between long, thin trunks, white and grey like beech trees, the same shade as Alondra's skin. "There has to be something!"

"You'll only be able to do so much. You can only offer a door. You can't make him walk through it."

"So, what are you saying? Don't try? Just let Morrow bleed him dry?" Leo could barely swallow; he hoped he wasn't being too literal. Alondra took a breath, then put a hand on his shoulder.

"I'm not saying that. I'm just trying to warn you what you're up against."

"I'm not scared of Morrow."

"Not Morrow," Alondra said. "Ares."

"I'm not going to let him get himself killed," Leo insisted. "And if you were his friend, you wouldn't either." Alondra leaned back on her heel, and blinked at him, and Leo found that more infuriating than anything else. He skirted around her, catching up quickly with Matilda, who'd walked past them. Clearly, Alondra wasn't the only one who knew her way to Mae's and thank God for that.

As he continued on, the trees quickly became shorter, the distance between them growing. The edge of the forest was younger, and after a few minutes, Leo could breathe easier. The air had a soft tang of salt, and as the tree line fell away, Leo discovered they were walking up a hill. He slowed as he came to the crest of it, Matilda continuing on down ahead of him toward a cottage in the valley between this knoll and the next. Down below, the sea stretched out a steely blue lined in rushing whitecaps. Leo took a deep breath. He was on edge still, but he'd exhausted himself enough that he could hear his intuition telling him he'd gotten something wrong. Something important. He swallowed as Alondra came up alongside him.

"Sorry," he said. She shook her head, adjusting her glasses on the bridge of her nose.

"In the summer, these hills are full of poppies," Alondra

said, smirking at the house. "And you'd never be able to find this place unless you already knew where you were going."

"I shouldn't have said—"

"Humans care about people in different ways than immortal creatures do," she said, quietly. "We're forgetful, I suppose, of how precious it all is. Still, it's refreshing to discuss life with someone who has such a passion for it."

"Are you immortal?" Leo asked as Alondra started down the hill. She laughed again, that throaty sound, but this time, Leo could almost hear the music in it, caught in the breeze from the water, suspended between them in the air.

"Yes," she said. "I am." Leo trailed down the hill behind her, thinking that that explained a lot of things.

What had looked like a cottage from far away, wasn't really a cottage at all now that they were close. It was much larger than it appeared, a grass-topped roof making it blend in easily with the hill behind it. There were four large stone chimneys letting out puffs of smoke, and the sides of the house were painted in a dark green and decorated in vibrant purple and red symbols and pictures. He didn't remember it, but it felt familiar all the same, and something about it soothed the anxiety that had tightened his chest.

They stepped up onto a wide front porch, and a shimmer of light off the waves gave Leo the sensation that there was something stuck in the corner of his eye. Alondra knocked, as Leo rubbed at his eye with his knuckle, but then, on the porch, where Leo had seen the strange wobble of light, a figure shivered into existence.

"Uh—" Leo took a step back, reaching for Alondra's arm. Alondra looked at him, her brow furrowing, and then turned her head in the direction he was staring, mouth agape. "Is that—"

"Sal," Alondra smiled, and dropped her hand as she took a step toward the figure. "So good to see you! Leo, this is Sal. They're a ghost," she said, glancing over her shoulder, beckoning Leo forward. Leo didn't move.

"A ghost?"

"Humans usually know about ghosts," Sal frowned, their dimples disappearing. Shaggy bangs fell almost into their eyes, and they lifted a muscular looking arm in a motion that suggested brushing the hair off their face. They were wearing a waistcoat with nothing on beneath it, and below the hips their body was little more than a haze.

"No, I... I know about ghosts," Leo said.

"Just never met one?" Sal asked, squinting a little judgmentally. "I mean, we did sort of meet, before. But I guess you probably don't remember." He absolutely did not. Leo scrambled to readjust his understanding of the world and how it functioned, particularly in regard to the afterlife. It made his brain fizzle out like an electrical short, and all he was left with was the echo of both his parents telling him not to be rude, so Leo stepped forward and offered his hand.

"Leo Quince. Pleasure to meet you."

"If I shake your hand your fingers will go all icy, and you'll probably pass out," Sal observed.

"Sal, where's Mae?" Alondra interrupted, before Leo could sort out how to respond to that.

"She's down digging for clams. I can show you where the key is, if you want to come in and warm up. I'll go fetch her for you."

"Oh, no," Alondra said, shaking her head. "It's perfectly fine. We can go down to the water."

"Are you sure? Quite a long walk from the Gamekeeper's place. Where's Ares? You know, he'll be needing—"

"He lost track of time, I'm afraid," Alondra said with a solemn shake of her head. Sal frowned, shoulders slumping.

"Too much time alone. I've always said so," they shook their head, disappointed, and then evaporated into nothingness.

27

Leo paused at the bottom of the steep set of roughhewn steps that led from the cottage down to the beach. Sand slid away under his boots, and Leo kicked them off, bending over to pull off his socks as well, not wanting to trek the miles back to Ares' cottage in sandy shoes. Alondra didn't wait for him, starting across the reedy dunes.

The water stretched out long in front of him, a steely blue, covered in a lace of whitecaps. Suddenly he found himself thinking of Hindry, the small house on the cliffside where Sidney was staying. He missed his brother, always, but especially now. Sidney had gone and gotten himself mired in all this magical stuff, and while Leo was worried for his brother, Sidney was so quick about everything, he probably already knew the way to help Ares. Or at least, he'd know where to start.

A yelp pulled his attention back to the present. A little way down the beach, Alondra and a shorter woman with flaming auburn hair were leaping up toward a purple and blue scarf that had been whipped out of their hands by a gust of wind. The scarf seemed to tumble through the air as Mae, the shorter woman, lifted a shovel, trying to snag it as it caught an updraft and swung out over the waves. It blew north, toward where Leo was standing, and landed ten yards away from him at the edge of the surf.

He jogged in for it, ignoring the sting of the icy water as it seeped into the fabric of his pants, and sucked at his ankles. The tide threatened to rip the scarf into the undertow, but Leo caught the end of the sodden fabric in his fist before it could sink under the waves, yanking it through the wet sand and back to safety.

"My hero!" Mae flung herself against Leo, nearly bowling him over. She wrapped her arms around his neck and kissed his cheek, Alondra's throaty laughter floating along in the air, as Mae stepped back and pulled the scarf from Leo's hands.

"Well! You're looking much keener than you were when I saw you last! I'm glad I saved your life, or I'd be out my favorite shawl!" Mae's accent was thickly and surprisingly Scottish. Leo hadn't remembered that. She wrung out the fabric onto the sand, as the wind whipped her dark green skirt up around her knees. A bulky orange knit sweater rolled up to her elbows, revealed peachy freckled skin, lined with tattoos. "Whatever you want, Leo, it's yours. Hopefully what you want is clam chowder because that's what we're having for lunch. I just have to go back for the bucket. Here," she tossed Leo the soaking shawl. "Carry that for me, will you? Alondra says you're here for Ares? Still hanging around with him then?"

"Yes," Leo said. "I suppose we—"

"Good," Mae said with a firm nod as she started back down the sand. "That boy needs some friends."

Leo followed dutifully behind Mae and Alondra, keeping quiet as the two women walked and traded gossip about people and places Leo had never heard of. It reminded him of being a child and listening to his parents talk over dinner, the conversation above his head, but desperate for scraps of it anyway, waiting to hear anything that applied to him. They were in the house before that happened. The wood floor was warped underfoot, and it was only when Leo stepped onto it that he realized he left his boots and socks down at the beach.

"That's alright. No one will be down there to take them," Mae said, setting her bucket of clams in the sink. The kitchen was wide and warm, even though all the windows were open. A breeze floated through the house, dragging in smells from the garden and the ocean. Leo stood useless in the center of the room, still holding the shawl, until Alondra plucked it out of his hands as she walked by, taking it out onto the porch.

Mae rolled up her sleeves even further as she rinsed clams in the sink. She glanced over her shoulder as Alondra went outside and smirked at Leo.

"Come on, then. Make yourself useful. There's a bowl of ice in the freezer box there, go ahead and grab it."

Leo did as he was told, meeting Mae at the sink. She told him where to put it, and then filled it with water and poured the clams inside, their elbows brushing as she finally glanced up at him with a smirk.

"So, you've been staying with Ares?"

"I have."

"No wonder he hasn't been to see me recently," Mae winked. Leo blushed, and wished he wasn't. Leo cleared his throat.

"Alondra said you know about Ares' deal with Morrow? She wouldn't tell me what it was."

"Ares hasn't told you?" Mae shoved her hands into the bowl of icy clams and stirred them around.

"He told me Morrow threatened his brother," Leo said. "That's it." Mae nodded.

"Ares is fiercely protective over the people he cares about," she said. "Ferocious, even. Not entirely unlike the bear that he is. I've known him for ten years now, and I've never seen him back down when he's defending someone else."

"That sounds right," Leo muttered. Mae laughed, nudging him with her elbow.

"You've seen him in action then?" Leo thought back to the night he'd arrived in Laurel Grove. The alleyway and the handsome stranger who'd come to his rescue. Leo nodded.

"I have."

"He's a good man, with a kind heart. And he's pulled the short end of the stick, as far as where he's gotten himself stuck." She glanced up at Leo, as she paused to push her tangled curls back over her shoulder. "What about you, though?"

"Me?" Leo asked.

"Alondra will be taking you back home tonight. We could do it here if you don't want to risk seeing him again."

"I can't leave," Leo said. "Not while Ares needs—" Mae grinned, and Leo kept stammering. God. What had gotten into him? He shook his head, trying to clear it. "I just don't like the idea of him trapped. Not if I can help."

"So, it's not just about his cock then?" Leo could feel every part of him flush. He opened his mouth to protest, but before he could speak, Mae chuckled. "Sorry, lovey. I couldn't help it, but you're really so obvious. As for Ares, he's losing track of time, and I think we can only place some of the blame for that on you. Not enough though."

"Wait," Leo willed his brain to put some of these pieces together. "I thought when Alondra said he was losing track of time, she'd just meant he was disorganized."

"Does he seem disorganized to you?"

"No," Leo said slowly. "But then... is something happening to him? Something physical?" Mae watched Leo for a moment. Then she sighed and pinched the bridge of her nose, her glasses riding up on her fingers, water droplet sliding down onto her cheek.

"He's working too much," she said, turning back to the sink. "Giving too much of himself to the land. There aren't boundaries here the same way there are back home. Energies are more malleable."

"It's his job," Leo said. Mae shook her head.

"Put too much into the ground, and eventually you can't tell the difference between your hands and the dirt." Leo looked down at his palms in the sink and frowned.

"You're not speaking metaphorically, are you?" he asked. Mae met his gaze with a frown.

"Have you ever heard of the Mycelians?"

"The what?"

"They're a type of Fae. A sort of—I suppose the most direct though perhaps unpolished way to describe them would be 'mushroom people.' They're so intricately interconnected with the earth that they've created a sort of hive entity below it. It's not any one of them, but it's sort of, all of them. They can communicate through it, which is damned useful, but there's also a transfer of energy, or magic, or even soul that can occur through it if they're not extremely careful about how much of themselves they're putting into it."

"And I suppose Ares... isn't being careful?" He tried to take a breath, but his lungs felt tight, like there was something pressing down against his chest. In his mind, Ares was being sucked into the tilled dirt of the garden, arms first. "Can we stop it?" Leo asked. Mae watched him carefully for a moment, her eyes scanning his face like she was looking for an answer in the tilt of his head.

"That's a tricky question," she said finally, digging her hands back in amongst the clams. "Stopping it would depend upon a couple of things."

"On what?"

"On him," she said. "And you."

ANOTHER TREE WAS UNDERPRODUCING. The third one in this row. Ares checked the side of the tank again. Barely ten gallons of sap, when it should have at least been fifteen by now. Eighteen in a strong month.

Ares walked around the tree, examining its barren branches, almost praying that there would be something visibly wrong with it. Some lichen or an infection. Something he could treat. Something that didn't mean the soul of the tree was dying.

"The soul of the tree," was a phrase Morrow had used since the beginning. It had taken a couple of years before Ares had learned what it really meant.

Morrow cultivated the seeds himself, structured them around bent and warped magical objects. That was all Ares thought they were at the time. The first time Ares reported a tree as underproducing, Morrow had it ripped up by the roots. And Ares had felt the pain of it. Like his own arm had been wrenched out of socket at the joint. Agony, sourceless but marrow deep, throbbing for days after the deed had been done. That was seven years ago. And he'd lost three more trees since then, each one hurting worse than the last.

His soul and his magic were, to the best of his knowledge, inextricably linked. The curse of being half human. And his magic, the nourishment he could provide, was the only thing keeping these other poor, stolen souls from blinking out of existence.

Ares came back around the tree and got to his knees about a foot from the base of its trunk. He dug with his hands; fingernails already caked in dirt. It was easier when he could feel the heat from the roots. It was how he knew he was deep enough. The knife he pulled from his coat pocket was still slick with blood. This wasn't the only underproducing tree he'd found today. It was the third.

Ares pulled back his shirt sleeve, ignoring where it streaked crimson up his skin, and dug the blade into his flesh. Blood to replenish the sap of the tree. His life for its. In some ways it only seemed fair. That they would pull from him as he would from them. A balancing of scales, in a way.

"The core of magic is exchange." Morrow's voice echoed in his head. Ares had been crying then. He was crying now. Blood pooled in the lines of his palm and he thrust his hand into the dirt, smearing his blood against the roots, the earth seeping the warmth from his skin.

28

The clam chowder was hot and rich, and Leo felt fortified, even as talk turned away from Ares and into topics Leo had no real interest in. As he scooped the last of the soup from the bottom of a brown earthenware bowl with the end of a loaf of bread, he weighed his options. Stay or go.

Ares was in trouble, no doubt about that. But if he'd learned anything from Mae and Alondra it was that he couldn't save Ares on his own. Even if he could work out a way to break Morrow's contract, Ares would still have to decide to leave. Or to agree to try. And if he knew anything for sure about Ares, it was that he was as stubborn as a mule. And if he felt some sort of obligation to the place, to his mother or even to the deal itself, was there any point in Leo trying to convince him to leave?

So then, what was the other option? Could Leo do the legal work of it himself and then seduce Ares into going? Ares wouldn't like it, if he found out. Leo didn't like it much as it was. But maybe it would be enough to open the door. Maybe if

Leo could remind Ares what was on the other side, perhaps he'd walk through on his own.

"You look pensive," Mae said. Leo nodded, grabbing his mug of hot cider and taking a sip.

"I was thinking about Ares. I'm wondering if I can find some loophole in his contract with Morrow. Get him out of the whole thing."

"Getting him to accept your help will be the challenge there, I think," Mae said.

"We could kill Morrow," Alondra offered. Leo choked, surprised at her expression of total sincerity. "His death voids all magical contracts," she added simply.

"Murder has its own set of consequences, of course," Mae smirked. "Not that you care about that."

"I grew up in the Abyssal Plane," Alondra scoffed. "No one from the Assembly would be able to catch me."

"I only know about half of those words," Leo said. "But I think we ought to keep murder as a last resort."

"You can't argue against its efficacy," she shrugged.

"I can argue against the practicality of being an immortal being who is also a fugitive."

"The Assembly's memory is shorter than my lifespan by a considerable amount," Alondra said haughtily, lifting her own cider to her lips. Mae rolled her eyes.

"Abyssal Demons all fancy themselves warriors of one sort or another. You'll never talk sense into her."

"Well, if we decide murder is the route we want, you'll be the first person I call," Leo said, Alondra sniffed, her gaze pointedly over Leo's shoulder. Then she sighed.

"It's snowing. You ought to be getting back."

"Snowing? Wait, are you not coming?"

"I have business with Mae," Alondra said. "I'll come back by the house this evening before I pass through. You'll have to have made a choice by then."

"Let me get those poultices for you," Mae said, getting up from the table. Matilda stood up from the hearth and stretched, walking slowly across the room to sit at Leo's side.

"That's a good sign," Alondra said. Leo glanced up at her. "What?"

"That she likes you. She's a good dog. Good instincts."

"Is there anything else you can tell me about Ares? Anything that might help?" Leo said, his mind still buzzing as he reached down to pat Matilda on the head, the feeling of her warm fur slipping between his fingers more grounding than he'd anticipated.

"I've influenced you enough. Ares will accuse me of meddling," she said, as Mae returned in a flurry of skirts.

"This should be everything he needs. I've packed extra. Give him at least a third more than he asks for of any of the tinctures. He's always under medicating. And he straight up refuses the good stuff." Leo got to his feet and Mae shoved the pack into his hands. Matilda stood, and nudged Leo's knee with her nose.

"Is it time to go?" Leo asked her. She rubbed her warm, furry body against his calf, and then started toward the door.

Roots. There was something about the roots crawling under his skin, the small dirt covered tendrils, that felt like longing and promised peace.

A fifth tree was underproducing. Ares had stopped binding his wound after the third, and he'd been right not to bother. Blood and the magic he resented and loved seeped out of him as one. The magic was slicker. Softer. Reminded him of his mother. There was less of her in the orchard with each passing year. Something about the natural rate of decay and the passage of time. In moments like these, his grief was still raw.

At first, he hadn't minded. His hands in the dirt, close to the roots, he could feel her again. Her presence or her magic. Like she was still alive. Every brush of fibrous roots against his skin was her lips against his forehead when he'd been a baby, soothing as she checked him for a fever. Not healing, she didn't have that power either, but a brush of her magic fortified him, nurturing and kind. The gentility of a love that asked for nothing in return. He could feel it in the dirt. The same gentle caress. A promise that it would all be alright. If not now, then soon.

But the ground was cold. Unfamiliar to his skin, his memories. The feeding roots crawled up his arms, the souls of strangers desperate for a body, a home that wouldn't eat them alive or bleed them dry. It was a perversion of magic, what he'd done. What everyone who had made and maintained the orchard had done.

Thin, white roots tugged at his flesh, peeling his skin aside. He watched them move, dazed and unfeeling. The pain was so constant that he'd become numb to it. He preferred numbness, actually. Grief ached the same from the living trees as it did from the dying ones, and it felt the same as his own.

A sound, far beyond the creaking of branches in the wind and his own blood and tears dropping in the dirt, wheedled its way into his consciousness. A starling answered by the chirrup of a wren. A wren with feathers the same brown as Leo's eyes. Ares would miss him. The feeling of his hands against Ares' skin. The warmth of him, and the way his kisses melted like water against Ares' lips. The way he didn't ask for much except honesty. Ares didn't want him to leave and would have nothing to give him except pain if he stayed. He was useless to anyone except the trees. Still, he would have liked to kiss him again. Make him laugh and sigh and smile.

Ares yanked his arms out of the hole he'd dug at the base of the tree, falling back into the dirt. Fuck. Everything hurt. He'd spent too much time crouched in front of the tree and his legs and shoulders were stiff. It was snowing and the sun was sinking low behind the thick grey clouds, light leeching from the sky. Ares was going to be sick. He rolled onto his elbow and waited, counting the seconds so that he wouldn't lose them. The tree above him shook angrily in the wind. Or maybe that was just the way trees moved. He wasn't sure anymore.

Head spinning, Ares struggled slowly to his feet. He hated this fucking place. He took two steps and had to brace himself against the nearest trunk, blood-soaked fingers digging against the damp bark. So stupid. He needed to get home to where Leo wouldn't be. Hopefully Alondra wouldn't be either. He didn't need to be scolded, he just needed quiet. To lay down on the floor in front of his fireplace and sleep in the heat, floorboards and foundation a hard barrier between him and the dreams of roots in the dirt that would come like they always did, unraveling in his mind and choking him in his sleep.

Seven days before he'd have to come back for the harvest. Seven days to get out to Mae's and see how far she could take what little sap they had. Far enough that Morrow wouldn't notice the diminished supply. The thought of Morrow uprooting five trees was enough to make Ares' stomach clench so violently that he nearly doubled over as he staggered out toward the gate. He needed to go home before he could think about coming back.

With shaking hands, Ares fumbled for keys in his pocket, locking the tall, iron gate and his coat somewhere inside. He didn't care. He was hot and woozy from the blood loss. Time was still strange. There was snow collecting on the ground. A quarter of an inch already, and melting through his curls, cold and dripping down his scalp. Ares left his hand on the stone wall, using it as a guide as he staggered around the perimeter of the orchard. When he made it to the small drop that would put him on the paved path that ran behind the wall, behind his house, he stopped. No handrail there. He should really install one. His balance was off as he tried to dig a heel into the dirt and stepped too far forward. His body sagged, exhausted, and he fell forward onto his hands and knees, injured arm giving away beneath him almost immediately. He tried to breathe through the pain, but he'd done enough of that already for the evening. So instead, he sighed and passed out on the pavement.

29

Ares woke to the sound of panting. Everything was cold, and someone was breathing hard over him. He might have passed out on the floor of the kitchen, Matilda standing above him, dripping drool onto his cheek. Snow tapped icily against leaves, filling his head with an easy, fuzzy sound. Or was it the crackling of a fire?

Hands, soft and warm, heat he'd craved, caressed his neck, and then pressed against his chest and back.

"Jesus Christ," Leo hissed. Ares closed his eyes tight before forcing himself to look. Leo's beautiful face hovered over Ares with a concerned grimace. Ares hated it, sort of. Hated that Leo was worried. He wanted to brush the distress off his mouth and reached toward Leo's face with his good arm.

Leo caught his hand in the air and held it gently, lowering it slowly. Ares frowned.

"Does that hurt?"

"'m fine," Ares grunted and hoisted himself up onto his elbow. He was not fine. Everything hurt.

"Uh, no. Don't do that."

"You're supposed to be gone," Ares said, his head swooping.

"And you're not supposed to be lying on the ground bleeding to death, yet here we both are. Would you be still please?"

"I'm fine," Ares repeated, trying to sit.

"You're covered in blood."

"Don't exaggerate."

"I wish I was." Ares looked down at himself. There was a large streak of blood and dirt where his arm had curled against his chest. And the arm itself didn't look good. He'd had worse. Out of the orchard was all that mattered.

"That's hardly *covered*."

"Ah, yes. Semantics. That'll be a fun argument to have right now. It's more blood than I'd like," Leo's tone was arid and his face looked pale. Wind blew hard, ripping through the thin fabric of Ares' shirt. He shuddered and Leo's lips thinned. "If I get you up, can you walk?"

"I'm alright," Ares lied. "Hungry, that's all. How long have you been out here?"

"Ares," Leo huffed without responding. Leo got one foot beneath himself and then wrapped his hands around Ares' good arm, pulling him up to a real seated position. Ares wasn't expecting Leo's strength, which was silly because Leo was so strong. And pretty. Ares' head throbbed, but he managed to balance without tipping back over, so that was good progress. He was relieved Leo was there. And guilty for being so relieved. He'd wanted him to stay. Or not to stay exactly. Some middle thing of being with Ares and not being trapped. How to explain it? His neck was stiff, and he groaned, turning his head at the sensation of something warm and solid at his back. Matilda was sitting against him. He smiled.

"I guess she got you home okay."

"She's a very good dog," Leo said, reaching up and brushing away the snow that collected in Ares' curls. Ares reached for his hand, his fingers colliding sloppily, fumbling with Leo's. His hands were so warm. It was the touch he'd craved in the orchard. Leo let him lace their fingers together, and maybe Ares was acting strange, because Leo's mouth had dropped open, his breath steaming up toward the night sky, head cocked to the side. Before Ares could explain, Leo tightened his grip and then looked up, squinting through the precipitation. "If you think you can sit here a few more minutes, I might be able to get the wagon."

"I don't need to be carted around like a prize-winning pumpkin," Ares chuckled, and with that he forced himself forward, rocking up onto one foot. He would have fallen forward and broken his teeth if Leo hadn't steadied him. As it was, Ares ended up leaning his forehead against Leo's shoulder, huffing into the skin of his neck. Fuck but he smelled good. Warm and lightly spiced like mulled cider. Then Leo's arms were looping beneath Ares' arms, around his back, as Leo tugged Ares against his chest and then up, standing them both at once. Ares found his feet, still gripping hard against the bend in Leo's elbows.

"There you go," Leo's voice was comforting, calm, and he took a deep breath. Ares was so grateful he hadn't gone, even though the cold that curled around Ares' neck reminded Ares that he should have gone.

"I thought you were leaving," Ares said again. Leo snorted.

"You should be thanking your lucky stars I haven't. I've got a whole pack full of insane medicine to give you, and I won't be going anywhere until I've seen you drink all of it—"

"I don't need all of it."

"Put your arm over my shoulder."

"I'm—"

"Shut up. Don't tell me you're fine because I won't believe it. And if I did, I'd be wrong to. Let me help you so we can get inside, please!" Ares was so startled by Leo's outburst that he swallowed down a laugh and did what Leo said, throwing his good arm over Leo's shoulder, first shuffling, then stepping down the snow-covered path.

It was slow going, but not too slow, and Leo was silent and stern the entire time. Ares could feel his anger, and it was sort of sweet actually. And strange. Did anyone care about Ares enough to be furious with him? His aunt and uncle, maybe, when he'd been a teenager inclined toward getting in fights. He'd sort of forgotten what that felt like.

On the patio, Ares fumbled getting his arm down from around Leo's shoulder, grazing the back of Leo's head with his fingers. And then he couldn't get his hand into his pocket, because it was wet and tight to his thigh.

"Move," Leo huffed, shoving his more delicate fingers into the soaked fabric, making something tighten in the small of Ares' back, a tangible realization that he had not died, was actually quite alive, and maybe that was a good thing after all. He choked down a stupid, likely delirious laugh, as Leo pulled the small ring of keys from his pocket and unlocked the door.

"I don't like our odds on the stairs," said Leo, as Ares staggered inside and braced himself on the mantle. "I'll run up and get you something dry to wear. Try to get out of your pants if you can."

"If not, you'll do it for me?" Ares asked, half joking.

"I will," Leo called as his footsteps were already echoing up the stairs. "And I promise I'll do it as unappealingly as possible."

"That's not likely," Ares muttered, rolling his eyes toward Matilda who blinked at him and then shook her fur off, spraying him with flecks of snow.

Horrifyingly, Ares had only managed to get his pants down to mid-thigh before he got dizzy again. He bowed his head, trying to ignore the heat in his cheeks as he heard Leo thundering down the stairs.

"For a man that's so small, you sure do make a lot of noise," Ares grumbled.

"For a man that's so big, you're really abysmal at taking care of yourself," Leo returned. And then his hands were on Ares' thighs. Ares squeezed his eyes shut tight as Leo tugged at the wet fabric, wincing as he heard Leo get to his knees.

Leo untied the laces on Ares' boots, and then got his shoes and socks off without a word.

"Put your hand on my shoulder before you step out of your trousers," Leo said. Ares did as he was told, telling himself that his eyes were still shut so that he wouldn't get dizzy, and not for any other reason. His head was clearer, and his mind was telling him that Leo should have gone. Never mind that Ares' heart was pounding in his chest because Leo was sliding his hands down Ares' legs, shifting the fabric around Ares' feet.

Ares had to change his grip, hand and fingers touching the skin of Leo's neck, thumb sliding accidently beneath the collar of Leo's shirt. Leo stood slowly, keeping himself steady so Ares could balance. He could feel Leo's breath against his chin, and Ares opened his eyes.

Leo was studying Ares' face carefully, his eyes narrowed in concern. Ares' hand had streaked blood on Leo's neck, a single red thumbprint on the center of Leo's throat. Leo's lips were pursed and Ares wanted to kiss them back to fullness. Ares wanted to kiss him, and after all the things they'd done, that didn't seem like it should be such an insurmountable thing to want.

Leo reached his hand up and brushed his thumb over Ares' brow, his hand resting against Ares' temple. He was so handsome, and he was going to be leaving soon. Ares wouldn't see him again after tonight. He would only have the memory of

Leo's mouth and skin and smile; the only reasons he'd been able to pull his arms away from that tree in the orchard.

Ares leaned forward and kissed him, trying to make it a real one, firm and sincere. Leo's mouth softened at once, opening for Ares just a little, enough that he could taste the warmth of Leo's breath, and slide his tongue against Leo's cold lips.

Leo's hand tightened in Ares' shirt, his body listing forward, though he should have been pulling away. Ares swayed, dizzy with wanting Leo. Or maybe just dizzy. He grabbed Leo's hip, but it wasn't enough. He could feel Leo curl under him, catching Ares as Ares collapsed, unconscious, in front of the fireplace.

30

Leo cursed a long, soft string of invectives as he eased his hands out from beneath Ares and rolled Ares onto his back, his fingers scrambling against skin for a pulse. It was there in Ares' throat, slow but steady, and Leo collapsed slightly, his forearms holding himself up against Ares' chest. He took a deep, shaking breath, ignoring the tears that filled his eyes.

He'd done nothing but panic since they'd found Ares' body on the path. It couldn't have been more than fifteen minutes ago, but it felt like hours. He was still alive. Alive was what mattered. Leo grabbed the bag of medicine that Mae had given him off the coffee table, and reached into it with shaking hands, quickly finding the ice blue liquid she'd said was a stabilizing tincture. He wondered if he ought to drink some himself first.

Leo forced himself up to his knees, clean strip of cotton waving like a flag between his fingers. He wet the fabric with the blue stuff and then held it to Ares' mouth, sliding it between his slightly opened lips, against his tongue.

Ares rolled his lips, dampening them against the cloth and Leo was both relieved and furious. How dare Ares kiss him at a time like this? But God, Leo wanted nothing more than to curl up on top of Ares and kiss him all day long. It wasn't the right impulse to have at the moment. There was something not right about him. About both of them. But Leo wanted Ares well enough that Leo could take him to bed again. He wanted him well enough that he could want to kiss him without feeling guilty. He wanted him well.

Leo soaked the fabric again and tucked it partially between Ares' lips, knowing it was the only way to get him the medicine without risk of choking him. Then he looked down at Ares' injured arm, the cut ragged and deep, destroying the etched vines that decorated his skin, and Leo got angry all over again.

"What are you doing in that stupid orchard?" Leo grumbled, grabbing for poultices and bandages and a cleaning salve. "Why on earth would you do this to yourself, and why... why would you think anything that made you do this was a good thing to do? You are absolutely the most impossible human being I've ever met, and I guess you aren't really even one of those, are you?"

Ares' head turned slightly, and Leo flushed and focused on cleaning Ares' wound for a moment before looking at his face again.

"Are you awake?"

"Kind of," Ares mumbled, reaching slowly up with his good hand to take the fabric from his mouth. "But don't let that stop you."

"Well, I'd say I'm sorry, but I'm not sorry. And I really hope this cleaning stuff stings."

"It doesn't."

"Well, then I'm going to suggest Mae change her recipe."

"Why are you so mad?" Ares asked. "And where's the blue stuff?"

"Here," Leo handed it to him, and Ares lifted his head

enough that he could drink a quarter of the bottle. "Drink more."

"You didn't answer my question."

"Why am I so mad? I thought you died!"

"Disappointed I didn't?" Ares smirked slightly as he laid his head back down.

"That's a horrible thing to say," Leo said, going back to mending Ares' arm. Ares was quiet for a moment, before he spoke again.

"I can do that. My arm, I mean."

"Shut up," Leo snapped, pressing poultices to the injury near the elbow joint and the wrist where Mae had told him to. Ares hissed.

"That stings."

"Good."

"Why didn't you leave?" Ares' eyes were closed again, his hand still holding the vial of blue liquid.

"I haven't decided yet," Leo said, mostly because he was irritated. Ares nodded, barely.

"I thought you'd gone," his voice was quiet. Rough. "If I'd known you'd still be here, I wouldn't have let it get this bad."

"What is it?" Leo asked. "I mean, why did you do this to yourself?"

"My mother's magic was special. Strong. I don't have as much as she did, and even if I did, it's not as potent. Mae told you, I guess?"

"A little bit."

"The orchard needs our magic to grow. And I give it what I can."

"It's killing you," Leo said. Ares snorted.

"Eventually," Ares opened his eyes, and looked at Leo, a small smile curling up the corner of his lips. "I'm a bad bet, Leo.

I know you can see it. Whether you leave or stay, it all ends up the same for me."

"It doesn't have to," Leo said.

"Yes, it does." Ares moved, pushing himself up to seated with a long, low grunt. He turned his back to press against the hearth. The bandages Leo had started twining around his arm trailed along the floor as Ares lifted the blue potion to his mouth again. He drank another quarter and set it down. Leo wanted to shout at him to keep drinking. He wanted to shake him by the shoulders and demand he was being unreasonable. He wanted to crawl into his lap and kiss him senseless. But he didn't think any of those things would gain him any ground in the argument he was about to make.

"What if I could break your contract?" he said. Ares looked up at him, then down quickly, his cheeks flushing, as he began to slowly wrap the bandages around his own arm.

"What do you mean?"

"I mean Morrow conscripted you to pour your soul into that orchard," Leo said, guessing mostly. Ares didn't confirm or deny it, so Leo pressed on. "He threatened your brother, you told me that. So, whatever happened between you two occurred under duress, so there's a legal standing—"

"The law doesn't work the same way here that it does back home," Ares shook his head. "It's fae law, and it's complicated and poorly weighted against the deal taker."

"I can figure it out," Leo said. "I can—"

"What if I don't want to break the contract?" Ares asked. Leo's hands clenched.

"Ares. It's killing you."

"It's more complicated than that."

"Then explain it to me!" Leo demanded, knocking his elbow into the table. "Everyone around here loves to tell me that things are so complex and that everything's so fucking complicated. I'm smart! My job is figuring things out and I can do this!"

"What if I don't want you to waste your time?" Ares asked.

"Waste my time because you don't think I can do it?"

"Waste your time because I don't think it would change anything," Ares said. He rested his hands on his thighs, arm wrapped from elbow to wrist. His shoulders sagged and he tried for another small smile, but this time it only looked weak and tired. "Leo. You don't doctor a lame horse, you kill it. That's what this is."

"That's not true."

"You don't want this."

"You don't get to tell me what I want!" Leo slammed his fists against his thighs. "I get enough of that at home. I get enough of everyone deciding what's important to me and where I have to go and what I need to say. I—" Leo bit his tongue, and then gave it up. He wanted to speak his mind, so he was going to. "I don't think you're a bad bet. I think you're a good person, and I think you got tied up in something that you didn't understand before you got involved—"

"Well, now who does that sound like?" Ares muttered. Leo rolled his eyes.

"Shut up. I'll do as I damn well please."

"You don't have any idea—"

"Well then enlighten me! Unless you don't actually know what you agreed to either, because you're just some dumbass demigod with a death wish!"

"And you're a smug little rich boy being led around by his cock," Ares snapped. Leo lunged for him, his fists clenching in Ares' still damp shirt. Ares caught his hips and Leo kissed him hard and furious. He hated him and he wanted him so badly. Leo's heart was pounding in his chest, and he could taste potion like blueberries on Ares' tongue. Ares grunted in surprise when Leo tackled him, but he was pulling him close now, his fingers tangling in the buttons on Leo's shirt, tugging as he tried to undo them. Which was stupid. It was more stupid that Leo was letting him. Was helping him.

Leo moved his mouth down Ares' jaw, kissing the dirt and sweat from the line of his throat, as Ares pushed his hips up, pressing them together. Relief and want and anger all swam through Leo's head; he'd never felt so much while he was kissing someone, and it made him dizzy. Ares yanked Leo close, pressed his mouth against Leo's collar bone and sucked. Leo arched his back, crying out, and then there was a knock at the door.

Leo heard it, Ares didn't. Or Ares was just too busy trying to slide Leo's shirt off to care. Leo fell back, pushed himself to his feet.

"There's a—" the knock came again. "It's probably Alondra."

"Alondra?" Ares asked, breathless, his chest heaving.

"In case I wanted to—" Leo couldn't say it. Ares blinked and then nodded, his gaze dropping. He straightened the collar of his shirt and looked away.

"You should go."

"Fuck you."

"I meant answer the door," Ares huffed, rolling his eyes. And Leo left to go do exactly that.

31

"How is he?" Alondra looked no worse off than if she'd taken a stroll through a gentle breeze, the top of her hood glinting with snowflakes. Leo tried to stifle his general frustration with a non-committal grunt.

"I thought you were staying with Mae?" What he'd really thought was that he'd have more time. He was so mixed up over Ares, he could hardly catch his breath. Frustration warred against desire and something deeper that threaded behind the others. An emotion Leo didn't understand so he couldn't name, and all he could parse from it was that it wanted to know Ares would be safe whether Leo stayed or went.

"I can travel much faster without a companion," Alondra said, shoving her way past Leo into the foyer. She looked him over and gave a small judgmental hum before shaking her head, unclasping her coat and shoving it into Leo's arms. "He's well enough I suppose, judging by the state of you. If you're going with me through the realms, now would be the time to gather your things," she said, before walking into the living room.

Leo tried to take a deep breath as he hung her cloak on the hook, ignoring the way his heart was in his stomach and pounding arrhythmically. How did anyone make decisions? A lifetime of doing what other people had told him to do had left him woefully ill-equipped for this, and it was beginning to look like Leo didn't really know how to do anything but panic. He shook out his arms and stepped into the study just long enough to remember that they'd moved all of his things up into Ares' room the night before. Going upstairs felt needlessly danger-ous. But if he *was* leaving... well, he should take his things with him.

At the same time, he considered as he walked up the stairs, he didn't really need to take anything with him at all. He'd left a full suitcase at Elmmond House. The stack of his clothes on the corner of Ares' dresser had been "fabricated" which might mean they were made of pumpkins and fairy dust and would dissolve upon first contact with reality.

Leo stood in the doorway, staring at his things, and then made the horrible mistake of glancing at the bed, which was all it took to unleash the memories he'd been diligently trying not to think about: Ares' hands on him, Ares beneath him, fucking him. 'You're mine,' he'd said. It was a thing people said during sex. Though, in Leo's experience, they usually had the courtesy not to look you in the eye when they said it. It still sent chills up his spine, brought his hand up to the back of his neck, as though he could rub away the sensation with the press of his palm.

"There are men who can fuck you at home," he muttered, annoyed at the way he wanted to grab Ares' pillow and shove his face into it like some kind of feral animal. He wasn't used to wanting a person more than an act, and it took him a full minute to realize that's what his strange desire really was. He wanted Ares.

Leo tried to swallow that thought. It was a problem for a number of reasons, and wasn't helpful at the moment. Leo's own ridiculousness could take a backseat. He needed to find a way out for Ares.

Ares thought that he was a lost cause, so that was a bad start. And he was trapped here, and stubborn enough that Leo didn't know if there was anything Leo could offer that would entice him to leave. Ares had said he liked Leo. Liked having sex with him at least. Could Leo be seductive enough to coax Ares back to Earth and out of his contract with Morrow? The man had been celibate for ten years, so probably not. Still, Leo had slept with people for worse reasons; he supposed he could always try. But that meant staying. And ignoring the way he felt about Ares, because his emotions were tender and strange and confusing. The easiest way to avoid them would be to go home. He didn't owe Ares anything. And the pragmatic side of him, the side that sounded most like his father, was begging him to remember that.

Leo finally got up the courage to walk into the bedroom. He ignored the bed and all of Ares' things, and went to the dresser, shifting through his small pile of clothes. Behind them was a clutter of Ares' affects: scraps of notes, a jar of some kind of salve with a note from Mae on it that read 'You're out in the sun all day. Please use this for the love of God.' The jar looked unopened. Beyond that, pushed against the wall, was a desktop radio Leo hadn't noticed before, the speaker protruding from the box just enough that Leo guessed it was likely broken. In front of that, a pile of sweaters, some with fraying strands visible, mending probably. And on top of those, Ares' sketchbook, open to whatever he'd been working on, grey charcoal in streaks against the cream-colored page.

He'd expected to see more wrens. Leo glanced at the paper, and then grabbed the sketchbook off the stack in disbelief. His own face, eyes turned down, looking at something out of frame. His curls soft, drooping, run through too many times by Leo's hands. His mouth relaxed, a curve at the corner of his lips almost a smile. Leo didn't know he had ever been so comfortable. He looked into the mirror over the dresser, almost to make sure the person in the drawing was him. He didn't look like this, did he?

He certainly didn't now. His jaw was tight, and his forehead was wrinkled in worry and confusion. His heart was hammering away in his chest, and he had no idea what he was doing.

"Leo!" Alondra called from the bottom of the stairs. "Time to go!"

§

"HOW ARE YOU FEELING?" Alondra asked as she strode into the living room, her eyebrows arched over the rim of her glasses. Ares had managed to tug on the joggers that Leo brought down for him, though he was still sitting on the floor in front of the unlit hearth. Alondra stopped in front of him, and Ares fought the urge to try and hide his bandaged arm behind Matilda, who was sitting at his side.

"I thought you'd be gone by now."

"You'd like me to be gone by now," she crossed her arms over her chest. It was true and not true. Ares swallowed.

"I'm alright. Between Leo and Mae..." he trailed off, patting the bag of medicine beside him. Alondra stayed silent and the back of Ares' neck began to warm under her scrutiny. He scowled. "You're taking him with, aren't you?"

"Not if he doesn't want to go."

"What he wants and what he needs—"

"The pot said to the kettle."

"He can't stay here."

"I'm sure Mae would be grateful for the company," Alondra

said. Ares huffed and she smirked. "It'd be so much easier to badger me if you actually wanted him to leave, wouldn't it?"

"I do want him to leave," Ares said firmly. "For his own sake."

"What a martyr. Saint Ares," she clasped her hands as if in prayer, and he rolled his eyes.

"You need to take him," Ares said again, trying to inject sternness over the fear that was tightening in his chest, making him sound more desperate than sincere. Leo couldn't stay. Ares was dangerously, frighteningly close to admitting something like affection for the other man, and that would be bad for both of them. For several reasons. But if Leo was gone now, these last five days could be nothing more than a memory that Ares would revisit and likely regret. The same way he did so many others.

"Ares, he's not a rucksack. I can't just pick him up and throw him over my shoulder."

"You could. You're strong."

"I have no interest in taking him anywhere he doesn't want to go."

"It's dangerous for him to stay here."

"It's dangerous for you to stay here," she said, her tone surprisingly sharp. Ares narrowed his eyes, frowning up at her. "You don't see me dragging you back Earthside."

"That's different."

"If he decides to stay—" Ares opened his mouth to protest, but Alondra held up her hand and continued before he could butt in. "If he decides to stay, will you please do me a favor?"

"No," Ares said. Alondra continued to ignore him.

"Consider that he may have reasons for staying that don't deserve your ire. Or your dismissiveness."

"I'm not—"

"His intentions are good. I know you're not used to that." Ares snorted. "Even if he's a little misguided."

"Misguided I agree with," Ares grumbled. Alondra smiled.

"I'll be back in a week either way, but especially if he does leave. You'll need help getting the sap down to Mae." He didn't need help, strictly speaking. But it would go faster with two. "Take it easy until then. Have Fen help with the garden. You need to rest."

"I'm fine," Ares repeated, though it felt hollow, since they both knew he was lying. Alondra only blinked at him.

"I imagine you want the floor tonight. No use in me trying to help you up the stairs?"

"I'll be fine down here," he said. Alondra sighed, stepping forward. She leaned around him, kneeling on the hearth, and he could hear logs scraping against the stone. There was a soft hum, and then a breath, and the crackle of dried, cold wood, as the logs caught fire. "Thanks," he said, as she backed up. Alondra patted Matilda on the head and then reached down and squeezed Ares' shoulder. Without another word to him, she turned and walked out of the living room and back down the hall.

Ares listened as Alondra called up to Leo. His footsteps on the stairs were only partially muffled by the crackling fire that warmed Ares' shoulder blades. He strained to hear the pattern of their hushed voices, and then did hear the sharp hiss of portal magic. Leo would be able to go through the portal now, since Ares had marked him. And that stung a little more than it should have. Ares sucked the inside of his bottom lip willing himself not to call out, to say goodbye. It was better that they didn't, because now that he was alone, sitting in the nearly silent living room, it was much easier to admit how badly he didn't want Leo to leave.

Matilda lay down beside him and rested her chin on his

thigh. He ran his fingers through her thick fur as he tried to focus on the sound of fire and not footsteps. He ignored the gasping, clawing sensation of tightness that wrapped around his torso and wanted to sob. Instead he let the feeling settle in the new trench that grief and loneliness were digging in his chest. It was stupid to be sad. He'd barely known the man. That was a lie, of course. Leo had been more forthcoming than anyone had any reason to be over the course of five days. Ares would miss him, his chattering, his aimless cheerfulness, the intimacy. And those few, precious moments, even if they'd only ever been in Ares' head, where Leo had been his.

The portal closed with a silent, gentle suction that shifted the air, like a vacuum removing all the energy from the house. The fire flickered behind Ares, casting long shadows on the far wall, as he slumped back against the stone, feeling more than hearing the echo of emptiness in the cottage. He forced himself to exhale around the tightness in his chest and the knot in his throat, thinking of only how much he wanted to curl up on the rug and go to sleep for a week. His dreams would be horrible, but at least there he'd be sure to see Leo's face again. And that was better than being awake.

32

"What do you want for supper? And don't say it's too late for supper because I know you need to eat. I doubt you've had anything all day." Ares' whole body stilled, his skin prickling as Leo strode into the living room and then through to the kitchen, flicking on the light as though this was the most normal thing he could be doing, still existing in Ares' house.

"What?" Ares barely managed a whisper, as Matilda leapt up, her tail wagging as she trotted into the kitchen, ready to beg for scraps.

"I can make grilled cheese," Leo called over the sound of the icebox opening and closing. "Not sure how filling that'll be. Maybe with some of that chicken. We have a little left." Ares fumbled to his feet as Leo rambled on. He nearly tripped over the rug as he staggered to the open archway that separated the kitchen from the living room and grabbed tight to the molding. Leo turned toward him frowning and shook his head.

"Uh, no. You need to sit somewhere and rest. I have dinner well in hand. I used to make grilled cheese on an ironing board in college. I think I can manage on a stove."

"You're not supposed to be here," Ares said, short of breath somehow. Leo shrugged and turned back toward the icebox.

"Alondra said she'd be back in a week, so that's how long you have to try and run me off." Ares stared at the back of Leo's head, waiting for the surge of anger that he'd expected. He was furious. He ought to have been furious. It was a horrible idea, that put them both in danger. But instead, all he felt was relief.

"Leo—" Leo didn't turn, waving Ares away over his shoulder.

"Genuinely, I could take you in a fight right now. You should sit down."

"Leo," Ares reeled forward, wanting nothing more than to put his hands on Leo, maybe to shake him, but mostly just to be sure he was real. Ares wavered and Matilda barked, causing Leo to turn and see Ares. He grabbed Ares by the forearms, before Ares could lose his footing. Leo's hands were strong and steady and blissfully real. Ares could have cried.

"Ares," Leo frowned. "Look, I know I'm likely not your—"

Ares closed the distance between them, lurching forward into an inelegant kiss. Leo's mouth was already open, and he gasped in surprise, taking the breath from Ares' lungs. Ares tugged him close, leaning into the softness of Leo's mouth, as Leo kissed him back, threading his arms around Ares' waist as he held them upright.

"I thought you'd be furious," Leo said, eyes wide in shock even as he leaned in and kissed Ares again. When Leo drew back, Ares tried to steady himself.

"I am furious," he said, though he didn't sound it. All the muscles that had been tensed for grief relaxed all at once. Ares was woozy on his feet still, and Leo nudged him toward the table.

"If this is how furious looks on you, I'm not sure what I was worried about."

"You can't make grilled cheese on an ironing board," Ares said, as Leo backed him into a chair. He sat heavily, and Leo smirked down at him, an impossibly handsome quirk to the corner of his mouth.

"Tell that to me at nineteen."

Ares reached up and caught Leo's wrist, pulling him forward. He just wasn't ready to let go of him yet. Stupid. Insane. Leo let himself be tugged astride Ares' right knee.

"Again, if this is you angry, I really think I've been given the wrong impression about—" Ares leaned forward, sliding his hands over Leo's hips and Leo's expression softened, his tongue darting over his lips before he wrapped his arms around Ares' neck and kissed him again.

Ares' arm throbbed when he moved it to wrap snuggly around Leo's waist, but he could barely feel the pain through the haze of bliss and exhaustion. Leo slid his fingers over the nape of Ares' neck, drawing back slowly, his thumb grazing the soft curve of Ares' jaw.

"A spoiled rich boy being led around by his cock?" he asked, eyebrow arched. Ares flushed.

"I'm sorry."

"An apology? Jesus. Now I'm really worried about you."

"You started it," Ares grumbled. "I don't have a death wish."

"That remains to be seen," Leo said, climbing off Ares' lap and turning back toward the stove. "And I might let you lead me around by the cock. But only if you ask very nicely."

Ares didn't allow himself to think too hard about that. He was already in dangerous territory where Leo and attraction intersected.

"You should have left."

"Oh, let's not start that again."

"Why didn't you?" Ares asked. Leo went over to the ice box, shuffling around inside, and for a moment, Ares thought Leo was pretending not to hear him. After a moment, Leo straightened up, knocking the door closed with his hip.

"I didn't want to," he said simply. "I want to see if I can get you out of your contract. And I like it here." The sentence hung, and Ares' chest tightened, something hard pressing against his shoulders, reminding him how bad of an idea all of this was. Dangerous. Not sustainable. Self-indulgent. Everything he'd been avoiding for the last ten years, all rolled up into one beautiful, impossible man. Who wanted to stay with him. Ares swallowed, watching as Leo began to scan the shelves above the counter, running his hand through his curls like he didn't know where to begin.

"Frying pan is above the stove," Ares said, closing his eyes.

"Shut up," Leo said, his voice accompanied by the abrupt clanking of cookware. "I know what I'm doing." And Ares did shut up, even if he knew what Leo said couldn't have been further from the truth.

GRILLED cheese sandwiches (with chicken and mushrooms) were easier to make on a stove than an ironing board. Ares ate two sandwiches and could barely hold himself up by the end of the meal. Before Leo even bothered to clear the table, he decided it was time to get Ares up to bed.

"Come on," Leo said, standing beside Ares and putting a hand on the back of his bicep. "Upstairs. Pajamas. Probably more blue stuff."

"No, I'm alright," Ares mumbled, bracing himself against the table and getting to his feet. "I'll sleep in the living room. You can have the bed."

"The living room?" Leo asked, as Ares slid past him, his gait slow and shuffling toward the fireplace. "You're going to sleep on the couch?"

"The floor," Ares said, grabbing a throw blanket off the back of the armchair.

"Ares, you need a good night's sleep—"

"I'll have nightmares in bed," he said, then yawned, sitting on the hearth. "Too squashy. Can you toss me a pillow from the couch?"

"I... can," Leo said, trailing behind Ares into the living room, where the fire still roared and the snow was tapping against the glass of the patio doors. "I can bring down your pillows and blankets from the bed too, but I really think—"

"The mattress is like..." he trailed off, making a squeezing motion with his hands. "Soil. Too soft. Roots can press through it. The ground—floor I mean. Foundation's stone," he stamped his foot lightly on the wood floor. Leo frowned.

"This is an orchard thing, then? Is that what happened to your arm? Roots? Like, tree roots?"

"Sort of," Ares yawned again and seemed to give up on the idea of a pillow, getting to his knees in front of the hearth.

"Wait," Leo sighed, holding up his hands. "Give me two minutes," he said, before he jogged up the stairs and stripped the bed of its blankets and pillows. It took less than two minutes, but Ares was already mostly reclined on the floor, nudging the coffee table out of the way with his foot. Leo tossed the pillows down and dragged the coffee table to the side, as Ares grabbed for the blankets, spreading them out over his legs. "You're really serious?"

"I'll be fine," Ares said, placing the leather pouch of medicines up on the hearth.

"Take more of the blue one," Leo said, unsure of what else he should be doing. A bad day at the boxing club usually meant painkillers and an extra inch of whiskey in his glass before passing out. But he would have gone an extra round in the ring with anyone before agreeing to sleep on the floor.

Ares grumbled, but he did what Leo said, draining the blue vial before laying down with his back against the hearth. Leo hesitated and then went into the kitchen, tossing the plates into the sink where they could wait until morning. When he turned out the light, he could see Matilda's shadow slink over to the fireplace, and Leo knew he was fooling himself if he really thought he was going to end up anywhere in the house that Ares wasn't. Ares was why he'd stayed, after all.

Leo got ready for bed upstairs where he could turn on a light. He tugged on his pajama pants and shuffled through the stack of Ares' holey sweaters on the top of the dresser. Beneath the mending was a few small paperbacks, the pages yellowing slightly at the edges, the titles tawdry and clearly from Earth. Leo smirked, tugged on one of Ares' sweaters and grabbed a book, padding back downstairs to the small nest of blankets where Ares was already softly snoring.

Leo crawled in beside him, laying on his stomach, shoving his pillow under his chest so he could read by firelight. He'd barely gotten the book open before Ares dropped an arm over his back and snuggled close, his head tucked against the side of Leo's arm. Leo leaned over and kissed him lightly on the temple.

"You don't have to sleep down here," Ares mumbled.

"It's fine."

"Might have nightmares anyway."

"No, you won't," Leo said, threading his fingers through Ares' hair. Ares hummed, his body warm and close. Leo exhaled, willing them both to relax, and Ares' hand found the small of Leo's back, sliding under the hem of the sweater, resting there as his breathing slowed again. Leo closed the book, and curled into Ares' arms, confident that he'd made the right decision, as he drifted off to sleep.

33

Ares was so warm when he woke up, he barely noticed how stiff and achy he was. Leo was curled at his side, snoring lightly, his whole body tucked beneath Ares' arm. Light poured in from the outside, a brighter day than the one before, despite the two inches of snow that covered the ground. Ares leaned his head back, squinting out into the garden, where Fen was walking toward the chicken coop.

Ares closed his eyes, trying to decide why that might be happening and if he really wanted to deal with it right now, even though he knew logically it was because he'd done nothing yesterday but work in the orchard, and today he'd slept in. Ares got slowly to his knees, bracing himself against the hearth, watching as Matilda stood up from in front of the still-glowing embers of the fireplace, and walked to the patio door. Ares looked down at Leo, who was curled on the edge of the rug, one hand tucked beneath his cheek, his chest rising and falling under the blanket of Ares' sweater.

Fen could get the eggs on her own. She didn't need his supervision. He could lay back down, thread his aching arms around Leo and fall back to sleep, responsibilities be damned.

Inconveniencing the others who worked at the big house made him feel guilty enough that he wouldn't actually lay back down. And the thought of what Morrow would do when he got wind of Ares shirking his duties... well, there'd be hell to pay. One more reason Leo should have gone, he was a distraction. The promise of comfort and a warm bed and gentle hands was too much, in the cold light of day. The need for human comfort should have been wrung out of him a long time ago.

He staggered to his feet and went to the front door as quietly as he could, stepping into gardening boots and tugging on his coat. Matilda followed, her nails clacking against the red tile floor and then the front stoop, as they headed around the side of the house, taking the long way, since opening the patio door seemed like an unnecessarily chilly and rude awakening for Leo.

The sun was out; the breeze was steady and cold. Ares hunched into his shoulders a bit, turning his head this way and that, just to stretch the muscles in his neck. He was stiff, but not as stiff as he'd been the month before. To be fair, he hadn't polished off a bottle of the blue stuff a month before either. Or eaten supper. Back then, he'd just collapsed in a bloody heap on the floor and slept until the nightmares came.

Ares almost tripped himself, skipping a step as he realized that he hadn't had any nightmares. He'd slept soundly the entire night, warm and relatively comfortable, and Leo's assurance from the night before, that he wouldn't have any nightmares, echoed suddenly in Ares' mind. Did Leo have some sort of ability that would have prevented them? Magic like that existed, mind readers and the like. And Leo did have a strange sort of way of knowing what Ares needed before Ares did.

But no. Ares wasn't sure Leo could keep any kind of secret, let alone something so easy to brag about as telepathy. Still, the idea of Leo having an ability would have been comforting because it would mean that Leo knew what Ares wanted because Ares wanted it, instead of the unsettling but more likely truth that Leo knew what Ares wanted because he was starting to know Ares.

Luckily, Ares didn't have any more time to think about that, because Fen was letting the chickens out of the coop, and Ares was at the gate to the pen. He swallowed, trying to shake the thoughts of Leo from his mind. He put his hand on the snow-covered fence to steady himself.

"Morning," Ares said. Fen jumped and twisted around, chickens clucking around her feet, waiting for feed.

"Oh my god!" Fen huffed, clutching a hand to her chest. "Saints, Ares! Don't do that."

"I would have thought you'd heard me," Ares said, coming into the pen, as Fen dug a fist into her pocket and threw feed down in the other direction, scattering chickens away from the gate.

"Sorry, no," she frowned. "Sorry to come down. No one's up at the house yet. But I know with the harvest coming—"

"No, I'm sorry," Ares said, taking the basket from her hand and ducking into the coop. "I'm late on your delivery."

"I know where the chickens live. And honestly, we're fine on supplies up at the house. I mean, you keep us well-stocked," her voice wavered, and Ares frowned down at the nests as he scooped up eggs.

"What's the matter?" he asked. He thought he heard her sigh, but the wind kicked up, gusting snow off the roof of the coop, muffling her reply. He turned as the wood planks that led into the enclosure creaked, and Fen ducked her head in, talking as though he'd heard the beginning of what she'd said.

"...so, he went on a rampage and dismissed two of the footmen and his valet."

"What?" Ares said, twisting back at an uncomfortable angle so that he could look at her face.

"I know! And Warren said it's all because Morrow was supposed to come last night but didn't and Warren's worried because well, Kephisto is in too deep with Morrow. That's what the rumors are anyway—"

"Wait, slow down," Ares held up a hand. "Kephisto dismissed three of the staff last night?"

"Two footmen and his personal valet. Had them escorted from the premises. And Warren's worried because one of them was supposed to go up to Warnock today, because Kephisto's on the warpath about any little thing and apparently all his good winter clothes are at Warnock. And Warren's basically the only footman available who's not terrified of Kephisto, so he's having to valet, but without the—"

"And no one can go up to Warnock?" Ares frowned. Fen shook her head.

"There's no one left. And it's a two-man job anyway, so unless you and Julian can do it—"

"Me and—me and Julian go?"

"Well, no one should go by themselves. It's a five-hour ride in good weather, which this isn't. It'll be a night there and then maybe a night on the road. And," Fen shook her head, worrying her bottom lip as she bent down to scoop up a couple of eggs. "I don't know. It'll be fine, I suppose. It'll have to be."

"I can't leave the gardens," Ares said. Though that wasn't precisely true. Now that the first snow had come, there wasn't so much he had to do that wasn't maintenance around the grounds. And of course, the cows and the chickens. The goats. Ares frowned, and Fen sniffed, her woolen mitten coming up to her cheek to swipe away a tear. Ares winced. "Fen..."

"No, it's alright. Sorry. Everyone's just tense, that's all. You know how Kephisto gets. And Warren's..." she trailed off, sniffing again as she shook her head. Ares pursed his lips, not quite sure why she was so worried about Warren in all this but appreciating it all the same. Fen was always overly compassionate. Ares ran his tongue along the back of his teeth and bit back a sigh.

"We can go. Julian and I can go today, if you don't mind checking on the chickens and the cows tomorrow morning. I'll do the milking before we go and—"

"Are you serious?" she asked, her eyes wide. Ares nodded, and Fen's expression softened, her jaw hanging open slightly, tears trembling at the corners of her eyes. "Oh, Ares! Thank you so much!" He held the basket of eggs out to her, primarily so she wouldn't try to hug him, and she looped the bag over her elbow and stepped toward him in the narrow aisle, pressing him into a hug anyway. "Thank you! Ares. That's a huge relief. I didn't know how Warren was going to manage being in two places at once. I think he was considering making a demon deal for it!"

"Well, there's no need for that," Ares said, patting her awkwardly on the shoulder.

"I'll stop by the stables on the way back up and tell the boys to get you a carriage ready. Just something small, but you'll need the room for all Kephisto's things." Ares grimaced at the thought, but nodded, as Fen stood on her tiptoes to press a kiss to his cheek, before practically skipping her way out of the coop.

34

"So, explain this to me again?" Leo said, receiving a mug of coffee from Ares as he sat next to Leo on the hearth. Ares' hair was wet from his shower, and it was becoming increasingly difficult for Leo not to try and close the distance between them just to feel the thick curls on his fingertips.

"Apparently Kephisto went on a tirade last night and fired three of the staff," Ares said, leaning against the pile of blankets Leo had folded. "He has his tantrums pretty regularly and levies threats all the time, but something set him off."

"Did Fen have any idea what it was?" Leo asked, taking a sip from his cup. Ares sighed.

"Rumor has it that Morrow was supposed to come to the house last night and then didn't."

"And why does Kephisto care so much about tha—oh." Leo paused as Ares raised his eyebrows in a significant way. "They're... oh." Ares shrugged. "What's the... I mean, how—?"

"I've done my absolute best not to think about it at all," Ares said, with a thin smile. Leo snorted.

"Fair enough."

"So, now, Warren has to take care of Kephisto and manage to go to the house at Warnock and get all the winter things that Kephisto doesn't need but has decided he wants."

"Right," Leo nodded. "And Fen is worried about Warren because," he paused and made the same significant eyebrow raise back at Ares. Ares cocked his head to the side.

"What?"

"Fen. And Warren."

"No," Ares shook his head. "Really?"

"Ares," Leo scolded, not bothering to suppress a smile. "Come on now. They're always together."

"They work together!"

"Two things can be true at the same time," Leo laughed. "They like each other! Why else is she crying about him to you? Why is he always in the kitchen, and she's sleeping over at his Nan's house?" Ares blinked and Leo shook his head, laughing again. "It doesn't matter. I'm happy to go. But should you be travelling? How far is Warnock?"

"It's about five hours northeast of here. By the time we're ready to set off, Fen will probably have a shopping list for us from everyone at the big house. It's fairly metropolitan."

"And should you be traveling?" Leo pressed. Ares scoffed and rolled his eyes.

"I'll be perfectly fine, thank you." Leo snorted but didn't argue. Ares did seem to be okay, for the most part. And even if he hadn't, it wasn't likely that he would stay put when Fen and Warren needed his help. Which was insufferable and charming both.

"Do they have a library in Warnock?" Leo asked, realizing suddenly that in a larger town he might be able to access law books for researching Ares' deal with Morrow.

"There's certainly a library at Warnock House," Ares said. Leo frowned. "Why?"

"I can't sustain myself on your smut novels," Leo teased, nodding to the one he'd left on the floor by the pillows. Ares looked down at it, his cheeks pinking slightly.

"Where'd you find that?"

"On your dresser."

"I think I remember telling you not to go through my things."

"That was a very long time ago," Leo said. Ares huffed and got to his feet.

"Shower and pack a bag. We'll leave after I've seen to the cows."

It was easy enough for Leo to throw his few items into a bag. He packed a lunch for them as well, and was showered and ready well before Ares was back.

While he packed, Leo considered what sort of law he'd need to know more about to help untwist Ares from whatever was binding him to that orchard. On a scrap of Ares' sketchbook paper, he jotted down 'contract inheritance,' 'indenture contract,' and 'duress and undue influence,' topics that had come to him as he showered. Last night Ares hadn't seemed uninterested, necessarily, though he sounded certain that anything Leo was able to find wouldn't be enough to help.

Leo thought again about Sidney, who seemed mired in this world, and in dealings with Morrow. Ares might know of a way Leo could get in touch with him. As little as Leo didn't want to involve Sidney in anything to do with Morrow, Leo couldn't help but want this solved. The state Ares had been in yesterday, while obviously not permanent, thank God, had been terrifying.

"Coat," Ares prompted, as he arrived in the foyer, where Leo had a borrowed rucksack over his shoulder and a small wicker hamper of food in one hand. "Even if you're in the carriage it'll take a while for the heater to warm up."

"Where will you be?" Leo asked, setting his bags down and grabbing his coat off the hook.

"Someone has to drive," Ares said, pulling a broad brimmed felt hat onto his head. "And of the two of us, I'm the only one who knows where we're going."

"Yes, alright," Leo rolled his eyes as he shrugged into the canvas coat. Ares frowned at him, then tugged a dark green scarf down off the hook, looping it around Leo's neck. Before Leo could say anything, Ares leaned down and grabbed the hamper, cheeks pinking.

"Come on. The boys will be waiting for us."

And he was right, of course. The stable boys had a small, covered carriage hitched to two black horses, waiting in the open bay of the stable. Ares took one large, graceful step up into the driver's seat, as Leo tried not to be mesmerized by the sight of him, flat-brimmed hat and broad shouldered, cutting an intimidating figure as he wrapped the leather reins around his hands.

"Get inside," Ares said, glancing down at Leo, who was standing beside the carriage staring up and trying not to drool. One of the stable boys was just behind his hip, valiantly attempting to take the bag off his shoulder and stow it.

"Can I sit up there with you?" Leo asked. Ares shrugged.

"If you like."

"It'll be far colder up front, sir," said the boy at his side, who'd finally managed to unthread the straps of Leo's bag from his arm.

"That's alright," said Leo, stupidly.

"A moment, then, sir," the boy said and then scurried into the carriage house before Leo could ask not to be called 'sir' again. In the meantime, he hoisted himself up, holding tight to the metal frame of the carriage, and then the boy was back, holding out to him a brown felt hat with a short, slightly curved brim. Leo thanked him and tipped the hat onto his head.

"How do I look?" Leo asked, tapping the brim toward Ares. Ares snorted.

"Like a character in a wild west sideshow," Ares said.

"Like a cowboy?" Leo smirked. Ares shook his head, and snapped the reins, starting the horses out of the stable and down the road.

"Like a rodeo clown."

While there was still snow on the ground, stretching out in a blanket of white as far as Leo could see, it was already melting on the roads. The sun was high in the sky, and it *was* chilly, but never worse than that. The road wended north, finally coming alongside the coast, dipping out and back from the cliffs, around the occasional building. Ares seemed to know the inhabitants of every house between the hall and the outskirts of the next town, and he passed the time telling Leo stories about all of them.

Outposts popped up occasionally too, and Ares would ask if Leo wanted to stop and stretch his legs, or if he wanted to go inside the carriage. By all accounts, Leo should have. He had planned on scouring his brain for every inch of contract law he remembered, but Ares was practically glowing in the warm winter light. His cheeks looked flush and healthy, and the further they drove from Leyland Hall, the happier he seemed, like the weight of the place had stifled him in a way Leo hadn't realized until he'd seen Ares properly away from it. It wasn't so bizarre to think of him as a demigod when he looked the way he did now.

As they passed near the edge of the forest, Ares tipped his head back, exposing the line of his thick throat, chest bulging out as he inhaled the scent of pine and sap, birdsong bright on the breeze, and Leo couldn't help but stare; he was barely able to catch his breath for how gorgeous Ares looked. Ares caught him at it, his eyebrow quirking up as he glanced at Leo. Leo quickly turned his attention back toward the road, ignoring the sudden hardness in his trousers as admiration and desire threaded tightly together beneath Leo's skin.

Leo missed several interesting birds that Ares tried to point out to him, his attention tripping instead on the way Ares threaded the reins over and under his fingers. Leo wanted Ares to slide the leather straps around Leo's wrists and tie his hands behind his back. Leo wanted to straddle Ares' lap and let the rhythmic bouncing of the carriage take care of the rest. He wanted Ares' bright smile to turn toward him. To turn into a kiss. He wanted the heat of Ares' body, and to feel the comfort of his heartbeat.

"Did you see that hawk? Look, up in the branch—"

"I must've missed him," Leo shrugged, attempting to feign interest by performing a studious backward glance, cracking his back in the process.

"Alright," Ares said, rolling his shoulders. "We've a river crossing up here, we'll stop for a bit. I shouldn't be able to hear your bones cracking over the rattling of the carriage."

"I was looking for the hawk."

"He was in front of us. There's another in the trees right there," Ares pointed again, and Leo only managed to see it because the bird chose that exact moment to take off into the bright blue sky visible between the naked branches of the trees.

The river crossing was a stone bridge that was wide enough for two carriages to pass each other, though, judging by the leaves that littered the path, it wasn't frequently traveled. Ares pulled them off the road and into a small copse before he hopped down off the bench.

"We'll eat here and stretch our legs. If we don't stay more than half an hour, we should make it to Warnock just after dusk." Before Leo could respond, Ares was already at work unhitching the horses and leading them a little closer to the river where they could eat shrubs and have their fill of water. Leo watched Ares move with an ease that only came from self-assurance and skill and tried to ignore the heat that crawled up the back of his neck and tinged his cheeks. As Leo climbed down off the bench, he tried to think of a time he had wanted someone so fiercely, and was a little bothered by the fact that he couldn't remember one.

Leo took a short stroll up the road and onto the bridge, where the river cut a path through the trees. He could see the winding water moving north to southwest, sliding back toward the ocean and the way they had come. He squinted toward the horizon, wondering how far they were from the coast, and took a deep breath, listening to the wind in the branches and the cawing of crows in the distance. Away from the world, away from everyone except the one person he wanted to be closer to, these woods had a freedom to them that was altogether different than being at Leyland Hall. It felt a little like heaven.

When Leo got back, Ares had taken his hat off and was sitting in the carriage with the door open, his legs stretched out under the opposite bench in the small space. He watched the horses grazing by the river, and Leo stood beside the doorway, one knee up on the step, and accepted a hunk of bread that Ares held out to him.

"It's nice out here," Leo said before taking a bite. Ares nodded, his chest rising and falling in a contented sigh. "Do you ever think about building a home in a place like this? When your contract is up, I mean." Leo had guessed that it wasn't exactly the kind of contract that had an end date, but Ares seemed to consider the question as though it was.

"Maybe. It is nice. Quiet. The soil here's likely not exactly what you want for a garden. And I imagine the nearest town is a little far away to suit you." Leo chewed his bread, trying not to read anything into the suggestion that Ares was considering what Leo might want when planning a future homestead. It was the politest way to keep the conversation moving, not a marriage proposal, for God's sake.

"Two hours, you said?" Leo asked, impassively. Ares nodded. "It's a little far. But, if I had a library of my own, and an office—"

"This is a funny place to practice law, I imagine."

"Andurnei, you mean?" Leo asked. Ares nodded. "You said the contracts here are unfairly weighted?"

"Well, you know the stories. Fairy tales, I mean. First born children and giving full names and all sorts of strange things. Magic hinges on interaction, though, so it's not like it's all lethal, or no one would bother. But it does tend to favor the fae, or whomever has more magic, in the long run." Leo had about a dozen questions on the subject, but he didn't want to press them toward anything that would change Ares' mood for the worse. There would be plenty of time for that later. That and Ares reached for a jug of cider, holding it up to his mouth with the crook of his arm, tilting his head back, Adam's apple bobbing as he swallowed, and it took all of Leo's questions and tore them completely out of his head. He wasn't going to be able to take two more hours of this.

Leo pulled himself up through the carriage door, stepping over Ares' legs and sitting on the bench opposite him. Leo took off his hat and ruffled his hair with his fingers, trying to decide how to start things, a little annoyed that he was nervous, because God, he'd done this sort of thing before. Ares wasn't even looking at him, his gaze still out the door, and Leo slid his tongue over his lips and told himself just to get on with it.

He ducked his head as he stood, and the motion of standing was all it took to close the distance between them. Leo put his knees on either side of Ares' hips and sat astride him, turning Ares' chin gently with his palm. Ares chuckled, as he slid his dark eyes over Leo's face, one eyebrow arched.

"Really?"

"Oh, shut up," Leo said, and kissed him.

Ares' kisses always had Leo craving more. The softness of his lips, paired with the desperate way Ares' hands clung to Leo's hips, then slid beneath his sweater made Leo's skin tingle. Ares pulled Leo in tighter, closer, as though there was any space between them to begin with. Leo turned his head, deepening the kiss, and Ares' fingers dug into the thin fabric of Leo's undershirt.

Leo ground down against him, desperate and losing himself in the way his body lit up as they touched, catching Ares' mouth mid groan. The sound of Ares wanting him was enough to destroy the last shreds of Leo's decorum. Leo shucked his coat and scarf, tossing both behind him. He wanted more of Ares arching his back in pleasure, stretching his throat long, moaning for Leo. And Leo knew how to get it.

He slid to his knees between Ares' thighs, and tugged at the belt that looped around Ares' hips. Ares stared down at him, eyes wide, mouth open, breathing ragged.

"What are you doing?"

"Think about it," Leo huffed, the belt finally giving way. "I bet it'll come to you."

"Leo—"

"Ares."

"You don't have to—" Ares stopped mid-sentence, as Leo slid his fingers up into the soft, dark hair that covered the bottom of Ares' belly, rucking his shirt up, before unbuttoning his trousers and tugging them down.

"I don't think you understand how much I want to," Leo murmured, nuzzling his nose against Ares' hip, relishing in the heat of him, his scent making Leo's mouth water in anticipation. Leo kissed Ares' belly, the curve of it, and then lower, against his hip and thigh. Ares' breathing was going ragged, his hand hovering over Leo's shoulder as though he was afraid to touch him. Leo looked up at him, leaning his jaw against Ares' fingers. "Is this okay?"

"Yes." Ares slid his hand to cup Leo's jaw, and Leo kissed his palm, the urge for tenderness warring with baser counterparts. As he usually did, Leo chose the satisfaction that was mere inches and moments away.

Leo slid his hands beneath Ares' hips, tugging his trousers down just enough to free Ares' cock. There were likely more seductive ways to give head, but Leo wanted Ares so badly, he didn't have the patience for any of them. He took Ares into his mouth, letting his tongue slide along the underside of Ares' cock, lips tight around Ares' girth. Ares groaned, his head hitting the back wall of the carriage as he leaned back, hands fisting on his thighs. Leo took him deeper, moaning his pleasure at Ares' reaction.

He eased off slightly, gripping Ares' shaft firmly at the base, sliding his hand up to follow his mouth, and Ares' eyes opened, lips parted, panting, as he stared down his body at Leo. Leo hummed around his cockhead, and Ares dug the heel of his boot into the floor of the carriage.

"Leo." Ares grunted, a command that sent a shiver down Leo's spine. Leo pulled off just long enough to make eye contact while he licked his lips.

"I'm busy at the moment."

"Can I— Fuck!" Leo interrupted by taking Ares as deep as he could, bobbing up and down sweetly on Ares' cock, letting his eyes close as he focused on the heat pooling low in his own spine. Leo pushed himself forward almost deep enough to gag, swallowing around the tip of Ares' cock. Ares moaned, his hand leaping to the back of Leo's head. Now they were getting somewhere.

Ares' fingers tangled in Leo's curls, and Leo could feel him hesitating to tighten his grip. Such a gentleman. Leo slid off Ares' cock again, stroking him with his hand in the same rhythm as he braced forearms against Ares' knees.

"Sorry," Ares said, and then bit his lip as Leo ran his fist over Ares' cockhead.

"I like it," Leo said. "You can tug on it if you want." Ares whimpered, his eyes closing, hips jumping, as Leo slowed his strokes. "I want you to feel good."

"It feels amazing."

"I've wanted to suck your cock all day," Leo purred. Ares' smile was crooked, teeth digging into his bottom lip as he whined at Leo's touch. Leo wanted more. He took Ares' cock deep, and Ares thrust, nearly gagging him.

"Leo! Fuck—Leo—" Leo stiffened, and Ares slid back, sensing something was wrong. Leo ignored the way his eyes were watering, slowing as he pulled off, swallowing the sensation of choking. Ares' fingers slid along the back of his neck, and Leo could feel more than see that Ares was about to ask if he was alright. Was about to stop them.

Leo hummed, bracing himself against the bench with one hand and took Ares' deeper, breathing through his nose, tightening the press of his tongue. It was enough that Ares grunted, fingernails scraping gently against Leo's skin. Leo moved forward, setting the pace again. He worked fast, tightening his lips around Ares' cockhead, making Ares moan and rock his hips forward. Good. Better. Ares' palm cupped Leo's jaw, and he tilted Leo's head up just enough that Leo could look into his eyes.

"Leo. You're so good. Please. I want you."

That was.

That was something.

Leo whimpered, his eyes fluttering closed as his cock throbbed, and something inside him ached too, for Ares to want him like this now and all the time. Leo moaned and Ares lost the rhythm of his movement, barely managing to gasp out, "Leo!" as a warning before he came. Leo swallowed around him, still wanting more. More of Ares' pleasure. And his praise.

35

res wanted to sit up but his legs had turned to jelly. He had to settle for grabbing Leo's arms and hauling Leo into his lap. Leo kissed him, deep and frantic, and the heat of Leo's mouth, the taste of himself on Leo's tongue, was doing strange things to Ares that were only made worse by the fact that there were no thoughts in his head anymore. He wanted nothing except Leo.

He half-pushed, half-placed Leo onto the bench seat beside him, taking advantage of Leo's splayed legs. Leo tried to balance himself, bracing one boot against the opposite bench of the carriage, as Ares nearly tore open Leo's trousers. Ares' skin felt hot all over, his mouth watering at the sight of Leo's cock straining and slick with precum. Practically on his hands and knees, bent over Leo on the bench, Ares took Leo into his mouth.

"Oh fuck," Leo moaned, his back arching, fingers gripping tight against the wall of the carriage. Ares relished the strain in his shoulders as he worked Leo's cock with his hand and mouth. He wanted Leo's sounds forever in his ears. The way Leo was whimpering, begging, thrusting. It was enough to make his own cock twitch again. And then, the long twisting vines etched into his forearms, trailing down over his wrist bones, began to glow.

"Ares! Please—" Leo's fingers dug into Ares' hair, and Ares hollowed out his cheeks, taking Leo to his base. He wanted. His magic wanted, and for the first time in a long time, Ares was happy to comply. "Ares!" His name turned into a desperate groan as Leo's hips lifted off the bench and he came, Ares swallowing as much of him as he could.

Ares straightened up, wiping his mouth on his sleeve. Leo was partially collapsed, braced awkwardly against the bench and the side wall of the carriage, his legs still splayed, and slightly shaking. He ran one hand through his hair, his head falling back against the far wall of the carriage. Ares could see the flush on his neck, and it made everything in Ares feel bright and alive.

"God," Leo said, looking up slowly, his eyes meeting Ares'. "I mean..." Ares laughed, shaking his head.

"You started it," Ares said, offering him a hand, and, when he took it, tugging him upright. Leo stretched his back as he tucked himself away, and Ares did the same, unsure of what to say now, and wondering what it meant that all he wanted to do was have Leo again. And again. And again.

But no. That was insane. And there were things to do. Ares glanced out the still open door to see that one of the horses had begun to wander back toward the carriage. The sun was still in the sky, but the light between trees was turning a soft shade of gold. They hadn't even eaten yet.

Ares felt Leo shift, and before he could turn, the man had collapsed against Ares' side. Ares wrapped an arm around him, and Leo leaned up and kissed the corner of Ares' mouth.

"Thank you."

"Shut up," Ares huffed. "If anyone should be giving thanks—"

"I'd been thinking about it for a long time," Leo murmured, resting his head on Ares' shoulder.

"How long?"

"How many days ago did we meet?"

"You're obnoxious." Ares smiled, nuzzling his nose in amongst Leo's curls, inhaling the smell of him, and feeling the way the scent made all his limbs go limp and relaxed, and trying not to think about how incredibly nice that was. "You know, if you were really worried about getting me to like you..."

"It's not exactly a guarantee of lasting goodwill," Leo snorted.

"It is the way you do it." Leo laughed then.

"Well, I don't go through all that for just anyone," Leo said. Ares arched an eyebrow, doubtful, but the way Leo blushed took Ares aback slightly. The warmth beneath his sleeves grew as something possessive and pleased twisted together in his chest. "Don't get a big head about it," Leo said, reaching across the carriage for the jug of cider, raising it to his mouth. Obviously, Leo was more experienced than Ares. And obviously, he'd pleasured other men in the course of whatever that experience looked like. But Ares had never been given a blow job like the one he'd just received. And the idea that Leo had never given a blow job like that either certainly occupied Ares' mind as he re-hitched the horses to the carriage and got them back on the road.

Leo brought the basket of food into the front of the carriage, and they spent the next half hour in comfortable silence, as the sunlight turned orange and began to sink toward the horizon. They ate cheese and apples and bread and when Leo slid closer on the bench seat, Ares draped his free hand around Leo's hip, his mind strangely at ease, his body sated in every imaginable way.

When they came into Warnock, the glow of the streetlamps reflected off the glistening pools of melted snow between the cobbles, and Ares couldn't help but remain unbothered. The task itself was stupid, but the journey had been an altogether pleasant one, if he ignored the fact that they were doing it so that Kephisto wouldn't fire anyone else. It was so good to be away from Leyland Hall, out from beneath the ever-growing shadow of Morrow's influence.

He'd known, in a sort of objective way, that Morrow was probably sleeping with Kephisto. It was interesting (horrible) that Kephisto's feelings had been so hurt by a snub from Morrow that he'd lost his mind. Ares wasn't sure if the idea of their connection being deeper than physical was more or less awful than the alternative, and as they entered the main square, where Warnock House sat opposite the Governor's Mansion, Ares resolved not to think about it.

The whole town had the aesthetic of an old-world Bavarian village. It reminded Ares of the old ceramic Christmas town his aunt would build on the mantle every year around the holidays. Little snowcapped houses, exposed dark wood against plaster and brick, triangle frames ornamented by carvings that looked like swirls of gingerbread icing.

Warnock House took up almost an entire side of the square, surrounded by tall iron fencing with gaps just wide enough that you could stick a hand or a nose through and admire the splendor of the thing without getting too close. Around the back of the house was an alley where deliveries could come through, and where there was a gate with a lock that Ares knew the combination to. He hopped down to open it and then back up, bringing the carriage even with the servants' entrance to the house. Because Kephisto wasn't in, there were no guards. Only a wide wooden door, firmly locked, and a bell pull.

Ares rang the bell and waited, bouncing on the balls of his feet as a cold wind raced down the narrow alley on the side of the house. Ares flipped his collar up against the gust and glanced at Leo just in time to see Leo tighten Ares' scarf around his neck. Leo was marked by him. His. Not that Ares deserved Leo, or that Leo was even aware of Ares' thinking, but it was there all the same. Ares forced himself to turn away, toward the door, just in time to see that it had been cracked and was now being pulled open with vigor.

Mrs. Goode was a short woman with close cropped white hair, and ruddy skin speckled with age and wrinkled with laugh lines. She was unreasonably strong for someone of her size and age, which Ares remembered as she grabbed him by the arm and yanked him to her chest in a tight hug.

"Ares Silva! Good Lord, it's been an age! What are you doing here?"

"Mrs. Goode," Ares returned her hug firmly, and then tried to step back. She only let him get about a half a foot away. "I honestly wasn't sure you'd still be here. I was hoping you'd retired."

"Oh, no! Retirement is for the birds, dear one. Absolutely not of any interest to me at all. His royal highness isn't in that carriage, is he? You know how he gets when he's been kept waiting."

"Thankfully no," Ares said.

"Ah, good! So, this really is a pleasant visit. Who's that handsome chap up there?"

"That is Julian Flint. He's my new assistant."

"Helpful, is he?" she asked, wiggling her eyebrows. Ares snorted, blushing.

"Mrs. Goode—"

"Get him down from there and bring him inside before anything important freezes off! Once we get in front of the fire you can tell me why you're here. You haven't eaten, have you?"

"Not for a few hours."

"Starving the poor thing!" she smacked Ares in the chest with the back of her hand. "Terribly rude. Your mother raised you better. I'll have Salz come up for the carriage and the horses. Just tie them there," she waved toward the hitching post, and Ares looked up to see Leo fumbling with the reins. He sighed and strode over to the front of the carriage.

"Give those here," he said, reaching his hand up. "Grab your things and go in with Mrs. Goode."

"Mrs. Goode?"

"She's the housekeeper here. She was a friend of my mother's. And she thinks you're handsome."

"Well, she's got good taste at least," Leo said, tipping his hat down and winking, as he tossed Ares the reins. Ares rolled his eyes, trying not to smile, as Leo hopped down, going around to the side of the carriage. Before Ares could ask, Leo grabbed Ares' bag as well as his own, and started toward the open door, where Mrs. Goode had lit the lamp above the stoop.

Ares led the horses forward, tying them to the hitching post and then locking the carriage doors. By the time he'd made it onto the steps, Leo and Mrs. Goode had gone inside, and Ares was left to navigate the narrow servants' halls on his own.

He hadn't been to Warnock House in about five years, which seemed absurd since it wasn't that far of a drive. The last time he'd come was when Salz had needed help re-shingling the carriage house, and Kephisto hadn't wanted the expense of hiring any additional day laborers. It had been an enjoyable week or so, mostly because he'd been away from Leyland Hall.

Orange sconces high on the walls lit his way to the kitchen, where Leo had already been bustled onto a stool, and Mrs.

Goode was gathering his outerwear in her arms as he shed it. A surly looking, speckle faced teenage boy was standing in an adjacent doorway, holding their bags.

"Ares, give your things to Graham. He'll take them up for you."

"Nonsense," Ares said, shaking his head, even as he pulled off his hat and tucked it under his arm. "We can do it. And, we can take rooms down here—"

"You could if we had any made up for you, which we don't, since we weren't expecting you. But we always have a room ready in the guest wing. And one of you can have the Lord's suite, since he's not in attendance."

"Mrs. Goode—" Graham protested before Ares could, his narrow face paling beneath his acne.

"Let's not risk his majesty's irritation," Leo said levelly. "If there's only one room ready in the guest suite, we can share it, and Graham, you can—"

"His job is to take things up, Mr. Flint," Mrs. Goode said, shoving Leo's outerwear into Graham's already full arms. "Go on, then," she said. "You can come back and finish supper when you're done." Graham left, stomping and audibly grumbling, and Leo looked at Ares with wide eyes and a slight shrug, indicating that he was currently helpless. Ares chuckled, shucking his coat, knowing neither of them would be able to make any headway on Graham's behalf, if Mrs. Goode had already decided not to let them.

36

Supper was some kind of delicious, gamey roast that Leo didn't think he'd ever had before, along with well-seasoned potatoes, carrots and zucchinis. Between the food, the red wine, and his back to the fire, any lingering chill that Leo'd felt from the end of their journey had vanished. Mrs. Goode was absolutely enthralled with Ares, cutting him an extra-large portion of meat, and hanging on his every word like a doting grandmother. She chided him for not visiting more regularly and then tried to get Leo to agree in loud whispers that Ares was overworked and didn't know the true value of rest, all of which Leo firmly nodded along with. Primarily because it was true. Ares only rolled his eyes, ignoring them both with a handsome smile on his face that Leo desperately wanted to kiss.

He was looking forward to the shared bedroom portion of the evening, as the final two hours of their trip had put him in a prime position to watch more of Ares' deftness with the horses and allowed him to identify that something Leo really wanted, both sexually and in more general terms, was for Ares to want *him*. Ares bent over him in the carriage, taking Leo like he was starving for him, made something flutter low in Leo's stomach even now. He hadn't parsed out the rest of it, yet, and he wasn't exactly sure he wanted to because he was beginning to feel like maybe the way he'd operated with past partners had been less about sex and more about overloading his senses until his brain whited out. The thought of doing that with Ares, of not really feeling Ares' hands on Leo's body, or the way their mouths fitted together, or the sounds Ares made when Leo swallowed around him, would be awful. And it was beginning to feel like that was the point of things. Which it never had been before.

The wine was strong enough that all these thoughts jumbled together, as Ares told Leo to go up and make himself comfortable, and he would be there just as soon as he'd finished helping Mrs. Goode with the dishes. Leo did as he was told, following surly Graham up into the main part of the house.

The foyer was large and beautiful, with a marble checkerboard floor and lush, carpeted steps that led up to the second, and then the third floor.

"Graham, is there a library at Warnock House?" Leo asked, remembering that Ares had said there was.

"On the second floor," Graham said with as little inflection as humanly possible. "East wing," he said, pointing in the opposite direction from the hall he'd just turned them down. "Your room's here," he said, pointing to a door about halfway down the hall.

"Thanks so much," Leo said, wishing he had a fiver for the boy, who had already turned on his heel, mumbling something that might have been 'no problem,' or 'fuck off.'

The bedroom was wide and brighter than Leo had expected given the darker tones of the rest of the house. The ceiling was a sculpted wood, planks wrapped into elongated ovals, receding into the arched ceiling. The walls were off white, painted with motifs of red and orange flowers with a shimmering coating that made them look almost metallic and reflected the light from the fireplace. The bed was massive, easily big enough for five people, and the headboard, footboard and the bedposts were made of the same dark wood as the ceiling, the bedposts carved into thick swirls that stretched as high as Leo was tall, at the foot, and nearly to the ceiling at the head. The effect was striking, intimidating, even, and Leo hesitated in the doorway for a minute, before stepping in and closing the door behind him.

Beside a wardrobe on the far wall was a door to a large bathroom where a white marble tub was lifted by thick, brown claw feet, the taps shining brass. Leo drew himself a bath because a bath sounded lovely, and he went briefly back into the bedroom to retrieve his bag of clothes, before stripping down and climbing into the tub.

He didn't soak for long. Ares was busy, and the water and a good scrub had cleared Leo's head enough that he knew now was as good a time as any to go to the library. He didn't have to read all the books tonight, he just had to find the ones that would be useful. If the library was big enough, he might even be able to take them without anyone noticing. Leo dunked himself under the water one more time, staring up at the ceiling above him through the ripples. He breathed out, sending up a stream of bubbles, thinking about Ares. About breaking this stupid contract. About what would happen if Ares could come home safely.

Home was a strange idea to Leo. When he was a kid, Sidney had been his home. And then, when their father began to run for office, Leo had had to put up walls between himself and his brother. It was that or watch Sidney flounder under their father's ridiculous, borderline cruel, demands. Sidney had always been the more bookish one, more intelligence than sense sometimes. When their father put Sidney to a task, it seemed like Sidney always chose to do it in the most challenging way imaginable, just to see if he could. As though everything was some wild endurance test. As though pleasing their father wasn't hard enough on its own.

All that to say, Leo'd done a lot to strip himself of any non-congressman approved attachments. Shaving off things that didn't suit the needs of the moment. The firm. His father. He missed Sidney. He'd been glad to see him, and then relieved that their bond from long ago had been enough to pull them through their encounter with Edmund Morrow, at least, for whatever part Leo had played in it. But he didn't know what really waited for him back home. And if Sidney would even be willing to be a part of it. And if he wasn't, would Leo just fall back into his old habits? Being whomever someone else needed him to be?

And Ares was in the same boat, in a lot of ways. Though Leo knew that Ares at least had a brother who was desperate to have him return. But maybe there would be space for Leo to build something there too. 'Together' seemed like too big a word to pin on it, but that's what it was. That's what it could be, if Leo would let himself think it.

Leo sat up, letting the water spill out of his hair, down his shoulders and chest, pulling out the drain plug with his toes before getting to his feet and grabbing a towel. He dried off and dressed, still thinking about the library. About Ares and Sidney, and what home might look like, if he could manage to get this right.

❧

"THANK you for helping with the washing." Mrs. Goode leaned her hip against the counter as Ares dried the platter the roast had sat on. He hadn't felt right leaving her to do the cleaning, even though she told him three times not to bother. Then she'd finally handed him a dishtowel. "Mr. Flint seems nice."

"He is nice," Ares agreed mildly. Mrs. Goode huffed.

"Come now, Ares! You aren't getting any younger, you know."

"I'm perfectly fine on my own, Mrs. Goode."

"Tsch," she shook her head. "Nonsense."

"He's not from here, anyway. He's got a job and a home to get back to." Ares balanced the platter on the drying rack and looked over at Mrs. Goode, expecting a response. Instead, she was frowning at him, her chin resting between her thumb and forefinger as she pursed her lips.

"Your mother wouldn't have wanted you to go through all of this alone," she said. It stung. He hadn't intended to talk about his mother, or what he was going through. Ares' stomach twisted, his chest tightened. He looked down into the sink, bubbles popping around the edge of the drain, and wished there was something else there for him to wash.

"I'd rather not get anyone else involved," he said slowly. Mrs. Goode scowled as though he'd gotten something wrong, but Ares pressed on. "Mom was by herself."

"She had me. She had you and Dominic."

"We weren't *with* her."

"You were always with her," Mrs. Goode insisted. "And she made friends. She didn't hide herself away. When I was at Leyland Hall, everyone knew your mother." It was true. He knew it, because of the way people had flocked to him when he took her place. Friends from Laurel Grove, others who worked at the big house. But Ares had grieved so intensely for so long that he'd pushed them all away. And he'd never bothered pretending that wasn't on purpose.

Alondra was the only exception. She'd sat through a number of his tirades, drunken, angry, tearful rants. She'd listened and not judged. Then she brought in Mae, somehow. He'd never thought to ask. And then Kephisto hired on Fen, but that was only a couple of years ago, and Warren was practically new. They didn't know about the orchard, though, even if they were his friends, as much as they could be when he'd kept them at arm's length.

"I can't feel her anymore," Ares confessed suddenly. "Mom, I mean." He didn't know why he'd said it, really, because his mother and the orchard were the topics of conversation he always did his best to avoid. But if anyone could understand, it would be Mrs. Goode. "In the orchard. The trees are dying. She was so much stronger than I was and she's... I think she's gone." Ares hesitated, sliding his tongue over his lips. "I think it might be killing me." Mrs. Goode stepped forward, taking his forearms in her hands and pressing her thumbs against the thin skin of his wrists.

"You can't pour water from an empty pitcher, Ares. Nurturing yourself is the first step. Otherwise, the spirit weakens, the magic fades. You have to let people in."

"So that they can get hurt? Get tangled up in the same mess I did, and end up... end up like me?" Trapped, miserable and alone, he didn't have to say. She knew how things were. How he'd made them.

"No, you stupid boy," she said with a soft smile, pressing her hands into his skin. "You have to let people in so that they can help you."

"They can't help me without getting hurt. He—" Ares gestured upstairs, to where Leo was waiting for him. Or was hopefully already in bed asleep. "He's already too— He should be back in his world. I'm sure he's—"

"When we care about someone, helping them is not a sacrifice. It is a joy. If he wants to help you, if he wants to stay with you, you'd be a fool not to let him."

"I don't think..." Ares swallowed, irritated that it was becoming hard to breathe. He shook his head. "Even if he does. I mean, I *can* let him in."

"Can you?"

"But even if I do, I'm not sure that there's a way out for me."

"Maybe," she said, her hands sliding down into his, "maybe not. But there's always the help he can give you right now. Good company is a better balm than you think. And if you give it space and time, you never know what might grow from it. Whether you intend it or not." She patted his cheek and gave him a small smile. "Believe me. I'm a very old woman, who's seen a lot of people come and go over the years."

"You're not that old," Ares protested. Her grin broadened, and she chuckled.

"Yes, I am. Which is why you should listen to me."

37

Ares went up to the bedroom, Mrs. Goode's words ringing in his ears. Letting Leo in seemed so reckless. So foolish. So what if it was the only thing he wanted to do? Ares could explain it all to Leo: Morrow, the orchard, his mother, his brother, the whole convoluted, ugly mess. It wouldn't change anything.

Unless Leo could fix it. Maybe the right angle of legal defense did exist that could unbind Ares from this stupid contract, one he'd spent years rehashing for loopholes and contradictions and found none. But what if Leo could?

Leo wasn't in the bedroom, which was probably good because Ares was so mired in anxiety about all the things Mrs. Goode had said, that if Leo had been there, Ares would have told him everything. Not because he wanted Leo to fix it, but mostly just to expunge it, get it out of him so that he could sleep well for one more night. Instead, he took a bath, sinking below the steaming water, holding his breath, pushing all his worries aside. There wasn't anything to be done. Letting Leo in would be dangerous, and he liked Leo too much to let him get tangled up in the mess that Ares' life had become.

Still, there was an idea that Mrs. Goode had put in Ares' head that Ares wasn't able to drown in the bathwater. The suggestion that he let Leo stay, if Leo wanted, had unlocked a strange sort of fantasy for Ares where Leo would be with him and be safe. It couldn't happen that way; it was technically impossible. But what if it wasn't? What if Leo was always there to help Ares with the chickens and the goats and patching holes in the fence? What if Leo was in Ares' bed every night, and woke with him every morning? Making coffee, sitting on the couch, pretending to read. What if Leo was his, even if it didn't change anything else?

Ares got out of the tub, his mind swimming with soft fantasies of a life that wouldn't be. It couldn't be. He would never let Leo stay because Ares had nothing to offer him aside from the promise of grief. Maybe not this month or this year. But soon. Soon enough that Ares couldn't make himself start something, because he already knew the end. But that didn't mean he couldn't think about it. That was nurturing in its own way, he supposed. It certainly made him feel warmer, as he walked into the bedroom with his towel knotted around his hips.

He pulled his bag up to the foot of the hideously ornate bedframe, balancing it on the thick footboard, a waste of good, furniture-quality wood, digging around for his clothes. He hadn't planned on having to share a bed with Leo, not that he was opposed to it either, but he was glad he'd packed the less-threadbare pair of pajamas that he owned.

As he tossed them on the bed and began fishing for his small kit bag, the bedroom door opened behind him. Leo was wearing a borrowed dressing gown, thick and burgundy, his thin white undershirt peeking out between the lapels. His hair was shining, curls still damp and drooping handsomely over his forehead, and he had two large books tucked under his arm.

"I found the library," Leo said, coming in and nudging the door shut behind him. His small, satisfied smile made him look irresistibly smug, and Ares almost laughed, shaking his head as he turned back toward his bag.

"That looks like light reading."

"I thought you might want a bedtime story."

"You spoil me," Ares deadpanned.

"I'd like to." Leo's response was so sincere that it made Ares stop and look over at him, while trying not to be obvious about how those three simple words had made his cock half hard. He arched an eyebrow, as Leo walked to a small desk on the side wall, smirking as he set the books down. "I don't think you'd let me though."

"I suppose that depends," Ares said slowly.

"On what?" Leo asked.

"Well, I won't call you 'daddy,'" Ares said. Leo laughed, his eyes crinkling at the corners as he shook his head and walked over to stand beside Ares at the foot of the bed.

"No one's ever called me that before," Leo chuckled again. "And frankly, I'm not sure I'm ready to start hearing it. Ask me in another fifteen or twenty years, and we'll see." Fifteen or twenty years. Ares smiled at the thought of them still knowing each other then. Still having whatever this was.

"I could spoil you," Ares said, his hand coming up to brush against the shining fabric of Leo's lapel. Leo licked his lips; gaze darting down to Ares' hand and then back up.

"My relationship with my father is too strange and strained to get off on calling anyone 'daddy' either," Leo said. Ares snorted.

"Not like that," he said, thinking instead of intimacy. Gentle caresses, slow, deep kisses. The way he'd want to take Leo to bed sometimes if they had all the time in the world. Months and years of being together, instead of hours and days.

Ares cupped Leo's jaw with his palm and tilted Leo's head up, bringing their mouths together in a soft, slow kiss. Leo let Ares lead, his mouth dropping open, making room for Ares' tongue. They melted into each other, breath catching in the small space between them, and Ares let himself loose in the heady fantasy that this thing with him and Leo was real. Could last.

Leo slid his palms down Ares' chest, dragging fingernails slowly against the sensitive skin of Ares' stomach, and then his ribs. Ares pulled back, straightening them both up, his hands dropping to the tie that held Leo's dressing gown closed. This was where he lost track of himself. Where things moved into hurried and frantic, or he would panic and falter and Leo would have to coach him through. But there was no rush now. Tonight, Leo was his. And Ares wanted it to feel infinite.

Leo bit his bottom lip, as Ares unthreaded the knot, letting the robe fall open. He was probably waiting for Ares to tear his clothes off, a blur of mouth and hands against skin. But the fantasy of languid, careful, lovemaking had overwhelmed Ares. Leo deserved to be worshipped, and Ares was determined to do exactly that.

Slowly, he pushed the robe off Leo's shoulders, reveling in the way Leo leaned up so that Ares' hands brushed his skin. Maybe because Leo was used to something faster, he seemed to be chasing Ares' touch, his body always pressing into Ares' palms as Ares held Leo's waist and kissed him again, long and slow, before tugging the shirt off over Leo's head.

"What are you doing?" Leo murmured, trailing fingers through Ares' still damp curls, as Ares knelt at Leo's feet, pressing kisses down Leo's chest, his abdomen. Leo's smooth, firm muscles twitched as Ares slid his mouth over them, kissing, nipping occasionally, once he'd discovered how that made Leo grunt, his hips canting up into Ares' chest.

"Ares," Leo moaned. Ares slid his tongue over Leo's hip bone and then bit the soft skin above it gently. Leo's fingers tightened in Ares' hair, and Ares smirked, thrilled to explore the expanse of Leo's skin. He wanted to be able to draw a map of Leo, mark all the places on it that made him whimper and moan. When Ares' towel slid from his hips, he barely noticed. He was too busy sliding Leo's trousers off, kissing the soft, pale skin of Leo's upper thigh.

"Ares," Leo said again, breathless, his fingers twitching against the shell of Ares' ear. Ares looked up at him then, pleased to find Leo's chest flushed, his cheeks rosy. "What are you doing?"

"Kissing you," Ares said with a small smile. "Is that okay?"

"Okay isn't—It's not—"

"You don't like it?" Leo rolled his eyes and gestured to his fully erect, and up to this point ignored, cock.

"I like it. I'm just not sure what I did to deserve it."

"Nothing," Ares shrugged, letting his fingers run light stripes over the outside of Leo's thighs before Ares reached up and grabbed the footboard, pulling himself to his feet, bracketing Leo's hips in with his arms. There was barely any space between them, and Ares felt as though he was balanced on a knife's edge in every conceivable way. "You're you. And I... I want you in ways I didn't know I could want someone."

"You can have me," Leo murmured. "I thought I'd made that very clear." Ares leaned closer, his lips brushing Leo's ear.

"Don't worry. I intend to."

38

Leo's thighs shook. His hands twisted in the soft, satiny fabric of the duvet, as Ares pressed his mouth against the back of Leo's knee. Ares had been methodical, focused on Leo's body, Leo's pleasure in a way no one ever had. There wasn't an inch of Leo's skin that had gone unkissed, except, torturously, his aching cock. Leo groaned at the prickling of Ares' stubble and the way he wanted to throw his leg over Ares' shoulder and thrust up into nothing. Leo reached for his cock, desperate for some kind of friction, knowing it would take almost nothing to push him over the edge. This was agony. It was also bliss. He'd never felt so much.

Ares lifted his head, chin briefly brushing Leo's inner thigh. He licked his lips as he looked at Leo's cock, and Leo moaned at the thought of Ares sucking him off, the carriage earlier, and how fucking good it would feel to have Ares' wicked, gorgeous mouth finally put to good use.

"Turn over," Ares said, nudging Leo's hip with his palm.

"Ares," Leo groaned. "I'm so fucking—" Ares got to his knees between Leo's legs, his thick cock ruddy and glorious, and fuck but Leo was going to turn over for him. Leo practically growled in frustration as he flipped over, Ares' hands immediately coming to his hips, lifting them up enough that Ares could shove a silk covered pillow beneath them. Leo whimpered, the sensation of the soft fabric against him making his back arch. Ares chuckled, leaning down over Leo, his cock resting in the cleft of Leo's ass. Leo ground back against him and Ares nipped at his neck in response.

"Tease."

"Oh, shut the fuck up." Leo rolled his hips again out of spite, and smirked as Ares grunted, his fist clenching beside Leo's elbow on the blankets.

"Do you want to stop?" Ares murmured. His hair brushed Leo's cheek, and Leo could feel Ares lifting himself off Leo's back, granting himself a bit of distance, something Leo had neither wanted nor asked for in the last half hour.

"No," Leo said. He didn't want to stop. He'd never been taken apart so slowly and thoroughly. Ares' calloused fingers had run delicately, reverently, across Leo's skin, setting him alight. Ares' mouth would follow, pressing kisses, murmuring praises after his hands. 'Fuck, Leo.' 'You're so gorgeous, Leo.' 'I want you.' Leo was more sensation than flesh now, bucking and moaning at things that were barely kisses, the lightest brush of fingers was enough to make his cock throb, and if Ares' plan was to continue in the same way down Leo's back, then Leo was going to orgasm whether Ares stroked him or not.

Ares kissed Leo's neck, Leo's shoulder blade, his lips parting in a huff of breath as Leo moaned.

"God," Ares murmured, his mouth inching down Leo's vertebrae, Leo arching up to meet him. "Look at you. So good for me."

"Ares," Leo begged, not for the first time, and he was rewarded with Ares' small smile against his skin.

"Yes?"

"Why?" Leo exhaled sharply, as Ares kissed his lower back, grabbed his ass.

"Why not?"

"I don't—ah!" Ares kissed Leo's tailbone, fingers sliding up the cleft of Leo's ass. God. He was trembling. "I don't need all this."

"Do you like it?" Ares asked, his breath warm on Leo's hip. Leo whined.

"Am I more aroused than I've—" Ares slid one hand around the curve of Leo's hip and Leo twitched, a full body shudder. "Than I've ever been? Yes."

"I told you, I want to spoil you."

"You've ruined me. I'll never—" Ares ran his fingers over Leo's entrance, pressing in gently before bowing his head and replacing his fingers with his mouth. "Ares! Good fucking—" Leo lost his cursing to a long low moan as Ares began to slide his tongue against him, inside him, fucking him. "Oh my God. Ares!" Leo shifted backward in earnest desperation, and Ares lifted up slightly, kissing the curve of Leo's ass, fingering him again.

"I'm going to fuck you now, if that's alright."

"Yes. Please," Leo gasped. "Ares. I want you." He wanted nothing else. Ares was the only thing he could think of, his body, twitching, aching, desperate for the ministrations of one man. There had been times in Leo's life where he had been overstimulated, his mind blanking out everything but sensation. But this was not like that. Ares was pressed against his back. Ares' fingers were inside him. Ares was delivering wave after wave of pleasure.

"I know you're going to feel so good." His lips were warm against Leo's ear.

"I need you, Ares. Ares!" Leo gasped, as Ares' careful, slick fingers opened him.

"I'm yours, Leo. I'm all yours." It almost tipped Leo right over the edge.

"Fuck me." And Ares pushed into him slowly, slowly. Leo tried to press back, take more of him.

"Easy," Ares grunted, his grip on Leo's hip tightening as he slid in deeper and then stilled. Leo panted, his head swimming with pleasure, every throb and ache ricocheting bliss across his nerve endings. He was going to come the minute Ares started fucking him, he knew. They'd toed all the way up to the edge of the cliff. All Leo needed was a little push.

"Ares," Leo moaned, leaning forward, creating space for Ares to fill. "I need it. I'm yours. Ares." Ares moved then, one hand coming up to grab Leo's shoulder as he began to fuck him proper. It was exquisite. Back bowing. Heart pounding. Leo babbled, begging for more, harder, just one more. And then somehow, Ares slid a hand around him and started to stroke him. Leo came moaning Ares' name, and it took everything in Leo to not just collapse forward and let Ares finish however he liked. The haze of bliss was thick, but Leo wanted Ares to feel good. To know how much Leo wanted him still.

Leo pushed himself up, palms pressed against Ares' thighs, so he was sitting back on Ares' cock and watched as Ares' come-slick hand grasped for purchase around Leo's hips, pulling Leo down as Ares thrust into him. Fuck, but Leo did love being manhandled. And then, for every point a counterpoint, Ares kissed Leo's throat, mouth soft, panting against his skin.

"I want you," Leo gasped. "Fuck me." Ares came, pinning Leo's hips down against his thighs, filling him with sharp, shuddering thrusts. Ares buried his face against the back of Leo's neck, mouthing desperate kisses against his skin, and Leo was overcome. What had just happened? He looked down at their bodies, at the mess they'd made of the duvet, and noticed the arm Ares had wrapped around Leo's waist, was glowing.

The lines that Leo had thought were scars were shimmering, golden and soft. Leo ran his fingers against Ares' skin in wonder.

"Up," Ares murmured against Leo's shoulder. Leo straightened, thighs shaking, body adjusting as Ares slid out of him, slowly, carefully. Leo sank onto his hip and rolled over on his back, watching Ares move. Both of Ares' forearms were covered in the softly glowing tendrils.

"What's that?"

"Magic," Ares said with a soft sigh, as he collapsed onto the bed beside Leo. He raised one arm above Leo's head, so that Leo could see. Curious, Leo reached up and traced the glowing threads with his fingers.

"Does it hurt?"

"No," Ares said. "Though, I haven't had them so bright in a while. I look like a bloody Christmas tree." He dropped his arm and tucked his head next to Leo's shoulder. "I'm sorry if I was too rough with you," his voice was a low murmur, and Leo turned to face him.

"You were perfect. But I don't think we can just brush past your glowing forearms quite so easily." Ares snorted.

"You can't, at any rate."

"Why does it happen?"

"They're called extolations," Ares yawned and closed his eyes, caressing Leo's ribs with his fingertips. "When you're a demigod, and you please the deity that heads your family line by doing something... I don't know, aligned with their ethos, sometimes, they bestow gifts. It's a strengthening of my magic. Temporarily. It'll fade in an hour or so."

"Your deity likes that you fucked me?" Leo asked. Ares snorted. "The implications of that are—"

"It's not just that we fucked. More the manner and the... I

dunno. Intention?" Ares' cheeks were pinking, and Leo was beginning to feel very smug.

"The intention?"

"I wanted you to feel good," Ares opened his eyes again, looking at Leo beneath his lashes. "To—I don't know. There's probably something about pleasure and nourishment and, I mean. It's all esoteric and vague. No one's ever given me a list of all the things that could trigger it."

Leo hummed, considering this. Considering how hard he wanted to press for more information, just now.

"It was *particularly* pleasurable. I feel thoroughly spoiled," Leo said with a small smile. Ares rolled his eyes, and Leo kissed him again, feeling Ares' lips curl into a smirk beneath his own. "I don't think I can ever have regular sex again. You've ruined me."

"Anyone who isn't willing to take the time to have you like that shouldn't be in your bed in the first place," Ares grumbled. Leo grinned, tucking his forehead against Ares' chest, feeling the pulsing beat of his heart.

"Still, I suppose it's a good thing I've got you," Leo said after a moment. "Since I know you'll make time."

"I'm all yours," Ares said, easily. And it might've been meant that way, just a simple turn of phrase, but Leo's foolish, stupid heart leapt like it was something more.

39

When Leo woke, he was draped over Ares' chest, his face buried in the crook of Ares' shoulder. It was barely light out, but perhaps he'd heard something, a sound that had roused him and then vanished before he could recognize it. Or maybe it was just the strangeness of being somewhere new.

Ares rolled toward him, kissing the hollow of Leo's throat as he tucked his head below Leo's chin. They shifted together beneath the blankets and Leo let his eyes sink closed again, even as other parts of his body came awake at Ares' touch. Half asleep himself, Ares slid his hands down Leo's ribs, the most unassuming caress Leo had ever experienced in his life. Ares wasn't asking anything of him; he was gentle, palms slowing over the curve of Leo's hips and then resting there, warm and heavy.

Leo's perception might have been hazy with sleep, but there was something about the way Ares was handling him, like Leo was something precious, valuable and fragile, that made him relax. There was nothing he had to do for Ares. Nothing to prove or show, and it made Leo want to pull their bodies together, just to feel the pleasure of Ares' skin against his own. So, he did.

Ares' hand dipped over Leo's backside, fingers soft, sliding over the curves of Leo's ass and onto his upper thigh. Ares' eyes were still closed, but he didn't seem surprised when Leo kissed him. Ares' movement stayed languid, syrupy, his tongue dragging over Leo's lips and into his mouth. He moved so leisurely that Leo had to relax further just to keep pace with him, his arousal growing as their bodies melted toward each other.

Leo hitched his thigh over Ares' hip and rocked against him. He could feel Ares' smile against his chest where Ares had been pressing kisses. When Ares slid his mouth over Leo's nipple, sucking gently, Leo moaned. Ares got slowly to his knees, his hands beside Leo's shoulders, and Leo spread his legs, enjoying the heat that coursed over his skin as Ares settled between Leo's thighs. He knew he tasted like morning and that his curls were a mess and that there was likely still dried cum on his stomach, but when Ares sank down, pressing Leo back against the pillows with a kiss, Leo didn't care about any of those things. He knew Ares was going to be gentle with him. That Ares wanted Leo like this, and that it would feel so good to have him.

Sex had never been so easy. Leo was used to the pressure of wanting something out of it. Wanting to please his partners and make sure that he was fucked so well that he wouldn't be able to think. It had never been like this. The dawn light was gentle, brushing over his skin as Leo lifted his hips, and Ares slid their bodies closer.

"I've never seen anyone as beautiful as you," Ares murmured. Leo wanted to say something. Wanted to tell Ares to look in a mirror sometime. Wanted to tell him that he'd never craved the touch of another person the way he craved Ares. But then Ares pushed into him, his cock thick and hard and Leo moaned, arching his back, his hands grasping at the sheets because nothing in his whole life had ever felt so good.

Ares stroked him slowly, the same agonizing pace as his thrusts, and Leo could hear his own gasping and begging get louder, more desperate as the minutes ticked on.

"Ares," Leo panted, eventually, fingers grasping at Ares' forearms, biceps, tugging on him. "Ares, please!"

"So good for me, Leo," Ares grunted, hoisting Leo's hips just an inch higher, sliding deeper. "Gods. You're gorgeous." Leo arched his back and saw stars, as Ares fucked him. "So pretty stretched around my cock." Leo moaned and came.

Ares rocked forward, putting more weight on his hands, enough that Leo could wrap his arms around Ares' neck and pull him down into a kiss. Ares filled him with a mumbled curse against Leo's mouth.

They both caught their breath, tangled together in the bedsheets and Ares kissed Leo gently again: his jaw, then his neck. Leo's hands slid down Ares' waist, his whole body feeling boneless, already ready to sink back into sleep.

Ares sat with his back against the headboard, letting his hand drag across the page, revealing the long curve of Leo's shoulder. He studied the paper and his sleeping model, ignoring the way looking at Leo made him breathless, and how he was dreading the moment that they'd have to get out of bed.

Leo was snoring into the pillow, but Ares hadn't been able to fall back to sleep, no matter how good it had felt to lay beside him. Maybe it was just because Ares was used to being up early. Maybe it didn't have to do with the creeping anxiety that he'd let this whole thing go too far.

Sketching was supposed to have been relaxing, but the

longer he worked on it, the more desperate he was to get it right. He needed to get the exact curve of Leo's nose, the way his hair was falling over his ear, his cheek in the pillow, because soon this drawing would be all he had left of Leo Quince. And maybe if he captured the man exactly, it wouldn't hurt so much when Leo had gone.

And Leo did, really, have to leave. Especially now, as Ares' feelings for him grew in depth and general tenderness. Pretending that Leo was Ares' for one night had felt so good, so right, that he'd forgotten to stop. He shouldn't have encouraged Leo the second time. Hell, if he was honest with himself, he'd practically instigated it. So stupid and self-indulgent. But even though he knew that, all he wanted was to kiss Leo awake, pack him up in the carriage, and take him home where they could build a life together. It was a dangerous thought, and it was impossible. Morrow was still out there. Ares had work to do. And he was dying besides. It wasn't right to put Leo through all that, even if Leo thought he wanted to. Just because he'd said Ares had ruined him for other men. Because he'd said, 'you can have me,' and the echo of it still sent chills running up Ares' spine. It didn't mean anything. Probably.

Ares bit his tongue and focused on his drawing, working on the details for longer than he should have been able to on what was such a small image. 'This will be all you have of him,' said a small voice in the back of his head. 'Better make sure you get it right.'

Before long, Leo was yawning, stretching one arm up, his bicep bulging as he folded his arm down, pressing his hand to the back of his head, turning toward the sun.

"Morning," Leo said, glancing at Ares out of the corner of his eye. Ares snapped the sketchbook closed, depositing it on the side table as discreetly as possible.

"Good morning," Ares said, trying not to smile at him. As

though Leo could sense what Ares was attempting to suppress, he smirked and turned his gaze up to the ceiling.

"So, what are we going to do today?"

"We're going to load the carriage with an obscene amount of fine fabrics and fur coats and drive it back to Leyland Hall." Leo hummed, pressing his head back into the pillow, his mouth curling into a tempting smile, his eyes fixed on the ceiling still.

"I could look obscene in a fur coat." Ares bit his bottom lip and snorted, refusing to respond. Instead, he moved to get out of bed, throwing the blanket off and intentionally over Leo's head. Leo pushed it off with a grin. "I wanted to spend a little more time in the library if I could. And maybe run by the Assembly Office. Graham told me yesterday that it's across the town square, and you can call between realms there."

"Who do you want to call?" Ares asked, immediately suspicious. Leo sat, rolling his eyes, and Ares tried not to let himself get distracted by the expanse of bare chest that was exposed as the blankets pooled around Leo's hips. Leo stretched his arms above his head, groaning, and Ares forced himself to look for his trousers.

"Sidney. I imagine he's wondering where I am by now. I don't want him to worry."

"Unless you know the runes for the place he's staying, you won't be able to call him."

"What do you mean?" Leo asked.

"It's like a telephone number," Ares said with a shrug, finally unearthing his trousers from a pile of clothes beside the bathroom door.

"Well, isn't there a directory or something?" Leo frowned, his hands hitting the bedspread with a quiet thud. "Everyone seemed to be coming and going from Elmmond House. Surely there's a record of their runes somewhere. I mean, people know about it, right?"

Ares rolled his lips between his teeth. His back was still turned to Leo, so he didn't have to work to keep the indecision from his face. What did he care if Leo called his brother? It wasn't any of his business. Maybe it would be good for Leo. Talking to his brother might encourage him to leave when Alondra returned. Ares was supposed to want that.

"I might still know them," Ares shrugged. There was no 'might' about it. He'd memorized them ten years ago, and never forgotten them, tracing them in his mind on his worst days, when he was so desperate to go home.

"Well, that's better than nothing," Leo said, his tone pleased, chipper even. Ares ignored the guilt curdling his stomach. He'd have felt worse if he hadn't said anything. Probably. It didn't matter; he'd never know.

40

After breakfast, Ares and Graham began loading Kephisto's luggage. Leo helped with the dishes and tried to subtly ask Mrs. Goode if she thought anyone might notice a few of the books from the library going missing. She cocked an eyebrow at him, her lips flattening into a thin line, and that said as much as the disapproving silence that followed.

"Take thorough notes," she said finally. And that was that.

Leo went back to the bedroom, gathering up the book from the night before, and borrowing Ares' sketchbook from his side table, since Leo hadn't brought a notebook of his own.

The library was a good size, and the shelves on it were packed and dusty, giving Leo the impression that the whole thing was more about appearances than function. He was used to libraries like this, his father's was similar, and it made him stand up straighter. And then slouch on purpose because his father wasn't about to walk into the room, no matter how much it seemed like he might.

The book he had found the night before was called *A Blink or a Wink? Proper Comportment for Interspecies Negotiations* and was more about behavior and cultural customs to be aware of during deal-making than about law itself. The reason Leo had kept it was because it had a section about the way some contracts followed bloodlines, and how children (particularly first born) should be invited to attend certain contract discussions. This section was followed by a reference to CSA 77§115.26B which meant nothing to Leo yet. But he had clocked a large, encyclopedic-looking set of books behind an over-sized desk that blocked most of the far wall. If studying law had taught him anything, it was that statutes and codes loved to be bound in unnecessarily extensive volumes. And if working with his father had taught him anything, it was that men of power liked to be seated in front of books of laws that they had every intention of breaking.

So, Leo was pleased (but not at all surprised) to discover that the large set of books housed *The Codices of the Sorcerers' Assembly.* Then it was a simple matter of locating statute 77, and section 115, subsection 26B. Contracts between parties that would transfer through multiple children, and further, should one child have children, and—

It was dense, and contained more minutiae than Leo was ready for. He grabbed Ares' sketchbook and flipped to the last page in it, before realizing he hadn't brought a pencil. The first drawer he yanked open was practically spilling over with correspondence, unfiled and all at odd angles. Leo shifted one corner of one envelope to see if he could spot a pen, and several letters fluttered to the floor.

"Damn." With a grunt and a sigh of frustration, Leo crouched down, gathering up what he could. As he stacked the letters on top of each other, he was struck by the fact that they were almost all the same handwriting. A glance at the signature made him stop. *'E. Morrow'*

Morrow was corresponding more than a little frequently

with Kephisto. Leo's stomach tightened anxiously, though he couldn't precisely place why. It just didn't seem like a good omen to be finding traces of Ares' jailer everywhere they went. So, he sat back on the floor and began to read.

Based on what Leo could suss out, Kephisto had been holding dinners and soirees with various members of the Assembly, shoring up support for different projects and amendments to the codex. Morrow was more influential than Leo had thought, which didn't exactly complicate things, but it didn't make them any easier. Leo started skimming after the fourth letter pivoted in a later paragraph from business to a detailed description of how Morrow wanted to fuck Kephisto on the dining room table during dinner. Leo winced and paused, closing his eyes as he considered whether or not he wanted to read further. He didn't. But he did pocket that letter, since whatever Morrow was doing to Ares, Leo wasn't above using blackmail to stop it.

He went back to skimming, working more quickly. Blackmail would be good, but it wouldn't be as effective as a decent legal defense, and so far, all Leo had found out was that Morrow was considerably well-connected. He ran his tongue along the back of his teeth, setting letters on top of the open drawer, looking for any words or phrases that stood out as possibly being tied to Ares. And then he found one:

Whether it causes strife with your mother or not, I have to insist you don't extend invitations to any of the Mycelian delegation. Were the dinner anywhere else, I would have no objection, but the proximity to the orchard is far too great a risk. They are a nuisance at a regular garden party, and at Leyland Hall, they would genuinely constitute a potential threat to our work.

It was innocuous otherwise. Lord Someone from Somewhere was to be invited, without his incessantly chattering daughter, and the Duchess was not to be allowed to attend without her wife, a friend of—It didn't matter. Leo read the paragraph again. Mae had mentioned the Mycelians to Leo. The mushroom Fae, with deep connections to the earth. Would they be able to tell what was wrong with the orchard? What it was doing to Ares?

Leo tucked that letter into his pocket as he suddenly became aware of the sound of approaching footsteps. The door swung open, and Leo could see Graham's thin pant legs from beneath the desk. Leo popped up, shoving the rest of the letters back into the drawer and sliding it shut, as Graham frowned at him.

"Just looking for a pen," Leo said, getting to his feet. Graham pointed, wordlessly, at the pen in the inkwell on the top of the desk, and Leo attempted his most charming grin. "Silly me! If it was a snake, it would've bit me."

"Mr. Silva is ready to depart."

"Thank you," Leo said. "You can tell him I'll be along in just a—"

"He said I was to fetch you. Or that otherwise you'd be all day."

"Ass," Leo grumbled, trying to suppress a small smile as he began to copy down the Codex page in front of him.

It took less than fifteen minutes for them to pull up to the Assembly building in Warnock, and Leo's mind was still sorting out what he'd learned from the library, formulating questions for Sidney as he rode along beside Ares. The sky was bright blue behind the high Assembly tower that rose up from the sharp lines of the austere-looking white marble building before them.

"They take the term 'ivory tower' rather literally here, don't they?" Leo mused, as Ares tied the horses to the hitching post and then reached up and wordlessly offered Leo his hand. Leo took it, appreciating the small smirk on Ares' handsome mouth. He was getting better at reading Ares' silences, interpreting his expressions and gestures and learning that those things were as revealing as what Ares' decided to say. Usually, moreso. Ares' hand drifted across the small of Leo's back as they walked into the atrium of the building, pressing against him for a moment, a quiet reminder of his presence and a promise of security, before it fell away.

The center of the room was filled by the giant black curve of a marble information desk, where a woman sat, her eyes scanning them briefly before dropping back to whatever was in front of her. Two long, hooked staircases curled toward the upper floors, each blocked by a hearty looking security guard. The guards looked at proffered badges and cards, allowing passage and thin smiles to whomever met their standards for entry. There were other halls shooting off the main space in multiple directions, though none of them were marked. Leo took a deep breath and strode up to the woman at the desk.

"How can I help you?" she said with a performative smile.

"We're hoping to make a call to—"

"An outer realm," Ares interrupted. "We were told there are hearths here for public use. Is there a fee?"

"No fee," she said brusquely. "Excepting blood for the spell work, of course. First hall on the right there. The flames reset every twenty minutes, and require additional payment, should the call go long. And there are no rune records here, so—"

"We have the runes," Ares said.

"There are instructions on the wall, should you have any other questions," the woman said, dismissing them by abruptly going back to her reading.

Leo had at least a half dozen questions, but Ares was apparently satisfied as he walked off in the direction the woman had indicated.

The hall reminded Leo of some of the smaller courthouses he'd worked in back home, tight and unnaturally warm. Outside of each room was a cord that looked like a bellpull, attached to a sign above the doorframe that read 'Available' or 'In Use' and Ares stopped them at the third 'Available' door they came to, nearly at the far end of the hall, where an uncomfortable looking bench sat beneath an over-filled bulletin board, notices hanging well over the bottom edge of the wooden frame. Ares ignored those things and pushed open the door, yanking on the bellpull before stepping inside.

The room was the size of a small closet and had to be about as hot as a sauna, without any of the dampness. The dry, ashy heat made Leo cough, as the door swung shut behind them. A fire roared in the grate, and it took Leo a moment before he realized that the flames that leapt up the chimney were tipped with purple and silver, and the fire itself was slowly changing colors.

Before Leo could ask what they needed to do, Ares got down on one knee in front of the hearth with a grunt. He reached into his boot and pulled out a small workman's knife, the blade tucked into the handle. Before Leo could speak to stop him, Ares dug the blade into the flesh below his thumb, blood spilling up slowly, trickling toward his palm.

"Ares!"

"It needs blood to work," he said. Leo suppressed a shiver, his stomach clenching in warning at the sight of Ares so casually injuring himself. He grimaced, trying to think of something scolding to say and ignoring the sweat that was beginning to prickle at the back of his neck. "Don't make a face. Everything here needs blood eventually." He held up his hand toward Leo. "Spit."

"What?"

"Spit in my palm."

"Onto your open wound?" Leo arched an eyebrow and Ares rolled his eyes.

"No. On my palm. Just a little. I don't know if their grates will be finicky about you seeing through them without something connecting you to the magic. Just—" Leo leaned forward and spit into the crease of Ares' hand, uneager to discover what else this spell might require. Ares leaned forward and scooped some of the ash from beneath the logs in the hearth and mixed it into a slurry in the center of his hand, his blood tinting the whole thing into a muddy grey. Leo swallowed, thickly, as something occurred to him.

"Should it have been my blood?"

"It could have been. But this is easier."

"Easier for who?" Ares ignored him, bending down again to trace lines on the stones closest to the fire with the slurry from his hand, as though the flames needed to read them.

"I'm irritated with you," Leo said, grabbing Ares' arm as Ares got to his feet.

"Be irritated with me later. There's about to be someone on the other end of the fire," Ares said, gesturing to the hearth. Leo leaned up and pressed his mouth to Ares, relaxing as the firm line of Ares' lips softened against him. He wanted it to have the same feeling of Ares' hand on his back, the possessiveness and the promise of safety. He would do the bleeding next time. He would be sure of it. Ares put a hand on Leo's hip and lightened the kiss. "I'm fine," he muttered, and Leo smiled, pleased that Ares had known what he meant. They were getting better at this. Leo kissed him again, briefly, before a voice came through the fireplace.

"Hello? This is Elmmond House. Can I help you with something?"

"I'll give you some privacy," Ares murmured, and then slid out the door, leaving Leo to get down on his knees in front of the fireplace, and talk to the man whose face shone out of the flames as though the smoke had turned to glass.

41

It took a minute for the butler at Elmmond House to realize that Leo was asking to speak to Sidney. He'd had to call him 'Rookwood's guest at the cottage,' before the man seemed to know who he meant, and then the man left, saying that he would check and see if they were in.

Leo began to get anxious as the minutes dragged on. The woman at the desk said they'd have to reset the spell if it took more than twenty minutes, and surely almost half of that had elapsed already. But then in a rush of legs and knees and huffing breath, Sidney was there, collapsed cross-legged in front of the fire. He hadn't known how much he'd been worried about Sidney until Sidney appeared. Leo's shoulders sagged, as tension he'd not been aware of melted away. Sidney's eyes widened in surprise as he leaned forward, still panting.

"Leo?! Shit! It really is you! Where *are* you?"

"Warnock. At the Sorcerer's Assembly building—"

"Warnock? I have no idea where that is."

"Neither do I," Leo said with a shrug, ignoring the scowl that crumpled Sidney's face. "Listen, I need a favor."

"Are you—Are you stuck? Are you safe?"

"Perfectly safe. Is Rookwood there?" Leo asked, realizing his mistake. "Damn. I should have asked for him as well as you. I need to know about contract law in Andurnei, and I—"

"He's on his way. You didn't make a contract, did you?" Sidney huffed, preemptively exasperated. Leo smirked. "I tried to tell you—"

"Not me. A friend." He wasn't going to get into specifics, he knew that would only muddy the waters and was likely to get Sidney more upset. The last thing he needed was Sidney running off to Ares' brother, telling him that Ares had been found before Leo had worked out a plan to get him back. "I need whatever information you can find for me about the way contracts get passed on via bloodlines. How are they nullified, or if they can be? And what sort of protections are put in place for unwilling or unaware—"

"Christ, Leo."

"Sorry. I just don't have a lot of time."

"Do you have a plan for getting back?" Sidney pressed. Leo huffed, grateful for Sidney's concern as much as he was irritated by it.

"I know what I'm doing, Sidney."

"You always say that."

"The law—"

"Wait a moment," Sidney grumbled, as he held up a hand, scrambling to his knees. "Let me get some paper."

ARES STOOD outside the door for a moment, the phantom press of Leo's lips still tingling against his mouth. He was impossibly tangled in his feelings. The silence of the carriage had been good, promising even. Leo hadn't shared whatever he'd found in the library, and maybe that meant there hadn't been anything. That Leo would distance himself naturally, as he realized that there was no way out of this for Ares. By the time Alondra got back, he'd have figured it out for himself.

Still, in spite of their silent carriage ride, Ares couldn't stop himself from touching Leo. Couldn't stop himself from returning Leo's kiss. He'd lost all self-control where Leo was concerned. And it was a bad sign that Leo had been scowling at him after Ares had cut himself. It meant Leo hadn't understood anything at all about the fate that awaited Ares. A little cut on his hand was barely worth mentioning in the grand scheme of things, but it had made Leo unhappy, and the stupid, selfish part of Ares' heart that he'd lost to Leo over the past week beat a little faster at the look of concern on Leo's face.

Alondra had told Ares to let Leo take care of him, but there had to be a line somewhere, didn't there? He couldn't let it go on like this, for both their sakes.

Ares walked back toward the atrium for something to do, pacing the hall a few more times and trying not to think about what the rest of the carriage ride home was going to be like if they weren't going to talk to each other. He was a little curious what Leo had found at the library, mostly because he knew that it was likely nothing, and maybe hearing Leo confirm that would be good for both of them. If he could get Leo to admit that this was all going to come to an end soon, that might give Ares some firmer ground to stand on when it came time to push Leo away.

Of course, then there was the small voice in his mind, in his chest, that sounded like Alondra and insisted that Leo might have found something really useful after all. It was an easy voice to quelch. There was nothing. He knew it. He'd lived the last ten years of his life knowing it. It was ridiculous that ignoring that knowledge for one night was all he'd needed to give himself hope.

Ares paused in front of Leo's door, listening, hearing Leo talking rapidly, his voice muffled by the fire and the door, so that Ares couldn't make any of it out. He'd definitely gotten a hold of Sidney though, which was good. Ares never called Dom. For the same reason that he was going to end this thing with Leo. There wasn't a way out. There was no reason to visit grief on people who didn't do anything to deserve it.

Christ, he couldn't go around and around like this anymore. Desperate for anything else to distract him, Ares stepped across the hall and began to study the notice board. It was a mix of information, most of the lower pages tattered and poked through with pinholes as other pages had been placed on top of them and then removed. There were signs advertising classes to be held at the Assembly, missing persons posters, and a few signs requesting information about wanted criminals, promising rewards that were enough to entice even the most loyal of fellow lawbreakers.

Most of the posters had hand drawn images instead of photographs, and Ares couldn't help but critique the proportions of the sketches. There was no way the gap between that man's eyes was that large. And another had a mouth that sat diagonally above his chin. A portrait on a poster tacked up halfway over another had a brow line and a chin that nearly, but not quite, had the proportions of Leo's face. The eyes were too wide, though, and the cheekbones too pronounced. His lips were actually quite a bit like Leo's, quirked up in a smug, know-it-all smirk that Ares had come to admire, even though it usually meant he was about to be treated to a sassy comment. Ares stepped closer, plucking at the bottom of the page to see what the man was wanted for.

Dead or Alive, a Handsome reward will be paid to any who provide information that leads to the apprehension and arrest of Leo Quince,

*for assault upon an officer of the Sorcerer's Assembly, unlawful entry
and various other crimes!*

Ares couldn't hear anything over the rush of blood in his
ears, and he didn't realize he'd torn the poster down until he
had it in his hand. He crumpled the paper, balling it up and
shoving it into his pocket. Ares' heart was racing, chest tight, as
he rapped hard on Leo's door with his knuckles, not waiting for
a response before he stuck his head in.

"We have to go," he said, trying to keep his voice from going
too stiff.

"Just a moment—"

"Now, Leo." Leo looked at him then, enough surprise on his
face that Ares knew he'd failed at keeping his voice even.
"Now."

"Is everything—?" A voice from the fire, faint but sounding
so remarkably like Leo that for a moment, Ares thought it was
Leo who'd said it.

"No, it's fine," Leo said quickly, pressing himself up onto his
knees. "I have to go."

"Where should we—?" A deeper voice, distinctly different
from the Quince brothers. Ares swallowed, his head spinning.

"Leo," he prompted again.

"I'll be in touch. I can sort something out, I'm sure," Leo
said with confidence that made Ares' heart ache. This was all
going to be over soon, and it was for the best. Ares would keep
him inside, not let him leave the cottage until Alondra was
back. Everything was going to be different from here on out.
The longing in his chest made him furious. Ares stepped back
into the hallway, yanking on the bell pull that doused the fire at
once, cutting Leo's goodbye short.

42

res insisted that Leo ride inside the carriage instead of up front. The argument was shorter than Ares had expected, and he was grateful the weather seemed to be getting worse, as that did a good part of the work for him. Unfortunately, without Leo as a distraction, the ride felt twice as long. It wasn't until Ares saw the first outpost in the distance that a horrible thought occurred to him. The likelihood that Morrow had only posted signs about Leo in Warnock was extremely low. The outpost buildings along the road. The town hall in Laurel Grove. It was possible that there were signs everywhere.

Ares stopped at the outpost, sticking his head into the carriage to feed Leo a ridiculous lie about seeing to a bit of business for Mrs. Goode. Leo was intent on working in a notebook, scratching away with a pencil nub, and nodded his agreement to stay in the carriage. Inside, Ares found the notice board without any trouble, Leo's face hanging in the center of it. He yanked it down without ceremony, only realizing afterward that he ought to have checked to make sure no one was watching. Ares balled up the poster, stuffing it into his coat pocket beside the first, before returning to the carriage and getting them back on the road.

Anxiety crowded his thoughts. How could he contact Alondra and get her back to the cottage tonight? He needed to get Leo Earthside as quickly as possible. But would that even help? Morrow had people everywhere, fewer in the human realm, but not none. He would have to tell Leo before he sent him back, at least enough so that he could take precautions. He would take precautions, Ares tried to assure himself. Leo was reckless, but he wasn't stupid. He would see reason about this. He had to. Ares would make him.

The next two stopovers on the main road yielded two more posters, and Ares twisted the leather reins around his hands so tightly that his fingers began to tingle. Night was fast approaching, faster, somehow than it was supposed to, and dark clouds were threatening on the horizon as the wind picked up. They still had at least another two hours to go, and Ares couldn't risk stopping at an inn. Though, he should have been stopping at inns and pubs the whole trip, anywhere Morrow might have had put up signs. His stomach tightened at the thought, nauseous at the attempt to calculate just how many posters he might have missed. How many people would have seen Leo's poorly drawn portrait and would be looking for him now.

"Ares!" The sound of Leo's voice through the window of the carriage made him jump. "Let's stop somewhere soon. I'm starving and it looks like rain." It'd looked like rain for the past hour, and Ares dragged a hand down his face as he pulled back on the reins. There was no place safe to go, and they were still an hour and a half from Leyland Hall, provided the storm kept at bay. Fat raindrops, thick and heavy with a coating of ice, began to splatter down around him. Ares closed his eyes and tried to breathe through the panic.

"Ares, are—"

"Half an hour," Ares called back, turning the horses with a jerk of his arms, taking the road south, deeper into the forest, toward the coast.

It took nearer to an hour to get to Mae's, but Leo hadn't bothered to stick his head out of the carriage again and ask where they were going. Ares could breathe slightly better once he could make out the golden lights of Mae's house in the valley between the two hills. The well-worn path into the gulley was fitted to carriage wheels, but still uncomfortably bumpy as the ice began to coat the road. By the time they'd reached the small stable, Ares could barely see through the sheets of steadily falling sleet.

Leo hopped down out of the carriage, and began to help Ares unhitch the horses, following Ares' lead without any questions. Ares was too cold and anxious to parse out what the silence between them was, but he could feel Leo's eyes on him as he worked. He told himself it was Leo watching the motions of putting the horses away so he could follow along, nothing more. After fifteen minutes, they were back out in the sleet, heads bowed, quiet stretching between them as they made their way around the side of Mae's house and up to the front door.

Ares knocked the mud and slush off his boots on the bottom step, and by the time he'd made it to the top step, Sal had appeared. They looked as haggard as it was possible for an incorporeal and infinite being to look, their form trembling at the edges, as though they were too busy to bother coming into focus.

"Ares. Mr. Quince," Sal nodded to them each in turn, and then shook their head. "You've picked a bad time to stop in, gents, if I can be so bold as to say." Their voice was a huff, as though they had breath they were trying to catch. "Mae's in the thick of an experiment at the moment. She won't be taking visitors."

"We were just hoping for a place to sleep," Ares said, thinking he'd take a blanket and one of the chairs on the front porch if he had to. "I know it's not long back to the house on foot, but the ice." Ares gestured over his shoulder. "Plus, we've got horses and a—"

"I know she wouldn't want me turning you away, Ares. Not after everything, but, uh..." They looked hesitantly toward the house, which seemed the same as usual, at least to Ares' untrained eye. Sal's shoulders dropped, as though they'd heaved a sigh. "Alright. The upstairs'll be mostly aired out by now. Just, uh..." they looked back at Ares and Leo and shook their head. "Cover your nose and mouth with something, alright? Tightly, too. Or it'll be on my head."

"What is it?" Leo asked, frowning, even as he tugged Ares' scarf out from beneath his collar.

"Just some fumes from a poculum amatorium. They can be a bit potent, that's all."

"And what is that?" Leo asked, drawing Ares' scarf up over his nose, his arm stretching back to clench the fabric tightly behind his head. Ares could feel the heat in his cheeks at the sight of the scarf he'd worn so often, his favorite, wrapped around Leo's face, keeping him safe from whatever the hell Mae was cooking up.

"Ares, come on," Sal nodded, waiting until Ares had tucked his chin down and pulled his collar up, tucking his nose and mouth into his shirt. "Alright, lads. Up the stairs. Have the Seas Room, in the back there. It's had a good breeze for at least a quarter of an hour now. You'll have to stock the stove, Ares, but there should be logs in there. Keep the door shut firmly, yeah?" And with that, Sal disappeared, and the door swung open.

It only took two steps inside for Ares to understand what

Sal meant. A thin, lilac mist seemed to hang in the air, which was thick with damp heat, like a steam room that had been left on too long. It didn't smell bad though. Like anise and clove, with notes of bourbon and apple, sweet and sharp. Ares suddenly had the urge to inhale deeply, and just barely stopped himself as Sal reappeared to herd Ares up the stairs behind Leo.

"It's her ninth go at it, and it never doesn't explode. If she'd been expecting you, she'd never have started it. Mr. Quince, left at the top, that first door on the far wall. There you are."

The air looked clear, though the scent remained, as Ares followed Leo into the suite at the corner of the house. It was cold and damp, but the air smelled more like ice and ocean. Ares could still feel the heat of the bourbon and spices in his nose, as he closed the door behind them.

The room was large, with faded teal wallpaper, and bedecked with drooping streamers of sea glass threaded onto twine. Windchimes made from shells clanked together quietly outside the open windows, and the dresser and the small bookshelves were covered with pots overgrown with green string of pearls and string of tears vines everywhere, giving a strong impersonation of seaweed. The whole place looked as though it had been ripped directly from a shipwreck, including the large fourposter bed that stood on the far wall, large arches of driftwood forming the headboard and the footboard.

"I'll bring up some snacks for you," Sal called through the door. "And I'll let Mae know you're in. Feel free to light the stove and close the windows!" And then there was silence.

Leo looked at Ares, revealing a barely suppressed grin as he tugged Ares' scarf down off his nose.

"This place is insane. And we're not more than an hour from home."

"It'll take longer if we stay on the roads," Ares said. "It's quicker to walk, but we can't take the carriage. And we had to back-track. Sorry," he added, for good measure. "I know you were hungry."

"It's fine," Leo said, his gaze up, lost immediately in the bizarre trappings of the space as he started over to the window. "I'm alright, honestly. It's just good to be out of the carriage. Sorry that you had to drive all this way."

"It's not a problem." Ares turned to find the wood stove pressed into the corner near a threadbare rug and a sagging leather armchair. He shoved a couple of logs into the belly of the thing, as Leo slid the windows shut. Having something to do was soothing in a small way, and Ares shucked his coat and hat as he waited for the fire to catch. He left the door of the stove open for a moment as he got to his feet, warming his hands to give himself time to muster up the courage to tell Leo that he had to leave. In no uncertain terms. Ideally from Mae's, and ideally tonight.

Of course, when he turned back, Leo was leaning against the foot of the bed, looking as relaxed and handsome as ever. He'd taken off his coat and hat, but his face was still buried in Ares' scarf, one hand holding the fabric to his nose, the other raking through his still damp hair. Then he lifted his chin and sniffed, furrowing his brow, as though he was expecting to smell something. Ares cleared his throat.

"We need to talk."

"A happy beginning to any conversation," Leo said, unthreading the scarf slowly from around his neck. "Are you going to tell me why we had to leave Warnock so fast? Or why I was sequestered to the carriage for most of the trip."

"It was cold," Ares said.

"But that wasn't the reason." Leo gave him a small smile that didn't quite reach his eyes. "I may not have known you for all that long, but give me a little credit. When you go all silent or demanding, it's a pretty good bet that something is up."

Ares swallowed. Being so exposed was somehow both embarrassing and elating. In any other situation, he might've blushed.

"You've got to leave."

"Ares," Leo sighed. "We've been through this."

"No," Ares turned, grabbing for his jacket and the pocket filled with wadded up posters. He'd throw the rest into the fire, but he managed to extract one and smoothed it out between shaking hands before holding it out toward Leo. "This isn't like before. This isn't about me." Leo stepped forward, frown crinkling his mouth, as he took the paper from Ares and studied it. Ares held his breath, waiting for the moment that Leo would finally see it too. Would understand that Ares wasn't worth this.

Time that had been in such a rush all day, slowed all the way down. Eventually, Leo looked up, folding the paper between his long fingers, his gaze distant. Ares could practically hear the gears in Leo's head spinning toward the inevitable conclusion, but he couldn't bear the silence anymore.

"You have to go," Ares said. Leo's eyes snapped to Ares, as though he'd forgotten Ares was in the room.

"I thought you said you weren't afraid of him."

"I was wrong."

"What changed?" Leo lifted his chin, and took a step forward, crumpling the paper in his fist. Ares swallowed.

"I thought Morrow had taken everything from me, but I..." he trailed off, the words sticking in his throat. He knew better than to say them out loud. Ares had thought he didn't have anything left to lose, but that was before Leo. Before whatever fragile thing that existed between them had bloomed into something beautiful and precious. Something else that Ares had to give up to protect.

"What?" Leo demanded. Another step. The paper in his

hand dropped to the floor, and Ares shook his head. "What else do you have for him to take?"

"Don't make me say it."

"If it's the reason you're going to send me away, I think I ought to hear it at least once."

"I'm not sending you away, I—"

"Of course not. You're not sending me away; you're just telling me I have to leave. But the decision's all mine? Is that it?" There was venom in Leo's voice, and it burned, making Ares' cheeks flush. "Lucky for everyone, isn't it? That I just go along with whatever choice has been made for me, no matter what it costs."

"And what is it going to cost you to stay? When he catches you," Ares gestured to the paper on the floor. "Those were posted up everywhere. People will be looking."

"What if I don't care?" Leo took another step forward, and Ares could feel the heat coming off him. He'd thought it was anger, and maybe some of it was, but beneath it was something far more dangerous and intoxicating.

"What could be worth it?" Ares choked. "Dead or alive? It's—"

"You aren't the only one who can make sacrifices for someone they love," Leo said. Ares' jaw dropped open, and he scrambled to come up with some protest that he could give voice to. Something that would hold water, that Leo couldn't argue against. But then Leo's hands were on Ares' chest, and Leo was kissing him, and Ares might have been a coward, but he wasn't stupid enough to push Leo away.

43

Leo hated Ares. His stupid, idiot face and how he thought he knew better than everyone else how to be a martyr. Well, Leo could be a fucking martyr too, though he wasn't planning on it. He'd made good headway on a strategy in the last three hours in the carriage, before it got too dark for him to scrawl notes in Ares' sketchbook. He had Sidney and Rookwood working on things on their end. All he needed to do was get more details out of Ares about what his deal with Morrow entailed, so he could make sure they were undoing it properly, and he could sew the damn thing up. It would be done, and when Leo went home, he'd have Ares with him. Simple. Easy.

Ares slid one hand over Leo's hip, as tentative as the first time they'd touched, and Leo almost growled in frustration.

"What's wrong?" Leo muttered, pulling back just enough so that he could drag his lips across the stubble of Ares' jaw. "Are you afraid of falling into bed with a dead man?"

"Shut up." Ares' hands tightened, and Leo tried not to enjoy it.

"Uh, no. You couldn't possibly want me. I'm one foot in the grave already. Haven't you seen the posters?"

"I won't let him touch you."

"Then what are you worried about?" Leo leaned back, creating space between them, room enough to breathe, room enough to think. Ares' hands dropped to his sides.

"I—I can't promise— Leo, he's stronger than I am."

"I doubt that."

"I can't lose you," Ares breathed out hard, reaching for Leo until he looked down at his outstretched hands, as though they'd moved without him meaning for them to. He curled his fingers against his palms.

"Why not?" Leo demanded. He didn't know why it mattered to him so much to hear Ares say how he felt. Except that, that morning, when they'd been together in Warnock House, Ares had said that he would be Leo's. And Leo had wanted him to mean it. "I'm tired of you telling me what to do, as if you would do anything different." Ares scowled, turning away, running his hands through his hair. "You're not going to be able to pull off your usual disappearing act without poisoning yourself, so you may as well talk to me."

"What do you want me to say, Leo? You know how much I want you."

"In bed. While you're fucking me."

"I'm not fucking you now!" Ares threw his hands up. Leo crossed his arms over his chest and leaned back against the footboard.

"So, say it, then."

"You need to go home, Leo."

"You're an ignorant bastard, Ares Silva." Ares snorted, his broad calloused hands running over his face again. It wasn't in Leo to let him off the hook, though perhaps that would have been the kinder route. He watched the shadows of the steadily strengthening flames play across Ares' face. His eyes looked dark, and his five o'clock shadow was heavier than it had been in all the days that Leo had known him.

"I don't know what I'd do if something happened to you because of me," Ares said. "I don't know how I would live with myself."

"I'm not going to leave you here to die," Leo bit. "I'm not doing it."

"I can't ask you—"

"I'm offering!" Leo threw up his hands. "Have you really been alone so long that you can't see that? I want to help you. I want you, Ares. It's not any more complicated than that. Do you want my help?"

"I want you alive."

"That's not what I asked," Leo snapped. Ares stared at him, his chest rising and falling slowly. Maybe he was angry. Maybe he was really considering what Leo had said. The wood in the stove hissed, ominous in the silence between them.

"I want you," Ares said finally. "I want you, Leo. And I can't have you like this. I'm trapped in this world. And I can't find a way out. Believe me, I have looked for ten years. And if you have an answer, or some other way that I don't know about, I'd love to hear it. But until then, I'll do what I can to keep you alive. Because I need you to be alive and living and... even if it's not with me."

"Shut up," Leo said quickly. He didn't want to think about that. Ares' confession, the thing Leo had wanted desperately to hear, was tangled up in grief so heavy it made Leo's chest ache. He stepped forward anyway, grabbing Ares by the wrists. "Let me try, Ares. Please."

For a long moment, everything stilled. Ares' deep brown eyes searched Leo's face, and Leo realized that his breath was caught in his throat.

"Could I stop you?" Ares smirked, but Leo could hear the pain in his voice. He bit his lip.

"I don't know. You can't stop me from trying, I suppose. I guess if I found an answer, you could refuse to take it."

"I don't know how to refuse you anymore," Ares murmured. "Worse than that, I don't want to."

It was all the permission Leo needed. He stepped forward and kissed Ares firmly. Ares listed toward him, like he had after the orchard, like he needed something to hold him up. Leo pulled back, trying to steady him, but Ares shook his head. His cheeks were flushed.

"Leo, you have to know how I—"

"I know," Leo said quickly. He didn't need to hear it. He'd never been the sort of person who needed to hear those three words. He didn't know what had come over him. "It's okay. I'm sorry." Ares shook his head, tugging Leo into his arms. When Ares kissed him, Leo could feel all the desperation and the longing, and everything it was costing Ares to let Leo get so close. And Leo promised himself then that he'd do right by Ares. He'd figure out how to fix this, no matter the cost.

Ares pulled away slowly, his chest aching with the pain of being honest and exposed. He hadn't told Leo everything there was to tell. About how much he cared for Leo. About the quiet embers of desperation and hope that were threatening to catch fire and destroy the tangle of roots that knitted together his ribcage. Those things were too precious, too fragile to put outside of him. He had been alone for too long. It wasn't everything, but it was what he could manage for now.

Leo ran his thumb across Ares' cheekbone, studying his

face, and Ares had no idea what he saw there. Ares had been stripped bare. No one had ever exposed him so thoroughly.

"I want you," Ares heard himself say, and it was true. "I don't want you to leave."

"I'm not leaving," Leo said. And then he kissed Ares again, with such surety that Ares melted against his mouth. Leo's presence seemed miraculous. It still felt indulgent, like Ares had let a joke go too far. Ares hesitated, not from lack of desire but simply out of habit, and Leo noticed, drawing back with a small frown.

"Why?" Ares asked.

"Why what?"

"Why do you—" Ares stammered. "I'm—I'm not—"

"Oh," Leo smiled. Then he laughed. "That. I mean, besides the fact that you've saved my life at least twice now, I think you're handsome. Extremely handsome. And kind. You do everything for others and nothing for yourself, and you are so, so wonderfully good in bed." Ares rolled his eyes, and Leo laughed. "After last night, there's no use in you denying it. But even if you weren't. You're a good person, Ares. And I am exceptionally lucky that you've let me hang around as long as you have."

"I did try to get rid of you," Ares said. Leo hummed noncommittally.

"I suppose. And it might've worked if you hadn't seduced me at the same time."

"You kissed me first," Ares said. Leo smirked.

"That's because I know a good thing when I see one." Ares kissed Leo then. He didn't know if he believed even half of what Leo had said. But he wanted it to all be as real as the feeling of Leo's mouth against his, and the way their bodies fit together in the soft warmth of their shared affection.

44

Leo woke slowly, curled in Ares' arms. The fire had gone out some time in the night, and the room was cold, but Ares' chest was warm, and Leo snuggled against him, still half-asleep.

He might've drunk too much the night before, a result of their unrepentant honesty, and that Sal had brought a basket of snacks that was primarily liquor and assorted cheeses. Leo and Ares had shared its contents on the floor in front of the wood-stove, and Leo had fallen asleep embarrassingly early against Ares' shoulder. The next thing he knew, he was being tucked in, and then it was morning.

Leo shifted closer, throwing his thigh over Ares' hips, trailing his fingers through the soft dark hair of Ares' chest and stomach. The ways Leo wanted Ares were tangled altogether, the threads of them impenetrably knotted in Leo's head. He wanted Ares sexually and emotionally and physically; for Ares to be free to be wherever Ares wanted. For all their decisions to truly be theirs. It felt like a fantasy, but Leo couldn't stop reaching out toward it, desperate with the knowledge that he could maybe grasp it if he just knew a little more and understood a little better.

But then, Ares rolled onto his hip and wrapped his arms around Leo's waist. When they kissed, Leo tried to memorize the way Ares opened his mouth for him. The way he sighed and gasped and shifted, and how it was all soft and vulnerable and real. Leo couldn't remember the last time he'd been made so desperate by something so tender.

Leo trembled with it, as Ares turned them over, laying Leo on his back, fucking him slowly. Leo moaned around the words that sat on the tip of his tongue and felt Ares say them in the brush of his stubble against Leo's neck. Ares was rough and then gentle and then filthy at exactly the right moments, and Leo had never known how good it could be to be known by another person so thoroughly. Ares pinned Leo down, murmuring praise in his ear, as he drove into him, and Leo came entirely undone, with "Ares" tumbling over and over again out of his mouth.

"I love the way you say my name," Ares breathed, his lips warm and soft against the shell of Leo's ear.

"Ares," Leo moaned again, relishing the feeling of Ares' hips stuttering as he gasped a curse against Leo's skin.

The afterglow was interrupted by a sharp knock at the door. They froze, still wrapped in each other's arms. Leo might have forgotten where they were, and that other people existed, his cheeks flushing as he realized how loud he'd been.

"Not trying to interrupt anything," Mae's voice was bright and cheerful, as though she was truly unbothered by the racket he'd undoubtedly been making. "The wind's changed, and it looks like a bad snowstorm is rolling in. I imagine you'll want to get a move on unless you're going to be here for a few days. It's no problem with me. I've got plenty of pairs of earplugs."

Properly abashed, they got up and dressed. Leo peered out the window, watching the tumble of grey-white clouds rolling across the horizon.

"Looks like she might be right," he said, turning around to find Ares halfway through stripping the bed. Ares nodded.

"We've got to get a move on."

"Enough time for breakfast?"

It was nearly noon. They'd slept in. Mae furnished them with sandwiches and several knowing looks, before helping them back to the stables. They got the wagon hitched just as the first few flakes were beginning to fall. After they'd said their goodbyes to Mae, and she'd turned to go back to the house, Ares held the door of the carriage open for Leo. Leo pursed his lips.

"Really?"

"Humor me. Please. We're so close to Leyland Hall."

"You don't even know if he's there."

"Leo," Ares frowned. "Please."

Leo gave in without grumbling. It wasn't that he understood the risks any better than the day before. But he understood what it meant to Ares, who kissed him firmly before closing the door and climbing up into the driver's seat.

Even racing the snow, the ride back to Leyland Hall took more time than Leo expected. There were almost two inches on the ground by the time the stable boys were fetching a cart and helping to unload everything into it. The sky was getting dark, though it was barely three in the afternoon, and the wind was beginning to howl. Ares came out of the kitchens with Matilda, and a large hamper with steam billowing out the top.

"What's that?" Leo asked, as they started down the snow-covered path to the cottage.

"Treats from Fen," Ares grunted, hoisting the hamper up to the crook of his arm. Matilda bounded out ahead of them, prancing in the snow. Leo couldn't help but smile.

"She's happy you're home."

"I'm happy we're home," Ares muttered. "And she won't be quite as pleased when I don't serve her beef tips for her supper like she's been getting up at the big house." He reached over Matilda and unlatched the gate, pushing it open. "Spoiled rotten." Matilda charged up the steps and onto the front stoop, turning back around to bark at them, as if they weren't moving fast enough. Ares stepped back and let Leo go through first.

Perhaps it was the shelter, the security that the cottage would provide, but even with its windows dark, it was remarkable how much this place really did feel like home. Leo took the hamper from Ares as Ares fumbled in his coat pocket for keys, and Matilda squeezed her massive body between their legs. Ares cursed. Leo laughed. And then they were all tumbling into the foyer.

"This storm is really impressive," Leo said, watching the snow gust up against the patio window as he wolfed down his second biscuit. The fresh bread Fen had packed for them had been the item billowing steam, and it seemed a shame to let it get cold. Ares had shooed Leo out of the kitchen as he started a 'proper dinner,' and Matilda was feasting on some kind of scraps that Ares had begrudgingly set on the kitchen floor. "Bizarre, since it was practically temperate last week," Leo continued. "Do you remember those trees in the glade when we were hunting? Still green." Ares murmured something, avoiding Leo's gaze as he stepped out of the kitchen and headed into the foyer. Leo pursed his lips and sprung up, following Ares.

"Stay inside with Matilda and keep an eye on supper. I just want to check the coop. Fen said she got all the sheep into the barn."

"Did you do something to those trees?" Leo pressed. Ares rolled his eyes, and bent down for his boots.

"If I did, it was your fault," he grumbled.

"My fault? Explain."

"Leo, the chickens—"

"I'm sure Fen took care of the chickens too."

"She didn't say," Ares said. Leo crossed his arms over his chest, and Ares sighed heavily.

"You saw the extolations when we were in Warnock. I told you, it's a strengthening of magic. Temporary only."

"And?" Leo prompted.

"I thought you said you were clever?" Ares needled.

"You were kissing me and then..."

"You were pinned to the tree, and I was holding you there, and some of the magic just—It makes things grow."

"Makes the air warm? Makes it feel like spring?"

"I really thought we've been over this," Ares huffed and grabbed for his coat.

"Are you making it snow?" Leo demanded. Ares grimaced.

"If I thought it was capable of making it snow, I'd be trying a hell of a lot harder to make it stop."

"But you've been so stressed—"

"Leo, trust me, my sphere of influence only goes about this far," Ares stretched out his arms. Then he grabbed Leo's waist and pulled him in for a kiss. "Watch dinner for me. I just want to check on the chickens."

"The chickens aren't stupid."

"Yes, they are. They're chickens." Leo groaned, pulling away from Ares, trying to process what he'd just learned. He'd known Ares was a demigod. He just hadn't guessed at exactly how powerful Ares' magic was. No wonder Morrow was so hellbent on keeping him here. Leo went into the kitchen, opening a covered pan on the stove to find that it was full of cut potatoes. A gust of wind rattled the windows, as Ares came back into the kitchen, bundled in a heavy winter coat, a knit cap, and Leo's scarf. Or rather, Ares' scarf, that Leo had mentally adopted.

"You're really doing this?"

"I need to check the coop. And the goats."

"Ares."

"That's it. It'll be five minutes. Don't ruin the potatoes."

"Don't go out to the barn," Leo said. Ares rolled his eyes.

"Who said anything about the barn?"

"If you die in a snowdrift, I'll have 'Leo told him not to go to the barn,' carved into your tombstone."

"You're going to buy me a tombstone?" Ares batted his eyelashes, pressing his hand against the center of his chest. "How romantic."

"Shut up."

"That's probably the most expensive gift I've ever gotten," Ares said as he walked across the living room. "Make sure you pick a pretty one. If I'm not back in five minutes, give the potatoes a stir."

"Don't go to the barn," Leo said, as Ares yanked open the patio door. The cold rushed in on the wind, snow a blinding swirl in its wake. By the time Ares had pulled the door shut behind him, he was already practically invisible, his figure little more than a shadow against the white.

Leo waited a few minutes, stirred the potatoes, and then waited some more, trying to puzzle out the extent of Ares' abilities. He wondered if Ares knew himself, or if it had all just been trial and error. He'd said that no one had ever explained the extolations to him, and if his mother was already gone by the time Ares reached Andurnei had anyone taught him anything about his magic? Would he tell Leo, if Leo asked? Usually, Ares was only vague and cagey because he was trying to hide the tender parts of himself. Or protect someone else's. It made Leo crazy. It made Leo love him. And ultimately, Leo supposed, it didn't really matter. If Ares didn't know, maybe they could figure it out together.

Leo fussed with the potatoes some more, and then opened the oven to reveal a chicken, roasting merrily away inside. He got himself a beer out of the icebox and leaned against the counter, thinking about how he was going to have to find another grate to fire-call from. Would any fireplace work? Could he use the one in the living room? He doubted Ares made too many calls. But Leo would need to get in touch with Sidney again soon to see if he and Rookwood had made any progress. And then, of course, there was Leo's end of things.

Leo had almost asked Ares last night about the terms of the contract he'd made with Morrow, but then their conversation had turned so intimate, it hadn't felt right. It would be easier now that they were home.

Thinking about the case, the terms of Ares' contract, made Leo want his notebook. He wandered into the foyer and then the study, where he'd deposited the sketchbook that he'd repurposed on their ride. He glanced out the front window and noticed that the wind, at least, had tapered off considerably, but there was still no sign of Ares. It had been at least twenty minutes, and the sky was dark. Leo put his notebook down and went into the foyer, shouldering into his coat.

"So ridiculous," Leo said, sitting down to put on his boots. The sound of motion by the front door alerted Matilda and she came padding in, watching Leo put on several layers of outerwear. "You're not coming," he said to her. "Stay here and watch the house." Matilda barked. "Look, I'm not really happy about it either, but someone's got to go pull Ares out of a snowdrift, and

I think I'll probably make quicker work of it than you will. Now be a good girl," Leo wedged himself between Matilda and the door and then tugged it open. Immediately, Matilda ran out the door and pounced on a figure who had just come through the cottage gate.

45

Oh, God. Leo hoped it wasn't someone elderly. Struggling to keep his footing on the slick path, he hurried after Matilda.

"Dammit, Matilda! Get off, you ridiculous creature. Get!" He managed to catch Matilda around the middle, and haul her backward, nearly knocking himself into the snow in the process. He reached forward, half to try and keep his balance, and half to give the stranger a hand up. "Christ, I am so sorry!"

The man who Leo only just managed to pull to his feet looked oddly familiar. Olive skin, dark hair tied back in an impressive knot, a solid bruise on his chin that fully distracted Leo from the fact that the man was wearing what looked very much to be a bathrobe.

"Oh, God. She didn't give you that bruise, did she? She's not usually like this with strangers, I don't—" The man's dark brow furrowed. Leo was talking too much, but his mind was reeling, trying to place him. And then Leo recognized him. "Dom Silva?" Oh, shit.

"Yes." Oh. Shit. "How do I know you?"

"Leo Quince," Leo said. It sounded like he was talking to a

client. He swallowed. "We met at the Ascension Party. And at your diner."

"Sidney's brother?"

"Yes! That's right. I—" Matilda barked so suddenly that Leo jumped. She was standing on the front porch, waiting again. Leo fumbled. "Fine. Alright." He couldn't leave Ares' brother standing out in the snow. What other choice was there? He'd just get Dom settled and then try to get outside quickly enough to intercept Ares. "You'd better come in. It's freezing out here. Are you wearing a robe?" Dom nodded as he followed along beside Leo, his gaze firmly set on the cottage.

Ten years, Ares and Dom hadn't seen each other, and somehow, Leo had stumbled into the middle of whatever their reunion was going to look like. Dom seemed shaken already, and Leo had no idea how Ares was going to react. Not to mention that Matilda was jumping around him the minute he'd stepped over the threshold like his pockets were full of beef tenderloin.

"She's gigantic," Dom said, patting Matilda with a small laugh.

"She's a menace." Leo reached over to help Dom, who was not only wearing a bathrobe, but had also, bizarrely, put on a wool cape. "Here, let me take your cloak, at least. Do you need ice for that jaw? It looks like you took a mean right hook."

"Where's Ares?" Dom asked, looking around as though he expected Ares to jump out of the woodwork.

"Ares is checking on the pasture. We only just got back—" He stopped himself. Dom didn't need the details, and Leo needed to hurry up and go find Ares. To warn him that the brother he hadn't seen in a decade was now standing in the foyer. "We've been out. It's a long story. But Ares is determined to get stuck in a snowdrift all for the sake of a few errant sheep."

"How do you know my brother?" Dom's gaze narrowed in on Leo so sharply, that Leo almost choked.

And then the patio door opened. Ares was back.

❧

Ares toed off his snowy boots at the door. He could see Matilda prancing around in the foyer. Presumably, Leo was trying to get her to go outside, which would be hopeless. She only liked to go out through the patio.

"Well, no damage to the hothouse," he called, walking across the living room in his socks, letting the warmth of the house thaw his numb toes. "The wind's died down again. I imagine we'll make it through the night without—"

Leo wasn't alone in the foyer.

Ares' body stopped as though he'd collided with a brick wall. He wasn't even sure his heart was still beating.

Gods, Dom had gotten tall.

He looked like their father. Would look even more like him in glasses. He remembered the way Dom had refused to wear his small tortoise shell frames when they'd first been prescribed. Two decades ago at least. They'd lost so much time, it made Ares' knees feel weak. Or maybe it was just that he'd stopped breathing.

"Dom?" Was it really him?

"Yes, Dom's here," Leo stammered. "I was just coming out to help, but then Dom arrived, and I thought it best to keep Matilda from mauling him." The bruise on Dom's chin was massive. His jaw was clenched tight.

"Are you alright?" Ares asked. Demanded. Dom nodded stiffly.

"Good," Leo said. "Good. So, I'll go check on supper and Dom needs clothes. Ares' room is—" he pointed up the stairs, and then slid around Ares, placing a firm hand on the small of Ares' back as he passed him, disappearing into the living room.

For a long moment, Ares tried to find words. Dom, his baby brother. The person Ares had done all of this for. Ares didn't want Dom in Andurnei with every fiber of his being. But he was relieved to see him.

It was relief that moved Ares. He was across the foyer, wrapping Dom up in his arms. He was real, solid, warm. It was wonderful and horrible all at once.

"What in Christ's name are you doing here?" Ares breathed. Something in Dom seemed to collapse, then, and Ares held him up as Dom sobbed into Ares' shoulder.

For years, Dom had held the last, biggest piece of Ares' heart. He was the person Ares treasured most. He was Ares' home. Ares' family. It was strange to be able to physically touch the reason for Ares' continued existence. He'd almost forgotten that Dom was a flesh and blood man, and not some phantasmic distillation of the idea of love and sacrifice. It was comfort that brought tears to Ares' eyes.

"How did you get here?" Ares asked, holding Dom at arm's length just so he could look at him again.

"It's a long story," Dom exhaled with a shudder.

"Upstairs," Ares turned him toward the steps, as a tidal wave of questions threatened to overwhelm him. "Let's get you changed. Why are you wearing a dressing gown? Dinner should be ready soon. What happened to your face?"

"I'm fine," Dom lied. Ares rolled his eyes. "It smells good in here. I guess you still know how to cook?" Ares snorted, nudging him in the back.

Dom was nearly as tall as Ares but wasn't as wide. Ares tore through his wardrobe and dresser, coming away empty handed for anything that would fit Dom, except for an undershirt, and a sweater Mrs. Goode had knitted him years ago. Dom stood in awkward silence behind him, and Ares tried not to think about what his room might be revealing about the person he'd become.

"Leo's trousers will likely fit you better. Give me a minute," he said, and left the room.

Ares shook the jitteriness out of his shoulders as he went downstairs, rolling up his shirtsleeves for something to do with his hands. What was he going to do with Dom? What was he going to say? How had he never planned for this happening?

He'd never thought it was going to happen. Dom had been sequestered, eternally nineteen in Ares' perception, because Ares was never going to get to see him grown. But now that he had, Ares' world had been jolted into perspective, and he still wasn't sure what he was seeing.

The door to the study was cracked open, a yellow light coming through the doorway told Ares that was where Leo had held up. He knocked once and then nudged the door open, not waiting for an answer. Leo was sitting in the corner of the over-stuffed couch, where Ares had put him when he'd first arrived. A book was spread across his knees and Matilda was curled up at his side, and Ares was surprised at how relieved he was to see Leo sitting there.

"How's it going?" Leo asked. Ares shrugged, tried to answer and failed to find any words that fit the bizarre mix of emotions he was feeling.

"I need to borrow a pair of your trousers for Dom. Mine won't fit him."

"Most of my things are up in your room," Leo said. Ares remembered then that they had moved them when Alondra had come to stay, and he flushed at the thought of Dom seeing that Leo's clothes on Ares' dresser. "Here." Leo got up and fished around on the desk beneath the coat and outerwear he'd stripped off. He produced a plain black pair of work pants. "I didn't like the cut of these, so I left them down here." He handed them to Ares, and Ares wanted to kiss him.

"Thanks."

"No problem. I'll have dinner in here. That way you two can talk."

"I don't know what to say to him," Ares confessed. Leo smiled and stepped closer, running a hand over Ares' exposed forearm.

"Just be honest with him. He'll understand."

"I don't think he will."

"Trust me," Leo said, and then he leaned up and kissed Ares gently. Leo lowered himself back down, the heat of him still warming Ares' lips.

Ares realized that he loved Leo very slowly and then all at once, the way the sun crept over the horizon at dawn. He couldn't say it. He couldn't do anything about it. But it was there all the same.

Ares turned around and left, going back up the stairs in a daze. He handed Dom the trousers and turned toward the door to give his brother some privacy and to try and catch his own breath. One thing at a time.

"You're alright?" he asked Dom again, remembering suddenly the bruise on his brother's chin. If there was someone Dom needed protection from, frankly that was an easier problem to solve than most of the other ones on Ares' docket.

"You can turn around," Dom said. "And what's on your arms?" Ares glanced down to see the extolations on his skin glowing faintly. He hadn't noticed.

"Oh—" Before he could figure out what to say, how to start revealing their family lineage, Dom tugged up the sleeve of the sweater he'd just put on and Ares could see the etched vines, curling their way up Dom's forearms. His stomach sank.

Dom had used magic. The thing Ares had swore to protect

him from. The whole reason Ares had trapped himself in Andurnei.

"Did someone tell you what we are?" he managed. "Or did you figure it out on your own?"

"A little of both."

"They're called extolations. When you make an offering to a deity, and they're pleased by it. Or if you cast something that they like, you might get them. Some people call them Atlasions. Marks that show you bear the weight of the gods."

"So, we are, then?"

"Great, great grandsons of Demeter. Yes." It was so strange to say it aloud, but Dom seemed to take it in stride, rubbing thoughtfully at the bruise on his chin. "I'm sorry about Matilda. She's usually better behaved."

"Oh, that's fine. She didn't give me this," Dom smirked as Ares opened his mouth to ask who did. "How long have you had her?" Dom interrupted.

"Since she was a pup. About five years or so."

"Have you been here the whole time? At Leyland Hall, I mean." Ares pursed his lips. He should've known that for every question he had, Dom would have one of his own.

"Pretty much. Come on. Supper's almost ready." And Ares would need it to help him get through the truths he suspected he was going to have to tell. Though, if he had his way, he was going to get to ask his own questions first.

46

res got Dom settled at the kitchen table and went to fetch a growler of beer from the icebox. Ares wasn't a big drinker, but alcohol was likely to make whatever came next easier to swallow.

"This is the part," Ares prompted while his back was still turned, "where you tell me how you got here."

"I will if you will," Dom returned, ever the obnoxious little brother. Ares could only pretend for a few moments that he hadn't missed it.

"You first."

"Do you remember Jonas Rookwood? He was a regular customer for years. Tall and broad with tattoos all over." Ares grunted in the affirmative. Intriguing would have been the word he'd have used to describe Rookwood ten years ago. Before Ares knew that the rumors the townsfolk liked to spread about him were probably true. "Well, he's not—I mean, he's a demon, as it turns out."

It was strange to have the rumors Ares was just thinking of immediately confirmed. He had nothing against demons or any other sort of magical being, but what made his chest tighten as

Dom continued his story, was the fact that Dom was speaking about this demon like he was a friend.

The reason Ares had come to Andurnei, had made a deal with Edmund Morrow, the whole of it, had been to protect Dom from magic. From the same fate had befallen Ares, and their mother, and meanwhile, Dom had been getting friendly with a Duke of Hell. And Rookwood's friend, a fae who'd fallen on hard times. Lost his magic. Asterion.

Ares clenched his teeth, trying not to have any reaction to the name at all. He'd never met Asterion. He'd seen him. It was hard to miss him. He was more handsome than his older brother Kephisto. And often more inebriated.

"So, I've been renting your room. Regularly, not just to Asterion," Dom said. He cleared his throat, and Ares glanced over at him. His brother was staring into a half-full glass of beer, his cheeks turning pink. "But also to Asterion. And, uh… I had told him about you. I mean, Jonas had already said he'd help me look for you, and we found out you were at Leyland Hall, and Asterion's brother— You probably already know that his brother—"

"Is my employer," Ares said shortly, stirring the potatoes with more vigor than was strictly necessary. Dom nodded.

"So, Asterion said he'd come through with me."

"Generous of him," Ares said. Dom's cheeks turned crimson. Good Gods. Ares didn't really need Dom to tell him more. But he was annoyed that he wasn't.

When they were younger, all serious conversations happened in the kitchen, one of them hunched over the stove or half in the icebox, the other rambling on about whatever incident had impacted them so dramatically that it needed a brotherly sounding board. Usually, it was some injustice leveled against them by their parents or teachers. Sometimes it was a crush or a friend. Very occasionally, it was actual major life choices. When Dom was choosing what college to go to, they'd been in the kitchen so long that Ares had basically cooked a four-course meal.

But now Dom was rushing through his story, talking around a fae prince who seemed like more than just a friend, and Ares was torn between being hurt that he wasn't being told the whole story, and furious about what he knew. Dom shouldn't have been within a hundred yards of Asterion of Andurnei, let alone traveling the realms with him!

Dom finished his story without sufficient explanation of what had happened to his face or where Asterion was now. They'd been separated by the Queen Dowager, which was frankly better than Ares had anticipated. It gave him an opening. Now he just had to sort out how to broach it. He dropped a plate in front of Dom.

"Let me take a plate to Leo. But you start. Don't wait for me."

"He's not joining us?" Dom asked, already digging in.

"He said he'll eat in his room. Trying to give us some privacy, I think."

"Oh. How long has he—?"

No. If Dom was keeping secrets, then so was Ares.

"Eat, Dom. I'll explain what I can in a minute." And with that, Ares took a plate full of chicken, potatoes and green beans down the hall to Leo. The door to the study was ajar, and Ares knocked it open with his elbow.

Leo was sitting on the sofa, pencil flying over the sketchbook he'd stolen of Ares. He barely glanced up at Ares' face, when his brow furrowed and he paused.

"What's wrong?"

"He's lying to me," Ares hissed, handing Leo his plate. Leo frowned.

"What do you mean?"

"He's been... Magic. He knows about it."

"Well, he lives in Hindry. And he's not an idiot. And also, isn't he magic? A demigod, like you." That was far too practical for Ares. He growled, his fists tightening at his sides. "Ares. Stop. It's okay. Just talk to him."

"I'm not good at talking."

"You're better than you give yourself credit for. Besides, he came looking for you. He wants to talk. You're his brother." Ares exhaled, deflated.

Leo was right, as much as Ares was loath to admit it. Dom had come all this way. He hadn't given Ares up for lost, which seemed impossible. But then, he wasn't doing anything the way Ares had thought he would. Ares took a deep breath and glanced at Leo, who was holding his plate and looking up at Ares with a softness that made the back of Ares' neck feel warm. Ares turned and left, cursing himself for wanting Leo when it was absolutely the least convenient.

Maybe he could send Leo and Ares back together. Just until Ares could figure out what to do about Morrow and those damned wanted posters. Dom shouldn't be getting mixed up with magic in the first place, and Leo could go back and keep an eye on him until... Ares didn't know when. Until Morrow forgot, or Ares could get back, or Leo figured out the contract. Something.

Ares thought more about it as he ate. By the time he'd cleaned his plate, Dom was having seconds (one of the first things he'd done that Ares whole-heartedly approved of) and Ares grabbed the bottom of his pint glass for stability, as he began.

"I've been here for a while. Leo's only been here for about two weeks. Maybe a little less. I have a supplier who goes back and forth between Andurnei and the human realm about once a month, and I was going to send Leo with her, but I'll feel better having him go back through with you."

"Wait, what?"

"Leo. He can't stay here. Once you figure out the runes you need to get back, you can take him with you." Ares did know the Elmmond House runes. He just needed to figure out how to say so without confessing what Dom would likely see as Ares' greatest sin: that, in theory, if he hadn't had a contract binding him, he could have come home at any time.

"Wait," Dom interrupted with a shake of his head. "What do you mean? What about you? And mom?" Mom. Somehow, Ares hadn't thought Dom would ask about her. That had been royally stupid. He looked up out the window over the counter, where the lights from the big house threw strange shadows over the trees in the orchard. "Is she...?"

"She's not here anymore."

"Not alive?"

"Not like she was." Ares cleared his throat. He wasn't ready for this conversation. He wasn't ready for any of this. "It's hard to explain."

"Try."

"Don't worry about it," Ares managed, though he hated the way it sounded coming out of his mouth. Dom did too, judging by the derisive snort he gave. Ares sighed and tried again. "Dom."

"If you have a way back, why didn't you come home? This supplier. Why couldn't you come with her? Is it because of Mom?" Ares' stomach churned. This whole conversation was headed toward disaster. The realization of how bad of a situation Ares had placed himself and his brother in landed on him like a boulder. He was going to be sick.

"I don't want to talk about this."

"Well, Ares, I came a hell of a long way to talk about it,"

Dom snapped. Ares fixed his gaze on the orchard over Dom's shoulder and tried to steady his breathing. He was floundering.

"It doesn't concern you."

"It doesn't concern me? Ares. You *disappeared*. For *ten years*." Ares forced himself to look at Dom, and the hurt was all over his brother's face. He didn't understand. How could he?

"I did what I—"

"You left me!"

"I was protecting you."

"From what?" Dom demanded.

"From all of this!" Ares gestured around. "This world is not—"

"Trust me, Ares. I know what this place is." He didn't. Because if he had, he wouldn't have come.

"Whatever you think you know isn't even half of it." Ares sat back and folded his arms over his chest to stop his shoulders from crawling up to sit beside his ears. He needed to explain. Apologize. Why couldn't he just do that?

"I know enough," Dom insisted with a sharp edge to his voice that brought Ares up short. He'd known his brother to be many things, but never bitter. Ares tried to diffuse.

"Dom, I'm not getting into this with you. I've got it handled, and you need to go home."

"And take Leo with me?"

"Ideally, yes." Though Ares doubted he could get Leo to go along with it. Before Ares could begin to puzzle that out, Dom pushed back from the table.

"You're being an ass. And I'm not going home. I'm going back to Paravel Palace."

Fuck. No. Dom could not stay in Andurnei. That, of all things, would be unacceptable.

"And that's how I know that you don't know how

dangerous this is," Ares said. "You'd have to be a fool to willingly get tangled up with these people."

"I need to help Asterion." So Dom *was* into Asterion. Great.

"You have no idea what you're talking about. He's a prince. He'll be just fine."

"You're being an asshole."

"Believe me, Dom. I know what I'm talking about."

"How can I believe you when you won't even tell me what's going on. Why didn't you come home?"

This was it. It was Ares' opportunity to apologize. To explain where everything had gone wrong: that Morrow had entrapped their mother into tending for his orchard, and instead of trusting that she knew what she was doing, Ares had come rushing in with ideas of heroism and caught himself in the same snare. Shame choked him. And fear that Dom would never forgive him held him back from saying the true thing.

"Because I'm doing what's best for all of us." It was what he had thought ten years ago. He wasn't sure it was what he thought anymore.

"You don't get to decide that!" Dom threw up his hands, and Ares suppressed the brotherly urge to turn over the table in response, since they'd moved swiftly into dramatics. "I'm not a kid anymore, Ares. You don't get to tell me what to do."

"You're acting like a kid."

"Oh my god," Dom leaned back in his chair, staring up at the ceiling. "I need a cigarette," he muttered. Spiteful little twerp.

"You're smoking again?" Ares demanded, because it was a far easier argument to have, and Dom stormed out of the kitchen with a huff.

A panic that Ares had not anticipated had him scrambling to his feet, calling out for his brother to wait. He couldn't lose him again. Ares charged through the house, into the foyer, just as Dom swung out the front door in Ares' coat and garden boots.

Ares steadied himself with a hand against the wall and tried to take a breath. Overall, it had gone about exactly as badly as he'd expected. That was comforting, at least.

Leo peeked out of the study just as Ares was pressing his forehead against the back of his hand on the wall. Ares closed his eyes and shook his head.

"That sounded... not great." Ares chuckled in spite of himself. Leo padded out into the foyer and put his hand on Ares' shoulder. Ares sank into his touch and opened his eyes to see Leo's sympathetic wince. "Do you want to talk about it?"

"Like I said earlier, talking isn't really my strong suit." Leo slid an arm around his waist, pushing his body close to Ares, and Ares leaned against him, glancing toward the door. "I should go get him."

"Let him cool off," Leo said. "Should take about fourteen seconds." Ares snorted, and Leo kissed him on the cheek, before tugging him back toward the kitchen.

47

Leo got the growler of beer from the icebox and joined Ares at the table, where Dom's empty plate still sat. Before he took a seat, he grabbed the plate and put it in the sink.

"So," he said slowly, pouring beer into a cup for himself. Ares shook his head, staring at his own half-full glass like it was saying something to him. Leo took a breath. "Can I guess?"

"Sure."

"You told him to leave."

"Of course I told him to leave," Ares looked at Leo with a furrowed brow. "The whole reason I'm here is so he doesn't have to be. That was—"

"In your deal with Morrow."

"He can't hurt Dom," Ares said vehemently. "I mean, that was part of my deal. Mom had tried... Our mother's deal said that he couldn't hunt us. He couldn't come to Hindry and try to bring us here. But of course, I came, so that—" Ares shook his head and swallowed. His gaze went back to his beer and guilt came off him in a wave. Leo's heart ached for him.

"You didn't know."

"No. I didn't. But I should have trusted that wherever she was, whatever she was doing, it was for us."

"You were just a kid," Leo offered. Ares scoffed.

"I think we're just bad at this. My family," he sniffed, looking up at Leo with a sardonic smirk. "It was stupid of me to think Dom would react any differently."

It was, but Leo wasn't about to say so. Instead, he took a drink and tried to think.

"You said Morrow can't hurt him?"

"He can't hurt either of us, physically," Ares said. "I made it a part of my deal with him, but I didn't know then about what caring for the orchard actually meant. That it wasn't Morrow I had to worry about, really." Leo mulled this over in the heavy silence that settled over the table. Morrow wasn't hurting Ares. The trees were. It was a nasty little loophole, but Ares had agreed to tend them. And his mother must have agreed to the same thing to keep her sons safe.

"Was she here when you got here?" Leo asked eventually. Ares' chest fell, and he took a drink before he shook his head.

"Not as I knew her. I mean, technically, she still *is* here. Or she was, for a long time. Maybe not anymore." When he looked up at Leo, his eyes were wet with tears. "I don't know how I'm supposed to tell Dom that, though. Maybe it was selfish, but I never thought I'd have to."

"He'll understand," Leo said. Ares snorted.

"Would you?"

"Eventually," Leo offered. "Probably. But I don't think you're going to be able to keep pushing him away. You can't really expect him to leave now that he's found you."

"Morrow might not be able to hurt him, but that's not enough to keep him safe. I didn't—I still don't understand the nuances of the contract. I know that now, but I can't—"

"You have to tell him," Leo said. It was the one thing he was certain of. "You can't keep this a secret. None of it. It's the only way to protect him. Please tell me you see that, Ares." Leo's chest tightened as Ares swallowed and breathed and didn't answer. Frustration bubbled up inside Leo, and before he could stop himself, he spoke again. "You really are bad at talking, aren't you?"

"Glad you're finally starting to get it."

"At least if you explain everything to him, he can make an informed decision."

"I don't want him to make a decision. And if he'd just leave, he wouldn't have to." Leo pursed his lips and stared at Ares. He was amazed at the man's pigheadedness. Which was really saying something, considering Sidney was his brother.

"That's stupid," Leo said. It was the kindest thing he could say. Ares gripped his beer bottle tight. "You can't make decisions for other people."

"I'm trying to protect him."

"You failed," Leo said. Ares' jaw dropped, his eyes wide in hurt. It would have been kinder for Leo to slap him, and Leo regretted it instantly. "I mean—"

"I failed," Ares' voice was rough and choked.

"Not—"

"No, you're right. Because he's here. So, I did fail."

"But he's not... he's not trapped. He can still leave," Leo said. There was a sharp knock at the door, and Leo stood as Ares sank deeper into his chair. "Look. Ares, I'm— You need to be honest with him, but we can figure this out." Silence. Nothing. Leo exhaled. "I'm going to let him in, and we'll get him a drink and we can all talk about it." He didn't wait for Ares' response, because he doubted there would be one. All he thought about as he walked to the door was that he'd fucked this, badly. But up until now, Ares had always met Leo's sharpness with barbs of his own. He hadn't expected him to wilt.

There was another knock, and Leo yanked open the door without bothering to look out the window. It was cold. Dom had been outside for at least twenty minutes, if not more. Frankly, Leo was surprised he'd lasted that long.

It took Leo half a second too long to register that it wasn't Dom standing on the stoop. It was a pale man with a stupid goatee and a cruel smile, that turned into wide-eyed shock. Leo took a step back, a retreat, and Edmund Morrow's expression morphed into a look of horrible glee.

"Mr. Quince. What a surprise."

Backward was the wrong motion. Leo needed to move forward so he could grab Morrow by the lapel and hold him still while he beat the shit out of him. He stepped up, into Morrow's outstretched hand, ignoring the immediate burn of it, the electric heat through his skin, white hot. He threw a haymaker with his right hand, connecting beautifully with Morrow's temple, knocking him into the wall.

Morrow scrambled, his arms stretched wide as he fell back amongst the coats and boots, against the bottom step of the staircase. Leo breathed out, stepped back, fists up and shoulders squared. It was a relief to be rid of hesitation. There was nothing in Leo's chest but rage. For Ares. For Sidney. For all of them. He could make Morrow pay, and he would. It was so much simpler than a court case.

But Leo had forgotten about magic. Which was stupid, because the muscles were still twitching painfully in his left shoulder where Morrow had run some sort of current through them. Leo took a step forward, and Morrow threw one hand down toward the ground, sending a bolt of sharp light to shatter the red tiles at Leo's bare feet. Leo jumped back, unable to avoid the shrapnel entirely, as Matilda and Ares burst into the room.

"Leo! Run!" Ares shouted, and then two things happened at

once. Morrow charged for Leo and Matilda tackled Morrow. Her teeth sank deep into his arm, and he fell halfway out the door with a yowl. Then there was a horrible, sickening crack, as a great black ball of fur came flying back into the house. Matilda's body skidded limp across the foyer floor. In the silence that followed, Leo couldn't make himself draw breath. And then Ares roared in fury.

The sound of Ares' rage could have spurred armies forward and it was enough to move Leo. He ran at Morrow, who was crouched on the stoop. Morrow ducked down and shoved up, pushing Leo hard enough that Leo flipped, landing painfully on his back in the snow.

"Shoot him!" Morrow shouted. Leo scrambled upright, his shoulders throbbing. Leo heard a gun go off in the same moment that he jerked forward with the force of the bullet that punched through his arm. Over Morrow's head, he could see Ares: wide-eyed, frightened, desperate, a hand reaching down toward his dog, the other stretching out toward Leo. Morrow lunged forward, and Leo ran.

48

The fur on Matilda's chest was scorched away in a wide stripe across her chest. Morrow was gone. Had chased after Leo. Gunshots that rattled through the endless dark, the only assurance Ares had that Leo hadn't been caught yet.

Matilda was panting but holding herself upright. She nipped at Ares' hand when he moved to touch her wound, and he swallowed and staggered to his feet. And then out the door.

If he could stop one of Leo's pursuers, that would be something. Give Leo a chance. A rifle cracked loudly. A rifle. Like he was an animal to be hunted. Morrow's quarry.

❧

IN THE HEDGEROW on the far side of the garden, a bullet came so close to clipping Leo's leg that he could feel the heat of it through his trousers. Or maybe that was just one of the hundreds of brambles that had torn their way through his clothes, finally catching and ripping at skin. He scrambled forward, down through the dirt, and then south, trying to loop back toward the cottage.

It was either there or Mae's. And there was too much exposed ground on the way to Mae's. The pasture between the garden path and the forest would be easy enough for Morrow and his men to watch. Leo could run, but if they'd gone back for horses, he wouldn't have a chance.

He'd almost made it out of the garden when he'd heard voices behind him. The rustling of plants, and footsteps in the snow. He ducked his head and ran, the glint of moonlight making the top of the orchard wall shine, turning great grey stones silver in the dark.

Leo charged forward, making peace with the reality of the hard, slick, unforgiving wall that he was about to attempt to leap up and grab the top of. If he missed, he'd be fucked. But likely he was fucked anyway, so he might as well try. The sound of his own breathing, each pounding footstep, thundered in his ears. There were a few spare feet of path below the orchard wall. It would be all he had to push off against. He had to get this right.

When his hand closed on top of the icy top of the orchard wall, his injured arm screamed out in pain. Leo grit his teeth to swallow a groan, flailed and then caught the top with his other hand. He pulled himself halfway up, his bare feet bloodied and scrambling on the stone below. There was no traction, and it took a second too long for him to find a foothold.

A bullet snapped into the stone beside his knee, sending another piece of shrapnel into the back of his leg. It was proper motivation. Leo dug in, pushing himself forward, and tumbled over the wall into the orchard, landing hard on his back against the ground.

THE SNOW BEGAN to fall more steadily as Ares got his feet under him and strode into the darkness, toward the sound of gunfire. Panic made sour bile rise in his throat, but the cold kept his eyes wide and focused. His mind attempted a half dozen warnings: you should have shoes on; you need a weapon; this is a bad idea. Ares ignored them all. He used to get in fights as a teenager. He'd gotten into fights with hooligans down in Laurel Grove. He didn't need a gun to hurt someone.

Ares stopped on the path between the house and the garden, squinting at the boot prints in the snow. He heard the crunch of footsteps before he saw the person making them and stepped back into the shadow of the big house. The moon was almost full and cast the grounds in shades of grey, but the glint of gunmetal telegraphed the guard's position.

Grabbing the barrel of the gun was easy. He yanked it out of the man's hands with a quick jerk, turning it around. The guard yelped, his eyes wide, hands up immediately in supplication.

"Where'd he go?" Ares didn't recognize his own voice, so full of hatred.

"I don't—"

"Quince. Where is he?"

"He ran toward the orchard, but he's not—I lost track of him! I don't—"

"I heard shots."

"I think it might have been a rabbit! I didn't—"

"Go back to the house," Ares said through gritted teeth. "Don't come outside again."

"But—" Ares cocked the gun.

"It wasn't a request," he said and turned toward the orchard.

LEO ROLLED onto his hands and knees as quickly as he could, wheezing, the wind knocked out of him from his fall. He heaved himself into the shadow of trees. Voices echoed behind the wall, but no one had tried to climb it. No one had followed him in.

Still gasping, Leo staggered deeper into the orchard. Every few steps he was tripping over tree roots, pain shooting across his chest, up his calves. One arm hung limp at his side.

He had to get through the orchard mostly because he didn't know if it would be safe to stay in it. Ares had been so injured here. The roots, he'd said. The trees were killing him, and through his own pain, Leo couldn't help but notice that the air was very still. The leaves and branches eerily silent, as the snow covered them in a heavy layer of white.

Leo slowed, risking a glance behind him as he came to a tree that seemed much larger than the rest. He caught himself on the rippled bark and winced at the sight of the trail of bloody footprints he'd left behind him. And the way small black tendrils began to lift out of the snow, curling into his tracks.

The tree beneath his hand made a sound. A low, echoing creak, the likes of which Leo had never heard before. He would have stumbled back if his legs hadn't felt so heavy. His breathing so labored. When he looked down, he couldn't see his feet anymore. Heavy, dark roots were wrapped around his ankles.

Leo leaned forward, pressing his forehead against the tree, trying to catch his breath enough so that he could scream for Ares. It would give away his position, but it was that or be eaten by a tree. At least a gunshot would be quick.

"Ares." Leo whispered. And then wheezed. Something in his chest was broken. Damaged. He tried to inhale. One shout was all he needed. He braced his palms against the trunk of the tree and took the deepest breath he could.

'Don't scream.'

Leo gasped. Nearly choked on air as he swallowed the breath that would have yelled for Ares. He whipped his head around, immediately making himself dizzy, but didn't see anyone. 'Be still, Leo. Let me help you.'

"Who are you?" Leo's voice was shallow again, burning in his throat.

'Leo,' she said. It sounded like a she, low and sonorous, almost echoing in his chest, as though her head was pressed against his sternum. 'Close your eyes and lean into me.'

"The... you? Are you— are you the tree?"

'Close your eyes, Leo. Let me take you home.'

❧

Ares' heart sank as he saw the four men standing outside the gate to the orchard. The lock lay broken on the snow by Morrow's feet, though even from a distance Ares could see that he was having trouble getting his guards to enter.

Three guns pointed at Ares as he began his approach, his own stolen rifle resting on his shoulder. Only Morrow didn't bother. He scowled at Ares; his face twisted in frustration.

"You've been harboring a known fugitive."

"To my credit," Ares said. "I didn't really know he was a fugitive until yesterday."

"Bullshit!" Morrow screeched. Ares ignored him. He walked through the cluster of guards and was too tired to be amused by the way Morrow took a faltering step back as though Ares was about to attack him. He could have, he supposed. But it wouldn't have mattered. Ares could no sooner raise a hand against Morrow than Morrow could against Ares. It was the most unfortunate feature of their contract.

Still, Ares had learned a long time ago that raging against Morrow was deeply and profoundly unsatisfying. It was better to scare him. And nothing frightened Edmund Morrow more than Ares not reacting to him. Ares pushed open the gate to the orchard with one hand and walked through it. He was halfway to the first row of trees before he could hear anyone follow him.

"Leo!" Ares called out. The trees threw Ares' voice back to him. He shouted for Leo again, and then Morrow was beside him.

"I didn't expect you to be so helpful."

"You won't touch him," Ares growled, starting forward again.

"He's a violent criminal!"

"He definitely isn't."

"He will be taken into custody, Mr. Silva."

"No, he won't." Ares said. "I'll open a portal and send him home, and that'll be the end of it."

"You don't get to order me around!" Morrow's voice was so grating when he got irate. High-pitched like a human mouse. Ares weaved between the trees and barrels of sap, scanning the snow for footprints.

"I'll kill myself before I let you hurt him." It wasn't a threat so much as a statement of fact. Morrow met it with a cracking laugh.

"Kill yourself then. Save me the trouble."

Ares frowned at this new development. Without him alive, who would tend the orchard? But still kept his head down. There was a divot behind his mother's tree, like the ground had shifted there. Ares held up a hand toward Morrow, and the man stopped just behind him.

"What?"

"I don't know yet." Really Ares just wanted a minute, if it was Leo, to figure out what he was going to do to get him out. He stepped up onto the roots that emerged from the ground, bracing one hand against the tree. In the dark it took him a moment to recognize the smear of dark blood against the bark. Footprints, red and wet, led up to the tree. But none led away.

"Is he there?" Morrow asked. Ares glanced up, looking into the lower branches of the tree as he turned back. He didn't see any sign of him. There were still leaves on the tree, but not so many that they would totally obscure someone. Where could he be?

"So, you're finally going to let me kill myself?" Ares asked. About five years ago, he'd been at his worst, and had strongly considered the option. That was when Mae had brought him Matilda. Ares stepped back onto the ground beside Morrow. "That's kind of you, I suppose. Done with the fucked-up tree magic then?"

"I've got another child of Demeter," Morrow said, crossing his arms over his chest. His mouth was a smug line. Ares considered what it would be like to punch Morrow.

"So, you've tricked some other poor fool into making a deal with you?"

"Not yet," Morrow shrugged. "I imagine it'll be soon coming though. He'll make one if it means stopping you from dying, I'm sure."

"Why does he care about me?"

"I don't know. By all accounts, you've been an abysmal brother."

Dom. In all the commotion, Ares had forgotten. He wasn't missing one person. He was missing two.

Ares' stomach sank. The blood froze in his veins. He couldn't breathe. He didn't think. Ares swung the gun from his shoulder, twisting the broad side of it toward Morrow, pinning him hard and fast to the trunk of the tree. Morrow yelped. Ares grit his teeth.

"Let him go."

"Why would I do that?" Morrow ground out, jerking his

shoulders, as though he would be strong enough to throw Ares off. Ares pushed back harder.

"I can think of at least one reason."

"You can't hurt me."

It was surprising to discover how little that mattered. Ares headbutted Morrow, with the desperate desire to draw blood. Just to cause him an iota of the pain that Ares was drowning in.

The magic that threw Ares onto the ground came out of the sky and earth with the force of thunder. A great crack of energy and a fission of golden light sizzled in the air between them. Ares was flat on his back in the snow, shoulders aching. He'd barely gotten himself up to his elbows when Morrow stepped forward off the tree and picked up the gun. His gaze was fixed on Ares, his eyes narrowed and suspicious.

Morrow lifted the gun to his shoulder slowly, raising the barrel in Ares' direction. It was an unfortunate time for Ares to discover how much he didn't want to die. How much he needed to be alive to rescue his brother and find Leo. If one attempt at an act of violence was enough to break the bonds of their contract, then it was all over. His mind raced with all the things he should have said when he'd still had the chance.

A small, bright burst of golden light, and Morrow fumbled the gun. It fell into the roots of the tree, and he shook his hand out with a hiss, glaring at Ares before storming back toward the gate.

Shaking, hollow, Ares got to his feet. He staggered over to where Morrow had dropped the gun, glancing up into the branches again. Still no sign of Leo. Ares leaned down, grabbing the barrel where it stuck up out of the ground. He tugged and couldn't shift it. The stock of the gun was sunk, not into the dirt, but into a small knot of slowly twisting roots.

49

Leo was dreaming. He had to be. Or he was dying, and his last words were going to be whatever he mumbled in a hallucinatory conversation with a tree.

He closed his eyes and leaned forward, hands pressing against the bark and into the solid, warmth of wood that gave way like the stretched canvas of a boxing ring beneath his palms. His chest was flush against it. Then his thighs, then his knees. And then his feet were loose, and he was stepping through. Space, air, stretched around him like elastic and he could feel pressure on every single part of his body all at once. He groaned at the pain of the bullet wound, the cuts on his legs and feet being pressed, his muscles aching with a tightness and a tingling too close. For a moment, even his lungs compressed, his throat so tight he couldn't even gasp for air.

'Come back for him.' The voice in his head was as clear and sharp as bell. 'Help my son. Come back for Ares. Promise me.'

'I promise,' Leo swore with the last, fleeting moment of consciousness. 'I promise.'

And then it was over.

Leo staggered forward, his feet dragging against a leaf

covered ground. It was cold, but there was no snow. And there was light. Dawn.

He tripped over a headstone and fell to his knees, catching himself with both hands in the dried leaves. The air had a briny tang to it, and Leo could taste it in the back of his throat as he inhaled through what he assumed was going to be a ferocious pain in his left arm. But there was no pain. Just the cool sharpness of damp, autumn air.

Leo could feel the blood drying on his skin. The sleeve of Ares' sweater was torn and soaked in crimson. Slowly, Leo sat back on his heels. He was breathing normally. He was not in pain. Was he dead? Was he dreaming? His toe hurt where he'd stubbed it against the headstone, but there was no bullet hole in his arm anymore. There were no cuts on his feet. Leo swallowed and looked up.

The graveyard wasn't large. It extended a little way up a hill, and to the right was a small chapel, white stucco, greying with age. Leo knew the chapel, where so recently his brother had been kidnapped and had nearly bled out. It was prettier now. The stained-glass windows were just beginning to catch color from the morning light. Less than two feet to his left was a tree. It was tall and thick, with grey-brown bark and bare branches that stretched high into the morning sky. Its roots were wrapped around the headstone that had brought him to the ground. Leo slid the leaves off the stone with a shaking hand.

Demetrius Silva
He passed the melancholy flood with that grim ferryman which poets write of, unto the kingdom of perpetual night. His blessing is felt to the most distant and far-flung shores.

It was, Leo reflected, the strangest way he had ever been

introduced to someone's parents. His breath shook as he wiped the tears from his cheeks with the back of his hand.

"Young man." Leo looked up to see the pastor of the small church, an elderly man with dark brown skin and a shock of white hair coming carefully down the hill toward him. It took Leo a moment to remember how he knew him, but again, the night of his brother's near-death was the answer. Father Michaels, Leo remembered, as the wind took one side of the man's brown tweed coat and threw it flapping open to reveal the simple black outfit of the clergy, collar and all. "Are you quite alright?"

Was he? Not really. He'd left Ares. And he had to get back to him. He'd made a promise. And even if he hadn't, getting back to Ares would occupy him from this moment until he accomplished it. It could be his life's work, he supposed. But he hoped it wouldn't take that long. The man knelt beside him in the leaves, and Leo swallowed.

"I've been better," he said, meeting the man's curious gaze with a weak attempt at a smile.

"Let's get you upright, then. I often find that helps." The clergyman offered Leo a hand, and Leo took it, slowly getting to his feet.

"Do you remember me?"

"Mr. Quince's brother? I hope we're meeting under happier circumstances."

"I suppose we are, in some respects. Have you seen Sidney recently, by any chance?"

"I know he and Mr. Rookwood have been traveling quite a bit, but you might check the cottage." The cottage. Of course. Leo nodded looking down the path in what he was fairly certain was the right direction. "Though I'd recommend shoes first. The path's only dirt and gravel."

"Of course," Leo said, taking a shaking step toward the road.

The man held firmly to his arm, and Leo turned back to look at him.

"Shoes, lad. At the very least."

It was only a twenty-minute walk to the garden cottage and was still early when Leo arrived. He was wearing spare shoes and a coat from the church donations shelf, which Leo had promised to return once he'd found his own. He'd left quite a bit of luggage at Elmmond House, and he was hoping it'd still be there. But he needed to speak to Sidney first.

Leo knocked hard and waited. No answer. He took a step back and looked up at the house. There was at least one light on on the second floor. Before he could step forward and knock again, a ghost appeared on the front stoop. Leo wasn't any more prepared for it than he had been when he met Sal, but he tried to wipe the shock from his face as quickly as he could. The ghost's arms were crossed over her chest, and she had her head cocked to the side, like he was a curio in a shop window. Leo leaned back on his heels.

"Hello. Sorry, is Sidney in?"

"You're his brother, aren't you?"

"I am," Leo nodded. "And I—"

"I thought you were in Andurnei at the moment."

"I was."

"He was hoping to find you. He and Jonas just left for there, not all that long ago. Paravel, I think." Leo stiffened.

"What?"

"I don't know when they'll be back. It had something to do with Asterion. They told me, but I wasn't really paying attention."

"Is there any way I can get in touch with them?"

"You could try a fire call, I suspect," she shrugged. "I don't suppose you know any runes?"

"Only the ones for... for here," Leo said. The ghost shook her head, small tendrils of hair floating down out of her braid, wisping into thin air at the edges.

"Well, that's not going to do you any good. You can come in, I guess. I might be able to talk you through a few."

"Thank you," Leo sighed, relieved. He took a step forward, and she didn't move out of the way quickly enough. His hand brushed through the side of her skirt, and it felt as though his fingers had all gone numb. Leo jerked back, and the ghost shivered off to the side.

"I am so sorry," Leo apologized, massaging his fingers. She trembled as though a chill had gone through her and arched an eyebrow in his direction.

"Not at all. It's rather intimate of you."

"I didn't mean—" he stammered, his cheeks heating. She laughed.

"I'm only teasing. You're a bit heartier than Sidney. He practically shrieked when we first met. Honestly, I felt terrible about it. That was before I got to know him, of course. Maybe he mentioned me? I'm Delilah. Delilah Heatherington."

"Leo Quince," Leo swallowed. She looked him over appraisingly, and then seemed to make some decision, nodding and putting her hands on her hips.

"Well, Leo— can I call you Leo? The key's under that planter there. Why don't you grab it up and come inside. You look a bit peaky, and I think there's scones in the breadbox leftover from yesterday."

"Thank you," Leo said. He tilted the planter to the side and found a small silver key. By the time he'd unlocked the door, Delilah had already vanished inside.

50

Ares walked back to the house in a daze. He'd spent the last two hours in the dark and cold, inspecting every single corner of the orchard and had found nothing. There was no sign of Leo beyond the bloody footprints. He was gone.

It would have been stupid for Leo to go back to the cottage. Morrow was almost certainly waiting to see if Ares came out of the orchard with Leo in tow, and there was no way he wouldn't be watching the cottage as well. It wasn't a surprise when Ares got home to discover nothing new. No Leo. Foreign boot prints in the hall, but no further, as though someone had tried to come in and then thought better of it. Ares locked the door behind him, exhaustion and despair warring in his chest.

Matilda was laying in front of the fireplace, her head down on her paws. Ares watched her from the doorway, trying to get a grip on himself. She blinked at him and made a soft snuffling that to Ares' grief-addled brain, sounded like an apology.

"Stay there, Matilda," he said. He swallowed down the knot in his chest and went upstairs to grab the bag from Mae that Leo had left on the foot of their bed.

It was soothing to take care of Matilda. He soaked one of her dog biscuits in some of the blue tincture and took it to her. Ares got onto the floor beside her on the hearth and let his mind be occupied with checking her injuries. The heat and softness of her fur was comforting, even though his hands were shaking. He cleaned her chest and kissed her head, and Matilda ate her biscuit and then crawled into his lap and fell asleep.

The floor in front of the hearth was the last place he and Leo had slept together in the cottage. Ares stared at the room from the floor and tried to think beyond how terrible everything was. Leo was out there somewhere and in danger. Dom had been kidnapped by Morrow. Ten years of isolation and depression and loneliness hadn't done anyone any good, and it seemed so stupid now that he'd thought it could help. There was no peace in martyrdom, only more grief. It was ridiculous that Ares had to learn that the hard way.

Ares let his fingers sink into Matilda's fur, stroking her head and back as the hours wore on. Part of him was waiting for Leo, which was a dumb thing to do. Leo was smart enough to know not to come back to the cottage tonight. He'd probably gone to Mae's, which meant Ares would need to go there tomorrow. She could draw up a portal for them to go back Earthside, where they could get reinforcements and figure out how to save Dom. It was a good plan with one massive flaw: it would break his contract with Morrow.

Ares was bound to tend the orchard and the grounds of Leyland Hall. The harvest was in just a few days, and while "tending" was a word with some flexibility to it, shirking the harvest would almost certainly put him in breach of contract. He didn't know what that would do.

Leo would know. It was reassuring because it was undeniable. Leo had been researching the law for days. He'd wanted this for Ares longer than Ares had known to want it for himself.

Wanting things had been such a waste of time for so long, that Ares beat it out of himself, but Leo had brought it back. First in ways that made Ares blush to think of them. But then in other ways. Ways that felt like the first days of spring, where buds were sprouting and every plant held the promise of something new. Ares had forgotten that feeling. And now that he'd found it again, he couldn't give it up without a fight.

Eventually, he fell asleep, curled on the ground next to Matilda. When he woke, it was afternoon. His feet and shoulders ached, and in the process of getting up and dressed, he downed the rest of the blue potion, regretting that he hadn't done it the night before. He fed the chickens, collected the eggs and then let the sheep and cows out to pasture. The sky was the grey blue of winter, but the snow clouds were gone, and Ares breathed in the frigid air before going inside to pack a bag.

He left a note for Fen when he delivered the eggs to the big house, asking her and Warren to keep an eye on the animals, and telling her that he would be gone for a few days to visit the alchemist before the harvest. It was the sort of note he'd left before, so hopefully it wouldn't arouse any suspicion.

Matilda and Ares went slowly around the orchard, checking to be sure he hadn't missed anything in the dark before starting across the snow-covered pasture. Matilda kept pace with him; the only way Ares knew she was still hurting was because she wasn't loping out ahead like she liked to do. At the edge of the forest, they stopped for a break. Ares looked up the hill toward the big house and took a deep breath. Resolve was fortifying. It was also terrifying. He didn't know how to live a life outside of this place. He'd come here young and had forgotten so much. And he couldn't rely on Leo to fix it. To fix who he'd become. It was almost embarrassing that he'd asked Leo to save him. He should have been trying to save himself.

When he knocked on Mae's door, Ares tried to temper the

small ember of hope that Leo would be there already. He hadn't seen any signs of him on the way. There was no reason to think Leo would have been able to make the walk in the dark without a guide. Still, he was a little disappointed when it wasn't Leo who answered the door.

"You look like shite," Mae said immediately, stepping back to let Ares and Matilda into the house. Ares didn't point out that her face was covered in soot and the purple grime that covered her hands had an unhealthy thickness to it.

"Is Leo here?" he asked. Mae frowned and shook her head, and Ares felt his heart sink in his chest.

"Did you get into a fight or something?" She took Ares gently by the arm and walked him to the kitchen, leaving purple smudges on his coat sleeve as he recounted for her the details of what had happened. By the end of it, he was slouched at her kitchen table, and she'd poured them each a glass of whiskey and a cup of tea. Her chin was in her hand, and she was staring out the living room window toward the water.

"If he's not here," Ares ran his hand over the table between the two cups in front of him. "I don't know, Mae. Where else could he be?"

"He's not got any magic," she said quietly. "So, portaling on his own is out of the question. Is it possible he went to the big house? Would anyone there have been able to get him somewhere else?"

"I don't think..." Ares considered. "He doesn't know anyone else here. Except, well. He knows Prince Asterion. Knows of him, at least. I suppose he could have tried to go to Paravel."

"But does he know Asterion well enough to trust him? That Asterion wouldn't have turned him right back over to Kephisto, who would undoubtedly hand him off to Morrow?"

"I don't think so." Ares took a breath and tried to steady

himself. Hoping, wanting things, not despairing, was exhausting. How did people do it?

"I can help you get back Earthside, Ares. But I can't see how he would have gotten there." Mae grabbed her whiskey and took a sip. "What if we focus on your brother instead? Leo can take care of himself, and if Morrow has Dom under his thumb, that could be more pressing."

"He's waiting for me to mess up," Ares said. "Then he'll wheel Dom out to keep me in line."

"Undoubtedly. Which is the perfect time to get your brother back."

❧

"I don't think it's enough," Delilah said. Her apparition was cross-legged beside Leo on the floor in front of the hearth in Jonas Rookwood's bedroom. Leo's palm throbbed where he'd cut it to draw blood, and his fingers were sticky with gluey ash-paste. He groaned and dropped his head into his hands, being careful to keep his fingers out of his hair.

It was bad enough that he'd walked into this bedroom and been assaulted by the sight of lubricant and a large stone phallus sitting out on the bedside table. Now the fire call wasn't working because he wasn't magic enough. Even though he'd been marked, which, according to Delilah, was a good starting point. But apparently Ares hadn't fucked enough magic into Leo to make it worthwhile. Leo hadn't known he could be angry about something that he didn't really understand. But it turned out he could be and he was.

"Magic is stupid," Leo said.

"Cheers," Delilah said. "If I could drink to that, I would." Out of the corner of his eye, he could see her form shimmer as she stood. "I guess it's back to the library then."

They'd started in the library. Leo had been happier there, but he'd also been eating a half a plate of day-old scones: lemon poppy seed, Leo's favorite, as though Sidney had made them for him on purpose. Amidst several large, half-packed shipping crates, Sidney's notebook, recounting everything Leo had told him, was sitting in the center of the first wide table of the library. Books were open, hefty tomes full of law, and notes made on slips of paper in Rookwood's handwriting, detailing the different ways magic contracts could be negated.

Leo had skimmed while he ate, but he hadn't been able to get his mind off calling back to Leyland Hall. He could speak to Warren or Fen, and they could go get Ares for him and God, poor Ares. He was all alone, unless Dom had managed to get back through all the chaos, and Ares would be... Well, Leo didn't know precisely how he would be. Surly was the first thing that came to mind. Maybe Ares would be pleased that Leo was back Earthside, though Ares would have had to talk to the tree to find that out. Maybe he did talk to the trees. Leo had no clue, and it was enough to make him throw up his hands.

But there wasn't time for exasperation. Leo didn't have enough magic to fire call or open a portal back to Andurnei. Sidney's new beau would, though. And, as Leo figured it, Jonas Rookwood owed him one, because of the mental trauma that came with knowing that his sweet, innocent little brother Sidney had been thoroughly corrupted by a literal demon.

While he waited for Sidney and Jonas to return, Leo decided the best use of his time would be to continue their research. That way, when he made it back to Andurnei, he would have a plan to get Ares out of his deal with Morrow. A project was comforting anyway, and Leo spent the better part of the day making his own notes on top of Sidney's and coming up with the loose beginnings of a defense strategy.

He only noticed that night was falling because of the way

the light shifted in the room. Before it got dark, Leo took a break, walking up to Elmmond House to see if his luggage was still there. The butler was quick to fetch it, and looked pleased to see him, remarking that it wasn't often that people came back for their things. Paul and Evie had left a note for him as well, on a scrap of the firm's letterhead. It was the first time he'd thought about the law firm in a bit, and Leo considered what that might mean as he walked back to the garden cottage. Halfway there, Delilah appeared beside him, with a small smirk.

"You and Sidney make the same face when you're thinking hard about something."

"Yeah?"

"Yeah. Like you've just smelled something horrible." Leo rolled his eyes and decided to vocalize his thoughts. Delilah had been a very reasonable sounding board most of the day, after all.

"Is there a comprehensive study of magical law?"

"What do you mean?" she asked, frowning. "Like a law school?"

"Sure," Leo shrugged. Delilah shook her head.

"The Assembly keeps track of the legal goings-ons between different magical creatures and humans and things."

"Right," Leo nodded. "But what if your problem is with someone in the Assembly?"

"Then you're shit out of luck, I guess."

"So, why hasn't anyone pushed back against them? Started a magical lawyer service or something like that?"

"Well, it's not easy, what you're talking about. Different creatures are governed by different rules. And magic always involves some human exploitation."

"I mean, 'informed consent' is a thing."

"It sounds like you're talking about sex," Delilah said, wrinkling her nose. Leo shrugged.

"It would be sometimes, just by the nature of how magical transference works. But that's sort of beside the point. What I'm talking about isn't changing the way magic works. It's just helping people navigate the rules that govern it. So that what happened to Ares isn't happening to other people."

"What happened to Ares is the sort of thing tricksters and sorcerers thrive on."

"Well, maybe they shouldn't," Leo grumbled. He paused to hoist his suitcase up onto the stoop and then into the garden cottage. Delilah reappeared in front of him in the foyer. Leo straightened up, dusting off his hands.

"This idea you're having. This sort of, magical lawyer thing... it'll make you some enemies."

"Anything that helps the powerless defend against the powerful is bound to get someone's ire up."

"But that doesn't mean you shouldn't do it," Delilah said. Leo chuckled, and she smiled at him, and for a moment, Leo felt like things might end up okay.

That feeling faded as evening sank into night and Sidney and Jonas didn't return. Eventually, Leo forced himself to go to bed, climbing up the stairs to the guest bedroom, and collapsing without changing into the pajamas out of his suitcase. He slept poorly, tossing and turning in the empty bed. Visions of Ares bleeding out on the floor in front of the hearth flooded his dreams and kept him awake long into the night.

51

It had been a long time since Ares had gone into Leyland Hall proper. Usually, he didn't stray far from the servant's area, only going upstairs as far as the armory, which was tucked away in the northwest corner of the house. He'd forgotten how wide and tall the halls were. How small they made him feel. That was their purpose, of course, and he suppressed the sensation as best he could, as he followed Warren down the hall to Kephisto's office.

It wasn't the most subtle plan, and it relied heavily on Morrow and Kephisto being exactly as self-concerned as Ares thought they were. Mae had helped him with the details, and, half drunk in her living room, it had sounded more foolproof than it looked in the cold light of sobriety. It didn't help that Warren had been throwing him skeptical glances ever since Ares had asked for an audience with the prince. He paused outside the door to Kephisto's rooms and looked at Ares again.

"Are you sure?" he asked. Ares nodded.

"It's urgent."

Ares had changed into his nicest sweater and work pants with the fewest stains on them. He'd combed his hair and trimmed his beard and did everything else he could think of to make himself look respectable and trustworthy. He'd even used some of Mae's face cream. Warren pushed open the door and gestured for Ares to wait by the sofa, before sliding through the servant's door that would lead him to Kephisto's study.

For several long moments, Ares was left alone. He stepped toward the window that looked down over the western gardens, the line of the woods dark across the late afternoon sky. It was a nice view of the grounds; strange to see it from above as Kephisto saw it, instead of down with his hands in it. There was a small pit in his chest at the sensation of being away from it. Not bad, just different, he decided. One he'd have to get used to, because if everything went according to plan, he'd be gone soon enough.

"Mr. Silva," Warren emerged from Kephisto's study, pushing the door open. "Lord Kephisto will see you."

The study was a circular room with an oblong desk that didn't quite suit the shape of the walls behind it. Books, bottles and trinkets filled the shelves behind Kephisto, who sat at the desk, hands folded in front of him on the leather inset. His seafoam green hair was shining around his fair, almost glowing, cheeks. A high-collared tunic didn't fully hide a purple love-bite just below the angle of his jaw. Ares swallowed and bowed at the waist.

"My lord."

"Mr. Silva." When Ares looked up, he was surprised to see the intense look of studiousness on Kephisto's face. The prince was clearly trying to read him, and Ares wondered if he'd ever garnered so much scrutiny from his employer at any point in the last ten years. "Warren said you needed to speak to me on a matter of some urgency."

"Yes, sir," Ares said. Swallowed. Took a breath. Kephisto raised an eyebrow.

"Does this have something to do with that unfortunate disturbance from last night? Because Viceroy Morrow assured me that he had the situation well-in-hand."

"No, sir. Not as such. But it... well," Ares hesitated. "It does have to do with the Viceroy, my lord." Kephisto's mouth seemed to shrink, his lips forming a thin line as his eyes flicked toward the door, which Warren had closed behind Ares.

"Very well then. Have a seat, Mr. Silva." Ares did as he'd been bidden, doing his best to look penitent and uncomfortable. Kephisto cleared his throat and Ares looked up at him.

"Has Viceroy Morrow mentioned to you the issue we've been having with the trees, m'lord?"

"What sort of an issue?"

"Ah, well, it's a matter of the saplings, sir. They're not taking root like they should, and Mr. Morrow—I mean, Viceroy Morrow, hasn't brought us any more of the additional nutrients," he paused for emphasis, an arched eyebrow and a nod from Kephisto, confirming that he did in fact know about the stolen souls buried beneath each tree. "As a result, our production is decreasing significantly. I just returned from a visit to the alchemist, and she has her own concerns about waning production."

"I see," Kephisto said slowly, and Ares bit his tongue and wondered how much more blatant he was going to have to be to make sure Kephisto really did see.

"It's my understanding that the sap yields may not be what Viceroy Morrow has told you and others to anticipate. And without more trees growing, I'm not in a position to remove underproducing ones." He held up his hands to forestall a protest from Kephisto that wasn't coming. "Now, sir, I'm not trying to imply that Viceroy Morrow isn't holding up his end of the bargain. I just couldn't bear the thought of your reputation suffering due to his negligence. Not that it's my place, sir."

"It isn't," Kephisto said, but he didn't sound sure. Ares pressed on.

"You've been so generous to allow the Viceroy use of your property and your social standing," he said, practically reciting Morrow's own words from the letter he'd found in Leo's coat pocket when he'd gotten back from Mae's. If Leo had been present, Ares would have kissed him on the mouth for the additional assistance. "I don't want to see your name muddled up in complaints and concerns when people aren't given what they've been promised."

"People have come to rely very heavily on that elixir," Kephisto frowned. Ares nodded solemnly. "My own sister, for one. She's with child, and the potions revitalize her."

"Of course they do. There's no problem with the product, my lord. Only that there isn't enough of it."

"And you're telling me that's Edmund's fault and not yours?" Kephisto challenged. Ares frowned down at his lap, as though this wasn't exactly what he and Mae had anticipated.

"I have been rigorous in tending to the orchard, sir," he said. Then he began to roll up his sleeves. Kephisto leaned forward, and when Ares held out his arms, the prince jerked back, a sound of revulsion escaping from the back of his throat.

Mae had done a damn good job with the gouges, mostly prosthetics with a bit of illusion magic thrown in. She'd given him an injection as well, that had bulged under his skin, making it look as though his arms were riddled with veins, infected and purple.

"When I ask the Viceroy for further assistance, he has denied my requests," Ares said, adding a little bit of extra desperation in his voice.

"But you have a special sort of magic," Kephisto protested. "You're a grandchild of Demeter—"

"As is my brother," Ares said. "Who Viceroy Morrow is

aware of. But for some reason, Morrow won't allow me to bring my brother to Andurnei. If my brother could assist me, and if I were given more nutrients for the trees, I believe we could make up the difference in the yield. His magic could supplement mine, and we could be even more productive than before. But as it stands, I'm sorry to say, I believe Viceroy Morrow has over-promised. And he may be about to under-deliver, which will not—"

"Yes, yes," Kephisto was frowning deeply, even as he waved Ares' words away with a flap of his hands. "I take your meaning, Mr. Silva. Why will he not allow your brother to assist you?"

"I don't believe he trusts my loyalty, sir. But I have given ten years of my life to this project, and I have been a good groundskeeper to you, and have no desire to go anywhere else." The lies were sticking in Ares' throat, even though he'd prac-ticed with Mae to make them sound genuine. Hopefully Kephis-to's ego wouldn't let him hear anything past the flattery. "I'm not one to turn up my nose at gainful engagement from a good and generous employer. Nor is my brother. He would be glad to work for you."

Kephisto was quiet, watching Ares again with that same studious look he'd had before. Ares' stomach twisted. He'd either fucked the whole thing, or it was going to work, and he doubted there'd be any in between. He bit down on the inside of his lip and then took a breath.

"If it would be possible to discuss the situation with Viceroy Morrow. Perhaps you could ask—"

"Viceroy Morrow will do as I tell him in regard to my prop-erty and my staff," Kephisto snapped. "That being said, I don't like the implication that he's keeping things from me. Espe-cially not when these problems have readily available solutions, which only require slightly more work from him." Ares ducked his head, giving himself a small smile.

"Yes, sir. Of course, sir."

"Morrow is at Kinclere Estate at the moment, but I anticipate him tomorrow or the next day. When he arrives, you will give us a tour of the orchard, and we will discuss its underperformance, and how to remedy that low yield. Thank you for bringing this to my attention, Mr. Silva. You are dismissed."

"Yes, sir," said Ares, getting quickly to his feet. "Thank you, sir."

52

He'd been back at the cottage for less than an hour before doubt began to set in. Trying to turn Kephisto against Morrow was a major risk. If it worked, it would mean that Morrow would have to bring Dom to Leyland Hall, which Ares struggled to think of as a good thing.

Mae had insisted it would only help to have an ally, using Leo as proof of how far Ares had come when he'd stopped isolating himself. But he still hated the thought of leveraging Dom. And it didn't help him figure out what had happened to Leo.

Ares went about his evening chores with unsteady hands. Dom was safe where he was, for now. Kidnapped, maybe, but Morrow wasn't about to let anything happen to his bargaining chip. Where was Leo? Mae promised she'd send word if he turned up. And Ares dragged his feet walking around the perimeter of the back pasture where it butted up against the woods in case Leo had been waiting for him there. He halfheartedly shooed sheep and cows toward the barn, keeping an eye on the fence, looking for anything that might have been a sign from Leo that he was there. That he was alive.

The sun slowly began to sink down toward the horizon, the sky vibrantly pink and orange behind the line of dark trees and the rolling field of the back pasture. Ares made his way back to the barn, the last of the livestock trundling inside, rounded up by Matilda. It was a beautiful sunset. The sort of vista that usually brought Ares some peace and comfort. Let him feel like he'd done the right thing and made the right choices. It was the sort of thing he wished he'd shown Leo before... before every-thing. It would have been the perfect time to say what he'd been thinking.

But Leo was gone, and between the pink and orange light in the sky the two colors bled together turning the distant clouds an unnatural shade of red. A gash in the sky. Blood in the snow and on Ares' mother's bark. And with it came the thought that Ares had studiously been avoiding: Leo might actually be dead.

Ares' throat was so tight he couldn't sob. He swallowed instead and called for Matilda, latching the barn door behind her once she trotted out. The walk back to the cottage was longer and shorter than Ares wanted it to be, and before he could think too much about it, he went into the kitchen and opened a bottle of cherry wine.

A mug was the nearest thing at hand, so that's what a third of the bottle went into. He didn't drink it fast, but he didn't let it linger either. Why not? There was nothing else to do until tomorrow. He could be sober by then. Ares was halfway through his second mug of wine when there was a knock at the door.

His heart leapt, even as he told himself firmly, 'no. Don't be stupid. He's gone. He's gone. He's gone.' Ares pulled open the door, half hoping it would be Morrow. Hoping for a fight. That would feel good. A fight. Someone to lay his fists into. Have some magic fling him into a wall and remind him what pain was really like.

But it wasn't Morrow. And it wasn't Leo. It was Warren, and a little behind him, Fen, both in their coats and hats and boots. Ares squinted at them.

"What's up?" he asked, trying to not sound like he was two thirds of the way through a bottle of wine. He wished he'd left the mug in the kitchen.

"We're going down into town," Warren said. "Kephisto's out so…" he trailed off, giving Ares a shrug and glancing nervously behind him at Fen.

"Where's Julian?" she asked. Ares had to think an extra moment before he remembered that Julian was Leo. It seemed like such a stupid lie now. He snorted and tried to cover his wine-stained mouth with his hand as a laugh became a whimper, and tears sprang to his eyes.

"Fuck," he gasped. Warren looked like a frightened rabbit and Fen's expression was a mask of barely contained rage. Her anger was so misplaced but devastatingly kind. Ares cleared his throat as best he could, shaking his head. "Julian's gone."

Fen pushed past Warren and pulled Ares into a hug. He was so startled he nearly dropped his mug. She pulled back, her lips pursed, her brows knitted together in a frown.

"Come on," she said. "Get out of your barn clothes and put on something else. We're going out."

And why not? He had nothing else to do but wait for his plan to blow up in his face. He stumbled upstairs to get dressed, and when he came back down, it seemed that Warren and Fen had agreed that the only topic of conversation that was off limits was Julian Flint. Which was perfectly fine. It was clear they thought he'd left and not been killed, which was alright too, because Ares couldn't manage anyone else's grief at the moment. He was barely managing his own.

The walk to Laurel Grove was spent listening to Fen and Warren speculate about where Kephisto had gone and which of the new valets that had just been interviewed would actually be brave enough to take the position. Ares was surprised when Warren steered them toward Fitzwilliam's instead of one of the livelier establishments. They settled at a table in the corner, and Warren went up to the bar to get drinks, as Fen looked around appraisingly.

"This is your favorite bar, isn't it?" she asked. Ares nodded.

"It is. But we can go somewhere else."

"No, no. It's nice. Quiet." She gave him a smile and then patted his forearm. "You'll be alright, you know?" Ares wanted to snort. In all likelihood, he was going to be alone until he ended up in an early grave. That was, he supposed, ultimately alright. Ares swallowed and forced a smile and a nod.

"I know," he said. Fen squeezed his arm and Ares appreciated it, for all the good it did.

After a few hours, Ares could barely stand, and he felt better primarily because he couldn't really feel anything at all. Halfway to Warren's nan's house, he started crying. Tears streamed down his cheeks unbidden; he hadn't even sobbed. He hadn't known that he could cry like that anymore, but he was. Fen curled around his arm and called Julian Flint a bunch of horrible names, and Ares started laughing, because what on earth was funnier than cursing the existence of a man who'd never existed at all? And then Warren was shushing them both and pulling them over his Nan's front stoop and into her parlor.

"Keep your voices down! Fen—No. Fen, shush!"

"He's a rat bastard, Warren!"

"Yeah, but Nan's not. And she's asleep!" Warren hissed. Ares stifled his laughter by collapsing onto one end of a sofa that was more cushion than proper seat. The next thing he knew, Fen was tipping him onto his side, throwing a massive, knitted blanket over him, and tucking him in. It reminded him of Leo. On the floor in front of the hearth, when Leo had taken care of him, even though Ares hadn't deserved it. Fen smiled at him, and Ares blinked at her.

"I miss Leo," he said. Her brow furrowed.

"Who's Leo?"

"Julian. Julian is Leo," Ares said. Yawned.

"Oh, well, then Leo is horrible."

"No, he's not," Ares shook his head. "Leo's perfect. Or he was perfect. And I should have told him. I should have told him that I love him because now he's gone." No more tears came, which was a strange sort of relief. If he could just ignore the hollow pit in the center of his chest for the rest of his life, he'd probably be alright. Fen took a deep breath, her chest rising and falling once, heavily, before she leaned over and kissed Ares' temple.

"Don't beat yourself up too badly about it," she said quietly. "It's hard to talk about the way somebody makes you feel. It's—"

"You've told Warren, haven't you?" Ares asked. It was hard to tell because the light was dim and he was drunk, but Ares thought Fen was blushing. "You should talk to him, Fen. He cares for you. Leo saw it. I see it too, I think."

"I'm not sure you're the love expert in the room," she said. Ares snorted, and Fen's hand leapt up to cover her mouth. "Ares, I'm sorry! That was so—"

"No," he chuckled. "No, you're right. But you should learn from my mistakes. Else you'll end up drunk on Warren's nan's couch."

"Alright," Fen said, patting his shoulder gently. "I'll think about it."

"Goodnight, Fen," Ares said.

"Get some sleep," she said, and he passed out before her footsteps had faded from the hall.

53

When Leo finally woke up, he wasn't sure if it was morning or night. A storm had rolled in at some point and had turned the light grey and strange as it filtered through the clouds. Leo lay in bed, still exhausted, staring up at the ceiling, listening to the rain and the wind, trying to decide what to do. If Sidney and Jonas didn't come back today, he would have to find some other way back. The tree, perhaps, in the graveyard. Or maybe Delilah knew who else in town might be able to help.

He stretched his arms over his head and then pushed his palms against his eyes, listening to his own pulse and trying to will himself into moving, when a different sound entered his consciousness. The front door opened, and muffled voices echoed up the stairs.

Leo barely managed to pull on a sweater before he was bounding down the stairs. Standing just inside the front door, Sidney stared at him, wide-eyed, as Leo collided with him, pulling him into a massive hug, more relieved to see his brother than he'd ever imagined possible.

"Where have you been?" Leo demanded, as Sidney spoke over him.

"How did you get here? Christ, Leo! What's going on?"

"Oh, everything is massively fucked. But I need to get back to Andurnei." Leo watched as Sidney glanced back over his shoulder at the seven-foot tall, brick-shithouse of a demon, standing behind him. Jonas Rookwood was holding his coat by his collar, like he wasn't sure if he was going to put it on or hang it up.

"I don't know if we can get back to Andurnei," Sidney said. Leo frowned at him.

"What?"

"Portals between realms have a cost."

"Marking isn't a problem—"

"Not just that. A cost. Magic."

"What?" Leo frowned. "Like, what? Like a—" Ares had explained that to him before though, hadn't he? But Leo hadn't given anything to the tree. "But not always, right?"

"Uh, no. Basically always," Sidney said. Jonas seemed to decide that they were staying for the moment and put his coat on the hook. Leo scowled.

"I'm making coffee," Jonas said, pressing a palm to the small of Sidney's back, before giving Leo a small smile. "Good to see you again, Leo."

"Yes," Leo nodded in his direction as Jonas started to the kitchen. "You too. But Sidney, they can't all need a sacrifice, because when I came through the tree I just came through it."

"The tree?" Sidney looked as though Leo was speaking to him in a foreign language. "What tree, Leo? What are you talking about? How did you get here?"

"The tree in the graveyard that's connected to the tree in the orchard at Leyland Hall," Leo said. "Although I guess, I did promise it I would go back. Is a promise something? Like—"

Sidney frowned at him, his gaze snapping again toward Jonas, who had stopped and turned to look at Leo, his brow furrowed.

"What graveyard?" Jonas asked.

"The one at the chapel," Leo waved his hand in the general direction. "The one where Ares' father is buried."

"Ares Silva?" Jonas asked. "What do you know about Ares Silva?"

It took almost an hour, and a bit of backtracking, for Leo to explain the short version of everything relevant that had happened over the last two weeks. He was so engrossed in his storytelling, that he didn't even mind all the glances and varied expressions that Sidney and Jonas were exchanging across the table from him.

"So," Jonas said slowly once Leo had finally finished. "Edmund Morrow was shooting at you, and you ran into the orchard, and a tree spoke to you, you promised you'd go save Ares, and then the tree spit you out at Bittergate Chapel. Do I have that right?"

"I think the tree is Ares' mother," Leo said, accepting another cup of coffee from Sidney, who also set down a second plate of scones. Leo did really love his brother. "She said—The tree called him her son."

"And Dom said Ares was in Andurnei because of something to do with their mom," Sidney said. Leo nodded.

"They got in an argument about it, like I told you."

"But we just brought Dom back," Sidney said. "I mean, like... last night, early this morning, brought him back. Rescued him from Morrow. That's where we've been."

"You saw Morrow?"

"Not," Sidney shook his head, frowning again. "Not as such." That was a problem. Potentially a very large problem. If Morrow had kidnapped Dom, where did that leave Ares? Did Ares know Dom had been taken? Would Morrow have told him?

Almost certainly yes if he could lord it over Ares. Or worse, use it to push Ares into doing something stupid. Leo's stomach soured, his whole body feeling tight enough that it was hard to take a breath.

"Dom's okay?" Leo asked. Sidney nodded.

"Okay enough. He's been beat all to hell, but—"

"We need to get back to Ares," Leo said. "If he knows something's happened to Dom, that's not good. He'll do something stupid."

"I thought he sent Dom away," Jonas frowned. Leo sighed.

"Only to try and keep him away from Morrow. Morrow wants them because their blood makes the trees in the orchard grow."

"Their... what? Grow what?" Rookwood asked. "What's he growing?"

"I don't know," Leo shrugged. He hadn't seen any fruit as he'd run through the orchard, just barrels and trees. Barrels. "Sap. It's not... they're not growing something magical; they're producing magical sap. For... something."

"But I thought you said the tree was Ares' mother?" Sidney asked. "Literally? Like—"

"Like she's buried there," Leo said. "Or she's a part of the tree somehow? Inside it. I mean, she was talking to me."

"Asking you to protect her son," Sidney frowned at Jonas. "That would be consciousness or... soul?"

"If he's imbuing trees with human souls..." Jonas trailed off, his eyes wide. "I mean, that could potentially create a substance, the sap in this case, with potent restorative abilities for creatures." It seemed like Jonas was getting excited about this. Leo wasn't sure he understood. "If dealing for human souls strengthens a creature's magic, then drinking or imbibing something that's been run through a sacrificed soul like a filter, could impart—"

"Yes! And it solves the problem of needing a sacrifice of soul to create a portal," Sidney chimed in, sounding more thrilled than Leo was sure he ought to. "If the very base of the portal is imbued with the soul of a human, then the portal is grown into the tree itself."

"None of that matters," Leo said firmly, because he had no clue what they were talking about. "We need to get back to Ares."

"It does matter," Sidney said. "Quite a lot, actually."

"It can wait, though," Jonas acquiesced. "We need to tell Dom and Asterion. They should know what's happening."

"We don't have that kind of time," Leo demanded. And then there was a knock at the door. Sidney got up and went to answer it, as Jonas leaned back in his chair.

"Morrow likely doesn't know Dom's gone yet. We do have a little time, and running off half-cocked isn't likely to do Ares any favors."

"If I can get Morrow to void his contract with Ares—"

"If Sidney and I are right about the trees and the souls, and Morrow needs Ares' magic to nurture the souls, then Morrow's not likely to give up his contract without a fight," Jonas said with a grimace.

"Well, no, but I have an idea. All we have to do is—" Sidney returned abruptly to the kitchen. His face was pale, and his shoulders were stiff, lips pursed, as though he tasted something sour. Jonas straightened up.

"Sidney?" Leo was bowled over by the shift in Jonas's voice, all quiet concern, so much gentler than Leo had expected from him. Sidney shook his head, his gaze on Leo.

"Dad's here," he said, his voice barely more than a whisper. "He wants to speak with you."

Leo helped Sidney into a chair before turning toward the hall door with a grimace, as though it concealed a gauntlet of horrors. Part of him was irritated that he was going to have to do this now. There were so so many more important things to deal with than whatever his father was about to berate him for. He didn't feel bad about missing two weeks of work and however many campaign events. Those things had never felt less important to him than they did now.

Still, maybe there was something of a little boy in him still. His father's silhouette against the front windows of the cottage was menacing. Tall like Sidney, broad-shouldered like Leo, their father cut an intimidating figure. His caramel-colored hair was unnaturally golden, recently dyed. His mouth was turned down at the corners as he frowned at Leo. And then at Leo's rumpled clothes.

"I hope I'm not disturbing your holiday." It was his Congressman voice. Used to bend opposing politicians to his will on the house floor. Leo exhaled.

"I was unexpectedly detained."

"For two weeks?"

"It's a long story. Why are you here, dad?"

"We're on our way to Brixton. For the—"

"The town hall. Right."

"Do you know how this looks for me? Your little sojourn. You were supposed to co-host a donor event yesterday."

"I—"

"I don't want to hear any excuses. Get dressed and get your luggage. Now." Leo stilled. He wouldn't be doing that. He didn't move, and his father growled. "I let you come up here to this house party with the understanding that you would use that time to network for the campaign and the firm. Your proclivities aside—" Leo bit his tongue and ignored the heat on the back of his neck.

"I'm not going with you. I'm not doing that anymore."

"Leo." The congressman grit his teeth. "I have been nothing

but accommodating to you. I have never asked too much of you, and I—"

"You never asked anything of me at all," Leo said. "You told me where to go and how to dress and who to be. I'm not doing that anymore." There was a beat where the two men stared at each other, and something settled in Leo's chest. He wasn't doing that anymore. He'd said it aloud, and the world hadn't ended.

"Leo," the congressman's voice turned coddling, almost gentle. Leo braced himself. "Your charisma and your success are important. People *like* you. You're a story that I can sell." A commodity. Not a person. Leo swallowed.

"That's not me."

"I can give you more time off," the congressman offered.

"That's not the point."

"Leo—"

"Dad," Leo took a step back into the house. "I'm sorry. I am. But I've been the man you want me to be and it's suffocating. I'm not him." The congressman stopped playing at warmth. His face was red, and his fists were clenched. When he spoke, his voice was sharp like a whip crack.

"Who are you then?"

Leo thought of Ares. He thought about how much he'd enjoyed working in the garden, and on the grounds. The relief at getting his hands dirty, and the thrill of working on Ares' case. The possibility he'd felt out in the wide newness of Andurnei. The comfort he'd felt being back with Sidney.

"I don't know yet," Leo said. "But I'm going to find out."

54

Ares woke up with a hangover, light pouring in the window above his head, illuminating an old woman who was seated across from him in a floral armchair. She was engrossed in her knitting, content to treat Ares as though he was little more than an additional throw pillow. He tried to swallow but his mouth was unnaturally dry. When he sat up, he was certain he could feel whatever was left in his skull sloshing from side to side.

The old woman didn't look at him until he was fully upright, and then she smiled, her eyes crinkling at the corners. Her nose and mouth were the same shape as Warren's. The infamous Nan. Ares opened his mouth to apologize for his existence on her sofa, but before he could, she spoke.

"There's tea on the hob and crumpets in the larder, dear. Help yourself. Fen went back up to the hall, but my Tom's waiting for you in the kitchen."

Tom? A husband, perhaps. Tea and crumpets were exactly what his unhappy stomach wanted.

"Thank you," Ares began, but she shook her head.

"My hearing's not right, love. It's all fine. Just go on. Enjoy your breakfast." Ares nodded to her, and her smile broadened as he got to his feet.

His legs were as shaky as a newborn calf, but he managed to make it to the kitchen, only stumbling a couple of times on the changing thicknesses of the variety of rugs. The kitchen was bright and warm, and Warren was the only person present, his back straight as he read a newspaper and sipped at a cup of tea.

"Are you Tom, then?" Ares asked. It came out a rough growl. Warren only laughed.

"Thomas Warren the Third, at your service. Sit down, I'll get you a crumpet."

"Why don't we call you Tom?"

"Kephisto's valet two valets ago was Tom. I came on after him, so I got to be Warren. Which is fine. I have been since school really," he said all of this as he got up to rifle around in the cupboard for plates and cups. The clanking of porcelain echoed in the chamber that used to hold Ares' brain, and he winced. Warren didn't notice.

"Fen left already?"

"Well, it's almost 11. She still makes breakfast for the maids and the other staff, even if his lordship isn't in."

"I see," Ares said. He supposed if he'd thought about it, he would have guessed as much, but thinking seemed beyond him. Except. "We ought to get back up to the house."

"Have a crumpet at least, and a cuppa. I doubt you'll make it back up the hill otherwise."

As much as Ares didn't want to admit it, it was true. Warren seemed more at ease in his Nan's house than in any other setting Ares had seen him, and they lapsed into a comfortable silence, while Ares ate and Warren read. Ares stared out the window over the sink that led out into the back garden, watching the birds swoop around the feeder. If Leo were dead, he would have felt it.

It was a strange thought to have apropos of nothing. But there was still something in him that believed it was true. Hope had steered him wrong plenty of times before. Hell, he'd been hoping he was doing the right thing for ten years, and he'd been proven wrong. Maybe it was the tea and crumpets. Maybe it was that Warren's company made him feel that much less isolated. It was stupid. He knew it was stupid. Leo was gone. The thought made his stomach clench, turned the cherry crumpet sour in his mouth. Ultimately, it would be best not to think about Leo until he'd gotten Dom back. One thing at a time.

When Ares and Warren finally arrived at Leyland Hall, Kephisto's carriage was still gone. Ares went back to the cottage, after thanking Warren again for inviting him out, and Warren told him he ought to come up to the house for dinner that evening. Fen's famous pot roast was on the menu. Ares promised he would.

The house was too empty. Ares took Matilda out to stretch her legs, and they let all the animals into the pasture again to enjoy the sun, despite the snow on the ground. Better to do it now before the clouds on the horizon blew in and brought more weather with them. The cold was making his headache worse, not better, so after an hour, he whistled for Matilda and started back inside.

The front foyer was still a mess from Morrow's invasion, the tile splintered, muck from boots splattered the floor. Ares dipped the last vial of blue tincture into a large mug of coffee and drank it as he got down onto his hands and knees and began to clean.

It was a pain in the ass to pry up the tiles that were cracked and not broken, and Ares took a break halfway through, drinking more coffee as the sunlight began to fade behind rainclouds. From where he was sitting on the bottom step, he could see Leo's plates still sitting on the desk in the study.

With a grunt, Ares got to his feet and stepped over the ruined tiles into the tiny room. Beside Leo's bowl was Ares' sketchbook, the small one he'd taken to Warnock. Ares frowned, expecting to see his last sketch: Ares' desperate attempt to get Leo out of his head and heart and onto the page. But no. It wasn't that. Instead, it was full of notes. Handwritten, scrawled at all angles, speckled with ash.

Ares turned the page. More notes. A quote from the Assembly codices, half of it scratched out. Below that, bullet points:

- *Induce a magical exchange. Provide Morrow with his own ability to feed the orchard?'*
  - *Consequences of magical removal/exchange?*
- *Contract negation. Contract is binding the assignee to illegal activity/Assembly malfeasance? Proof of malfeasance is—?*

Ares kept skimming through Leo's extensive brainstorm that went on for pages, his heart aching as he smiled despite himself. Leo had been seriously trying to free Ares. Not that Ares had doubted him, but it was different to see it, scrawled and scratched out in black and white. Missing Leo felt like a new appendage, and Ares flexed it, sitting with the pulsing ache for longer than he needed to. Leo had wanted to help Ares. He'd been going to save Ares, just like he'd said. And as much as it hurt to know it, Ares was glad for it. If he couldn't have Leo anymore, at least he had proof that he'd had him once. That Leo had loved him. And Ares was better for it.

A thundering pounding against Ares' front door had him jerking upright, just as Matilda began barking furiously. Ares closed the notebook and stepped back into the hallway when a blast of magic blew the lock off the door. Ares took a step back, stopping Matilda with a hand at the nape of her neck as Edmund Morrow glared in at them, chest heaving, face contorted in rage.

"Where is he?"

"Who?" Ares asked. Why was he so hung up on Leo after everything else that had happened?

"Your brother!" Morrow snarled. "Where the *fuck* is your brother?"

Ares took a half a step back, primarily to drag Matilda away from the door. She was growling, teeth bared, and Ares was trying to understand what was happening.

"How should I know? You took him," Ares said.

"He's not where I put him," Morrow snapped, striding in through the cottage door and looking around as though Dom was going to pop out from behind the curtains.

"Well, he's not here," Ares said, doing little to mask his elation.

"Fuck you, Silva! I'll have my men come down here and tear this place apart!"

"You might want to ask his lordship about that first," Ares said, nodding to the figure coming down the garden path. A fresh-faced teenage valet chased after Kephisto holding an umbrella aloft, as Kephisto strode down the cobbles toward the cottage. Two guards followed in their wake.

"Hello, Morrow," Kephisto said with a thin smile, his eyes bright. "How convenient I find you here. I was hoping to take a stroll around the orchard with you and Mr. Silva. He says the yields are—"

Morrow swung toward Kephisto before schooling his expression, anger bright, his mouth an ugly snarl. To his credit, Kephisto didn't step back. He did arch an eyebrow and give a small, judgmental cough. The guards shuffled audibly behind him.

"He's ruining everything!" Morrow swung an arm back in Ares' direction, sounding like a petulant child, and Ares attempted to look as innocent as humanly possible. Kephisto's expression remained unchanged.

"Be that as it may, I'd like to go assess the current sap production and see if we can't come up with an actionable solution."

"Bleed him dry," Morrow hissed, pushing out the door past Kephisto and striding in the direction of the orchard. "Feed his body to the trees."

"A temporary solution to a permanent problem, I believe," Kephisto said, still standing in the doorway. Ares blinked at him and Kephisto rolled his eyes. "Hurry up, Mr. Silva. I don't fancy spending my whole evening out in the rain."

It wasn't the plan Ares had in mind.

He'd hoped to leverage the poor sap production into revealing that Morrow had another child of Demeter at his disposal. If Ares could have secured Dom a position working for Kephisto without a contract, they would have been able to figure something out together. But now, Dom had escaped on his own. It was just Ares again. And in many ways, that was easier.

Ares trailed behind as Morrow and Kephisto walked out in front, leaning toward each other, hissing in furious low tones. Ares couldn't really hear them over the sound of the sleet that had begun to fall, tapping against the leaves and branches of the trees in the orchard, and it didn't matter. A new plan was forming as they walked further in. Reckless, maybe. Leo wouldn't like it. But Leo wasn't there. And if it worked...

"Why isn't this tree tapped?" Kephisto said, pointing to Ares' mother's tree. "It seems to be thriving. The largest one here by a considerable amount." Ares' stomach swooped, and finally Morrow looked over at him. They both knew what the tree was. That Morrow hadn't forced Ares to tap it might have been the only mercy he ever showed Ares. Or it might have just been that Morrow thought the same thing Ares did: the whole orchard was feeding on the magic that still eked out of her tree. It was why Ares never had to tend it. Never had to bleed for it. Morrow would have to kill another demigod to replace the drain on her magic.

"It's a wellspring of power," Morrow said.

"Power that's already fading," Kephisto replied, tersely. "Is there a way to replenish it?" He looked at Ares, and Ares made a choice.

"I can try." He stepped forward and rolled up his sleeves. Kephisto took a step back, and Morrow watched him with a furrowed brow, his lips pursed as though he wanted to say something but was stopping himself.

The roots were still under Ares' feet, slick with the ice and snow that was caking into the cracks in the bark. He could hear the guards, their guns clanking as they shifted their weight. Beyond that, there was only the quiet hush of ice tapping against the tree branches above them, the patter of it against the shoulders of his coat.

Ares bent down near the base, his back to the tree, his hands outstretched, and it was only then that he realized he didn't have his knife.

He looked up, thinking he'd ask one of the soldiers, when a sudden, bright light threw everything in front of him into stark relief. Everyone's eyes were wide, mouths open in gasps of surprise that Ares couldn't hear. The tree at his back groaned, an ancient, creaking sound that muffled all the others. The guards had their weapons up, though everyone was wincing, temporarily blinded. Only Ares, who'd had his back to the worst of it, could see Leo walking through the side of the tree.

Leo was alive. More than that he was here. Ares splayed his palms against his knees, trying to force himself not to cry out in relief. Something loosened in his chest, snapped maybe. Leo was here, and the rest of Ares' doubts flooded away. He could do this. He would do anything to get Leo back in his arms. To get them both home.

LEO STAGGERED THROUGH THE PORTAL. He'd expected darkness, but the light was blinding and sharp. And then it was gone. Ares was on his knees on the ground and Leo lurched forward.

"Ares!"

"Stop." Ares' voice cracked. The desperation in his tone made Leo's heart freeze, as he stilled and took in the rest of the scene. The guns. Morrow, looking like he wanted to breathe fire, and then Kephisto, his mouth an amused smirk. Asterion had warned them that there would be an order to these things. They were still on his brother's property, after all. And his brother was still royalty. Leo jerked his head around, his stomach souring. Where the fuck were Dom and Asterion? They should have been right behind him.

"Welcome back, Mr. Quince," Morrow simpered, his voice lilting. Teasing. Leo's fists clenched.

"Ares," Leo started, ignoring Morrow as best he could. Ares was giving him a small, soft look of relief and it took everything in Leo's power not to lunge for him. Wrap his arms around Ares, pull him back into the tree. If it would even open again. "Ares, you've got to— We figured it out. There's a—"

"It's alright, Leo." Ares' voice was low and soft. Leo's stomach lurched into his throat.

"No. It's not."

"Yes," Ares said. "It is. It's alright. I promised to give my magic to this orchard and help it grow. There's no changing that."

"Don't do this, Ares. Please!" Ares ignored him, turning to Morrow with a small smile.

"Can I borrow your knife?"

"My casting knife?" Morrow drew back slightly. When Ares nodded, Leo groaned in frustration. He should have known Ares would be pigheaded until the bitter end. Morrow hesitated, then drew a thin, silver switchblade out of his pocket. It caught the wide, white light of the moon as a cloud slid away.

"Ares," Leo warned. Pleaded.

"Leo, bring me the knife, please." For a moment, Leo couldn't get his feet to move. He stumbled, his own footsteps echoing in the unnatural quiet of the orchard, his stomach swimming and sick. Morrow sneered at him as Leo took the knife from his outstretched hand, and Leo swallowed down the urge to free the blade and jam it into Morrow's eye socket. He took a deep breath and picked his way back to Ares between the roots. It would have felt strange to step on them, now that he knew who she was.

Ares sat back on his heels. His perfect mouth was curved into a small smile, his shoulders relaxed. Leo's hand shook as he held the knife out to Ares.

"Ares, whatever you're doing—"

"I thought I lost you," Ares said quietly. Leo ignored the heat of tears behind his eyes. The way his legs wanted to collapse underneath him.

"I'm here now. Whatever this is, there are other ways."

"This is simplest, I think."

"Ares." Ares shook his head.

"When we argued at Mae's. I was so stupid that night."

"No, Ares—"

"I love you, Leo," Ares said.

Everything in Leo, his thoughts, his racing heart, his pulse, came up short. He couldn't swallow, he couldn't think of anything except the one thing that he already knew.

"I love you too." Ares smiled, his hand tightening around Morrow's silver knife.

"Then trust me. Alright?"

"I do," Leo said. "But Ares—"

"Get back a bit," Ares murmured. He turned away from Leo, bowing his head.

"Ares," Leo protested. If he would only listen.

"Now." Ares snapped, a harsh sound, more in line with the person he was always pretending to be. It irritated Leo out of his fear, maybe. Or it was just enough of a surprise to send him stepping backward, stumbling over a root as he reached back and steadied himself against the tree.

Ares dug the blade of Morrow's knife into his forearm, and Leo looked away. He couldn't watch. He couldn't bear it. His fingers dug into the bark with frustration and guilt. He'd promised he'd help Ares and now what the fuck was he doing?

But, in spite of it all, Leo trusted him. He'd trusted Ares since the moment he'd met him. And Ares had saved Leo's life over and over again.

The tree began to shake. Tremble, really. If Leo hadn't been clutching it, he might not have noticed. He didn't want to portal through. Not now!

Leo jerked back, stumbling over roots, but no one noticed. Ares' eyes were closed and Kephisto and Morrow watched with careful attention as Ares let blood pool in his palms before shoving his hands into the dirt.

❦

'You brought him back to me,' Ares thought. Could have sobbed. He didn't know how she'd done it. But it was a relief to see Leo's face. And the sting of the knife always dulled here, in this soft place between soil and roots. He could feel the hum of magic. The magic he'd thought he'd lost. His mother.

'I'm sorry,' she said. 'I was trying to protect you.'

'I know.' The tears on his cheeks were as hot as the blood on his arms. Power boiled beneath his skin. 'Help me end this,' he said. Begged. 'Let me be free.'

'I love you, Ares.' Her voice was just as he remembered it. Melodic, soft and calm. 'And I will do for you now what I should have done then.'

'I love you,' Ares said. The dirt clumped, wet with blood, in the grip of his fingers. His body swayed as the tree began to move beneath him and around him. They could end this. He could end this. Ares breathed in and let the magic flow out.

⚘

THE TREE CREAKED FURIOUSLY, the sound of a trunk swaying just before a tornado ripped it out of the ground. Leo tumbled as the massive root in front of him twisted itself up out of the earth, before flattening itself out straight and long. He scrambled around, trying to see Ares, to make sure he wasn't being pulled under the writhing waves of roots.

Guns snapped, bullets bouncing uselessly off the trunk of the massive tree. And then there was a scream. In the moonlight, Leo could make out a shape, a man, thin, his limbs flailing as a root hoisted him high into the air, and then with a sound like a whip-crack, plunged him down into the dirt. There was a horrible sickening thud, followed by an earthen splatter, mud and gore flinging into the air.

"Ares!" It couldn't have been Ares. It hadn't been Ares, but it terrified Leo all the same. He charged forward, and then all at once, everything went still.

Ares lay face down in the dirt. Leo staggered toward him, the sickly smell of wet blood mixed with fresh earth, made his stomach churn.

"Ares. Shit. Ares." Ares' name became like a litany, as Leo fell to his knees, grabbing Ares as best he could by the shoulders, dirt and ice and snow and blood caking his hands. Finally, he rolled Ares onto his back. For a moment, Leo couldn't breathe. Leo's fingers slid through blood on Ares' arm, still searching for his pulse. When Ares' chest rose and fell beneath Leo's, Leo slumped forward and sobbed.

"Morrow!" Kephisto's voice rang out through the silence. "Edmund! Where are you?"

"Leo." Ares' voice was soft. Leo pressed himself up immediately, swiping the tears off his cheeks. Ares was pale, but he was smiling, his heavy hand stroking the small of Leo's back. "Were you crying over me?"

"Crying because of how much you irritate me."

"Relieved because you thought you were rid of me?"

"Don't say that," Leo choked. Ares reached up and pulled Leo down into a kiss. After a moment, Leo tugged away, breathless.

"I had a better plan than yours."

"I know. I read all of your notes. But mine was more efficient." Ares propped himself up on one elbow. Kephisto and the guards were walking unsteadily through the orchard, calling out for Morrow. Ares pursed his lips. "Not going to find him up here."

"Parts of him, maybe," Leo offered. Ares shuddered as he sat up, bending toward Leo. Leo helped him upright, settling in the churned earth beside him. "But that should be it, then. End of your contract?"

"You're the legal expert, not me."

"Oh, now you're interested in the plan that uses laws?"

"This worked out fine!"

"It was entirely reliant on chance and magic that you don't actually have control over."

"Enough of it was me," Ares shrugged, looking past Leo at the tree beside them. "The rest of it was her."

"She's been very busy these last couple of days," Leo said. Ares frowned at him, and Leo shrugged. "She let me through. Got me back home."

"She..." Ares trailed off, his gaze shifting between Leo and the tree, his eyes widening. "She portaled you through? But how?" Leo shrugged again.

"I don't know. I was hiding from Morrow, and then the next thing I knew I was in the tree. She asked if I'd come back for you, and I promised. Sidney and Jonas say that could have been a contract if she thought it was. And then she let me back here because of Dom. He's got enough magic that we didn't have to make any deals, so, here we are. Or I am. Dom and Asterion were supposed to be right behind me, but..."

"Gods," Ares huffed, shifting forward as though he was going to get to his feet. Leo put his hands firmly on Ares' shoulders.

"Uh, no. I think it's probably best if you stay put."

"I'm done taking orders from anyone for a bit," Ares said. Leo blinked at him, and Ares smirked. "Certain circumstances notwithstanding, of course." He reached forward, putting his hands on Leo's hips, and Leo couldn't even manage to stay annoyed with him for five seconds, when Ares tugged him forward.

"I was planning on saving your life you know. It was going to be incredible."

"I don't doubt it," Ares smirked. "You are an incredible man."

"Remember that, won't you?"

"I doubt you'll let me forget it," Ares murmured. When Ares kissed him, Leo melted. He sagged against Ares, chasing the flick of Ares' tongue against his lips, relishing in the rise and fall of Ares' chest beneath his own. He couldn't feel the cold anymore, and the fading adrenaline was rapidly being replaced with the euphoria of being back in Ares' arms, curled against him. There was nowhere else Leo would have rather been. A root slithered past, nestling itself back into the soil, and a bright, white light lit up the night.

56

Dom came through the tree, followed by a man who looked like Kephisto, but was not Kephisto. Immediately, Dom went to his knees, and Ares' stomach clenched at the sound of vomiting.

"Oh shit," he muttered. Leo was already on his feet, reaching for Ares' hand to pull him up, and Ares was so, so grateful for him. Leo steadied Ares as they both staggered toward Dom and the stranger, who Ares could only imagine was Asterion.

"What the hell happened?" Leo asked.

"She held us in an interdimensional portal space for an absurdly long time," Asterion seemed to be wavering. Ares dropped to his knees beside Dom, smiling as he heard Asterion say, "Christ. Did I just get lectured by a tree?"

Ares rubbed his palm down the center of Dom's back. He was suddenly, sharply reminded of a time when they were much younger. Dom had come back from a school party, so drunk he couldn't see straight. They'd done this, exactly this, in their aunt and uncle's backyard, Dom vomiting off the side of the porch.

"Mom's a tree," Dom wheezed.

"Yeah, I know."

"You should have told me, you asshole."

"I think that's a fair assessment of the last ten years," Ares agreed. Dom punched him in the arm. It would have hurt, probably, if Dom hadn't spent the last two minutes hunched over and puking.

"Where're Morrow and Kephisto?" Dom asked, pressing his palms against his thighs and lifting his head to loom around. "Did Leo manage to—"

"Morrow's dead," Ares said. "Kephisto's looking for him."

"Oh shit," Asterion sighed, sounding put upon. Then he paused. "Not about Morrow's death. Good. Good job whoever did it. I'll buy you a cake. I owe you one." Dom narrowed his eyes at Ares.

"You killed him?" Dom asked. Ares shrugged.

"Mom helped."

"Someone ought to tell him," Asterion said, his gaze searching the orchard for the silhouettes that kept popping in and out behind the trees. He took a step forward and Dom lurched in his direction.

"Asterion, wait—" Ares ached at the worry in his brother's tone, and was impressed when the prince fell back at once, kneeling in the dirt on Dom's other side. Hunched over Dom, Asterion and Ares met each other's gaze over Dom's head, and Ares knew he was being assessed as much as he was doing the assessing.

Dom rested his head on Asterion's shoulder but grabbed for Ares' hand. Leo, who was standing over them all, had a small smile on his face.

"Don't look so smug," Ares grumbled. Leo chuckled.

"I'll look however I please."

Dom straightened up, and everyone's attention shifted again to him. He pursed his lips and sighed.

"I'm sorry," he groaned. "It's just been a very long couple of days."

"No more portals tonight," Ares said, getting slowly to his feet. "We can sleep in the cottage. We'll sort out the rest tomorrow." Agreement came in the form of a general exhausted silent acquiescence. Together with Asterion, Ares got Dom upright. Dom was bruised and tired, leaning against Asterion, as Ares stepped back to look at him. A long overdue apology tried to leap out of Ares' throat, and Ares swallowed it down. He had so much he needed to say to Dom, and if he tried to do it here and now, he would fuck it up. There would be time enough for his apologies soon. Ares would make time.

Once he was sure that Asterion and Dom could navigate over the tree roots, Ares turned to Leo who was waiting off to the side. As they walked toward the gate, Leo wrapped an arm around Ares' waist.

"I'm glad they're staying, but where are they going to sleep? The cottage only has one bed."

"Not so," Ares smirked, leaning into Leo's warmth.

"What do you mean?" Leo frowned.

"The sofa in the study is a pullout."

"You're an asshole, Ares Silva," Leo laughed, shaking his head in disbelief. Ares grinned and kissed him.

THE WALK back to the cottage was full of quiet relief. Ares was free and frankly, Leo thought, if anyone deserved an early grave, it was Edmund Morrow. When Asterion gently suggested to Kephisto, as their party walked past, that further searching might be in vain, the prince only crossed his arms over his chest and huffed back toward the big house, which looked darker and more dismal than ever.

The cottage was bright and welcoming, though not warm, as the front door was ajar, Matilda's shadow visible in the crack. Ares shooed her off with a weary wave of his hand, as she pranced around Leo and sniffed curiously at Asterion. Several long licks over Dom's hand and arm finally brought a smile to his face. Leo herded Ares upstairs to the bathroom and the medicine cabinet.

Ares stripped slowly, as Leo went about looking for any more of Mae's potions in the bedroom, to no avail. He came back into the bathroom, and Ares glanced up at him, as he adjusted the taps.

"You think I can't get into the shower on my own?"

"You've proven to me many times over the past two weeks that you can't take care of yourself."

Ares chuckled and then winced as he straightened up.

"Do you have any more of the blue stuff anywhere?"

"Gave it all to Matilda, after Morrow."

"Right," Leo sighed. Ares leaned forward and kissed him, just a brief thing, that settled the roil of anxiety in Leo's stomach. Then Ares braced himself on Leo's shoulder and got into the shower. "Shout if you need me," Leo said. Ares grunted, and Leo retreated, because if he didn't, he knew he'd end up in the shower too.

In the living room, Asterion was stoking the fireplace, and he looked up as Leo walked in.

"Oh, thank Gods. Please tell him he's allowed to cook dinner." Asterion waved a hand toward the kitchen, where Dom stood in front of the stove, glaring at Asterion.

"Help yourself," Leo said. "I'd offer to make something, but I know you're the expert. And your brother has had to suffer through several of my feeble attempts at meals."

"I don't want to—" Dom hesitated, glancing around, before looking back at Leo. "Maybe just chicken and rice?"

"Fine," Leo said with an enthusiastic nod. He'd not eaten much besides scones at Sidney and Jonas' place. "Sounds great. Anything you need I'll try to find it for you." Dom nodded as he turned away, already reaching for the canisters of dried goods above the sink.

It was clear Leo wasn't needed in the kitchen, so he went over to Asterion instead. His steps stalled when he saw the outline of runes in ash on the hearth. Asterion glanced up at him, as Leo leaned back.

"Sorry," Leo said. "I didn't realize you were making a call." Asterion shook his head, robin's egg blue flyaways escaping the knot of hair at the back of his neck. He was paler than Leo remembered. Thinner. So much had happened since the Elmmond House party and even in Hindry, there hadn't really been time to discuss it.

"Normally, I wouldn't bother, but Jonas will worry if he doesn't hear anything."

"Right. Of course." Jonas and Sidney had stayed behind. The calvary, they'd said, in case they didn't receive any word within a few hours. Somehow the idea that they were calling off their backup finally made Leo's shoulders fully relax. They'd done it. Ares was truly free.

"No chance you've got any magic, do you?" Asterion asked, head cocked to the side. "I need some blood with power to start it."

"No," Leo shook his head. Then he frowned. "Wait, don't you?" Asterion shook his head, a small smile turning up the corner of his handsome mouth.

"Not anymore," he said proudly, getting to his feet with a

small huff of breath, and going into the kitchen. Asterion wrapped his arm around Dom's waist, leaning against his hip, and murmured something into Dom's ear. Dom nodded, held out his spare hand as he stirred whatever was frying on the stove with the other. Leo blushed and turned back toward the foyer as Asterion kissed the side of Dom's neck.

"Leo? Can I feed this dog?" Dom called from the kitchen.

"Scraps from the counter, you mean?" Leo said, pausing before he put his foot on the stairs.

"Yeah."

"It's fine. Just don't tell Ares." Not that Ares really cared. But he would pretend to.

He'd thought he was going up to get blankets and sheets from the chest in Ares' bedroom, but he didn't make it that far. Instead, at the sight of Ares' pile of clean clothes, Leo undressed, tugging Ares' undershirt over his head, and then a sweater on top of that. Every time he stopped to take a breath, he caught himself smiling. It was hard to believe it was really over.

Instead of doing anything useful, Leo stretched across the foot of the bed, collapsing, face down against the mattress, and inhaled the scent of Ares on his clothes and blankets, grateful to be home.

"Leo! Ares!" Dom's voice was distant. Bottom of the stairs at least. "Dinner!" Leo opened a bleary eye. Ares was in front of him, dressed, wrapping his forearm in bandages.

"Want me to bring something up for you?" Ares asked. Leo shook his head.

"No, no. I'll come down," Leo yawned. Ares snorted and helped him off the bed.

Dinner was quiet at first, though it didn't stay that way for long. Asterion seemed unable to stand much silence and began regaling them with an overdramatized version of his recent rescue of Dom from Morrow's fortress in someplace called Kinclere. Dom shook his head, amused smile relaxing onto his face as he denied each of Asterion's embellishments in turn. Ares ran his thumb over the top of Leo's knee under the table. It was wonderful. Comfortable. Homey, even. Leo hadn't thought being with Ares could get any better, but he'd never guessed that it might come with something like a family.

After supper, Ares helped Dom get the pull-out set up and Asterion and Leo did dishes as quietly as two men attempting to eavesdrop on an apology from several rooms away could possibly do. They couldn't hear anything. But there was no shouting, and Leo remarked that that alone was a vast improvement on the brothers' last conversation.

The domesticity continued, and Leo enjoyed it thoroughly, as he and Ares got ready for bed upstairs. When they were both lying beneath the sheets, Ares rolled toward him.

"Thank you," Ares said. Then he yawned. Leo laughed.

"I didn't really do anything. It was all you."

"You showed me that I could. That I should."

"Persistence is my strong suit," Leo said. Ares chuckled and pulled him close, a heavy, solid arm around Leo's waist.

"You said something at Mae's—"

"That I loved you?" Leo asked. Ares hummed, pressing a kiss against Leo's temple. Leo snuggled closer, using Ares' chest as a pillow. "I do love you, Ares."

"I love you too," Ares shifted down slightly, tucking his chin onto the top of Leo's head. "I'm sorry I waited to say it. That I couldn't believe it. That was the stupidest thing I've ever done. Which is saying something, considering."

"It's alright," Leo tilted his face up and kissed Ares. It started out slow and gentle, and Leo relished it. Every place their bodies touched, every soft caress, Leo was fully aware of.

He'd never been so present in an embrace. Until it was interrupted by a hesitant knock at the door.

They stopped kissing. Ares frowned and Leo shrugged.

"What?" Ares called. The door swung in two inches, and Asterion's face poked in.

"Sorry, chaps. Dom told me not to bother you, but I was just wondering, is there any hints you can give us about getting sweet Matilda off the bed? It's barely big enough as it is."

"No," Ares shook his head. "Sorry. She sleeps where she sleeps."

"Ah," Asterion pursed his lips for the briefest of seconds, before shifting his expression into a diplomatic smile. "Of course."

"Ares," Leo murmured, arching his eyebrow. "Come on. I can go get her." Ares chuckled, shaking his head.

"No need for you to get out of bed."

"But Ares—" Ares kissed him, then drew back and whistled. "Matilda! Up here, darling!"

The sound of four legs bounding up the stairs seemed instantaneous. Asterion stepped aside, pushing the door out of the way, so that Matilda could take a running leap onto the end of the bed. Which she did, settling promptly on Leo's feet.

"Cheers," Asterion said, winking at them before closing the door behind him and retreating down the stairs.

"Ares," Leo said, as Ares turned over to shut off the bedside lamp.

"Hmm?"

"She nearly crushed me to death every night for a week."

"I didn't want you to get lonely," Ares settled on his back, and Leo pinched him. "Ow!"

"You're a menace."

"Only when it's amusing," Ares said. Leo rolled his eyes before he closed them, his head resting on Ares' shoulder. Ares kissed him on the cheek, his voice low, breath warm on Leo's skin.

"I love you, Leo." Leo stirred. Not much. Just enough to open his eyes and smooth his thumb over the curve of Ares' jaw.

"I'm yours, Ares. I meant it."

"Me too," Ares kissed his shoulder, and it was the last thing Leo felt before he drifted off to sleep.

EPILOGUE

"But I don't understand the name thing."

"What's not to understand?" Asterion's legs were stretched out long, his feet crossed at the ankles and resting on the top edge of Leo's desk. He pointed his toes for emphasis, as if his arms lifted high above his head in an exaggerated shrug weren't emphasis enough. "They *take* your *name.*"

"Yes. But what does that do?" Leo demanded again. "It doesn't do anything! So, I give my name to a faerie. So what? I'll just change it."

"Change your name?" Asterion arched an eyebrow, his hands collapsing in a heap into his lap. "Just change it? Like to what?"

"I don't know," Leo shrugged. "Anything. I'm Barnabus now. Also, you're putting wrinkles in your silk." Asterion frowned down at the white silk shirt he wore beneath his ice blue suit and straightened the fabric.

"Thank you," he said. "I appreciate that. Even though you're entirely missing the point of the name exchange. It's not just any name. It's your name. Not like a 'given' name," he fluttered his fingers above his head as though it was a silly concept. "When they take your name, they take *your* name," he pointed at Leo, and then touched his own chest. "In here. *Your* name that you call yourself. Your true name. And then they have control over you."

"That's not explicit in any of these binding contracts I'm seeing." Leo gestured to the pile of contracts on his desk. It was one of several piles that he, Sidney and Asterion had amassed over four or five months of research.

Leo hadn't thought it would be easy to start a law firm to help humans navigate deals with magical creatures. But he hadn't realized that the body of work would be so massive and varied. Some of it had been simple enough to get his head around. But other elements, the name exchange among them, had been more esoteric than he'd anticipated.

"Karolina would be able to get into the weeds with you about it, but you may be better off looking for some fae scholars. Though, honestly *Mr. Quince*, I wouldn't have thought the power of a name would be beyond you."

It was true that the Quince surname had made it much easier to start a new practice of his own out of a small town like Hindry. And they had decided early that the location was a necessity. Since it had been a waypoint between realms for so long, if they were going to attempt to take cases that specifically dealt with magical law then Elmmond House would be the best place to do it.

But, whether he was stuck using his family name or not, Leo refused to regret that they were rapidly gaining clients; they'd only had their doors officially open for two months and were already approaching a full docket. Leo was behind in his reading, behind in his research, and he'd never been happier. He shrugged.

"Your name on the letterhead isn't hurting either," Leo pointed out.

"It's only there to keep the fae court from getting their knickers in a twist about the whole enterprise. You don't want them to get their dander up before you even get started. Believe me."

"You said Cressida would keep them in line."

"She has an infant and a husband and a kingdom to be tending to. Anything she does for me is an afterthought at best."

"She's leasing Leyland Hall to Sidney and Jonas."

"That's got nothing to do with me. She's always liked Jonas, and for reasons I don't understand, she finds your brother exceedingly charming. Besides, it was too big of a property to let rot away once Kephisto decamped, and Jonas promised her he'd act as lord of the manor. I assume she thinks the people of Laurel Grove need an aristocrat nearby."

"Speaking of Andurnei," Leo checked his watch. There was still time, but he needed to get cleaned up here. Before he could call for Delilah, there was a knock on the door frame.

Dom was dressed in a well-tailored linen suit, his hair tied back at the nape of his neck. Beneath the suit was a light blue cotton shirt that he wore open at the throat. Leo could just see the gleam of the silver necklace he always wore, shining against his skin.

"You two aren't still working, are you?"

"I'm not," Asterion said, getting to his feet immediately. "Not anymore. Gods." Leo busied himself moving paper around, as Asterion pushed Dom just out of sight into the hall. There was a loud thud against the wall. Asterion murmured something, and Leo could hear Dom chuckle in response.

"Uh, no. We don't have time for that."

"This is how I know you have no idea how good you look."

"Asterion."

"Twenty minutes. A room with a door."

"We don't have time!" Dom insisted.

"Ten minutes, then. Door optional."

"How would the presence of a door make any difference?"

Leo cleared his throat, fully aware of what he might hear if he didn't remind them that he was still very much within hearing range. Thankfully, Asterion's voice dropped. After several moments, Dom chuckled dryly.

"Oh, do you promise?" It was one thing to catch Asterion being filthy, but hearing Dom's low, rough tone made Leo blush. Leo stood and slammed a drawer more loudly than was necessary.

"Fuck off, Barnabus," came Asterion's muffled voice.

"This is my house, Asterion."

"Debatable."

"It really isn't," Leo replied. Asterion poked his head in around the door frame and stuck his tongue out at Leo. "We finished painting the study upstairs over the weekend," Leo said, locking up his desk drawer. Asterion arched an eyebrow at him. Leo smirked. "The study you had said was going to be yours, when you're consulting for us? I believe we did keep the door. But it should currently be unoccupied. If you wanted to take a look." Asterion grinned.

"You're a true friend, Barnabus. I adore you. Never forget that. Now, Dom, I need to go see my office."

"Is it a study or an office?" Dom asked, unwrapping himself from Asterion and starting toward the stairs. "And why did you call him Barnabus?" Leo wasn't sure he'd ever seen Asterion move so quickly, catching up to Dom in two hurried strides.

"Long story. One I think we can discuss most effectively *in my office*."

"Gods," Dom laughed.

"Don't be late," Leo called into the hall after them. "Ares will have a conniption."

"Ten minutes," Asterion said over his shoulder. He ducked down to wink at Leo just below the top of the door frame, before taking the stairs two at a time until he was out of sight.

The main foyer of Elmmond House looked the same, but that was the only thing that had survived the last six months unchanged. It had been the work of a couple of weeks to rearrange all the furniture, gut some of the bedrooms and repaint, but the first floor of Elmmond House now held Quince Law.

Leo's firm specialized in dealing with legal questions and contracts between humans and magic users. He couldn't stomach the fact that what had happened to Ares (and Sidney and Jonas) could be happening to others. It was finicky work, but Leo liked the challenge. And with Sidney, Asterion and Jonas all willing to consult, they'd managed to help a few clients already.

Delilah was in the parlor behind the reception desk, reading a crumbling issue of *Vogue*. She glanced up when Leo came in, but only for the briefest of moments.

"I thought you were taking off early today?"

"I am," Leo said. "Are you alright to hold down the fort?" Delilah gestured around at the empty reception area, turning the page of her magazine.

"This crowd? I think I'll manage."

"Thank you, Delilah," Leo turned to go get dressed and then he paused and glanced back. "Have you seen Matilda?" Delilah smirked.

"Outside with Verne, I think."

THE WALK up the path from the garden shed was warm, sunlight streaming through the trees where the new leaves were still the bright crisp green of early spring. Ares had two wooden folding chairs slung over each arm. He could have taken a couple more, they were light as anything, but he was enjoying being back in the garden. He wouldn't mind having to walk through again.

Not that he hadn't been tending to the plants at the cottage on Earth. And slowly planning a much larger garden to fill the lawn behind Elmmond House. It had been revelatory to work with Dom and Hector, planning a farm to table menu for The Silver Platter based on whatever he thought he could grow. He could supplement in the first few years with whatever extra Fen had from the gardens at Andurnei.

"And there's bound to be plenty of extra," Fen had said. "His Lordship and Mr. Quince don't seem to be as keen on entertaining as Kephisto was." Apparently, he, Leo, Dom and Asterion no longer counted as guests in the eyes of the staff that remained at Leyland Hall.

The birdsong echoed out of bushes and above Ares in the trees. He breathed in the sweet scent of new blooms and decided to take the long way around to the alcove, basking in the sun. It was just warm enough that he'd sweat if he stayed out of the shade for too long. But the breeze was cool, and he was still in his work clothes besides.

About fifty feet along the outside path, Ares stopped. There'd been a row of azaleas here (too much sun, they'd never done well, but they'd been planted before his time) but now instead there was a long line of shrubs with vibrant red blooms. Ares set the chairs down, resting them on either side of his hips, and reached out to touch the soft petals, shaking his head.

"Flowering quince," Jonas said. Ares nearly jumped out of his skin. For a being so incredibly large, Jonas Rookwood was light on his feet. And Ares still wasn't used to not being the biggest man in the room. Jonas hadn't noticed the way Ares startled. Or, he probably had, he was just too polite to comment on it. "Mae said she needed them for something, but I'm beginning to think it was just her idea of a joke. We moved the azaleas to the far side of the garden and took out some of the hedgerow. I hope that's alright."

"It's not my garden anymore," Ares said. Jonas snorted and lifted two of the chairs from Ares' side.

"Yes, it is. It's yours for as long as you want a say in it. It was just the right time to move the plants and you were still on sabbatical." Ares rolled his eyes as he hoisted the other chairs back into his arm and began to follow Jonas up the path.

Sabbatical was a generous term for it. When they'd decided the thing doing the most damage to the trees in the orchard were the taps, Ares was effectively banished from Andurnei by Dom and Leo both. Not that he'd been keen to see if he would still experience the pain of the orchard when he hadn't bled for it in a few months. It had felt like an easy decision, to stay away while the trees began to heal. And some days it had been easy. Other days it had ached.

But that was all changing now. Six months had gone by. Perhaps things just felt easier because they were all settling into new routines.

"How's the library coming?" Ares asked. Jonas smiled.

"The builders would be farther along if Sidney didn't insist on using the damn thing every day. I think we're going to have to go abroad if I want it done before the fall."

"Abroad Earthside? Or abroad here?" Ares asked. Jonas shrugged, and Ares noticed that he was already dressed in his navy-blue waist coat and trousers. He was getting stains on his sleeves. "Let me take those chairs."

"No," Jonas chuckled.

"You're getting dirt on your shirt. These chairs have been in the shed for at least a year."

"Gods," Jonas shook his head, barely glancing down at his sleeves. "It's fine."

"Asterion won't think so."

"Well, it's a damn good thing that I don't give a fig what Asterion thinks."

"I'm not sure his lordship should be attending formal events with stains on his clothes."

"Formal event? We're in my back garden," Jonas said. "And don't call me 'his lordship.' It's the worst thing about living in this house."

"But, you have to admit, the view of the stars at Leyland Hall is unmatched," Ares prodded. Jonas rolled his eyes, but his smile was wide and genuine.

"True enough. The things we do for love."

"Much to his lordship's chagrin," Ares teased.

"If I was really a lord, I'd have you banished for that sort of talk."

"And have a Quince brothers mutiny on your hands? Good luck to you." Jonas chuckled, and Ares was struck again by how ridiculously handsome he was. Leo had picked up on Ares' infatuation with Jonas before Ares could even confess to it. Ares had found it a little embarrassing. And confusing.

"Of course you have a crush on him," Leo had said, entirely unphased. They'd been in their bed upstairs in Elmmond House, drinking coffee. Leo was working on some legal brief while Ares had been staring at the ceiling lost in strange, half lewd thoughts that he was feeling inordinately guilty about. "Ares," Leo continued, "you didn't let yourself have feelings for ten years. Jonas is a walking, talking beefcake, with giant horns. He's gorgeous. He's nearly as smart as Sidney. Plus, he's taller than you, and that goes a long way. You've probably never had the chance to have a height-based crush before."

"Is that a thing?" Ares asked.

"That's a question that only people taller than six foot two ever ask."

"Were you attracted to my height?" Ares rolled onto his hip, as Leo glanced at him overtop the papers in his hands.

"Of course I was. I'm not a monk."

"So, if I was three inches shorter?"

"It wasn't your height that was the main draw," Leo said, finally twisting to set his papers on the bedside table, before rolling over to face Ares.

"No?" Ares smirked, tugging Leo close under the blankets.

"Of course not," Leo grinned. "It was your terrible attitude."

As Jonas and Ares turned the corner, coming along the north side of the garden, Jonas told Ares about the meeting he'd had with the new Assembly viceroy, after his mother had reinstated his title.

"I swear, you get half an ounce of magic back, and people are leaping all over themselves trying to get you to solve their problems. Not that I'm any more capable of solving a problem than I was six months ago."

"I think they missed you," Ares suggested, half joking. Jonas rolled his eyes.

"Missed having someone to pass the buck to anyway."

It was true that Morrow's death had had much further reaching implications than granting Ares' freedom from his contract. Since Morrow had named no heir and had never bothered to put his affairs in order because he was obsessed with immortality, all the deals Morrow had made over his lifetime became null and void all at once.

The first weeks after his death were filled with more

disarray than any of them had imagined. Asterion's sister had apparently experienced seven months of morning sickness over the course of one week. Assembly members were physically metamorphosizing into older, uglier versions of themselves in the middle of session, and apparently Jonas Rookwood had been returned what little magic of his Morrow hadn't managed to spend.

They made it to the alcove, where rows of chairs were set on either side of the aisle, leading to the wooden bower that Ares had interwoven with greenery and flowering boughs earlier that morning. It looked good, if he did say so himself.

He and Jonas placed the chairs at the ends of the first two rows, and Ares shook his head as Jonas tried to swipe the dust off his sleeves.

"You better go up to the house and change."

"I could say the same to you. You're still in your work clothes." Before Ares could retort that he'd already been planning on it, footsteps on the far path drew their attention. It took several moments, but then Warren was walking slowly into the alcove, helping his Nan along by her arm.

Ares and Jonas both moved to help her, and she giggled, taking Jonas' arm over Ares', which Ares decided not to be too hurt over. He stayed next to Warren, who was looking over the garden with slightly misty eyes.

"It looks incredible, Ares. Thank you. Nan wanted to see it before the guests and everything." Ares nodded then glanced up at the sun.

"Won't be long until people start showing up." He did need to go to the house and get dressed.

"It's nicer than I ever thought," Warren stammered. Ares smiled and patted him on the shoulder.

"It's alright," he said. "You deserve it." Warren hugged him, tightly. It took Ares a moment, but then he hugged him back.

"Do you know if Fen is alright?" Warren asked, sniffing as he pulled away. "Does she need anything from the house?" Warren and Fen had moved into the groundskeeper's cottage a few weeks after Ares had left. It more than suited them.

"I can check, but I'm sure she's fine."

"Would you?"

"Go get dressed, Warren," Ares laughed. Warren sighed.

"Ugh, I can't leave Nan with his lordship. She'll try and climb him like a tree." They both looked to where Warren's nan was leaning heavily on Jonas' arm. More heavily than was probably necessary. Ares snorted.

"Good luck. I'll go check on Fen."

Ares still went into Leyland Hall through the back door, keeping to the servant's stairs. He knew Jonas and Sidney had set aside the largest suite upstairs for Leyland Hall's first bride, but Ares couldn't help but check the kitchen first anyway.

Sidney was humming, looking a little frazzled and covered in icing sugar. It took him a full minute before he noticed Ares standing on the opposite side of the kitchen island, taking in the scene of destruction before him. Sidney scowled.

"Don't give me that. I literally only got her out of the kitchen half an hour ago. She wouldn't leave until all the hors d'oeuvres were in the icebox. It's a damn good thing I made the cake yesterday. Of course, hiding it was a different story altogether." Sidney and Fen's wars over the kitchen of Leyland Hall had become half farce, half genuine battle. When Sidney and Fen had agreed that Sidney would make the wedding cake, everyone at the dining table had winced.

"Do you need any help?" Ares asked hesitantly.

"No," Sidney said, turning around with a mixing bowl in his hands. "Well, sort of. But not from you. Dom promised he'd be here to do the icing but he's twenty minutes late, and I can't do the roses as well as he can."

"I can get you some real ones from the garden," Ares said. Sidney paused, considering this, but before he could respond, Dom strode into the room, already pulling off his jacket.

"Sorry, I'm late. I got held up."

"Problem with mom?" Ares asked, before he noticed that Dom's suspenders were twisted and there was a fresh red love bite on his collarbone.

"No," Dom shook his head, blush rising to the top of his cheekbones. "Just—"

"Your suspenders are twisted," Sidney said, shoving the icing bowl into Dom's hands with a smirk. "Stir, while I get the piping bag ready."

Ares left them to it. Upstairs, the formerly austere great hall seemed like it had come from an entirely new building. It was filled with rugs and tapestries, making it warm and less echo-y. The windows were open upstairs and down, letting in the breeze. In the center of the floor was a table, stacked with books in several small piles, surrounding a massive spray of flowers from the garden. It wasn't Ares' home. But it was a home now more than it had ever been.

In the bridal suite, Fen and Asterion were both lounging and drinking champagne, and that was far too dangerous a combination for Ares to get involved with. He left quickly, going back to the cottage where he would get ready with Warren and the other groomsmen.

They were a nice bunch of lads, and after they were all dressed and lining up to do a round of shots, Ares backed slowly out of his old front door. It was getting on to afternoon, the sun throwing shadows toward the back of Leyland Hall. The orchard glowed with dappled sunlight, as Ares walked through. The trees were flowering now. They'd never done that before. And there was a hum of magic in the air that seemed to draw bees and butterflies from everywhere else on the property. Starlings and their chicks nested in the tree branches, and even the grass was looking lush and vibrant. If he didn't have somewhere to be, he would have taken his shoes off and sat in it for a while. Let the magic twine up between his toes and fingers.

The bright light of the portal wasn't so blinding in the daylight. Matilda bounded over to him, and Ares managed to catch her before she could put paw marks on his suit. A nearby tree intentionally dropped a stick, and Matilda bounded off toward it, as Leo came through the portal.

Leo's suit was sage green, and his collar was open, bowtie hanging loose around his neck. He was really, unfairly beautiful. Before Leo noticed Ares, Ares watched as Leo picked his way over the roots, careful not to step on any of them too hard. When Leo paused at the trunk of the tree and placed his palm gently against Ares' mother's bark, Ares could hardly breathe with how much he loved the man.

Ares took a step forward, and Leo glanced up at once, his smile going wide.

"Hello, handsome."

"Hello," Ares said, offering Leo his hand, which Leo took so he could step over a particularly large root. When Leo was beside Ares, he slid his arms around Ares' waist and kissed him.

"I didn't think you were going to meet us. I assumed you'd be busy with Warren."

"I snuck out. It's fine," Ares said, sliding his fingers between Leo's. "I wanted to see mom. And I'd hoped I'd catch you."

"Well, you did," Leo leaned on Ares, as they looked up at the tree that still held the spirit of Ares' mother. "She looks gorgeous."

"Dressed for the occasion," Ares smiled. The wind blew then, sending a rain of his mother's white flowers down over their heads. Leo laughed, tipping his head back, and Ares smiled at the brush of the petals against his skin.

Ares had never thought he would feel peace within the four walls of the orchard. But for the space of the next several breaths, with the bright, fresh air of spring in his lungs, and Leo at his side, Ares was the happiest he'd ever been.